高等学校英语应用能力考试 · 高职突破系列

级考试真题
分类解析与模拟冲刺

主　编：张玲　黄立进　向云夫
编　者：（排名不分先后）

张　玲　纪淑军　刘　湘　张颖青
陈　萍　王　婷　顾晓晶　李世业
唐取文　欧建明　何　燕　杨绣妃
胡　雯　邱泳惠　石　波　黄高超
何云英　陆海涛　阮黎帆

中国人民大学出版社
·北京·

图书在版编目（CIP）数据

英语B级考试真题分类解析与模拟冲刺/张玲主编.—1版.—北京：中国人民大学出版社，2011.8
（高等学校英语应用能力考试·高职突破系列）
ISBN 978-7-300-14134-3

Ⅰ.①英… Ⅱ.①张… Ⅲ.①大学英语水平考试–题解 Ⅳ.①H319.6

中国版本图书馆 CIP 数据核字（2011）第 158812 号

高等学校英语应用能力考试·高职突破系列
英语 B 级考试真题分类解析与模拟冲刺
主 编 张玲 黄立进 向云夫
Yingyu B-ji Kaoshi Zhenti Fenlei Jiexi yu Moni Chongci

出版发行	中国人民大学出版社	
社 址	北京中关村大街31号	邮政编码 100080
电 话	010—62511242（总编室）	010—62511398（质管部）
	010—82501766（邮购部）	010—62514148（门市部）
	010—62515195（发行公司）	010—62515275（盗版举报）
网 址	http://www.crup.com.cn	
	http://www.1kao.com.cn（中国 1 考网）	
经 销	新华书店	
印 刷	北京东君印刷有限公司	
规 格	185 mm×260 mm 16 开本	版 次 2011年 8 月第 1 版
印 张	20.75	印 次 2011年 9 月第 2 次印刷
字 数	475 000	定 价 39.00 元（附赠光盘）

前言

　　高等学校英语应用能力考试是面向高职高专非英语专业学生的英语水平考试，分 A、B 两个级别。就目前我国高职高专学生应对全国高等学校英语应用能力 B 级考试而言，相当一部分学生仍感到力不从心。主要原因有：（1）中学英语基础比较薄弱；（2）应试复习时抓不到要领。为了切实提高高职高专学生的英语应用能力和应试能力，全面提高他们的 B 级考试通过率，我们依据《高等学校英语应用能力考试大纲（B 级）》，特组织全国部分高职院校教师编写了本书。

　　本书严格按照《高等学校英语应用能力考试大纲（B 级）》所规定的考试内容，参照历年真题及其难易度而编写，素材的背景知识都在高职高专学生应掌握的范围之内。

　　本书依据 B 级考试大纲所规定的考试模块，分门别类地对 B 级考试真题进行了解析。每一章节后用于巩固提高的专项模拟训练参考了各大出版社的主流高职高专公共英语教材以及国外的报刊、书籍等，有利于学生将平时的教材学习与应试能力的提高相结合。

　　本书选材和章节编排注重自身的系统性和难易梯度。无论是听力理解、词汇用法、语法结构部分，还是阅读理解、翻译和写作部分，都遵循从易到难、从浅到深、从简到繁的原则。

　　本书共分五个部分：第一部分 "B 级考试真题分类解析及解题技巧"；第二部分 "B 级考试全真试题"；第三部分 "B 级考试模拟试题"；第四部分 "B 级考试全真试题及模拟试题听力原文"；第五部分："B 级考试全真、模拟试题参考答案及解析"。

本书具有以下特色：

　　（1）配有外国专家录音的 MP3 光盘，方便广大学生反复听地道英语。

　　（2）选材新颖，具有鲜明的时代感。

（3）语法讲解深入浅出，解题技巧和真题分析讲解透彻，非常方便学生自主学习。

（4）语言测试训练与能力培养相结合。许多学生在应试时总是抓不到有用的信息，尤其是对于听力考试和阅读考试中出现的大量信息，更是抓不住要点，致使考试成绩不理想。为此，本书在选题时，非常注重试题的实战性和针对性，使学生在做题的过程中既能锻炼应试能力，又能发现自己语言知识上的漏洞，从而巩固语言知识，同时提高应试和应用能力。

（5）词汇和语法部分大多是原汁原味的当代英语，且都配了参考译文，以帮助读者理解。

本书对高职高专学生备考英语 B 级考试极具实用价值；对各类自学者测试和提高自己的英语水平同样具有一定的参考价值。

承担本书编写工作的老师是：刘湘、张颖青、陈萍（听力理解部分）；王婷、顾晓晶（翻译——英译汉部分）；张玲、欧建明、何燕、杨绣妃、胡雯、邱泳惠、石波、黄高超、何云英、陆海涛（阅读理解部分）；李世业、唐取文（词汇、语法结构和应用写作 / 汉译英部分）。本书由张玲、黄立进、向云夫统稿、定稿和审稿。

本书资料主要选自国内外新近出版的图书、杂志、报纸以及互联网等多种媒体材料，在此特向这些文献的作者和出版者表示感谢。

由于时间仓促，水平有限，书中难免有疏漏和不足之处，恳请广大读者和同行提出宝贵意见，以便日后对本书修订，使之更加完善。

编者

2011 年 7 月

C目 录
ontents

第四部分　　B级考试全真试题及模拟试题听力原文（参见附件）

第五部分　　B级考试全真、模拟试题参考答案及解析（参见附件）

B级考试真题分类解析及解题技巧

第一章　听力理解

第一节　题型介绍和解题方法指导

题型介绍

高等学校英语应用能力 B 级考试听力理解题的方向主要是日常交际和简单的业务交际。其中日常交际涵盖感谢、致歉、指路、询问天气、道别等；而业务交际则涉及宴请、送迎、就诊、客房服务等。B 级听力理解以测试考生对日常用语以及简单涉外活动用语的理解和应用能力为目的，测试时间为 15 分钟，共计 15 分，语速为每分钟 100 个词左右。测试分为三个部分：

Section A: 简短问题或句子（Short Questions or Sentences）。此题型共五题，每题由一两个短句组成。每题录音播放两遍。

Section B: 简短对话（Short Dialogues）。此题型共五题，每题由一组简短对话及针对对话的问题组成。每题录音播放两遍。

Section C: 短文（Short Passages）。此题型由一篇五处内容缺失的小短文组成，缺失内容可能是词、短语或数字。整篇短文录音播放三遍。第一遍与最后一遍均为正常语速，第二遍在所需填写的内容处有所停顿。

解题方法指导

高职高专学生英语基础相对薄弱；大部分学生在单词习得中，偏重于中文解释，而忽略了单词读音；有些学生在考试过程中受到心理压力过大、情绪紧张、不自信等因素的影响，听力理解能力相对薄弱。针对这一情况，在 B 级考试的听力理解中首要应掌握"3P"：

（1）Peace: 平静的心态是听力考试的关键。在考试过程中，考生首先应该放松心情，平和心态，集中注意力。

（2）Pace: 速度是听力考试成功的法宝，包括听力开始前的预览考题、听力过程中的摘录关键词以及听力结束后的总结。

（3）Prediction: 通过所给的听力选项，预测可能的提问是做好听力理解题的重要策略。

以下分别以近几年的 B 级考试真题为例，通过对题型的分析和总结，探讨考生在听力理解中的常见问题，找出解题技巧。

第二节　历年考点统计、考点解读和解题技巧

SECTION A

考点统计

	陈述句	特殊疑问句	一般疑问句
2005 年 6 月		2. What's the best time for us to leave? 询问 3. What do you study… 询问 4. How much… 价钱	1. Would you like… 提议 5. Would you like… 提议
2005 年 12 月		2. When… 时间	1. Could you please… 请求 3. Is that… 询问 4. Would you please tell me something… 咨询 5. Shall I… 提议
2006 年 6 月			1. Can I see… 咨询 2. Is this your first trip… 询问 3. Is there anything… 询问 4. Would you like… 提议 5. Will you attend… 询问
2006 年 12 月	2. 道歉 3. 致谢	5. How does… 询问	1. Can I speak to… 电话 4. Shall we need again to… 提议
2007 年 6 月		3. What time… 时间	1. Are you going to… 询问 2. Have you… 询问 4. Have you… 询问 5. Do you often… 询问
2007 年 12 月		3. When… 时间 4. How often… 频率 5. How… 询问	1. Would you please… 求助 2. May I speak to… 电话
2008 年 6 月		1. Why not… 建议 2. When… 时间	3. Did you enjoy… 询问 4. Can we… 询问 5. May I… 求助
2008 年 12 月		3. How long… 时间 5. What do you think of… 观点	1. Can I… 询问 2. May I speak to… 电话 4. Is this… 询问
2009 年 6 月		2. When… 时间 4. What do you think of… 观点 5. What's the weather like… 天气	1. Are you… 询问 3. Would you please… 求助

（＊统计表格中的数字为真题题号）

考点解读

　　从上表统计得出，其内容涵盖询问、求助、征求意见、咨询观点以及日常生活中打电话、谈论天气、咨询价格等等。其中有陈述句也有疑问句，而疑问句在 Section A 中占有

相当大的比例，在九套真题中，陈述句占的比例为 4%，除 2006 年 12 月的考题中涉及陈述句之外，其余全为疑问句。

疑问句分为以下四种：

（1）一般疑问句：Is she from America? 她来自美国吗？

（2）特殊疑问句：When is your birthday? 你的生日是哪天？

（3）选择疑问句：Is this a grapefruit or an orange? 这是柚子还是橘子？

（4）反意疑问句：You are a student, aren't you? 你是学生，不是吗？

而在近几年的考题中，以一般疑问句和特殊疑问句为主，其中特殊疑问句占 33.6%，而一般疑问句则占 60%，比重颇大。

解题技巧

1. 一般疑问句

不用疑问词，而且需要用 yes 或 no 回答的疑问句，叫一般疑问句，句末用升调。

（1）be 动词的一般疑问句

句型：Be 动词 + 主语 + ~?

Is your father angry? 你父亲生气了吗？

Yes, he is. 是的，他生气了。

No, he isn't. 不，他没生气。

（2）情态动词的一般疑问句

句型：情态动词 + 主语 + 动词原形 + ~?

Can you bring me some apples? 你能给我拿来些苹果吗？

Yes, I can. 是的，可以。

No, I can't. 不，不可以。

（3）一般动词（实义动词）的一般疑问句

句型：Do (Does, Did) + 主语 + 动词原形 + ~?

Does he have supper at home every day? 他每天在家吃饭吗？

Yes, he does. 是的。

No, he doesn't. 不。

（4）完成时的一般疑问句

句型：Have (Has) + 主语 + 动词的过去分词 + ~?

Have you known her since your childhood? 你从小就认识她吗？

Yes, I have. 是的。

No, I haven't. 不，不是。

2. 特殊疑问句

用疑问词引导的疑问句叫做特殊疑问句。回答特殊疑问句时不能用 yes 或 no，句末用降调。

疑问词分为三类：

疑问代词：what，who，which，whose，whom

疑问副词：when，where，why，how

疑问形容词：what (which，whose) + 名词

所以在听力理解中很快听清第一个词往往可以判断句子是什么类型的问句，该选择什么类型的答案。

在近几年真题中最常见的有以下几类：

关于"时间"的问答

（1）When 引导的疑问句：询问时间

　　When were you born? 你什么时候出生的？

　　I was born on June 5, 1962. 我是 1962 年 6 月 5 日出生的。

（2）How long…

　　How long have you been here? 你待在这里有多久了？

　　Two years. 两年了。

（3）What time is it now? 现在几点了？

　　It's 12 o'clock. 现在 12 点整。

与"how"相关

how 引导的疑问句可分为两类：

（1）"How…?" how 可单独置于疑问句的句首。

　　询问如何做某事，即做某事的方法、手段及健康、天气……

　　How are you?（问健康）你身体怎样？

　　How is the weather today?（问天气）今天的天气如何？

（2）How + 形容词（副词）+ ~?

　　询问年龄、身高、数量、次数、距离……

　　How much 多少（接不可数名词）

　　How much is the book? 这本书多少钱？

　　How long 多少时间（多久）

　　How long will you stay here? 你将在这里待多久？

　　How often 多久（频率）

　　How often do you visit here? 你多长时间来参观一次这里？

SECTION B

考点统计

　　Section B 的对话部分共五组，多以一问一答、男女声交替的形式出现。测试的内容和句子结构比较简单，内容涵盖日常生活、工作、交际中的基本对话，如谈论学习、工作、健康、时间、度假计划，发表意见，看医生以及宾馆、银行等商业对话等。旨在测试考生

对简单对话的理解能力和信息处理、推理及应变能力。

	特殊疑问句							
	what	where	how	how much	why	when	who	which
2005年6月	3	1		1				
2005年12月	5							
2006年6月	3	1				1		
2006年12月	3	1			1			
2007年6月	5							
2007年12月	4		1					
2008年6月	4		1					
2008年12月	2	2	1					
2009年6月	3	1				1		
总计	32	6	3	1	1	2		

由上表的总结可得出，在近几年的对话理解中，以 what 引导的特殊疑问句占 71%，列居首位。其次是以 where 引导的特殊疑问句，占总数的 13%。以下以表格形式对近年来 what 引导的特殊疑问句进行分析。

	what	what引导的句型	
2005年6月	3	7. What would the man probably do?	内容提问
		9. What does the man think of the fast food?	观点
		10. What does the woman think of the new boss?	观点
2005年12月	5	6. What can we learn from the dialogue?	推断
		7. What does the man say about the local calls?	内容提问
		8. What happened last night?	内容提问
		9. What does the woman ask the man to do?	内容提问
		10. What are they talking about?	内容提问
2006年6月	3	6. What are they talking about?	内容提问
		7. What do we know about the woman?	推断
		8. What does the woman want?	内容提问
2006年12月	3	6. What kind of food does the man ask for?	内容提问
		8. What can we learn from the conversation?	推断
		10. What does the woman want to do in the hospital?	内容提问
2007年6月	5	6. What's the weather like this morning?	天气
		7. What will the woman probably do?	内容提问
		8. What does the woman think of her new boss?	观点
		9. What does the man mean?	推断
		10. What does the woman mean?	推断

续前表

	what	what引导的句型	
2007年12月	4	6. What's the weather like?	天气
		8. What's the man doing?	内容提问
		9. What's the probable relationship between the two speakers?	关系判断
		10. What's the woman's suggestion?	内容提问
2008年6月	4	6. What does the woman like to have?	内容提问
		7. What does the man mean?	推断
		8. What's the probable relationship between the two speakers?	关系判断
		10. What does the woman think the man should do?	内容提问
2008年12月	2	7. What's the woman going to do?	内容提问
		10. What did the man do in that company?	职业判断
2009年6月	3	7. What's the man probably going to do?	推断
		8. What can we learn from the talk?	推断
		10. What does the woman ask the man to do?	内容提问

解题技巧

从上面两个统计表格可以看出，"是什么"的题目最多。其目的在于测试考生理解对话的表面内容和潜在内容，不仅要了解对话涉及的场景、人物的内容表达，还要通过对话了解人物关系、人物身份职业以及回答中的潜在意思。因此在答题中掌握技巧对于听力理解很重要。

（1）拿到试卷时，要做到抓紧时间，预先浏览，初步预测可能提问。例如：A. 1:30 B. 1:40 C. 2:00 D. 3:00，那么这一题必定是对时间的提问，在听力过程中对于出现的时间应保持高度敏感。

（2）放松心态，听清疑问词。例如：how much 问的是价钱，when 问的是时间，why 问的是原因，where 问的是地点等，听清疑问词对于听力理解有很好的导向性。

（3）有取有舍，在听力理解中如果遇到难题没听清，应该懂得放弃，及时进入下一题的答题，而不是苦苦思索，丧失信心。

SECTION C

考点统计

Section C 部分是一篇小短文，其中有五个单词或词组用空格代替，要求考生填入适当的内容。短文听写旨在测试考生的词汇和短语的听写能力，并不要求对全文主旨的理解，也不要求根据文章内容判断。但是要考查考生的基本单词拼写能力。单词涉及面较广，以下就近年来填空的单词、词组进行分析。

	动词	名词	形容词	副词	数词	其他短语
2005年6月	discuss	day	boring far away	as long as		
2005年12月	talk		wonderful	really as much		next year
2006年6月	deal with effect		useful wonderful	totally		
2006年12月	protect lead to		medical lower popular			
2007年6月	lost grow crops	building rain				every year
2007年12月		service	more information cheaper		3	as you like
2008年6月		degree training class work	better			other kinds
2008年12月			safe helpful	always		on business for example
2009年6月	welcome arrive stay	rain				local time
总计	11	8	13	5	1	7

从 2000 年 6 月到 2005 年 1 月十套真题统计，动词比例最高，占 40%，名词及名词词组为 22%，形容词为 14%。

而从 2005 年 6 月到 2009 年 6 月九套真题统计，形容词的比例上升到 29%，动词由原来的 40% 下降到 24%，名词占 18%。考查的方向从动词为重到动、名、形均衡分布，各方面均有涉及。

解题技巧

这类题型要求考生分四步走：

第一步：了解短文的大致意思，尤其注意单词和短语所在句的内容，作大致推测。

第二步：听第一遍的时候，将听到的十分肯定的单词填上，对于有疑问的单词或短语，可以从全文的时态和该单词、短语所在位置的前后内容判断词性。

第三步：在听第二遍的时候，着重听有疑问部分的单词，并且查看已填内容的准确性。

第四步：核对所填内容是否正确，检查拼写、单复数以及时态、语态。

第三节　典型真题分析和专项模拟训练及答案解析

SECTION A

典型真题分析

1. Excuse me, are you Mr. Smith from America?（2008 年 12 月真题）

　　A. Thank you.　　B. With pleasure.　　C. Oh, yes.　　D. Here you are.

　　【解析】听到此句时，只要通过"Are you…"判断出是一般疑问句，就可以得出答案为 C，因为只有 C 是以"Yes"作答的。

2. Have you received my letter?（2007 年 6 月真题）

　　A. Nothing serious.　　B. No, thank you.　　C. Yes, I have.　　D. It's terrible.

　　【解析】听到此句时，通过"Have you…"判断出是一般疑问句，就可以得出答案为 B 或 C。而根据句型：Have (Has) + 主语 + 动词的过去分词 + ~? 当主语是 I 时，肯定和否定的回答分别应是 Yes, I have. 和 No, I haven't. 因此，得出答案应为 C。

3. Shall we meet again to discuss it further?（2006 年 12 月真题）

　　A. Well, how?　　B. Well, who?　　C. Yes, when?　　D. Yes, what?

　　【解析】听到此句时，只要通过"Shall we…"判断出是一般疑问句，就可以得出答案为 C 或 D。这句话的问题为："我们什么时候再碰面做进一步讨论？"通过句中单词"meet"，可得答案 C。

4. Is this your first trip to Beijing?（2006 年 6 月真题）

　　A. Yes, it is.　　B. Yes, I have.　　C. I like the city.　　D. It's a famous city.

　　【解析】听到此句时，只要通过"Is this…"判断出是一般疑问句，就可以得出答案为 A 或 B。Is this 的回答应是 Yes, it is. 因此答案应该为 A。

5. Would you like another cup of tea?（2006 年 6 月真题）

　　A. I often drink tea at home.　　B. No, thanks.　　C. Not likely.　　D. No, it isn't.

　　【解析】根据此句中"Would you like…"的提问，可首先排除选项 A。根据句意："你要再来一杯茶吗？"可得答案应为 B。

专项模拟训练一（Exercise One）

1. A. Yes, please do.

　　B. Yes, I can.

　　C. Not at all.

　　D. I'm glad.

2. A. It's not far from here.

　　B. Sorry, I'm new here.

　　C. I work in a post office.

　　D. Yes, please.

3. A. I'm afraid you should.

  B. Yes, I am a doctor.

  C. Yes, let's go.

  D. I'd love to.

4. A. Yes, you will.

  B. Yes, you mustn't.

  C. No, you needn't.

  D. No, you mustn't.

5. A. Yes, I do.

  B. It's kind of you.

  C. That's all right.

  D. Yes, I'm glad to.

6. A. No, it's not mine.

  B. Yes. Here you are.

  C. Sorry, I don't know him.

  D. Ask Lily, please.

☞*Keys:* 1~6 A B A C D B

听力原文:

1. May I take this plate away now, sir?

2. Could you show me the way to the nearest post office?

3. Do you think I should go to see a doctor?

4. Must we hand in our homework now?

5. Will you go to Shanghai Library with me?

6. Have you got a map of the world?

典型真题分析

1. What do you think of the film we saw yesterday?（2009 年 6 月真题）

  A. Of course.   B. You are welcome.   C. It was excellent.   D. Yes, I do.

  【解析】"What do you think of…" 这个句型是征询他人意见，因此回答应该是对某人或某事的观点、看法。符合这一条件的只有 C，所以本题答案为 C。

2. Mr. Johnson, when is the library open?（2008 年 12 月真题）

  A. From 9 a.m. to 6 p.m.   B. Far from here.   C. Five people.   D. One hundred dollars.

  【解析】"When…" 与时间有关。选项 B 是距离，选项 C 是人数，选项 D 为价钱，符合句意的只有 A，因而答案为 A。

3. How often do you go on line?（2007 年 12 月真题）

  A. Yes, please.   B. For two months.   C. Every day.   D. Not bad.

  【解析】"How often…" 表示频率。答案为 C。

4. What time do you usually go to work?（2007 年 6 月真题）

    A. It's early.   B. Eight hours.   C. Yes, I'd love to.   D. At half past eight.

【解析】"What time…" 引导的是特殊疑问句。句子意思是询问具体上班时间，因此 D 是正确的答案。

5. How does the new product sell in the market?（2006 年 12 月真题）

    A. Quite well.   B. Not likely.   C. I'm afraid I can't.   D. Never mind.

【解析】"How…" 引导的特殊疑问句表示 "怎么样"。句子意思是问新产品在市场上销售的情况。A 选项 "quite well" 是相当不错的意思。因此 A 是符合题意的答案。

6. Janet, what do you study at college? (2005 年 6 月真题)

    A. Too difficult.   B. I'm twenty.   C. Chinese history.   D. I like football.

【解析】"What…" 引导的是特殊疑问句。句子意思是询问大学里学习的课程。A "太难了"；B "我 20 岁了；C "中国历史"；D "我喜欢足球"。因此 C 是符合题意的答案。

专项模拟训练二（Exercise Two）

1. A. For two weeks.

    B. Once a week.

    C. Since last week.

    D. The day after tomorrow.

2. A. Sorry, I don't know.

    B. Yes, it is.

    C. No, there isn't.

    D. Yes, there are.

3. A. At 2:30.

    B. Yes, I can.

    C. In Tianhe.

    D. At the train station.

4. A. Surely.

    B. Yes, of course.

    C. Good idea.

    D. At the train station.

5. A. It's five miles away.

    B. Two hours if we drive fast.

    C. By plane.

    D. Walking through the park.

6. A. Yes, I'll be in Beijing.

    B. Three weeks.

    C. Yes, it's a long way to Beijing.

D. Since yesterday.

Keys: 1~6 B A D C D B

听力原文：

1. How often do you have an English test?

2. What's on at the Xinhua Cinema this week?

3. Where can I catch the afternoon train to Hongkong?

4. What about going to the cinema tonight?

5. What's the best way to get to your house from here?

6. How long will you be away from Beijing?

SECTION B

典型真题分析

1. 职业判断

在此类对话中，可以通过说话者之间的用词和语言环境判断说话人的身份和职业。考生在听的过程中把握关键词，在此基础上加以推断，最终找出对话中人物的身份。

1. W: Did you work as a salesman in that company?

M: No, I was an engineer.

Q: What did the man do in that company? (2008 年 12 月真题)

A. An engineer.　　　　B. A doctor.　　　　C. A salesman.　　　　D. A secretary.

【解析】本题考查的是对对话细节的掌握。女士问："你在那个公司是一名销售员吗？"男士回答说："不是。我是一名工程师。"根据本题所提问的问题"这位男士在那个公司是做什么的？"可选出本题的答案为 A。

2. M: What's wrong with me, doctor?

W: Nothing serious. You've just got a cold.

Q: What's the probable relationship between the two speakers? (2007 年 12 月真题)

A. Patient and doctor.　　　　　　B. Husband and wife.

C. Teacher and student.　　　　　　D. Manager and secretary.

【解析】判断说话者之间的关系是 B 级考试比较常见的题型,在听的过程中抓住和身份有关的关键词非常重要。该句的关键词为 "doctor" 和 "got a cold"，不难判断出正确答案为 A。

对于这类题型，常见的提问形式有：

(1) What might be the relationship between the man and the woman?

(2) Who are the two speakers?

(3) What is the man/woman's job?

(4) Who is the man/woman?

(5) What is the man/woman?

专项模拟训练三（Exercise Three）

1. A. A salesman.
   C. A craftsman.
   B. A firefighter.
   D. A policeman.

2. A. Boss and secretary.
   C. Doctor and patient.
   B. Hotel manager and customer.
   D. Husband and wife.

3. A. Husband and wife.
   C. Salesman and customer.
   B. Waiter and customer.
   D. Host and guest.

Keys: 1~3 D B B

听力原文：

1. W: What kind of job did you have before your current job as a policeman?

   M: I used to work as a salesman.

   Q: What is the man?

2. M: Hello, I want to book a room which faces the sea.

   W: Hold the line, please. I'll find out.

   Q: What's the relationship between the two speakers?

3. M: Good evening, Madam. There is a table for two over there. This way, please.

   W: Thank you. Could I see the menu, please?

   Q: What's the relationship between the man and the woman?

2. 内容提问

从统计表中可见，内容提问类的题型频繁出现，每次考试均有涉及。这类题型又称细节辨析题，提问的方式多样。在B级考试中，这类内容提问题的答案一般在对话中都有提及。因此在做此类细节题时，把握关键词、句很重要，特别要关注回答问题那个人的说话内容。在听的过程中，养成随听随记关键语句的习惯很重要。

1. M: What's the matter, Mary?

   W: My computer doesn't work. Can you help me?

   Q: What does the woman ask the man to do?（2009年6月真题）

   A. Tell her the price.
   C. Examine her computer.
   B. Wait for a while.
   D. Go shopping with her.

【解析】句中关键的单词是computer，四个选项中只有选项C涉及电脑，因此该题的正确答案是C。

2. W: Can you stay for dinner?

   M: I'd love to, but I have to go to meet a friend at the airport.

   Q: What's the woman going to do?（2008年12月真题）

   A. Attend a meeting.
   C. Take an interview.
   B. Hold a party.
   D. Meet a friend.

【解析】该句中有两个关键词 "dinner" 和 "airport"。选项 A 中的会议、选项 B 中的宴会以及选项 C 中的面试与飞机场均不符。只有 D 是正确答案。

3. M: I wonder if you have a special menu for children?

W: I'm sorry! But we don't have one.

Q: What kind of food does the man ask for?（2006 年 12 月真题）

A. Children's food.　　　　　　　　B. Chinese food.

C. Holiday food.　　　　　　　　　 D. Western food.

【解析】把握句子中的两个关键词："menu" 和 "children"，如果对于 menu 这个单词不熟悉，可以通过问题中的 "food" 一词，在四个选项中运用排除法得出正确答案为 A。

4. M: Shall we have the meeting at 10 o'clock on Wednesday morning?

W: Wednesday morning at 10. It's OK for me.

Q: What are they talking about?（2005 年 12 月真题）

A. Where to have the meeting.　　　 B. When to have the meeting.

C. Who to attend the meeting.　　　 D. What to discuss at the meeting.

【解析】句子当中出现 "10 o'clock"、"morning" 和 "Wednesday" 等时间词，可推断出谈论的内容与时间有关，选择表示时间的疑问词 when。因此选项 B 是正确的。

　　细节题是听力考试中所占比例最大的一类考题，其出题形式多样，常常根据对话的内容提问，例如：

(1) What happened last night?

(2) What does the woman ask the man to do?

(3) What are they talking about?

(4) What does the woman like to have?

(5) What's the woman going to do?

专项模拟训练四（Exercise Four）

1. A. The address is not correct.　　　B. It needs more stamps.

　 C. It is sent without an address.　　 D. The envelope is broken.

2. A. She was sick.　　　　　　　　　B. She went to London with her mother.

　 C. She went to see her sick mother.　 D. Her mother went to see her yesterday.

3. A. Give a message to Mr. Jones.　　 B. Wait for Mr. Jones.

　 C. Write a note to Mr. Jones.　　　 D. Keep Mr. Jones' note.

4. A. He was sitting in the garden.　　 B. He was sweeping his garden.

　 C. He was mending his bike.　　　　D. He was riding his bike.

5. A. He was having breakfast.　　　　B. He was working.

　 C. He was cooking.　　　　　　　　D. He was staying at home.

↪*Keys:* 1~5 A　C　A　C　A

听力原文：

1. M: I wonder why the letter was returned to me.

   W: You didn't write the address properly.

   Q: What does the woman say about the letter?

2. M: What happened to Alice?

   W: She was visiting us when she learned that her mother was sick, so she left for London.

   Q: What happened to Alice?

3. W: Mr. Jones will be back in just a few minutes, you can wait if you want to.

   M: No thanks, I'll just leave this note for him.

   Q: What does the man ask the woman to do?

4. W: Where were you yesterday afternoon?

   M: In my garden. I was repairing my bike.

   Q: What was the man doing yesterday afternoon?

5. W: What were you doing when I called you an hour ago?

   M: Having breakfast. I stayed up late last night, and I worked until 12.

   Q: What was the man doing when the woman phoned him?

3. 推测

推测题型应该是听力考试中对话部分最难的一类题了。因为它的答案不是简单的表面听到的内容，而要深入到弦外之音中。因此，必须通过上下文和字里行间的意思来判断说话人的意向、态度和评价，从而选择准确的选项。

1. W: Excuse me, can you call a taxi for me?

   M: Sorry, the telephone is out of order.

   Q: What does the man mean?（2008 年 6 月真题）

   A. The line is busy.   B. There is no taxi.

   C. The traffic is heavy.   D. He can't call a taxi for her.

   【解析】此句中的关键是词组 "out of order" 的理解。在本句中该词组的意思是 "出故障了"，而不是其本意 "混乱的，杂乱的"。当然考生还要从 "电话出故障了" 结合一开始要求去找出租车的请求推断出不能帮忙打电话叫车，因此 D 为正确答案。

2. M: I'm afraid we'll be late for the party.

   W: Don't worry. There is still 20 minutes to go.

   Q: What does the woman mean?（2007 年 6 月真题）

   A. They will stay at home.   B. They will be late.

   C. They won't go to the party.   D. They won't be late.

   【解析】在听力理解中，尤其是推断类型的考题，第二说话人的观点是很重要的。因此我们在听完第一个人说的话之后不要着急做题，一定要留意第二说话人的语言，往往信息就在第二说话人这里发生改变。该句的改变就在 "Don't worry" 上，D 为正确答案。

3. M: Someone is knocking at the door.

   W: I think it is Jack again.

Q: What can we learn from the conversation?（2006 年 12 月真题）

A. The woman is calling Jack.　　　　B. There is a visitor at the door.

C. The door is open.　　　　　　　　D. The telephone is ringing.

【解析】该题是通过两位说话人的对话推断出有客来访。"knock at the door"在该句中很关键，通过这个短语就可以很好排除 A 和 D。再通过第二说话人的信息不难判断出答案为 B。

对于这类题型，常见的提问形式有：

(1) What does the man/woman mean?

(2) What does the man/woman imply?

(3) What can we learn from the conversation?

(4) What do we know from the talk?

专项模拟训练五（Exercise Five）

1. A. He didn't do well in his lessons.　　B. He is good at his lessons.

　　C. His parents will be happy about it.　D. He studies very hard.

2. A. The woman is busy working.　　　B. The woman can't take the message.

　　C. Mr. Jackson is in his office.　　　D. Mr. Jackson will be back soon.

3. A. Both of them like the painting.

　　B. Neither of them likes the patinting.

　　C. The man likes the painting but the woman doesn't.

　　D. The woman likes the painting but the man doesn't.

4. A. Children are normally silly.　　　　B. Children are short of good books.

　　C. Many children's books are not interesting.　D. Children have no taste at all.

Keys: 1~4 A　B　B　B

听力原文：

1. W: Have you got your test paper, Jim?

　M: Yes, I think my parents will be sad about it.

　Q: What do you think of Jim's school work?

2. M: Would you please give Mr. Jackson a message?

　W: Sorry, Mr. Jackson is having a holiday in Chicago.

　Q: What can we learn from the conversation?

3. M: I don't like the painting, either. Just looking at it gives me a headache.

　W: But we can't throw it away. It's a present from your mother.

　Q: What can we learn from the conversation?

4. W: Why do you think *Harry Potter* is so popular these days?

　M: Because there are not many good children's books available.

　Q: What does the man mean?

SECTION C

典型真题分析

Welcome to the Public Bus System. Its bus network operates 365 days of the year and has ___11___ that can take you to your destination quickly and easily.

You can travel round the city for just $ ___12___ a day with Type-A bus tickets. Type-B bus tickets are even ___13___ . You can get on and off as many times ___14___ , so you can tour the city at your own pace.

You can buy tickets at most newspaper stands.

If you want to get ___15___ , call the office of the Public Bus System.（2007 年 12 月真题）

【解析】欢迎来到公共交通系统，该公交系统全年无休，方便又快捷。

你只要花费 3 美元就可整天乘坐 A 型公交车环游这个城市，而 B 型价钱更实惠。并且可以随意上下车，游览进度由你来决定。

你可以到大多数的书报亭买票。

如果还想咨询其他消息，请拨打公共交通系统服务电话。

11. services　　12. 3　　13. cheaper　　14. as you like　　15. more information

在听之前可以预测在第 11 题中应该填入的是一个名词，因为动词 has 在前面，后面又是一个定语从句。

从 $ 这个符号可判断第 12 题应该是一个数词。

第 13 题可以通过比较 Type-A 和 Type-B 得出应该是比较级。

第 15 题的空格前为动词 get，所以判断应该也是一个名词。

专项模拟训练六（Exercise Six）

1.

Recently, a well-known man said that teaching one's wife to drive a car was a difficult job. He said it was the worst job he could think of. However, no one has ___11___ that women cause fewer accidents than men do. We hear hundreds of suggestions for ___12___ the number of road accidents. But men are not willing to admit that women drivers are more ___13___ than men. If more women and fewer men were ___14___ to drive cars, the number of deaths on the roads would soon ___15___ .

☛*Keys:* 11~15 pointed out　　reducing　　careful　　allowed　　go down

2.

China's gradual change into a market economy, which has been going on for several ___11___ , has put China among the world's ___12___ growing economies. While economic growth has increased incomes and improved health conditions, ___13___ reduced overall poverty levels, growth has not been totally good. Environmental pollution from coal burning is damaging human health, air and water quality, agriculture and ___14___ the economy. New laws have begun to control this environmental damage. On the national level, policies are made and ___15___ by the State Council.

Keys: 11~15 decades   fastest   as well as   finally   accepted

第二章　词汇和语法结构

第一节　词汇题型介绍和解题方法指导

题型介绍

　　词汇和语法结构部分在试卷中共 20 题，考试时间为 15 分钟。其目的是测试考生运用词汇、短语及语法的能力。该部分包括两节：Section A 共 10 题，为选择题，每题 0.5 分。Section B 共 10 题，为填空题，每题 1 分。主要包括句法结构、词形变化、词类用法、动词用法等。

解题方法指导

（1）理解题意，找准题眼，判断成分。
（2）推断词性，选用构词法，派生词形。
（3）明确英语四大实词的定义和语法功用。
（4）明确语法结构，多重思考，严密思维。

第二节　历年词汇考点统计、考点解读和解题技巧

历年考点统计与考点解读

2006 年—2009 年词汇题型考点分布图

年份	谓语	非谓语结构	虚拟搭配	固定搭配	词形转换	合计
2006年6月	2	/	/	3	5	10
2006年12月	3	2	/	/	5	10
2007年6月	2	/	1	2	5	10
2007年12月	3	1	/	2	5	11
2008年6月	3	/	1	2	5	11
2008年12月	1	2	/	1	5	10
2009年6月	1	1	/	3	4	9

解题技巧与历年真题点评

1. 理解题意，找准题眼，判断成分

　　理解题意、找准题眼、判断成分是做词汇填空的"三步曲"。理解题意是至关重要的

第一步，如果不能理解句意，就不能做出正确的选择；理解题意之后，要明确每一道题目命题者的意图，这称为题眼或考点，这是做题的关键一步，对历年英语应用能力测试 B 级试卷分析研究后发现，题眼主要包括谓语和非谓语动词、语法搭配、句法结构、固定搭配等几个方面；最后，运用掌握的各项基础知识加以分析判断。完成这"三步曲"之后，在很大程度上就能提高该项题型的正确率。如以下两题：

1. We usually (go) ___ abroad for our holiday, but this year we are staying at home.

（2005 年 6 月真题第 29 题）

经过分析发现前半句中缺少了谓语动词，是一道典型的谓语动词题。在做这类题时主要考虑时态、语态、人称三个方面，因此，根据括号里所给单词，该动词与主语是主动关系，并且"usually"这一单词在这句话中起了至关重要的作用，"usually"意为"in the way that is usual; most often 通常地；惯常地"。所以，按照我们所掌握的知识，应该采用一般现在时，这道题目的正确答案应是"go"。整句话的意思是"我们通常到国外去度假，但今年我们待在家里"。

2. There was a stranger (stand) _____ at the door.

（2002 年 6 月真题第 33 题）

经过分析看出本题已经有一个谓语动词"was"，我们应该确定这是一道非谓语动词题，意思是"有个陌生人站在门口"，根据题眼"was"，那么我们就要把动词"stand"处理成非谓语动词形式，"stranger"和"stand"之间是一种主动关系，所以我们应该采用表示主动意义的现在分词形式"standing"，而且"standing at the door"现在分词短语应该放在所修饰词"stranger"后面。

2. 推断词性，选用构词法，派生词形

词性转换类题型在词汇填空题当中占40%，此题型考点是将所给单词根据语法要求进行不同词性间的转换，其中大部分是通过增加或减少前后缀来实现词性转换。可见掌握词形派生法是十分必要的，要求考生注意平时词汇的积累，着重掌握 B 级考试词汇表中单词及有关前缀、后缀构词法的知识。

派生是通过在词干上加上词缀而生成新词的过程，词缀大致可分为前缀和后缀两种。在做题过程中，我们要先根据句子的意义和句子结构，推断出应填词的词性，然后运用已掌握的派生法，使单词进行相应的变化。

至于派生法，在对历年英语应用能力测试 B 级试卷研究中，还未涉及对前缀用法的测试，所以此处只总结出测试中常见的后缀现象。考生掌握了这些常见后缀的基本功用，领会其中的基本规律之后，应该能在以后的考试中举一反三，以不变应万变。

历年 B 级考试中常见后缀总结如下：

（1）在英语中，后缀"-en"可加在名词或形容词后构成动词，意思是"使……变得"。

He is told to <u>shorten</u> (short) his report to one page.

（2004 年 12 月真题第 30 题）

It is well-known that sports will <u>strengthen</u> (strength) the friendship between nations.

（2006 年 6 月真题第 35 题）

（2）在英语中，后缀"-ion"和"-ment"可以加在动词之后构成与原意相同的名词。

Mary told me not to worry because the <u>operation</u> (operate) on Mr. Smith was very successful.

（2002 年 12 月真题第 30 题）

The fast <u>development</u> (develop) of the local economy has caused serious water pollution in this region.

（2007 年 12 月真题第 30 题）

（3）在英语中，后缀 "-y" 和 "-ly" 可以加在名词之后构成形容词，意思是 "多……的" 或 "像……的"。

The sellers allowed the US to pay them on a <u>monthly</u> (month) basis.

（2001 年 6 月真题第 30 题）

The children looked <u>healthy</u> (health) with bright smiles on their faces.

（2005 年 12 月真题第 26 题）

（4）在英语中，名词后缀 "-ence" 可以转换成形容词后缀 "-ent"，构成形容词，意思是 "具有……的特性" 或 "处于……的状况"。

Although the small town has been changing slowly, it looks quite <u>different</u> (difference) from what it was.

（2007 年 12 月真题第 27 题）

（5）在英语中，后缀 "-er"，"-or" 和 "-ar" 可以加在动词之后构成名词，意思是 "该动作的执行者"。

Yao Ming, our favorite basketball <u>player</u> (play), is becoming a super star in the world.

（2004 年 12 月真题第 35 题）

The flexible working time system will enable the <u>employee(s)/employer(s)</u> (employ) to work more efficiently.

（2005 年 12 月真题第 32 题）

3. 明确英语四大实词的定义和语法功用

英语中，四大实词是指名词、动词、形容词和副词，它们是句子中的中心词和关键词。名词，表示人、事物、地点或抽象概念的名称，在句中常做主语或宾语；动词，表示人或事物的动作或状态，一般做谓语；形容词，说明人、事物或现象的性质和特征，常做定语修饰名词，或置于系动词之后做表语，或做宾语补足语；副词，用来修饰动词、形容词、副词或整个句子，说明时间、地点、程度等。对这四类词汇意义和用法的掌握是做好相关词汇填空题的前提，所以先确定好所填词在句中充当的成分，按照四大实词的定义，来确定是哪一类词汇。如以下四组例句：

(1) The <u>management</u> (manage) of a company is a very important part of the working process to its development.

（2002 年 6 月真题第 28 题）

It is difficult for a <u>foreigner</u> (foreign) to learn Chinese.

（2004 年 6 月真题第 29 题）

所填词在句中充当主语，体现出了名词的具体用法。

(2) As soon as we <u>got</u> (get) home，it started to rain heavily.

（2003 年 12 月真题第 32 题）

Next week we <u>will sign</u> (sign) the sales contract with the new supplier.

（2006 年 6 月真题第 29 题）

所填词在句中充当谓语，所以用括号内的动词本身，再附以一定的时态来体现。

(3) Your ideas are very interesting，but we need some <u>practical</u> (practice) advice for getting out of the trouble.

（2002 年 6 月真题第 35 题）

John's performance in this exam made us feel rather <u>disappointed</u> (disappoint).

（2003 年 12 月真题第 33 题）

所填词分别是句中的定语和宾语补足语，应当用形容词。

(4) I didn't attend the evening party: but <u>apparently</u> (apparent), it was a great success.

（2001 年 6 月真题第 33 题）

(5) <u>Unfortunately</u> (unfortunate), she has got a bad cold and can't attend the conference.

（2001 年 12 月真题第 34 题）

很显然，能修饰整句话的只能是副词。

4. 明确语法结构，多重思考，严密思维

语法结构题是词汇填空的第二类题型，根据对历年英语应用能力测试 B 级考试卷的研究，其语法范围主要包括：时态、语态、语气、非谓语动词、主谓一致、倒装句以及形容词副词的比较级和最高级等多方面。正如本节开头所说，词汇填空需要考生从多角度、多方面进行思考，有时甚至需要考生利用两种或是三种语法现象进行多重综合思考，体现了句子的整体性和语法的连贯性，同时也体现了思维的严密性。如以下例句：

(1) Hardly had we gathered in the square when it <u>began</u> (begin) to rain.

（2004 年 12 月真题第 31 题）

(2) Jane <u>had been praised</u> (praise) many times by the general manager when she was working as the office secretary.

（2005 年 12 月真题第 33 题）

以上两道题目，都是多种语法现象的叠加，需要考生进行多重思维。如：第 1 题考虑了 "hardly…when…" 这一基本句型结构之后，再考虑主从句各用何种时态，然后再体会否定词置于句首要采用倒装语序；第二题考虑时态的同时还要思考语态问题，句子涉及过去完成时和被动语态。

第三节 词汇典型真题分析

2006 年 6 月真题

26. Of all the hotels in the city, this one is the ＿＿＿ (good).

【答案】best

【解析】主句中缺少表语，应填形容词补上，另外，"of all the hotels in the city" 说明是两家以上，所以形容词用最高级。

【译文】这座城市中的所有酒店里，这家是最好的。

27. Yesterday they received a written _____ (invite) to a dinner from Mr. Black.

【答案】invitation

【解析】句中缺少宾语，而且空格前有形容词 written 修饰，应补上名词形式。

【译文】昨天他们收到了布莱克先生寄来的手写的晚宴邀请书。

28. That new film is worth _____ (see) for the second time.

【答案】seeing

【解析】be worth doing sth.

【译文】这部电影值得去看第二次。

29. Next week we _____ (sign) the sales contract with the new supplier.

【答案】will sign

【解析】next week 说明是将来时，所以 sign 要加 will 表示将来。

【译文】下星期我们会与新的供应商签订销售合同。

30. _____ (general) speaking, he is a person that you can trust.

【答案】Generally

【解析】固定搭配

【译文】一般而言，他是一个值得你相信的人。

31. The new machine ought to _____ (test) before it is put to use.

【答案】be tested

【解析】"ought to do" 表示应该，等于 "should do"，另外句子主语为 "machine"，应用被动语态。

【译文】这部新机器在投入使用前应该经过测试。

32. If your credit（信誉）is good, you will be allowed _____ (use) the credit card.

【答案】to use

【解析】allow sb. to do sth. 为固定搭配短语，表示 "同意某人做某事"。

【译文】如果你的信誉良好，你将会被允许使用信用卡。

33. It will be very _____ (help) if each member presents his or her own opinion at the meeting.

【答案】helpful

【解析】句中缺少表语形容词，应补上 helpful。类似变形的单词：colourful, mouthful, careful。

【译文】如果每个会员都在会议上提出自己的观点，那将会很有帮助。

34. The number of sales people who have left the company _____ (be) very small.

【答案】is

【解析】主语是 "the number" 指数量，因此要用谓语的单数形式。

【译文】离开公司的销售人员的数量是很少的。

35. It is well-known that sports will _____ (strength) the friendship between nations.

【答案】strengthen

【解析】strength 是名词，这里缺乏一个动词，表示 "增强、巩固" 的意思，所以要用动词形式 "-en" 后缀，一般可以与形容词结合，使其变形为动词，表示 "使变得……"，类似的单词有：widen, sharpen, shorten, whiten 等。

【译文】众所周知，体育可以增进各民族之间的友谊。

2006 年 12 月真题

26. It is a fact that traditional meals are ____ (healthy) than fast foods.

【答案】healthier

【解析】"than" 暗示了两种事物相比较，所以要用形容词的比较级。要注意形容词比较级的构成规则。

【译文】事实上，传统的膳食比快餐健康得多。

27. Nurses should treat the sick and wounded with great _____ (kind).

【答案】kindness

【解析】with 后缺少介词宾语，因此要补上名词。"-ness" 为名词后缀，加在形容词和分词后，构成表示状态或情况的抽象名词，如：darkness 黑暗。

【译文】护士应该亲切地对待病人和伤者。

28. All visitors to the lab _____ (expect) to take off their shoes before they enter.

【答案】are expected

【解析】固定搭配短语 sb. be expected to do sth.，某人应该做某事。

【译文】所有来访者要脱下鞋子才能进入实验室。

29. _____ (personal), I think he is a very nice partner, though you may not agree.

【答案】Personally

【解析】personally 通常放在句首，表示发表自己的个人见解。

【译文】就我本人而言，我觉得他是一个很好的合作伙伴，可能你未必同意。

30. They talked to him for hours, ____ (try) to persuade him to change his mind.

【答案】trying

【解析】现在分词做伴随状语，它所表达的动作或状态是伴随着句子谓语动词的动作而发生的。

【译文】他们和他谈了数小时，试图说服他改变想法。

31. His efforts to improve the sales of this product have been very ____ (help).

【答案】helpful

【解析】句子属于 be + adj. 的系表结构，很明显缺少一个形容词。

【译文】他作出的努力对改善这个产品的销售已经有很大的帮助了。

32. When we arrived, there was a smell of cooking ____ (come) from the kitchen.

【答案】coming

【解析】"come" 的逻辑主语是 "smell"，当动词和前面的主语是主动关系时，用 doing；"coming" 在这里是做 "smell" 的补语。

【译文】当我们到达的时候，闻到一阵从厨房里传出来烹饪的香气。

33. We have to find new ways to _____ (short) the process of production.

【答案】shorten

【解析】find ways to do sth., to 后面要接动词原形，句中给出的形容词要改成动词。

【译文】我们不得不找出新方法去缩短生产过程。

34. By this time next year my family ____ (live) in this small town for 20 years.

【答案】will have lived

【解析】"by+ 将来的一段时间"是表示到将来某个时间为止，句中要用将来完成时，所以谓语要用 "will have lived"。"by+ 过去时间"，则用过去完成时。

【译文】到下一年的这个时候，我家住在这个小镇就有 20 年了。

35. Jane, as well as some of her classmates, ____ (work) in the Quality Control Department now.

【答案】works

【解析】在 A as well as B 的结构里，谓语动词取决于句子的第一个主语。

【译文】现在，Jane 和一些同班同学在质量控制部门工作。

2007 年 6 月真题

26. She managed to settle the argument in a ____ (friend) way.

【答案】friendly

【解析】从句法分析，空格前后分别为介词和名词，显然应填形容词做名词的定语，后缀 "-ly" 加在名词后构成形容词或副词，如：monthly, weekly, costly, timely, likely 等。

【译文】她打算用友好的方法解决这个争论。

27. I would rather you ____ (go) with me tomorrow morning.

【答案】went

【解析】考到 would rather sb. did sth. 固定搭配。

【译文】我宁愿你和我明天早上一起去。

28. If I ____ (be) you, I wouldn't ask such a silly question.

【答案】were

【解析】句中条件句做了假设，主句谓语用了 "would do"，根据下表，判断从句谓语应填 were。

	If从句中动词形式	主句中动词形式
1. 与现在相反	were 过去式	would/should/ could/might + do
2. 与过去相反	had done	would/should/ could/might + have done
3. 与未来相反	were to do	would/should/ could/might + do
	should do (万一)	

【译文】如果我是你，我不会问这么愚蠢的问题。

29. You should send me the report on the program ____ (immediate).

【答案】immediately

【解析】副词做状语，"-ly" 加在形容词后构成副词。

【译文】你需要马上将程序报告交给我。

30. As soon as the result ＿＿＿ (come) out, I'll let you know.

　　【答案】comes

　　【解析】as soon as 引导条件状语从句，句中谓语用一般现在时表将来。

　　【译文】一旦结果出来，我就告诉你。

31. If you smoke in this non-smoking area, you will ＿＿＿ (fine) $50.

　　【答案】be fined

　　【解析】fine 表罚款，句中应用被动形式。

　　【译文】如果你在无烟区抽烟，你将会被罚款 50 美元。

32. It is quite difficult for me ＿＿＿ (decide) who should be given the job.

　　【答案】to decide

　　【解析】考到了 It is difficult for sb. to do sth. 固定搭配。

　　【译文】我很难决定谁将获得这份工作。

33. The new flexible working time system will enable the ＿＿＿＿ (employ) to work more efficiently.

　　【答案】employees

　　【解析】固定搭配短语 enable sb. to do sth. 使某人有能力做某事，判断句中缺少名词做宾语，另外，后缀 "-ee" ① =the object 表示受动者，如：appointee 被任命人；② =person receiving 表示处于某一种情况下的人，如 absentee 缺席者；③ =the object 表示"与……有关的人"，如：committee 委员会。

　　【译文】这个新的灵活的工作时间系统将能够使员工们更加有效地工作。

34. The more careful you are, the ＿＿＿ (well) you will be able to complete the work.

　　【答案】better

　　【解析】考到比较级固定搭配，the + 比较级 …the + 比较级，表示"越……越……"。

　　【译文】你越是认真你就越有能力完成这个工作。

35. I'll put forward my ＿＿＿＿ (suggest) now so that he can have time to consider it before the meeting.

　　【答案】suggestion

　　【解析】句中缺少名词做宾语，后缀 "-tion" 加在动词后构成名词。

　　【译文】我现在将提出建议以便他可以有时间在会议前考虑。

2007 年 12 月真题

26. David will go on holiday as soon as he ＿＿＿＿ (finish) the project.

　　【答案】finishes

　　【解析】as soon as 引导条件状语从句，句中谓语用一般现在时表将来。

　　【译文】戴维一完成这个项目就去休假。

27. Although the small town has been changing slowly, it looks quite ＿＿＿＿ (difference) from what it was.

　　【答案】different

　　【解析】句中缺少形容词做表语，应补上 different。

　　【译文】虽然这个小镇变化缓慢，但它看起来与过去大不一样了。

28. My father is a sports fan and he enjoys _____ (swim) very much.

【答案】swimming

【解析】固定搭配短语 enjoy doing sth.。

【译文】我爸爸是个体育迷，他很喜欢游泳。

29. The small village has become _____ (wide) known in recent years for its silk exports.

【答案】widely

【解析】句中 "known" 为表语形容词，应补上副词修饰形容词。

【译文】这个小村庄由于它的丝绸出口在最近几年变得非常知名。

30. The fast _____ (develop) of the local economy has caused serious water pollution in this region.

【答案】development

【解析】句中缺少主语，应补上名词做主语，后缀 "-ment" 附在动词或动词词根后构成名词，如：amendment, management 等。

【译文】本地经济的快速发展引起了这个地区严重的水污染。

31. Thank you for your letter of April 15, _____ (tell) us about Mr. John Brown's visit to our company on May 10.

【答案】telling

【解析】现在分词在句中做伴随状语。

【译文】谢谢你 4 月 15 日的来信告诉我们，约翰·布朗先生将于 5 月 10 日访问公司。

32. The _____ (late) model of the racing car will be on display at the exhibition this week.

【答案】latest

【解析】latest，表示 "最新的"。

【译文】最新型号的赛车将在本星期的展览上展出。

33. Miss Li was _____ (luck) enough to get the opportunity to work in that world-famous company.

【答案】lucky

【解析】句中缺少表语形容词，应补上形容词，后缀 "-y" = full of，如 clumsy 笨拙的，tricky 狡猾的，hairy 毛茸茸的。

【译文】李小姐获得在世界知名公司工作的机会是相当幸运的。

34. Last year, customers _____ (buy) a total of 90 million iPods and 2 billion songs from the iTunes store.

【答案】bought

【解析】句中 "last year"，明确表示过去时间，因此用过去时。

【译文】去年，消费者从 iTunes 商店购买 9 000 万台 iPods 的机子和 20 亿首歌。

35. Yesterday, the secretary _____ (give) the task to make arrangements for the annual meeting.

【答案】was given

【解析】句中 "yesterday"，表示过去时间，而且主谓关系为被动，因此填上被动语态。

【译文】昨天，秘书接到的任务是为年度会议做安排。

第四节　词汇专项模拟训练及答案解析

（一）

26. I prefer to spend the weekend at home rather than _____ (go) to the concert.

27. Since there is so little time _____ (leave), nobody can fulfill the task.

28. John and Mary arrived, the _____ (late) wearing a green wool dress.

29. We surely _____ (find) a good solution to the technical problems in the near future.

30. If you _____ (sharp) an object, you will make its edge thin or make its end pointed.

31. It is absolutely essential that all facts _____ (examine) first.

32. The swimmer failed _____ (reach) the shore.

33. The date of our _____ (arrive) is postponed once again for the thunderstorm has blocked the air traffic since Wednesday.

34. It was recommended that we _____ (wait) for the authorities.

35. If you don't want to get wet, then you had better _____ (take) this umbrella with you.

（二）

26. It's very _____ (thought) and very kind of you to offer me a job in your company.

27. _____ (judge) from previous experience, he will be late.

28. I would rather our team members _____ (prepare) for the worst.

29. I was so _____ (embarrass) that I didn't know what to say.

30. He insists that students _____ (have) the freedom to choose what to learn.

31. The girls next door used _____ (like) making clothes, but they seem to have stopped doing that now.

32. Before you mail the application letter, read it over again, _____ (make) sure that it is perfect.

33. The two _____ (develop) countries are now working together to improve their economies.

34. Future cars will _____ (tight) your seat belt automatically in time of danger.

35. I have no choice but _____ (accept) the fact.

答案解析

（一）

26.【答案】go

【解析】prefer to do sth. rather than do sth. "宁愿……而不……"。

【译文】我宁愿周末在家而不愿去音乐会。

27.【答案】left

【解析】原句可以在 "time" 后面加上 "which is left"，剩下的时间，表示被动，"which" 和 "is" 可同时省略，作为时间的修饰，使句子看起来简单。

【译文】由于剩下的时间不多，没有人可以完成这个任务。

28.【答案】latter

【解析】根据语境判断"the"后面应该加名词,"latter"表示"后者"。

【译文】John 和 Mary 到了,后面的那个穿着绿色羊毛衣服。

29.【答案】will find

【解析】"in the near future"是表示将来的时间,所以要用 will find。

【译文】我们一定会在不久的将来为这些技术问题找到很好的解决方案。

30.【答案】sharpen

【解析】句中缺少谓语,因此空格应填动词 sharpen。

【译文】如果你把一个物体给削锋利了,你会磨掉它的边缘或是让它的头变尖。

31.【答案】(should) be examined

【解析】在 "It is (was) + 形容词(或过去分词)+ that..." 结构中,主语从句的谓语要用 "should + 动词原形"表虚拟语气。由于"all facts"与"examine"是被动关系,所以"examine"用被动式。

【译文】对所有的事实先加以检验是非常重要的。

32.【答案】to reach

【解析】fail to do sth./fail in doing sth. 都是表示不能成功做某事。

【译文】这名游泳选手没有成功游到岸边。

33.【答案】arrival

【解析】句子中缺少名词,需要把动词转换成为名词,因此该名词应为 arrival。

【译文】自星期三开始,雷震雨造成了航空交通的堵塞,使我们的到达日期再次推迟了。

34.【答案】(should) wait

【解析】在 "It is (was) + 形容词(或过去分词)+ that..." 结构中,主语从句的谓语要用 "(should) + 动词原形"表虚拟语气。

【译文】有人建议我们有必要等待那些专家们。

35.【答案】take

【解析】had better do sth. 最好做某事。

【译文】如果你不想被淋湿,你自己最好带把雨伞。

（二）

26.【答案】thoughtful

【解析】"very"是修饰形容词的,因此本句的动词要转换成为形容词"thoughtful"。

【译文】你在贵公司给我提供一份工作,真的感谢你的关照和好意。

27.【答案】Judging

【解析】"judging"表示"从……判断",用动词的主动形式表示原因,做原因状语。

【译文】从先前的经验来判断,他将会迟到。

28.【答案】prepared

【解析】would rather + 从句,是一个常用的虚拟语气句型,从句中谓语一般用过去时来表示现在或将来。其意为"宁愿……,还是……好些","一个人宁愿另一个人做某事"。引导从句的 that 常省略。在谈到过去的动作时，谓语则用过去完成时。

【译文】我宁愿我们团队的成员做好最坏的打算。

29.【答案】embarrassed

【解析】句子缺少表语，"so"是修饰形容词的，所以应填上形容词，因此该形容词应为"embarrassed"。

【译文】我很尴尬以至于我不知道说些什么。

30.【答案】(should) have

【解析】在表示建议、命令、要求、忠告等动词的后面，其宾语从句的谓语用"(should) +动词原形"表示虚拟语气。

【译文】他坚持每个学生都有自由选择学什么。

31.【答案】to like

【解析】从句意可以知道是以前和现在的对比，used to do sth. 意为"过去常常做某事"。

【译文】隔壁的女孩们以前常常喜欢做衣服，但是她们现在似乎已经不做了。

32.【答案】making

【解析】原句可为：you must make sure that it is perfect. 把句子转化为状语，去掉主语，用现在分词表示主动，主句和从句的主语一致。

【译文】在你邮寄申请信以前，请再次阅读以保证它是完美的。

33.【答案】developing

【解析】句子中缺少定语，动词要转换成为形容词，做定语，因此该形容词应为 developing。

【译文】这两个发展中国家正在共同努力，以改善其经济。

34.【答案】tighten

【解析】"will"是情态动词，"tight"是形容词，所以 tight 要转换为动词。

【译文】未来的汽车在遇到危险时将自动收紧驾驶者的安全带。

35.【答案】to accept

【解析】but 是转折，在这句子里面做介词。在含介词 but 的句型中，but 前有 do，则 but 后的不定式不能带 to；相反，but 前若找不到 do，则 but 后的不定式必定带 to。

【译文】除了接受现实，我没有其他选择。

第五节　语法结构题型介绍和解题方法指导

题型介绍

B 级考试语法结构题为单项选择题，共 10 道题，每题 0.5 分。主要的测试题型为谓语动词题、非谓语动词题、语法搭配题、句法结构题和常用句型题等。

解题方法指导

考生在做题时应该培养以下解题习惯：

1. 读懂句子，理解题意

这是做题的第一步，也是关键的一步。题意没有看懂，就很难选择出正确答案。首先要读懂句子，分析该句的结构以及主要成分（主语、谓语、宾语等），大致理解该题的意思。做题时应记住该题是"英语"题，不是"汉语"题，因此不要用汉语的习惯进行思考、分析、判断和选择。

2. 认准考点，明确意图

读懂题意之后，要大致推断出该句的测试题型，即考点，明确命题者的意图。按照上述的五大考点：谓语动词题、非谓语动词题、语法搭配题、句法结构题和常用句型题，结合该题的题干和选项进行分析，认准该题的考点。抓住了考点就抓住了关键，其他问题就能迎刃而解，然后运用掌握的词汇、短语和语法知识进行分析、判断和选择。

3. 意义和语法并重

正确选项必须满足题目意义和语法结构两方面的要求。除了保证语法结构正确，还应考虑题目意义方面的需求。英语中有不少的惯用词语搭配、习惯表达法和特殊用法等，都需要考生特别注意。

4. 思路开阔，做题细心

要利用题目中所给出的信息开阔自己的思路和分析方法，不要用一成不变的思路和方法去选择答案，可以从不同角度去思考和分析每道试题。因为试题中多一个词或少一个词，就可能完全改变该题的测试要点。要细心地分析，判断是否有更合适的选择项，因为只有一个选项是正确的。做题细心不仅是好的态度，也是好的方法。

第六节　历年语法结构考点统计、考点解读和解题技巧（B级考试重点考查的九种语法现象）

历年语法结构考点统计

考试时间 考点	2009年 6月	2008年 12月	2008年 6月	2007年 12月	2007年 6月	2006年 12月	2006年 6月	2001年 12月
词汇	7	6	6	7	5	5	6	
非谓语动词		2	1	1	1	2	1	
时态、语态		1			1	1	1	
复合句	1	1	2	1	3		1	
虚拟语气			1	1				
情态动词						1		
倒装句型	1				1			
强调句	1							
主谓一致								1

从上表统计结果可以看出，B 级考试中词汇考点占相当大的比例，词汇测试的重点是：（1）动词（短语）；（2）近义词和近形词辨义；（3）习惯搭配。

考点解读

（1）词汇题主要考查动词或动词短语、近义词和近形词辨义和习惯搭配等。

（2）非谓语动词主要考查不定式、分词（现在分词 / 过去分词）、动名词。

（3）时态主要考查一般过去时、过去完成时、将来完成时等，语态主要考查被动语态。

（4）复合句主要考查定语从句、状语从句、表语从句、同位语从句等。

（5）虚拟语气主要考查常见的虚拟形式。

（6）情态动词主要考查 must, could, should, would, might 等的用法。

（7）倒装句型主要考查部分倒装。

（8）强调句型主要考查其基本的结构以及识别被强调的成分。

（9）主谓一致主要考查主语和谓语动词在人称和数上的一致性。

解题技巧

1. 解题步骤

1.1　大致浏览所给四个选项和句子，迅速判断该题是语法题还是词汇题。如果是语法题要通过一些标志词来判断该题涉及哪些语法内容，再进一步回忆该语法内容的要点。如果是词汇题就要先看一下所给四个选项的词是否都认识。

1.2　在第一遍的大致浏览过程中，有些题很容易就可以选出肯定的答案。然后再从头开始仔细看没有选出答案的题。遵循先语法后语意的原则解题。

1.3　利用暗示进行选择：注意考题设计的语境范围。平时应注重对习惯用语表达、惯用法和中英文化差别等方面知识的积累。

1.4　运用排除法：可采取语言排除、逻辑排除、语法排除或选择排除等方法。先排除掉较容易、较明显的错误选项，缩小范围，而后对剩余的选项进行比较分析，最后确定答案。

2. 注意事项

2.1　先易后难：一些考题的答案比较容易选定，可以先从这些考题入手。平时练习时，应以基础为主，主要精力不应放在偏题、怪题上，因为 B 级考试考查的主要是常见的语法现象。

2.2　注意考试时间的分配，对不会做的题目不要恋战，尽量把时间放在后面分值较高的题上。

2.3　在选定答案时要根据每题的实际情况进行综合的分析判断，先排除较容易、较明显的错误选项，缩小范围，而后对剩余的选项进行比较分析，最后确定答案。

2.4　对于经过分析判断得出的答案不要反复进行检查，要相信自己的直觉和判断。

3. 各题型应对策略

3.1　词汇题

解答词汇题首先要读懂题意，了解和辨别所提供的不同词的词义和用法，熟悉固定的习惯搭配。这要求考生平时要注意区别一些容易混淆的同义词、近义词；注意形式相似，但意思截然不同的词；掌握一定数量的词组的含义和用法；掌握一些常见动词与副词或介词所构成的词组的含义。同时，词汇选择题需要注意以下原则：意义一致原则、单（复）数一致的原则、时态一致原则等。

3.2　非谓语动词题

3.2.1　非谓语动词的做题步骤

第一，判定是否用非谓语形式。方法：看看句子中是否已有了谓语动词。

第二，找非谓语动词的逻辑主语。方法：非谓语动词的逻辑主语一般是句子的主语。

第三，判断主被动关系。方法：判断非谓语动词与其逻辑主语是主动还是被动关系。

第四，判断时间关系。方法：分析句子，看看非谓语动词所表示的动作发生在谓语动作之前、之后还是同时。之前常用 done; 之后常用 to do; 同时常用 doing。

3.2.2　非谓语动词语法归纳

非谓语动词可分为三种：不定式、分词（现在分词 / 过去分词）、动名词。

3.2.2.1　动词不定式

不定式具有名词、形容词、副词的特征。

（1）不定式的形式：(to) + do

否定式：not + (to) do

1）一般式：不定式的一般式所表示的动作与谓语动词动作同时发生或发生在谓语动词动作之后，例如：

He seems to know a lot.

2）进行式：不定式的进行式所表示的动作与谓语动词动作同时发生，例如：

The boy pretended to be working hard.

3）完成式：不定式的完成式表示的动作发生在谓语动词表示的动作之前，例如：

I regretted to have told a lie.

（2）不定式的句法功能：

1）做主语：

To finish the work in ten minutes is very hard.

动词不定式短语做主语时，常用 it 做形式主语，真正的主语不定式置于句后，例如上句可用如下形式：

It is very hard to finish the work in ten minutes.

常用句式有：① It + be + 名词 + to do；② It takes sb. + some time + to do；③ It + be + 形容词 + of sb. + to do；④ It + be + 形容词 + for sb. + to do。常用 careless, clever, good, foolish, honest, kind, lazy, nice, right, silly, stupid, wise 等表示赞扬或批评的形容词，不定式前的 sb. 可做其逻辑主语。

2）做表语：

Her job is to clean the hall.

3）做宾语：

常与不定式做宾语连用的动词有：want, hope, wish, offer, fail, plan, learn, pretend, refuse, manage, help, agree, promise, prefer, 如果不定式（宾语）后面有宾语补足语, 则用 it 做形式宾语, 真正的宾语（不定式）后置, 放在宾语补足语后面, 例如:

Marx found it important to study the situation in Russia.

动词不定式也可充当介词宾语, 如:

I have no choice but to stay here.

动词不定式前有时可与疑问词连用, 如:

He gave us some advice on how to learn English.

4）做宾语补足语:

在复合宾语中, 动词不定式可充当宾语补足语, 如下动词常跟这种复合宾语: want, wish, ask, tell, order, beg, permit, help, advise, persuade, allow, prepare, cause, force, call on, wait for, invite。

此外, 介词有时也与这种复合宾语连用, 如:

With a lot of work to do, he didn't go to the cinema.

有些动词如 make, let, see, watch, hear, feel, have 等与不带 to 的不定式连用, 但改为被动语态时, 不定式要加 to, 如:

I saw him cross the road.

He was seen to cross the road.

5）做定语:

动词不定式做定语, 放在所修饰的名词或代词后, 与所修饰名词有如下关系:

① 动宾关系:

I have a meeting to attend.

注意: 不定式为不及物动词时, 所修饰的名词如果是地点、工具等, 应有必要的介词, 如:

He found a good house to live in.

如果不定式修饰的名词是 time, place, way, 可以省略介词:

He has no place to live.

如果不定式所修饰名词是不定式动作承受者, 不定式可用主动式也可用被动式:

Have you got anything to send?

② 说明所修饰名词的内容:

We have made a plan to finish the work.

③ 被修饰名词是不定式的逻辑主语:

He is the first to get here.

6）做状语:

① 表目的:

He worked day and night to get the money.

② 表结果（往往是与预期愿望相反的结果）:

He arrived late only to find the train had gone.

③表原因：

They were very sad to hear the news.

④表程度：

It's too dark for us to see anything.

7）做独立成分：

To tell you the truth, I don't like the way he talked.

8）不定式的省略：保留 to 省略 do 动词。

If you don't want to do it, you don't need to.

9）不定式的并列：第二个不定式可省略 to。

He wished to study medicine and become a doctor.

3.2.2.2　动名词

动名词既具有动词的一些特征，又具有名词的句法功能。

（1）动名词的形式：V + ing

　　　否定式：not + 动名词

1）一般式：

Seeing is believing. 眼见为实。

2）被动式：

He came to the party without being invited. 他未被邀请就来到了晚会。

3）完成式：

We remembered having seen the film. 我们记得看过这部电影。

4）完成被动式：

He forgot having been taken to Guangzhou when he was five years old. 他忘记五岁时曾被带去过广州。

5）否定式：not + 动名词

I regret not following his advice. 我后悔没听他的劝告。

6）复合结构：物主代词（或名词所有格）+ 动名词

He suggested our trying it once again. 他建议我们再试一次。

His not knowing English troubled him a lot. 他不懂英语给他带来许多麻烦。

（2）动名词的句法功能：

1）做主语：

Reading aloud is very helpful. 大声朗读是很有好处的。

当动名词短语做主语时常用 it 做形式主语。

It's no use quarrelling. 争吵是没用的。

2）做表语：

In the ant city, the queen's job is laying eggs. 在蚂蚁王国，蚁后的工作是产卵。

3）做宾语：

We have to prevent the air from being polluted. 我们必须防止空气污染。

注意动名词既可做动词宾语也可做介词宾语，如上面两个例句。此外，动名词做宾语时，若跟有宾语补足语，则常用形式宾语 it，例如：

We found it no good making fun of others. 我们发现取笑他人不好。

要记住如下动词及短语只跟动名词做宾语：

enjoy, finish, suggest, avoid（避免）, excuse, delay, imagine, keep, miss, consider, admit（承认）, deny（否认）, mind, permit, forbid, practise, risk（冒险）, appreciate（感激）, be busy, be worth, feel like, can't stand, can't help（情不自禁地）, think of, dream of, be fond of, prevent… (from), keep …from, stop… (from), protect…from, set about, be engaged in, spend… (in), succeed in, be used to, look forward to, object to, pay attention to, insist on, feel like.

4）做定语：

He can't walk without a walking stick. 他没有拐杖不能走路。

5）做同位语：

His habit, listening to the news on the radio remains unchanged. 他收听收音机新闻节目的习惯仍未改变。

3.2.2.3 现在分词

现在分词既具有动词的一些特征，又具有形容词和副词的句法功能。

（1）现在分词的形式：V + ing

否定式：not + 现在分词

1）现在分词的主动语态：现在分词主动语态的一般式表示的动作与谓语动词所表示的动作同时发生，完成式表示的动作在谓语动词所表示的动作之前发生，常做状语。

They went to the park, singing and talking. 他们边唱边说向公园走去。

2）现在分词的被动语态：一般式表示与谓语动词同时发生的被动的动作，完成式表示发生在谓语动词之前的被动的动作。

The problem being discussed is very important. 正在被讨论的问题很重要。

（2）现在分词的句法功能：

1）做定语：现在分词做定语，当分词单独做定语时，放在所修饰的名词前；如果是分词短语做定语则放在名词后。

In the following years he worked even harder. 在后来的几年中，他工作更努力了。

The man speaking to the teacher is our monitor's father. 正与老师谈话的那个人是我们班长的父亲。

现在分词做定语相当于一个定语从句的句法功能，如：in the following years 也可用 in the years that followed; the man speaking to the teacher 可改为 the man who is speaking to the teacher。

2）做表语：

The film being shown in the cinema is exciting. 正在这家上演的电影很让人兴奋。

be + doing 既可能表示现在进行时，也可能是现在分词做表语，它们的区别在于 be + doing 表示进行的动作是进行时，而表示特征时是系动词 be 与现在分词构成系表结构。

3）做宾语补足语：

如下动词后可跟现在分词做宾语补足语：

see, watch, hear, feel, find, get, keep, notice, observe, listen to, look at, leave, catch 等。

4）做状语：

① 做时间状语：

(While) Working in the factory, he was an advanced worker. 在工厂工作时，他是一名先进工人。

② 做原因状语：

Being a League member, he is always helping others. 由于是共青团员，他经常帮助他人。

③ 做方式状语，表示伴随：

He stayed at home, cleaning and washing. 他待在家里，又擦又洗。

④ 做条件状语：

(If) Playing all day, you will waste your valuable time. 要是整天玩，你就会浪费宝贵的时间。

⑤ 做结果状语：

He dropped the glass, breaking it into pieces. 他把杯子弄掉了，结果摔得粉碎。

⑥ 做目的状语：

He went swimming the other day. 几天前他去游泳了。

⑦ 做让步状语：

Though raining heavily, it cleared up very soon. 虽然雨下得很大，但不久天就晴了。

⑧ 与逻辑主语构成独立主格：

I waiting for the bus, a bird fell on my head. 我等汽车时，一只鸟落到我头上。

All the tickets having been sold out, they went away disappointedly. 所有的票已经卖光了，他们失望地离开了。

Time permitting, we'll do another two exercises. 如果时间允许，我们将做另两个练习。

有时也可用 with (without) + 名词（代词宾格）+ 分词形式。

With the lights burning, he fell asleep. 他点着灯睡着了。

⑨ 做独立成分：

Judging from (by) his appearance, he must be an actor. 从外表看，他一定是个演员。

Generally speaking, girls are more careful. 一般说来，女孩子更细心。

3.2.2.4　过去分词

（1）过去分词的形式：过去分词只有一种形式：规则动词由动词原形加词尾"-ed"构成。不规则动词的过去分词没有统一的规则，要一一记住。

（2）过去分词的句法功能：

1）做定语：

Our class went on an organized trip last Monday. 上周一我们班开展了一次有组织的旅行。

注意当过去分词是单词时，一般用于名词前，如果是过去分词短语，就放在名词的后面。过去分词做定语相当于一个被动语态的定语从句。

2）做表语：

The window is broken. 窗户破了。

注意：be + 过去分词，如果表示状态是系表结构，如果表示被动的动作是被动语态。区别：

The window is broken.（系表）

The window was broken by the boy.（被动）

有些过去分词是不及物动词构成的，不表示被动，只表示动作已经完成。如：

boiled water（开水）fallen leaves（落叶）

newly arrived goods（新到的货）the risen sun（升起的太阳）

the changed world（改变了的世界）

这类过去分词有：gone, come, fallen, risen, changed, arrived, returned, passed 等。

3）做宾语补足语：

I heard the song sung several times last week. 上周我听见这首歌唱了好几次。

4）做状语：

Praised by the neighbours, he became the pride of his parents. 受到邻居们的表扬，他成为父母的骄傲。（表示原因）

Once seen, it can never be forgotten. 一旦它被看见，人们就忘不了。（表示时间）

Given more time, I'll be able to do it better. 如果给予更多的时间，我能做得更好。（表示条件）

Though told of the danger, he still risked his life to save the boy. 虽然被告知有危险，他仍然冒生命危险去救那个孩子。（表示让步）

Filled with hopes and fears, he entered the cave. 心中充满了希望与恐惧，他走进山洞。

3.3 时态语态题

3.3.1 时态语态题命题有三个角度：一是直接给定时间状语，考生可直接根据所给时间状语作出选择；二是给定时间状语，但所给时间状语有着较强的干扰性和迷惑性，考生不能直接根据时间状语进行选择；三是题干中不提供任何时间状语，而给出一个上下文情景或一个结构较为复杂的句子，考生必须仔细分析语境，才能作出判断并选择最佳答案。要解答时态语态题，必须研读题干，搜索出尽可能多的"时间参考信息"，如：haven't said, was doing 等，这些表达中都含有时间信息，发现和有效利用这些信息是解决问题的关键。解决时态和语态问题，要遵循如下解题思路：

（1）这个动作可能发生在什么时间？题干句中可参照的时间信息有哪些？

（2）这个动作处于什么时态，是进行中，还是已经结束（完成）？限制或修饰这个动作的状语信息有哪些？

（3）这个动作与主语的关系，是主动还是被动？

3.3.2 时态语态归纳

3.3.2.1 一般现在时

（1）概念：经常、反复发生的动作或行为及现在的某种状况。

（2）时间状语：always, usually, often, sometimes, every week (day, year, month…), once a week, on Sundays, etc.

（3）基本结构：动词原形（如主语为第三人称单数，动词还要改为第三人称单数形式）。

（4）否定形式：am/is/are+not; 此时态的谓语动词若为行为动词，则在其前面加 don't, 如主语为第三人称单数，则用 doesn't, 同时还原行为动词。

（5）一般疑问句：把 be 动词放于句首；或用助动词 do 提问，如主语为第三人称单数，则用 does，同时，还原行为动词。

（6）例句：It seldom snows here.

3.3.2.2　一般过去时

（1）概念：过去某个时间里发生的动作或状态；过去习惯性、经常性的动作、行为。

（2）时间状语：ago, yesterday, the day before yesterday, last week, last (year, night, month…), in 1989, just now, at the age of five, one day, long long ago, once upon a time, etc.

（3）基本结构：be 动词；行为动词的过去式。

（4）否定形式：was/were + not; 在行为动词前加 didn't, 同时还原行为动词。

（5）一般疑问句：was 或 were 放于句首；或用助动词 do 的过去式 did 提问，同时还原行为动词。

（6）例句：She often came to help us in those days.

　　　　　I didn't know you were so busy.

3.3.2.3　现在进行时

（1）概念：表示现阶段或说话时正在进行的动作及行为。

（2）时间状语：now, at this time, these days, etc.

（3）基本结构：am/is/are + doing.

（4）否定形式：am/is/are + not + doing.

（5）一般疑问句：把 be 动词放于句首。

（6）例句：How are you feeling today?

　　　　　He is doing well in his lessons.

3.3.2.4　过去进行时

（1）概念：表示过去某段时间或某一时刻正在发生或进行的行为或动作。

（2）时间状语：at this time yesterday, at that time 或以 when 引导的谓语动词是一般过去时的时间状语等。

（3）基本结构：was/were+doing.

（4）否定形式：was/were + not + doing.

（5）一般疑问句：把 was 或 were 放于句首。

（6）例句：At that time she was working in a PLA unit.

　　　　　When he came in, I was reading a newspaper.

3.3.2.5　现在完成时

（1）概念：过去发生或已经完成的动作对现在造成的影响或结果，或从过去已经开始，持续到现在的动作或状态。

（2）时间状语：recently, lately, since, for, in the past few years, etc.

（3）基本结构：have/has + done

（4）否定形式：have/has + not + done

（5）一般疑问句：把 have 或 has 放于句首。

（6）例句：I've written an article.

The countryside has changed a lot in the past few years.

3.3.2.6　过去完成时

（1）概念：以过去某个时间为标准，在此以前发生的动作或行为，或在过去某动作之前完成的行为，即"过去的过去"。

（2）时间状语：before, by the end of last year (term, month…), etc.

（3）基本结构：had + done。

（4）否定形式：had + not + done。

（5）一般疑问句：把 had 放于句首。

（6）例句：They didn't arrive as soon as we had expected.

By the end of last month, we had reviewed four books.

3.3.2.7　一般将来时

（1）概念：表示将要发生的动作或存在的状态及打算、计划或准备做某事。

（2）时间状语：tomorrow, next day (week, month, year…), soon, in a few minutes, by…, the day after tomorrow, etc.

（3）基本结构：am/is/are/going to + do；will/shall + do。

（4）否定形式：am/is/are/+not going to + do；will/shall +not do。

（5）一般疑问句：be 放于句首；或 will/shall 提到句首。

（6）例句：They are going to have a competition with us in studies.

It is going to rain.

3.3.2.8　过去将来时

（1）概念：立足于过去某一时刻，从过去看将来，常用于宾语从句中。

（2）时间状语：the next day (morning, year…), the following month (week…), etc.

（3）基本结构：was/were/going to + do; would/should + do。

（4）否定形式：was/were/not + going to + do; would/should + not + do。

（5）一般疑问句：was 或 were 放于句首；或 would/should 提到句首。

（6）例句：He said he would go to Beijing the next day.

I asked who was going there.

3.3.2.9　将来完成时

（1）概念：在将来某一时刻之前将完成的动作或状态。

（2）时间状语：by the time of; by the end of + 时间短语（将来）; by the time + 从句（将来）。

（3）基本结构：be going to/will/shall + have done。

3.3.2.10　现在完成进行时

（1）概念：在过去某一时刻之前开始的动作或状态一直持续到说话为止。

（2）基本结构：have/has +been+doing。

3.3.2.11　被动语态

语态是动词的一种形式，它表示主语和谓语的关系。语态有两种：主动语态和被动语态。如果主语是动作的执行者，或者是说动作是由主语完成的，要用主动语态；如果主语是动作的承受者，或者是说动作不是由主语而是由其他人完成的，则用被动语态。

3.4　复合句

3.4.1　复合句的解题关键是正确使用连接词，然而连词的使用绝不是将连接词简单地与其表面汉语意思相对照就能决定的。连接词的使用务必遵循以下八条原则才能清楚地进行分析与判别：

（1）连接词所引导的从句种类。

（2）连接词自身含义的区别。

（3）了解连接词在从句中与从句谓语动词的关系。

（4）确认连接词在从句中的位置与作用。

（5）在陈述语序下对全句进行分析。（疑问句，从属连接词的前移，被动语态均属于倒装。）

（6）删除干扰成分，在词句基本结构下进行分析。（插入语，各种词的修饰语均属干扰。）

（7）补齐省略成分，在句子完整结构下进行分析。（避免用词重复，无必要提及的成分均属省略。）

（8）注意某些须牢记的特殊情况要求。

3.4.2　复合句归纳

3.4.2.1　引导词的分类

（1）连接代词：what, who, whom, whose, which, whatever, whoever, whichever, 且这些词在从句中担当主、宾、表、定语作用。

（2）连接副词：why, when , where, how, 在从句中充当时间、地点、原因、方式、程度状语。

（3）连词：that, whether, if

whether, if 在从句中不充当成分，但整个句式中不可缺少，用以体现事件的不确定性，翻译成"是否"。

that 在从句中不充当成分，只起连接作用，陈述某一事实，引导宾语从句时某些情况可以省略。

针对如下情况，可进行对比：

1) _____ he will come to call on is uncertain .

2) _____ he will come to call on us is uncertain.

3) _____ he will come to call on us makes us unhappy.

从第一句中我们可以看出主语从句本身并不完整，缺少"call on"的宾语，应加

who;

第二句中表语为"uncertain",可知主语部分为未知信息,可加入 when, why, how, whether 等;

第三句表一种已知事实,应加入 that。

3.4.2.2 that, whether, if 在名词从句中的使用情况

(1) that 在宾语从句中大多数情况下可以省略,在主语从句、同位语从句、表语从句中不可省去。

但注意以下宾语从句中 that 不可省。

I know nothing of him except that he is from Henan.(介词后宾语从句中的 that 不可省。)

(2) whether, if 在宾语从句中可换用,但在主语从句、表语从句和同位语从句中不可用 if。

但注意在宾语从句中不能用 if 的情况:

It all depends on whether they will support us.(从句做介词宾语时不可用 if。)

He doesn't know whether to stay or not.(后有 or not 时,不能用 if。)

Please let me know if you like it.(这句是有双重意思的,如果视为宾语从句,就应换为 whether,否则就引起歧义。)

3.4.2.3 从句的区分

(1) He tells me his idea ＿＿＿ we reduce the cost.

(2) We are discussing the idea ＿＿＿ he came up with yesterday.

第一句中"we reduce the cost"应视为是 idea 内容的一种说明,是同位语从句,而第二句中"idea"可视为"come up with"的宾语,缺少引导定语从句的关系代词 that 或 which,当然可以省去关系代词。

3.4.2.4 应注意的问题

(1) 在主语从句中 it 的使用

That he will come to the party is certain. 表意上并没有错误,但实际上并不太符合用语习惯,因此采用 it 做形式主语,使句式平衡。

It is certain that he will come to the party.

同样道理,it 也可做形式宾语。

(2) 宾语从句中的情况

1) 时态的呼应问题

2) 特殊句式:

动词 suggest, insist, demand, order, request, require 等接的从句需用虚拟句式。

主语 + should + 动词原形 , should 也可省。

He suggested that we should pay a visit to that town.(建议)

但注意:

What he said suggested that he had known the truth.(表明)

同样,insist

He insisted that we do it at once.(坚持要做)

He insisted that he had done nothing wrong.（坚持说一种事实）

（3）whatever 与 no matter what 的区别

It is generally considered unwise to give a child _____ he or she wants.

A. whatever
B. no matter what
C. whenever
D. no matter when

此题应选 A。容易误选 B。选项 C，D 显然是错的，因为句中的 wants 缺宾语，而 C，D 两项不能做宾语。至于 A，B 的区别，可这样描述：no matter what 只能引导状语从句，而不引导名词性从句。而 whatever 既可引导名词性从句（= anything that），也可引导状语从句（= no matter what）：

1）引导名词性从句（只用 whatever）：

无论他做什么都是对的。

正：Whatever he did was right.

误：No matter what he did was right.

山羊找到什么就吃什么。

正：Goats eat whatever they find.

误：Goats eat no matter what they find.

2）引导状语从句（两者可换用）：

无论你说什么，我都不会相信你。

正：Whatever you say, I won't believe you.

正：No matter what you say, I won't believe you.

无论发生什么，都要保持镇定。

正：Keep calm, whatever happens.

正：Keep calm, no matter what happens.

（4）如何区分引导名词性从句的 what, that

—I think _____ he needs is more practice.

—Yes. _____ he needs more practice is clear.

A. what, What
B. that, That
C. what, That
D. that, What

此题应选 C。其余三项均可能被误选。what 和 that 都可以引导名词性从句，但有区别。

1）what 引导名词性从句时，它在从句中要充当句子成分（主语、宾语等）；而 that 引导名词性从句时，它在从句中不能充当句子成分。

2）what 引导名词性从句时，它有词义，表示：什么；所……的（东西）；而 that 引导名词性从句时，它没有词义。

请做以下试题，注意区别 what 和 that：

例1. _____ you said is different from the thing _____ he told us.

A. What, what
B. That, that
C. What, that
D. That, what

例2. —I think _____ he said is true.

—But don't forget the fact _____ he is a cheat.

A. what, what   B. that, that

C. what, that   D. that, what

例 3. _____ surprised us most is _____ he spoke English so well.

A. What, what   B. That, that

C. What, that   D. That, what

答案：例 1. C   例 2. C   例 3. C

（5）引导名词性从句的 whether 与 that

_____ we'll go camping tomorrow depends on the weather.

A. If   B. Whether   C. That   D. When

此题应选 B。容易误选 A，C。

1）关于 if 与 whether：两者都可引导宾语从句，常可换用；但若引导主语从句，则用 whether（不用 if），排除 A。又如：

他是否会来还是个问题。

误：If he will come is a question.

正：Whether he will come is a question.

2）关于 whether 和 that：两者都可引导主语从句，其区别主要应从句意来考虑：whether 表示"是否"，由它引导的主语从句的意思通常是不确定的；that 引导主语从句时，本身没有词义（that 在其他名词性从句中也没有词义），但是由 that 引导的整个主语从句的意思通常是确定的。试比较：

① a. That we'll hold a meeting is decided.
　　我们要召开一次会议，这已决定了。

　　b. Whether we'll hold a meeting is not decided.
　　我们是否要开一个会，这还没有决定。

② a. That he has left here is clear.
　　他已离开了这儿，这点很清楚。

　　b. Whether he has left here is not clear.
　　他是否已离开这儿，这还不清楚。

（6）引导名词性从句的 what

_____ he said at the meeting astonished everyone present.

A. What   B. That   C. If   D. Whether

此题应选 A。选项 C "if" 显然不能选，因为 if 不能引导主语从句；选项 B "that" 和 D "whether" 虽然都可以引导主语从句，但两者除了意思不合题意外，还有它们在主语从句中都不充当句子成分，而此句中的 "he said" 缺宾语。

3.5 虚拟语气

3.5.1 解答虚拟语气题，除了掌握基本的结构外，还要注意句子所表达的意义与现在、过去还是将来事实相反，看清时间状语，另外还要注意在其他结构中虚拟语气的运用。

3.5.2 虚拟语气的概念

虚拟语气用来表示说话人的主观愿望或假想，所说的是一个假设条件，不一定是事实，或与事实相反。

3.5.3　虚拟语气的用法

3.5.3.1　虚拟语气在非真实条件状语从句中的用法

条件句可分为两类，一类为真实条件句，一类为非真实条件句。非真实条件句表示的是假设的或实际可能性不大的情况，故采用虚拟语气。

（1）真实条件状语从句与非真实条件状语从句

例如：

If he doesn't hurry up, he will miss the bus.（真实条件状语）（不是虚拟语气）

If he was free, he would ask me to tell stories.（真实条件状语）（不是虚拟语气）

总结就是四个字："主将从现"，主句用将来时，从句用一般现在时。

If I were you, I would go at once.（非真实条件状语从句）

If there were no air, people would die.（非真实条件状语从句）

（2）虚拟语气在非真实条件状语从句中的用法及动词形式

1）表示与现在事实相反的情况

从句谓语动词形式	主句谓语动词形式
谓语动词用一般过去式 （be用were）	should/would/could/might +动词原形（过去将来时）

例如：If I were you, I would take an umbrella. 如果我是你，我会带把伞。（事实：我不可能是你）

2）表示与过去事实相反的情况

从句谓语动词形式	主句谓语动词形式
had+过去分词（过去完成时）	should/would/could/might + have+过去分词（现在完成时）

例如：If I had got there earlier, I should/could have met her. 如果我早到那儿，我就会见到她。（事实：去晚了）

3）表示对将来情况的主观推测（可能相反或可能性很小）

从句谓语动词形式	主语谓语动词形式	例句
If+主语+ ① should+动词 ② did ③were to do （①通常与一个表示时间状语连用）其中were to do可能性最小	should/would/ could/might+动词原形	If it rained tomorrow our picnic would be put off. 万一明天下雨，我们的郊游就推迟。

例如：If he would come here tomorrow, I should/would talk to him. 如果他明天来这儿的话，我就跟他谈谈。（事实：他来的可能性很小）

3.5.3.2　特殊用法

（1）在主语从句中谓语动词的虚拟语气结构为：should + 动词原形，表示惊奇，不相信，惋惜等。

例：It is advisable/important/natural/necessary that sb. (should) do

（2）固定句型：It is time/high time that sb. should do sth. 或 It is time that sb. did sth.

（3）固定句型：would rather sb.+ 过去时，指现在或将来。

例：I'd rather Father were here now.

I'd rather they came here tomorrow.

（4）but for..., without 短语译为"要不是……"，句子谓语也常用虚拟。

3.6 情态动词

3.6.1 情态动词题一般通过以下途径来解决：

（1）定意义

所谓定意义就是分析语境并确定应填情态动词的含义。

情态动词常见含义表：

情态动词	含义
can	能够（表能力）；可以（表许可或征询许可）；可能（表推测）
may	可以（表许可或征询许可）；可能（表推测）
must	必须，应该（表责任）；一定（表推测）
will	愿意（表意愿）
shall	需要（表征求意见）；必要，命令，禁止（表强迫性动作）；允许
used to	过去常常
need	必要，必需
dare	敢
ought to; should	应该

（2）定句型

所谓定句型，就是分析所给句子的句型特点，再选用具有特定句型特点的情态动词。

例如：

Peter _____ come with us tonight，but he isn't very sure.

A. must   B. may   C. can   D. will

【解析】选 B。根据语境，彼得拿不定主意是否来，说明他可能会来而不是一定会来，所以，A 为错误答案。may 和 can 都可表推测，意为"可能，或许"，但 can 通常用于否定句和疑问句，所以此句只能用 may。

（3）定人称

所谓定人称就是在解情态动词题时，应确定所填情态动词是否符合特定的人称。例如：

— _____ he wait for you at the school gate at the same time？

—No，he needn't.

A. Will   B. Shall   C. May   D. Can

【解析】选 B。根据语境可知，该句表征求对方意见，考生可能会认为 shall 只能用于第一人称，而误选 A，实际上表征求对方意见时，shall 可用于第一、三人称，而 will 用于第二人称，所以 A 为错误答案。

（4）定情感

所谓定情感就是在解情态动词题时，应确定所需情态动词是否符合特定的情感需要。

例如：

You _____ the exam，but you didn't study hard.

A. could pass   B. should pass

C. could have passed　　　　　　　　D. were able to

【解析】选 C。该句句意为：你本来能通过这次考试，但你学习不认真，实际上你没有通过这次考试。很明显该句应用 could have passed 来表示你本来能够通过这次考试，但实际上你没有通过的遗憾之情。

（5）定时态

所谓定时态就是在解情态动词题时，应确定所需情态动词是否符合特定的时态需要。例如：

You needn't do it today, but you will _____ do it tomorrow.

A. must　　　　　B. need　　　　　C. have to　　　　　D. be able to

【解析】选 C。该句表示：你今天没必要做这件事，但你明天将有必要做这件事。在"有必要做某事"的种种表达法中 must 是不能用于将来时的，所以 A 为错误答案，need 作情态动词不能用于肯定句，所以 B 也为错误答案，而 have to 是一个实义动词，可用于各种时态，所以 C 为正确答案。

3.6.2　情态动词语法归纳

情态动词是一种本身有一定的词义，表示说话人的情绪、态度或语气的动词，但不能单独做谓语，只能和其他动词原形构成谓语。

情态动词有四类：

（1）只做情态动词：must, can (could), may (might), ought to

（2）可做情态动词又可做实义动词：need, dare

（3）可做情态动词又可做助动词：shall (should), will (would)

（4）具有情态动词特征：have (had, has) to, used to

3.7　倒装句

3.7.1　倒装句的解题技巧主要是掌握倒装语序，区分部分倒装和全部倒装，熟记引起倒装的条件以及相关的词语。

3.7.2　倒装句语法归纳

3.7.2.1　全部倒装

（1）there be 句型是一种全部倒装句。例：

Something must be wrong. = There must be something wrong.

No one was waiting. = There was no one waiting.

有时为了生动地描写事物，其他一些表示存在意义的不及物动词也可以用于此句型，这些动词有：exist, lie, stand, live, remain, appear, come, happen, occur, rise 等。如：

There exist different opinions on this question.

（2）以 here, there, now, then, thus, hence 等引导的句子，习惯上主谓语全部倒装，其谓语动词通常是不带助动词或情态动词的不及物动词。如：

Here is a ticket for you.

（3）表示方向、地点的状语置于句首，而谓语又是表示运动的动词或表示存在的动词时，句子的主、谓语通常全部倒装。如：

Following the roar, out rushed a tiger from the forest.

这种表示方向、地点的词或词组有：up, down, away, here, in, out, off 等。

这种表示运动或存在的动词有：go, come, fall, rush, be, stand, lie 等。

注：主语是人称代词时一般不能倒装。如：

There it comes. Away they went.

（4）有时表语前置或分词前置也构成全部倒装。

Seated in the cinema are the workers from the watch factory.

3.7.2.2　部分倒装

（1）否定词或具有（半）否定意义的词语置于句首做状语时，一般必须采用部分倒装语序。具有否定或半否定意义的词和词组有：no, never, seldom, little, few, rarely, hardly, nowhere, no longer, no more, not often, not until, not only, at no time, in no way, in/under no circumstances, in no case, on no account, hardly...when, scarcely...when/before, no sooner...than, not only...but (also) 等。如：Seldom does he go to see his uncle.

注：当句子的主语由 little 修饰，或主语本身就是 not a word, not a soul 等时，主谓不必倒装。如：Little help can be expected from Peter.

（2）当置于句首的宾语是 nothing, no one, nobody 等否定词，或被 not a 修饰时，句子要部分倒装。如：Not a single word did Tom say.

注：但主语为代词时，仍可以不倒装。如：Not a word he said.

（3）"only + 副词，介词短语，状语从句" 位于句首，即当句首状语由 only 修饰时，需要采用部分倒装。如：Only when he works harder can Tom pass the exam.

（4）"so...that" 结构中的 "so + 状语" 位于句首表示强调时，需要部分倒装。

（5）由 so (neither, nor) 指代前面一句的内容表示 "也是（也不）" 的意义时，通常位于句首，并引起倒装。例：

Tom can't speak French.　Nor (Neither) can Jack.

注：当 so 引出的句子是对上文的内容加以证实或肯定时，不用倒装，例：

—"Bill will win the prize."

—"So he will."

（6）当以下几种状语置于句首表示强调时，一般可以采用部分倒装。

频度状语：often, many a time, every day, now and then 等。

程度状语：especially, to such an extent, to such a degree, to such extremes, to such length, to such a point 等。例：

Many a time has he given me good advice.

（7）由 were, had, should 等词开头的虚拟条件句（即省略了 if 的虚拟条件句中），也需要部分倒装。例：

Had he worked harder, he would have passed the exam.

（8）当对 as/though 等引导的分句中的形容词、分词、副词强调时，一般采取的倒装结构为：形容词/分词/副词 + as/though + 主语 + 谓语。例：

Young as he is, he has proved to be an able salesman.

3.8　强调句

3.8.1　强调句的解题技巧首先要熟悉强调句的基本结构以及强调句的特征，懂得解读题干以及还原句子本身的结构，只要能判断出考点为强调句，只要根据强调句的结构就可以很快找出正确答案了。

3.8.2　强调句语法归纳

强调句基本结构为：It + be + 被强调部分 + that + 句子其余部分。

（1）在强调句型中，能够被强调的句子成分通常为主语、宾语、时间状语等，不能用来强调谓语动词、表语、补语、让步状语、条件状语等。当被强调部分为 sb.，且在句中做主语时，可用 who，也可用 that，其他情况一律用 that。强调主语时，that 后的谓语动词必须与被强调的主语人称与数量保持一致。如：

I'm going to meet my friend at the airport tomorrow. →

It is I who am going to meet my friend at the airport tomorrow.（强调主语）

It is my friend that I'm going to meet at the airport tomorrow.（强调宾语）

It is at the airport that I'm going to meet my friend tomorrow.（强调地点状语）

It is tomorrow that I'm going to meet my friend at the airport.（强调时间状语）

（2）在强调结构中，无论被强调的是人还是物，单数还是复数，be 动词一律用单数 is/was 形式。如果原句的谓语动词时态是过去范畴，就用 was；如果原句的谓语动词时态是现在范畴，就用 is。也可以用"情态动词 +be"形式。如：

It is Tom and Mary who will be fined.

It was yesterday that he arrived here.

It might be in the morning that he broke into the house.

（3）强调句的特征是：如果我们把"It be...that..."从句中划去，所剩的正好是一个完整的句子。如：

It is not only blind men who make such stupid mistakes. 绝不只是盲人才犯这样愚蠢的错误。

Not only blind men make such stupid mistakes.

它的意思仍然是完整的，只是强调意味已经失去。实际上"It be...that..."只不过是一个框架而已，它的各部分在句子中均不担当成分。

3.9　主谓一致

3.9.1 主谓一致有三个原则：语法一致、意义一致和就近原则，无论哪一种，重要的是分清一个句子中，哪个是主语，主语是单数还是复数，分清题目属于哪种一致的情况，然后确定谓语形式。

3.9.2 主谓一致常见原则

（1）and 连接两个名词，但表同一事物，谓语用单数。如：

The writer and singer is my best friend.

（2）each, either, one, the other 及不定代词等做主语时，谓语常用单数。如：

Everybody is here.

（3）由连词 or, either...or, neither...nor, not only...but also 等连接并列主语时及 there be 句式，谓语动词应用就近原则。如：

Neither you nor I am to blame.

（4）国名、人名、报纸名、书名等专有名词虽以"-s"结尾，形式上是复数，但谓语动词常用单数。如：

The United States is a developed country.

但以"-s"结尾的山脉、岛、瀑布等做主语时，谓语一般用复数。如：

The Philippines lie to the southeast of China.

（5）由 each 修饰的名词做主语，谓语用单数。如：

Each student has an English-Chinese dictionary.

They each have an English-Chinese dictionary.

（6）表示时间、距离、钱、重量的名词做主语，若表示整体谓语用单数，但如强调具体数量，谓语则用复数。如：

Five hundred miles is a long distance.

Twenty years have passed since he began to work here.

（7）表示数量的 one and a half 后面要用复数名词做主语时，其谓语要用单数形式。

（8）定冠词 the＋形容词/分词表示一类人，谓语动词用复数。

（9）表示成双成套的名词，如 trousers, shoes, glasses, compasses 等用做主语时谓语用复数。如：

His black trousers are too long.

主谓一致的考查一般不会单独考查，常与时态、语态及句式（如倒装句）等相结合考查，此时如不能准确判断，不妨结合其他要点共同确定正确答案。

（1）语法形式上要一致，即单复数形式与谓语要一致。

（2）意义上要一致，即主语意义上的单复数要与谓语的单复数形式一致。

（3）就近原则，即谓语动词的单复数形式取决于最靠近它的词语。

一般来说，不可数名词用动词单数，可数名词复数用动词复数。如：

There is much water in the thermos.

但当不可数名词前有表示数量的复数名词时，谓语动词用复数形式。如：

Ten thousand tons of coal were produced last year.

第七节 语法结构典型真题分析

典型真题分析一

2007 年 12 月真题

16. It suddenly occurred to me that we could ＿＿＿＿＿ the police for help.

    A. ask   B. look   C. tell   D. meet

【答案】A

【解析】本题考查固定搭配的用法。ask sb. for help 意为"向某人求助"；turn to sb. for help 也表示向某人求助的意思。句中："It suddenly occurred to me that...", 意为"我突然想起……"。

【译文】我突然想到，我们可以求助于警察。

17. Many companies provide their employees _____ free lunch during the weekdays.

    A. by   B. with   C. to   D. for

【答案】B

【解析】本题考查介词的用法。"为……提供……"可以表达为"provide sb. with sth."或"provide sth. for sb."，比较：

The farm provides us with fresh fruits and vegetables.

The farm provides fresh fruits and vegetables for us.

【译文】许多公司在工作日期间都为员工提供免费的午餐。

18. Life is more enjoyable to people _____ are open to new ideas.

    A. whose   B. whom   C. who   D. which

【答案】C

【解析】本题考查定语从句关系代词的用法。定语从句中缺少主语，关系代词指代"people"，因此，选择"who"。在定语从句中，关系代词 whose 充当主语或宾语的定语；whom 指代人，充当宾语；which 指代物，充当主语或宾语。

【译文】易于接受新想法的人会活得更开心。

19. I _____ my former manager when I was on a flight to Beijing.

    A. ran into   B. put on   C. took away   D. shut down

【答案】A

【解析】本题考查固定词组的辨析。run into 偶然遇到，碰上；put on 穿上，上演；take away 拿走，没收；shut down 使关闭，使停产。run into 符合本题含义。

【译文】在我去北京的航班上，我偶遇我的前任经理。

20. It has been quite a long time _____ the two companies established a business relationship.

    A. although   B. because   C. if   D. since

【答案】D

【解析】本题考查连词的用法。"It is (has been) + 一段时间 +since…"，此句型表示"自从……以来已经有（一段）时间了"，since 引导的从句，常用一般过去时。如 It is (has been) a long time since I last visited Macao.

【译文】两家公司建立贸易关系以来有相当长的时间了。

21. The house was sold for $60,000, which was far more than its real _____.

    A. money   B. payment   C. value   D. profit

【答案】C

【解析】本题考查词义辨析。money 金钱，货币；payment 付款（方式）；value 价值，价格；profit 利润，赢利。

【译文】这座房子卖了 60 000 美元，这远远超出它本身的价值。

22. Customers consider location as the first factor when _____ a decision about buying a house.

A. make   B. made   C. to make   D. making

【答案】D

【解析】本题考查非谓语动词的用法。make 和它的逻辑主语 "customers" 的关系是主动的，因此使用现在分词 making，之前加上 when 用来加强语气。"when making …" 在句中充当时间状语。其他均不符合句子含义和结构。

【译文】顾客在决定买房子时，（房子的）地理位置会被考虑为第一要素。

23. The work seemed easy at first but it _____ to be quite difficult.

A. broke out   B. turned out   C. worked out   D. set out

【答案】B

【解析】本题考查固定词组的辨析。break out 爆发，突然发生；turn out 结果是，原来是；work out 算出，制定出；set out 出发，开始。turn out 通常用做 It turns out to be…。如：What you said at the meeting turned out to be wrong.

【译文】这项工作刚开始似乎很容易做，但结果证明是相当难的。

24. The small company is _____ to handle this large order.

A. able   B. probable   C. reasonable   D. possible

【答案】A

【解析】本题考查形容词的辨析。be able to do sth. 表示某人具有做某事的能力；probable 和 possible 表示"很可能的，大概的"和"可能的，潜在的"，两者均不用做 be probable to do … 和 be possible to do ….；常用做 It is probable/possible that... 等形式；reasonable 表示"合理的，明理的"。

【译文】这家小公司能够处理这个大的订单。

25. If I _____ that your business was growing so rapidly, I wouldn't have been worried about it.

A. know   B. knew   C. had known   D. have known

【答案】C

【解析】本题考查虚拟语气的用法。通过主句的结构 "wouldn't have been worried …" 可以判断是与过去事实相反的虚拟语气，其虚拟条件句的结构为 had done。因此，选择 "had known"。

【译文】要是我知道你们的生意发展如此之快，我早就不用担心了。

典型真题分析二

2007 年 6 月真题

16. This new style of sports shoes is very popular and it is _____ in all size.

A. important   B. active   C. available   D. famous

【答案】C

【解析】本题考查词义辨析。available 意为"可利用的，可获得的，有空的"。如：The equipment is available to teachers only. 这些设备只提供给老师使用。

That new novel is not available in the bookstore. 这本新出的小说在书店买不到。

Are you available this Sunday? 你这个礼拜天有空吗？

【译文】这种新款的运动鞋深受欢迎，各种鞋号的都可以买到。

17. _____ a wonderful trip he had when he travelled in China.

    A. Where   B. How   C. What   D. That

【答案】C

【解析】本题考查感叹句用法。how 用来感叹形容词或副词；what 而用来感叹名词，本题感叹 trip。

【译文】在中国旅游时，他度过了十分精彩的旅途。

18. She gave up her _____ as a reporter at the age of 25.

    A. career   B. life   C. interest   D. habit

【答案】A

【解析】本题考查固定搭配。give up one's career 意思是"放弃……的职业"。

【译文】25 岁那年，她放弃了当记者的职业。

19. She didn't receive the application form; it _____ to the wrong address.

    A. sent   B. be sent   C. was sent   D. being sent

【答案】C

【解析】本题考查时态语态的用法。通过前一句可以判断，句子的时态为一般过去时。"it"指代"the application form"，因此，应使用被动结构。

【译文】她没有收到申请表，（因为）寄错了地址。

20. Time _____ very fast and a new year will begin soon.

    A. takes off   B. goes by   C. pulls up   D. gets along

【答案】B

【解析】本题考查固定搭配的辨析。本题中只有"go by 流逝，经过"符合句中上下文的意思。take off 脱下，起飞；pull up 拔起，停止；get along 进展，相处融洽。

【译文】时间过得飞快，新的一年又快来到了。

21. I didn't answer the phone _____ I didn't hear it ring.

    A. if   B. unless   C. although   D. because

【答案】D

【解析】本题考查连词的用法。根据上下文的含义，可以判断 because 用于说明主句的原因。if 和 unless 引导条件状语从句，although 引导让步状语从句。

【译文】我没有接电话，是因为我没有听到铃响。

22. We're going to _____ the task that we haven't finished.

    A. take away   B. carry on   C. get onto   D. keep off

【答案】B

【解析】本题考查固定搭配的辨析。take away 拿去，带走；carry on 继续开展，从事；get onto 登上，踏上；keep off 让开，不接近。因此，carry on 为正确答案。

【译文】我们打算继续完成我们尚未完成的任务。

23. The general manager sat there, _____ to the report from each department.

    A. to listen   B. listen   C. being listened   D. listening

【答案】D

【解析】本题考查非谓语动词的用法。"listen"与"the general manager"的关系是主动的，所以使用现在分词。本题中，现在分词短语做方式状语，伴随句子中谓语的动作"sat"。如：

The pupils rushed into the classroom, talking and laughing.

The teacher came in, carrying a book in his hand.

【译文】总经理坐在那儿，听各个部门汇报。

24. In his report of the accident he _____ some important details.

    A. missed   B. wasted   C. escaped   D. failed

【答案】A

【解析】本题考查词义辨析。miss 遗漏，错过；waste 浪费，消耗；escape 逃避，避免；fail 失败，不及格。因此，A 是正确答案。

【译文】在这个事故的报告中，他遗漏了某些重要细节。

25. It is necessary to find an engineer _____ has skills that meet your needs.

    A. whom   B. which   C. whose   D. who

【答案】D

【解析】本题考查定语从句的用法。定语从句中缺少主语，关系代词用来指代先行词"the engineer"，因此选择 who。

【译文】找到合乎你们需求的有技能的工程师是必要的。

典型真题分析三

2006 年 12 月真题

16. It is the general manager who makes the _____ decision in business.

    A. beginning   B. finishing   C. first   D. final

【答案】D

【解析】本题考查关系词的用法。本句是强调句。强调句的结构是：It is/was + 被强调部分 + that/who + 句子其他部分。"who"用来指代"the manager"。如：It wasn't until this morning that I got your letter.

It was he that/who broke the window.

【译文】生意上，是总经理做最终的决断。

17. Never _____ such a good boss before I came to this company.

    A. do I meet   B. had I met   C. I met   D. I had met

【答案】B

【解析】本题考查倒装句型的用法。由 only, little, never, seldom, hardly 等词或引导的短语放在句首时，句子要使用倒装句型。倒装句型分为全部倒装和部分倒装。本题属于部分倒装，结构为"倒装部分 + 助动词 + 主语 + 其余部分"。如：

Only in this way can we solve the problem.

【译文】在我来到这家公司前，我从来都没遇到过这么好的老板。

18. If the machine should _____, call this number immediately.

    A. break down   B. set out   C. put on   D. go up

【答案】A

【解析】本题考查固定搭配辨析。break down 出故障，倒塌；set out 出发，开始；put on 穿上，上演；go up 上升，提高。因此 break down 符合句子的含义。

【译文】假如机器出故障，请立即拨打这个电话。

19. The manager showed the new employees _____ to find the supplies.

    A. what   B. where   C. that   D. which

【答案】B

【解析】本题考查固定搭配 show sb. sth. 的用法。

【译文】经理向新员工们说明在哪儿找到供应材料。

20. Look at the clock. It's time _____ work.

    A. we started   B. we'll start   C. we're starting   D. we have started

【答案】A

【解析】本题考查虚拟语气的用法。"It is (high/about/nearly) time + 从句"中要求用虚拟语气。该结构表示早该做而未做的事，并含有建议的意味。其动词形式用过去式。有时也可用 should + 动词原形。如：

It is high time (that) we began to work.

Isn't it (about) time that children went to school?

It is time we should leave.

【译文】看一下表，我们应该开始干活了。

21. The sales department was required to _____ a plan in three weeks.

    A. turn up   B. get up   C. come up with   D. put up with

【答案】C

【解析】本题考查固定搭配的辨析。turn up 开大，出现；get up 起床，起立；come up with 赶上，提出；put up with 忍受，容忍。因此，come up with 为正确答案。

【译文】要求销售部在三个星期内提出计划来。

22. Price is not the only thing customers consider before _____ what to buy.

    A. deciding   B. to decide   C. decide   D. having decided

【答案】A

【解析】本题考查非谓语动词的用法。"decide"和它的逻辑主语"customers"的关系是主动的，因此使用现在分词"deciding"，之前加上"before"用来加强语气。"before deciding …"在句中充当时间状语。其他均不符合句子含义和结构。

【译文】顾客在决定买东西前要考虑的因素不仅仅是价格。

23. All the traveling _____ are paid by the company if you travel on business.

    A. charges   B. price   C. money   D. expenses

【答案】D

【解析】本题考查词义辨析。charge 费用，收费；expense 费用，花费。如：no charge for window-shopping 免费浏览橱窗；an expense of time and energy on the project 在这项计划上花费时间与精力；a trip with all expenses paid 此次旅游已付了所有的费用。

【译文】如果你是商务旅行，所有的差旅费都由公司支付。

24. Sorry, we cannot _____ you the job because you don't have any work experience.

    A. make   B. send   C. offer   D. prepare

【答案】C

【解析】本题考查动词的辨析。offer sb. sth./offer sth. to sb. 意为"（主动）为某人提供某物"。如：offer me a drink 请我喝一杯。

【译文】抱歉，我们不可能给你提供这份工作，因为你没有任何工作经验。

25. This article is well written because special attention _____ to the choice of words and style of writing.

    A. had been paid   B. has been paid   C. will be paid   D. will have been paid

【答案】B

【解析】本题考查时态语态的用法。通过上下句可以判断，本题使用现在完成时为最佳（已经关注到了），"special attention"作为原因状语从句的主语，又为单数，因此应选用被动结构，所以答案是"has been paid"。

【译文】这篇文章写得很好，因为（文中）尤其注意到了词的选择和写作风格。

典型真题分析四

2006 年 6 月真题

16. David has _____ much work to do that he is staying late at his office.

    A. such   B. so   C. very   D. enough

【答案】B

【解析】本题主要考查 such...that 与 so...that 的区别。so 常与 many/much/few 等连用。如：

There are so many mistakes in your composition that you have to spend more time to correct them.

He ran so fast that I couldn't catch up with him.

These are such fine oil paintings that we don't know which one to choose.

It was such bad weather that we decided not to go for a picnic.

【译文】戴维有这么多的工作要做，所以他在办公室待到很晚。

17. I tried hard, but I couldn't find the _____ to the problem.

    A. solution   B. help   C. reply   D. demand

【答案】A

【解析】本题考查名词 solution 的用法。solution 后要接介词 to，意思为"解决某问题的方法"。因此，正确的答案为 A。

【译文】我努力尝试，还是找不到解决问题的办法。

18. I can't find the key to my office. I _____ have lost it on my way home.

    A. would　　　　　B. should　　　　　C. must　　　　　D. ought to

【答案】C

【解析】本题考查情态动词的用法。对已经发生的情况表示揣测，结构为"情态动词＋have＋过去分词"；但 must 表示揣测的语气较有把握，译为"一定……"。如：

It must have rained last night. The ground is wet. 昨晚一定下雨了。地上是湿的。

Could they have arrived there already? 他们会不会已经到了那儿呢？

I should have seen you yesterday. 昨天本应该来看你的。（实际没来）

【译文】我没有找到办公室的钥匙。我一定是在回家的路上弄丢了。

19. There are three colors in the British flag, _____ red, white and blue.

    A. rarely　　　　　B. namely　　　　　C. really　　　　　D. naturally

【答案】B

【解析】本题考查词义辨析。rarely 很少地，罕见地；namely 即，就是，换句话说；really 实际上，真实地；naturally 自然地，天生地。根据句意，应选择 namely。

【译文】英国国旗上有三种颜色，就是：红色、白色和蓝色。

20. As far as I'm concerned, I don't like _____ in that way.

    A. to be treated　　　B. to treat　　　　C. treated　　　　D. treating

【答案】A

【解析】本题考查非谓语动词不定式的用法。like 后既可接动名词，又可接不定式。根据题意判断，"treat"和"I"的关系应是被动的，所以，选择 to be treated。

【译文】就我而言，我不喜欢受到那种方式的对待。

21. My impression of the service in the hotel was that it had really _____.

    A. imagined　　　　B. implied　　　　C. imported　　　　D. improved

【答案】D

【解析】本题考查词义辨析。imagine 想象，设想；imply 暗示，意味；import 引入，进口；improve 改善，提高。因此，improve 符合题意。

【译文】我的印象是：这家旅馆的服务（质量）大大地提高了。

22. The policeman stopped the driver and found that he _____ alcohol.

    A. drinks　　　　　B. has drunk　　　　C. is drinking　　　　D. had drunk

【答案】D

【解析】本题考查动词时态的用法。that 引导的宾语从句的谓语动词的动作"drink"先于主句的谓语动词"stopped"和"found"，表示动作发生的时间是"过去的过去"，因此应使用过去完成时。如：

He said that he had seen the movie many times.

No sooner had we reached home than it began to rain.

【译文】警察让司机停车，发现他喝了酒。

23. There was a heavy fog this morning, so none of the planes could _____.

    A. get through　　B. take off　　　　C. pull out　　　　D. break away

【答案】B

【解析】本题考查固定词组的辨析。get through 通过，办完，结束；take off 脱下，起飞；pull out 拔出，抽出；break away 突然离开，脱离。根据句子上下文的意思，可以判断是 take off。

【译文】今天早上雾气很大，所以飞机都没有起飞。

24. _____ writing a letter to the manager, he decided to talk to him in person.

    A. Instead of   B. Because of   C. As for   D. Due to

【答案】A

【解析】本题考查介词短语的辨析。instead of 代替，而不是；because of 因为，由于；as for 关于，就……而言；due to 由于，归因于。

【译文】他没有给经理写信，而是决定亲自去和他交谈。

25. Lisa was busy taking notes _____ Mark was searching the Internet for the information.

    A. until   B. unless   C. while   D. if

【答案】C

【解析】本题考查连词的用法。在四个选项中，只有 while 可以引导表示对比的状语从句，与前一句进行对比。类似的词还有 whereas。如：

I like tea while she likes coffee.

Whereas he's rather lazy, she's quite energetic.

【译文】丽萨忙于做笔记，而马克在因特网上搜集信息。

第八节　语法结构专项模拟训练及答案解析

（一）

16. The machine is making terrible noise. It wants _____.

    A. to oil   B. oiling   C. to be oiling   D. being oiled

17. The reason _____ he gave me is not adequate for his being late for class.

    A. why   B. what   C. that   D. for

18. A traffic accident happened and the wounded _____ to hospital at once.

    A. sent   B. sends   C. were sent   D. are sent

19. The fact suggested that the situation _____ very serious at that moment.

    A. was   B. were   C. should be   D. to be

20. Not until last week _____ the sad news.

    A. that I knew   B. did I know   C. did I knew   D. that did I know

21. Teachers will _____ a lot from this advanced teaching method.

    A. benefit   B. value   C. interest   D. advantage

22. I consider _____ necessary to store sufficient information for our future work.

    A. this   B. that   C. which   D. it

23. My daughter has a headache and a fever. She appears _____ a cold.

    A. to has caught   B. to catch

C. to have caught   D. to have been caught

24. Jack stays at home all day and feels lonely. He needs a friend _____.

 A. playing   B. to play with   C. to play   D. playing together

25. _____ of the two books holds the opinion that the danger of nuclear war is increasing.

 A. Neither   B. Some   C. None   D. Both

（二）

16. The actor, _____ name I forget, has played in several successful films.

 A. whom   B. whose   C. who   D. which

17. Alice is fond of light music, _____ her brother is keen on rock and roll.

 A. when   B. as   C. for   D. while

18. Mary did nothing but _____ the whole time she was there.

 A. complain   B. to complain   C. complaining   D. complained

19. Smoking will do harm _____ your health.

 A. with   B. to   C. at   D. for

20. _____ had Jane reached the airport when the plan took off.

 A. No sooner   B. Only   C. Seldom   D. Hardly

21. _____ today, he would arrive in Washington by next Wednesday.

 A. If he leaves   B. Were he to leave   C. Would he leave   D. Was he leaving

22. The old man couldn't help _____ of what his wife said once again.

 A. to think   B. thought   C. thinking   D. have thought

23. It is _____ a difficult problem _____ nobody can solve it.

 A. such, that   B. so, that   C. so, as   D. such, as

24. The manager together with his colleagues _____ a warm welcome then.

 A. were receiving B. receive   C. is receiving   D. was receiving

25. _____ we are concerned, failure is not always a bad thing.

 A. As long as   B. As far as   C. So long as   D. As good as

答案解析

（一）

16.【答案】B

【解析】本题考查某些谓语动词（情态动词）的用法。在谓语动词为 want, need 等时，如果主语和其后的宾语动词是被动的关系，宾语用动名词形式或动词不定式的被动形式。如：My hair needs cutting. / My hair needs to be cut.

【译文】机器的噪声很大，需要给它上点儿油了。

17.【答案】C

【解析】本题考查定语从句关系词的用法。从本句的含义和结构可以看出，代替先行词"reason"的关系代词在定语从句"he gave me …"中充当（直接）宾语，而不是充当原因状语，因此不能选择关系副词 why。that 和 which 在定语从句中可以充当主语和宾语。比较：The reason why he was late for class is not clear.

【译文】对他上课迟到一事，他给出的理由不充分。

18.【答案】C

【解析】本题考查被动语态的用法。句中动词"send"与主语"the wounded"是动宾关系，且前一句为一般过去时，所以，后一句的谓语动词要用一般过去时的被动结构。

【译文】发生了交通事故，受伤的人被马上送往医院。

19.【答案】A

【解析】本题考查谓语动词 suggest 的用法。当 suggest，demand，insist 等充当"建议，要求，坚持"等含义时，其后的宾语从句的谓语动词为 should do 或动词原形的虚拟语气形式。但当 suggest 充当"暗示，表明"等含义时，要根据句子的具体情况，来确定宾语从句中谓语动词的时态。比较：We suggest that he should make a trip plan. 又如：He insisted that John should be punished. / He insisted John was foolish. 本题中的 suggest 的含义为"表明，暗示"。

【译文】事实表明，当时的形势很严峻。

20.【答案】B

【解析】本题考查倒装句的用法。当 not until 置于句首时，句子应采用倒装句型，本题为部分倒装，时态是一般过去时。

【译文】上个星期我才知道了这个让人难过的消息。

21.【答案】A

【解析】本题考查词义辨析。词组 benefit from 的含义为"从……中受益"。value 价值；interest 利益，利率；advantage 优势，长处。

【译文】老师们从这种先进的教学方法中受益匪浅。

22.【答案】D

【解析】本题考查形式宾语 it 的用法。此题中，"it"做形式宾语，动词不定式短语"to store sufficient information for our future work"做真正的宾语，"necessary"做宾语补足语。

【译文】我认为，为我们将来的工作存储足够的信息是必要的。

23.【答案】C

【解析】本题考查非谓语动词的用法。后一句中动词短语"catch a cold"的动作发生在谓语动词"appear"之前，所以，应该用不定式的完成形式，其结构为 to have done。如：I'm glad to have seen your mother.

【译文】我女儿头痛、发烧，好像是感冒了。

24.【答案】B

【解析】本题考查固定搭配的用法。play with sb. 意为：和……一起玩；逻辑关系上，a friend 可以理解为 play with 的宾语。playing together 中的 together 为副词，不可跟宾语；playing 动名词也不合适。

【译文】杰克整天都待在家里，感到孤单。他需要个朋友和他一起玩。

25.【答案】A

【解析】本题考查代词的用法。neither 表示两者任何一方都不，谓语动词用单数；none 表示三者或以上人或物都不，谓语动词用单数；both 表示两者都，谓语动词用复数。

【译文】这两本书的观点都是：核危险并没有增加。

（二）

16.【答案】B

【解析】本题考查定语从句的用法。在非限定性定语从句中，缺少宾语的定语。关系代词 whose 在定语从句中可以充当主语或宾语的定语。因此，答案是选项 B。如：The old man there owns the house whose walls were made of wood.

【译文】这个演员在几部成功的电影中都有参加表演，我记不起他的名字了。

17.【答案】D

【解析】本题考查连词的用法。在四个选项中，只有 while 可以引导表示对比的状语从句，与前一句进行比对。类似的词还有 whereas。如：

I like tea while she likes coffee.

Whereas he's rather lazy, she's quite energetic.

【译文】爱丽丝喜欢轻音乐，而她的弟弟钟情于摇滚乐。

18.【答案】A

【解析】本题考查非谓语动词的用法。本题中，but 用做介词，与 except 同义。英语介词一般不用动词不定式做宾语。然而，but, except, than 等几个表示"免除"意义的介词却属例外，它们之后经常接动词不定式。当前面句子以 do 做谓语（或以 to do 做定语）时，but（或 except) 后的动词不定式一般不带 to。此句中，谓语动词是 "did"，所以动词不定式不带 to。如：We do nothing but wait till he comes. / There is no choice but to wait till the rain stops.

【译文】玛丽待在那儿，除了抱怨，无所事事。

19.【答案】B

【解析】本题考查固定搭配的用法。词组 do good/harm/bad to 表示"对……有好处 / 害处 / 坏处"。

【译文】吸烟有害你的健康。

20.【答案】D

【解析】本题考查副词的用法。hardly (scarcely)... when... / no sooner ...than 均表示"一……就……"，当 hardly (scarcely), no sooner 等置于句首时，其主句的谓语要部分倒装，时态多用过去完成时，而从句中谓语动词用一般过去时。如：No sooner had he left than the police came. / Scarcely had he gone out when it started to snow.

【译文】简刚到机场，飞机就起飞了。

21.【答案】B

【解析】本题考查虚拟语气。此句表示的是与将来事实相反的虚拟语气，这一点从主句的结构 "would arrive" 和句子的含义（他尚未动身）可以判定，所以，从句的结构只有选项 B 符合与将来事实相反的虚拟语气条件句的结构。当虚拟条件句中有 were，should, had 等时，可以置于句首，省略 if，形成倒装句式。

【译文】他如果今天动身，那么在下个星期三之前可能就会抵达华盛顿。

22.【答案】C

【解析】本题考查非谓语动词的用法。短语 can't help / couldn't help 后接动名词，表示"情不自禁地……"。

【译文】这位老人情不自禁地又一次想起他妻子的话。

23. 【答案】A

【解析】本题考查 such…that 与 so…that 的区别。

so 的用法：（1）…so + 形容词/副词 + that…（2）…so many / much / few …that…

such 的用法：（1）…such + a/ an + 形容词 + 单数名词 +that …（2）… such + 形容词 + 复数名词 +that…（3）…such + 形容词 + 不可数名词 +that…

本题属于 such 的第一种用法。因此，答案是选项 A。

【译文】问题这么难，谁也解决不了。

24. 【答案】D

【解析】本题考查主谓一致的用法。在主语后接有 together with, along with, as well as 等时，谓语动词要与第一个名词一致。本题的主语是 "the manager"，谓语动词应该用单数。根据 "then" 一词，可以判断时态是过去，因此，答案是选项 D。

【译文】当时，经理和他的同事都受到了热烈欢迎。

25. 【答案】B

【解析】本题考查固定搭配的用法。As far as we are concerned / As far as we know 等作为固定句型,表示"就……而言"。选项 A 和 C 都表示"只要……"引导条件状语从句。

【译文】就我们而言，失败不总是一件坏事。

第三章　阅读理解

第一节　题型介绍和解题方法指导

题型介绍

　　阅读理解部分主要测试考生从书面文字材料获取信息的能力。总阅读量约 800 词。本部分测试的文字材料包括一般性阅读材料（科普、文化和经贸等内容）和应用性文字，如：简明广告、便条、通知、简短信函、简明说明书、简明规范等。题型为单项选择、填空、匹配、简答四种类型。

　　主要测试以下阅读技能：

　　（1）了解语篇和段落的主旨和大意。

　　（2）掌握语篇中的事实和主要细节。

　　（3）理解语篇上下文的逻辑关系。

　　（4）了解作者的目的、态度和观点。

　　（5）根据上下文正确理解生词的意思。

　　（6）了解语篇的结论。

　　（7）进行信息转换。

　　本部分的得分占总分的 35%。测试时间为 40 分钟。

解题方法指导

　　（1）根据题干到文章中去查找到恰当的地方，运用推理判断得出正确答案，切不可凭空猜测想象，所选答案一定要有据可依。

　　（2）正确选项不可能和文中的原句完全一样，大部分情况下是原文信息的同义或近义改写。措辞过于绝对化的选项，一般不是正确答案。

　　（3）注意解题步骤。迅速浏览问题，通读全文并答题。

　　（4）灵活采用解题方法。认真阅读题目及每个选项，找出每个选项之间的不同点，灵活运用排除、推理等各种解题方法。

　　（5）做完一篇文章的所有题目后，把五个题目的答案连接起来，看看与文章的大意是否相符，是否存在自相矛盾的地方。

第二节 历年考点统计、考点解读和解题技巧

TASK 1 AND TASK 2

考点统计

这两部分均为单项选择题，从 2005 年 6 月到 2009 年 6 月的考试真题来看，考点多为对文字材料细节的理解，其次是对文章的归纳及判断推理，也就是通常所说的事实细节题、主旨大意题和判断推理题，还有考查考生通过上下文准确理解单词含义的语义题。涉及的文章体裁及大致内容详见下表。

考点 ＼ 考试时间	2005年6月	2005年12月	2006年6月	2006年12月	2007年6月	2007年12月	2008年6月	2008年12月	2009年6月
一般性阅读材料	个人征税	节日习俗	医疗服务介绍	夜班工作生活	公路交通系统	汽车的安全带和气囊的重要性	如何避免家中意外摔跤事故		城市交通工具
简明广告				运输业务广告			租车业务广告	招聘志愿者广告	
启事					旅行饮食安排说明	博物馆项目介绍			
信函		求职申请信	公司告用户书						朋友通信
产品使用说明	压力锅使用说明							英语词典简介	

考点解读和解题技巧

1. 事实细节题

细节题是对文章重要事实细节的考查，如事情发生的原因、经过、结果以及涉及的人物、时间等，典型的提问方式有：

Which of the following statements is TRUE according to the passage?

According to the passage, when/where/who/why/what/which…?

Which of the following is (not) mentioned?

解题技巧：

（1）认真审题，使用排除法排除干扰项：内容是原文中的信息，但与题干要求不完全相符的选项；符合常理，但文中并未提及的选项；含有原文原句中的单词，尤其是生词、难词，但所答非所问、张冠李戴、偷梁换柱的选项；含全肯或全否的选项，也就是将文章

中不是绝对的观点绝对化的选项。

（2）仔细对照、比较选项的特征：如果题干中的选项可以在文中找到确切依据，可以确定为正确答案。

（3）认真核算涉及时间和数量的选项。

（4）注意否定句的用法：如篇中出现的是双重否定，答案一般会以肯定形式出现。如：

According to the growth pattern of Los Angeles, homes were mainly built _____.

A. in the city center   B. along the main roads

C. around business districts   D. within the business districts

（2007年6月真题 Task 2）

【解析】根据原文中第五段的句子 "So Los Angeles developed several business districts and built homes and other buildings in between the districts." 选项 C 中的短语与原文中画线的短语是近义短语，意思一致，故为正确答案。

2. 主旨大意题

此类题主要考查考生对所读文章的理解和归纳能力，常见的问题有：

What is the main idea/point of the passage?

What is the passage about?

What is the main purpose of the passage?

Which is the best title for this passage?

What does the passage mainly discuss?

Which of the following best summarizes the passage?

解题技巧：

（1）准确地找到文章的主题句，也就是通常所说的 topic sentence, 主题句的位置主要有以下两种情况：

1）文章开头第一句。其后的句子则是论证性细节，即通常所说的 supporting details。这种类型的文章我们可以用倒三角（▽）来表示，主题句位于文章的开头，其论证性细节的重要性是递减的。

2）文章段落的末尾一句。一般来说，当一种观点不易解释清楚或不易被理解接受时，作者为了说服读者，就会把主题句保留到文章的末尾出现。此种类型的文章，可用正三角（△）来表示，其论证性细节的重要性是递增的。有时候作者为了突出主题，也会采用首尾呼应的方式，在段落的开头和结尾用不同的陈述方式表述主题。

（2）认真审题，快速浏览所提供的选项，注意各个选项之间的差别。

主旨题的考点在于对文章的整体理解，考查的是文章最核心的内容。正确的选项应含有文章所涉及的中心词，简明扼要但概括全面，不能只反映文章某一细节或某一段落的内容的观点。如：

Which of the following would be the best title for this passage?

A. Types of Doctors.

B. Health Care in the United States and Britain.

C. Treatment of Sick Children in the United States.

D. Medical Insurance in the United States and Britain.

（2006年6月真题 Task 1）

【解析】从原文的第一段第一个句子可以看出，本篇文章的主题是关于医疗服务，而且是比较美国和英国的医疗服务状况，所以 B 为正确答案，其他几个选项不符合原文的内容。

3. 推理判断题

推理判断题多出现在主题句不明确的文章中。由于作者的观点和看法并没有明确的表述，需根据文章所提供细节的含义及上下文就作者的意图、态度和文章的主题进行推断和概括。答题时需特别注意作者描述事实时所用的词汇，尤其是含有强烈的感情色彩的用词，再根据上下文的线索领会其字里行间所隐含的意义，典型的提问方式有：

What is the author's attitude（态度）towards…?

What is the author's opinion?

What can be concluded from…?

From the passage, it can be inferred（推断）that…

What does the author think of…?

4. 语义题

语义题考查考生对文章中某一重要词语、短语或句子的理解。如出现此类考题，需要考生根据上下文推测及准确理解词义。常见典型问句为：

The word/phrase "…" in the passage means …?

What does the phrase/word "…" in Line/Paragraph… mean?

解题技巧：

（1）注意运用上下文中的定语从句和同位语（从句）进行推测（这两类从句通常起到解释和说明的作用）。

（2）注意利用上下文中的对比或类比关系进行推测。

（3）根据上下文中表示转折关系的词进行推测。

（4）根据文章中所给定义的解释进行推测。文章中出现的生僻词或专业术语，一般会通过下定义的方式给出解释。如：

The word "down-to-earth" (Line 4, Para. 3) most probably means _____.

A. changeable   B. expensive   C. reasonable   D. fixed

（2007 年 6 月真题 Task 1）

【解析】根据原文中第三段中的最后一句话 "Years of research have taught us which restaurants <u>reliably</u> serve a <u>good</u> choice of <u>delightful</u> dishes at down-to-earth prices" 中画线的几个词 reliably（令人信赖地），good 和 delightful（让人高兴的）可以推断出，题目中的这个词应该是指价格公道实惠，因此选项 C 为正确答案。

TASK 3

考点统计

这部分为填空题，主要考查考生对文章重要细节的理解和把握，需要填写的内容一般都能在原文中找到，通常要求填写的词汇不得超过三个。从分析 2005 年 6 月到 2009 年 6 月的真题来看，这部分涉及的体裁和大致内容见下表。

考试时间　　　考点	2005年6月	2005年12月	2006年6月	2006年12月	2007年6月	2007年12月	2008年6月	2008年12月	2009年6月
简明广告	信息中心服务广告					旅行社广告			
启事			地铁系统介绍						案件举报热线
信函		工厂新址报告		投诉信			求职申请信	会议邀请函	
简明规范					出差报告写作说明				

解题技巧

（1）可以采用"先看问题，后浏览全文"的方式。这样带着问题按图索骥，目的明确且定位准确，不但可以正确答题还能节省时间。

（2）注意把握整体信息，切忌遗漏了某些细微的信息，最好在答完题目后再检查一遍，以防写错、写漏。

（3）注意句子中与文章主题相关的关键词如主语、动词等，这些往往是考查的重点词汇。

（4）根据题干意义，"左顾右盼"，在文章的上下文中判断该填什么词，注意是否需要改变词性或词形。

TASK 4

考点统计

这部分测试考生阅读列表的能力，要求考生通过查读方式迅速准确地完成汉英信息匹配。常用的材料为公共场所的标志用语、故障说明、各种目录、表单等常用专业词汇。近几年涉及的术语包括医疗服务、电话操作、公共标识、企业管理、铁路服务、移动电话、邮政特快专递、进出口贸易及天气预报。

解题技巧

（1）掌握大纲要求的基本词汇。本题虽然会涉及一些行业的专业词汇，但只要掌握基本词汇，对照所给的中文表达，在英文表达中找到熟悉的词汇，就不难推断出整体的含义。

（2）广泛阅读，拓宽知识面。本题主要测试考生实际应用英语能力，考试材料多为实用性材料，如公共场所的标志用语以及不同行业领域的常用术语。这就要求考生平时要有意识地通过阅读中英报刊、杂志、书籍积累一些类似的应用性素材，扩大自己的知识面。

（3）答题时要看清题目要求 (Directions) 以及所给的例子 (Example)，以便了解测试的题材内容，然后根据题目中的汉语术语，寻找相应的英语进行配对。

（4）要注意某些英语的表达方式在某个专业领域的特定含义，如 note 的本义为"笔记，钞票"，但在商务英语中 blank note 的意思为"空白汇票"。

TASK 5

考点统计

这部分的文字材料主要是应用文（文摘、函电、广告、说明书、序言和文件等），一般在 250 个单词以内。所提问主要是针对文章的主题、某个特别的数字和时间或事物发生的原因或结果，而回答问题一般要求在三个单词以内。所提问题大多数能在文章中直接找到答案。因此考生应该充分理解并运用这些信息，这对于准确找到答案很有帮助。

Task 5 的问题一般不会是一般疑问句或选择疑问句，大多是以 what/how 开头的特殊疑问句，主要考查考生对关键信息的理解和把握能力，因此要求一定要对文章的细节内容作出具体的回答。

常见的提问方式有：

How much should be paid for the bidding documents?

Where will they stay when they are in China ?

What is enclosed with the letter?

How many aspects does Chapter 2 describe?

When will the final result come out?

从 2005 年 6 月到 2009 年 6 月的真题涉及的体裁和大致内容见下表。

考试时间 考点	2005年 6月	2005年 12月	2006年 6月	2006年 12月	2007年 6月	2007年 12月	2008年 6月	2008年 12月	2009年 6月
简明广告	新加坡航空公司广告	安利公司招聘广告						招聘广告	招聘广告
信函			索赔信和回复	求职信		饭店告顾客书			
产品使用说明					微波炉故障查找说明		洗衣机使用说明		

解题技巧

（1）仔细理解所提问题。

（2）带着问题快速阅读。抓住问句和答句中的关键信息，寻找其在文章中的对应位置。特别要留意文章标题及开头部分的句子，往往这个部分就能体现出文章的主旨。

（3）要注意所提问题的关键词语（例如：单数、复数），以及问题中表明数量、时间、地点的词语。如果问句中的关键词没有在原文中出现，就应该留意文章中该词的同义或近义词。

（4）注意区分不同类型的文章，有针对性地答题。如果是信函，应该分清楚信头部分的写信人和收信人，同时也要注意写信日期。如果是招聘广告，应该注意文中的黑体字和斜体字部分，因为招聘的职位通常会以醒目的方式标出。若是有标题的应用文，则应注意标题中的产品或注意事项，它们往往就能为答题提供重要线索。

（5）检查问句与自己所找的信息与文章中相关句子意思是否一致，最后确定正确答案。

第三节　典型真题分析

典型真题分析一

2008 年 12 月真题

TASK 2

Directions: *This task is the same as Task 1. The 5 questions or unfinished statements are numbered from 41 to 45.*

Each time we produce a new English dictionary, [41]our aim is always the same: what can we do to make the dictionary more helpful for students of English? As a result of our research with students and discussions with teachers, we decided to focus on providing more examples for this English dictionary.

Examples help students to remember the word they have looked up in the dictionary [42]because it is easier both to remember and to understand a word within a context（上下文）. The examples also show that words are often used in many different contexts. For these reasons, [43]we have included 40% more examples in this new book.

[44]We edit all the examples to remove difficult words and to make sure they are easier to understand.

We very much hope this new book will be of use not only to the students of English but also to the teachers.

41. The aim of the author in producing this new dictionary is to _____.

    A. correct mistakes in the old dictionary   B. make it more helpful for students

    C. increase the number of words   D. add pictures and photos

42. A word is easier to remember and understand if it is _____.

    A. included in a word list   B. pronounced correctly

    C. explained in English   D. used in a context

43. What is special about this new dictionary?

    A. It is small and cheap.   B. It has a larger vocabulary.

    C. It has 40% more examples.   D. It is designed for students and teachers.

44. The purpose of removing difficult words in the examples is to _____.

A. make them easier to understand　　　　B. provide more useful words

C. introduce more contexts　　　　D. include more examples

45. The passage is most probably taken from _____.

A. a letter to the editor　　　　B. a comment on a novel

C. an introduction to a dictionary　　　　D. a news' report in the newspaper

41. The aim of the author in producing this new dictionary is to _____.

【解析】本题是事实细节题，问作者编写这部新的字典的目的是什么。答案在文章第一段第一句 "our aim is always the same: what can we do to make the dictionary more helpful for students of English?"（我们的目的总是一样的：我们如何才能让字典对学英语的学生更有帮助）中能够找到，因此选项 B "make it more helpful for students"（让它对学生更有帮助）是正确答案，A（改正老字典中的错误），C（增加词的数量）以及 D（增加图片和照片）均未在文中提及。

42. A word is easier to remember and understand if it is _____.

【解析】本题是事实细节题，问在什么情况下更容易记住和理解单词。答案在第二段第一句 "because it is easier both to remember and to understand a word within a context（上下文）."（因为在上下文中更容易记住和理解单词）中能够找到，文章作者强调字典中举出的例子可以为学生提供单词的上下文，这样能够帮助他们记住单词。因此选项 D "used in a context"（用在上下文中）是正确答案，A（列在单词表中），B（正确地发音）以及 C（用英语解释）都未在文中提到，故应排除。

43. What is special about this new dictionary?

【解析】本题是事实细节题，问这部新字典的特别之处是什么。答案可以在文中第二段最后一句 "we have included 40% more examples in this new book."（我们在这本新书里收录了多于 40% 的例子）中找到，所以选项 C "It has 40% more examples." 是正确答案，A（字典体积小且便宜），B（收进的词汇更多）及 D（为老师和学生设计）都不是文章提到的该字典的特别之处。

44. The purpose of removing difficult words in the examples is to _____.

【解析】本题是事实细节题，问去掉例子中的难词的目的是什么。答案可以在文中第三段的句子 "We edit all the examples to remove difficult words and to make sure they are easier to understand."（我们编写例子时去掉难词可以确保读者更容易理解例子）中找到，因此选项 A "make them easier to understand" 是正确答案，B（提供更多有用的词），C（介绍更多上下文）及 D（收进更多的例子）都与原文的意思不符。

45. The passage is most probably taken from _____.

【解析】本题是推理判断题，需要考生在看完全文后通过归纳文章大意判断该文的出处。从原文的整体内容可以看出是在介绍一本新字典的特别之处：收录更多例子、去掉例子中的难词，这样能让读者更容易理解例子，从而更容易记住单词，所以可以推断该文是选自一本新字典的介绍，选项 C "an introduction to a dictionary" 是正确答案，A（写给编辑的信），B（小说评论）及 D（报纸上的新闻报道）都与原文的主题不符。

典型真题分析二

2008 年 12 月真题

TASK 3

Directions: *The following is a letter. After reading it, you should complete the information by filling in the blanks numbered from 46 to 50* ***(in no more than three words)*** *in the table below.*

Dear Dr Yamata,

　　[47]The Association of Asian Economic Studies is pleased to invite you to be this year's guest speaker at its annual international symposium（研讨会）. The symposium will be held for three days from [48]December 22nd to 24th, 2008. This year's topic will be [50]Economic Development in Asia. [49]About 100 people from various countries will be attending the symposium. They would be pleased to meet you and share their views with you.

　　The Association will cover all the expenses of your trip to this symposium.

　　As the program is to be announced on December 1st, 2008, will you kindly let us know before that time whether your busy schedule will allow you to attend our symposium? We are looking forward to your favorable reply.

Yours sincerely,

[46] John Smith

Secretary of Association of Asian Economic Studies

Letter of Invitation
Writer of the letter: ___46___
Organizer of the symposium: Association of ___47___
Guest speaker to be invited: Dr Yamata
Starting date of the symposium: ___48___
Number of guests invited: about ___49___
Topic of the symposium: ___50___ in Asia

46.【答案】John Smith

　　【解析】由书信的 "Yours sincerely, **John Smith**" 的署名可知写信者的姓名。

47.【答案】Asian Economic Studies

　　【解析】本题问该研讨会的组织者是谁，由书信的第一句话 "The Association of **Asian Economic Studies** is pleased to invite you to be this year's guest speaker at…" 和信的最后一行的地址可知。

48.【答案】December 22nd

　　【解析】本题问的是该研讨会的开幕时间。由书信的第二句话 "The symposium will be held for three days **from December 22nd** to 24th, 2008." 可知，开会的第一天是 22 日。

49.【答案】100 / one hundred

【解析】本题是问邀请与会人员的数目，从书信第四段 "**About 100 people** from various countries will be attending the symposium…" 可知应该是大约 100 人。

50.【答案】Economic Development

【解析】本题问的是会议的主题，第三句说 "This year's topic will be **Economic Development in Asia**"，这就是会议的主题：亚洲经济发展。

典型真题分析三

2008 年 6 月真题

TASK 4

Directions: *The following is a list of terms used in the waybill（详情单）of the Express Mail Service. After reading it, you are required to find the items equivalent to（与……等同）those given in the table below. Then you should put the corresponding letters in the brackets on the Answer Sheet, numbered from 51 to 55.*

A—original office（原办公室）   B—accepted date（收件时间）

C—posting stamp   D—delivery stamp

E—company name   F—sender's address

G—customer code   H—document

I—parcel（包裹）   J—name of contents

K—insurance amount（保险金额）   L—sender's signature

M—postal code   N—insurance fee（保费）

O—total charge   P—receiver's signature

Q—remark（说明）

Examples: (D) 投递日戳   (L) 交寄人签名

51.（O）费用总计	（B）收寄日期
52.（H）文件资料	（M）邮政编码
53.（G）用户代码	（P）收件人签名
54.（J）内件品名	（F）发件人地址
55.（C）收寄日戳	（E）单位名称

【解析】做这道题时只需要先看清中文术语，再在选项中找到能够匹配的英语术语，特别需要留意一些容易混淆的术语，如：L—sender's signature（交寄人签名）与 P—receiver's signature（收件人签名）。在看过例子后可以在选项中划掉这两个，每选一个就划掉一个，避免重复选择。

典型真题分析四

2008 年 12 月真题

TASK 5

Directions: *The following is an advertisement. After reading it, you are required to complete the answers that follow the questions, numbered from 56 to 60. You should write your answers **(in no more than three words)** on the Answer Sheet correspondingly.*

[56]Yanton Playingfield Committee
Grounds' person（场地管理员）Wanted

The Yanton Playingfield Committee has for many years been fortunate to have Eddie Christiansen as grounds' person at its sports ground in Littlemarsh. However, after ten years of service, [57]Eddie has decided it's time to retire in July. The committee wishes him the best for his retired life.

However, [56]this leaves us needing a new grounds' person. This role is part-time, averaging around five hours per week. [58]The duties involve the mowing（除草）rolling, and trimming（修剪）of the field edges. [59]Applicants（求职人）need to be able to drive and use the equipment needed for the above-mentioned duties.

Applicants can either [60]contact Hugh Morris, 42 Spencer Avenue, tel. 765-4943780, to discuss or register an interest in the position, or any member of the Playingfield Committee.

56. Which organization is in need of a grounds' person?

The Yanton Playingfield Committee.

57. Why is a new grounds' person needed?

Because the former grounds' person, Eddie Christiansen, has decided it's time to retire.

58. What are the duties of a grounds' person?

His duties involve the mowing, rolling, and trimming of the field edges.

59. What should applicants be able to do?

They should be able to drive and use the equipment needed for the duties.

60. Who is the contact person?

Hugh Morris or any committee member.

【解析】在回答问题时，需要找到题干中的关键词，如第 56 题的关键词是 "organization" 和 "grounds' person"，从广告的题目和第二段的第一句话中可以找到答案。第 57 题的关键词是 "Why"，答案在第一段的第二句 "Eddie has decided it's time to retire in July."（埃迪决定在七月退休）中能找到。第 58 题的关键词是 "duties"，答案就在第二段第三句 "The duties involve the mowing（除草）, rolling, and trimming（修剪）of the field edges."（职责包括除草、碾平和修剪场地边缘）中。第 59 题的关键词是 "applicants" 和 "be able to do"，答案在第二段最后一句 "Applicants（求职人）need to able to drive and use the equipment needed for the above-mentioned duties."（求职人必须能够驾驶和使用履行上述职责所需要

的设备）中。第 60 题的关键词是"contact person"（联系人），答案就在最后一段的第一句话中。从这里可以看出，所有问题都是针对文章的细节信息，需要根据原文做出准确具体的回答，答案都能在文中找到。

第四节 阅读理解专项训练及答案解析

专项训练一

2007 年 6 月真题

Part III Reading Comprehension

Directions: *This part is to test your reading ability. There are five tasks for you to fulfill. You should read the reading materials carefully and do the tasks as you are instructed.*

TASK 1

Directions: *After reading the following passage, you will find five questions or unfinished statements, numbered from 36 to 40. For each question or statement there are four choices marked A, B, C, and D. You should make the correct choice and mark the corresponding letter on the Answer Sheet with a single line through the center.*

We've found that eating habits vary（变化）so much that it does not make sense to include meals in the price of our tours. We want to give you the freedom of choosing restaurants and ordering food that suits your taste and budget（预算）.

As our hotels offer anything from coffee and toast to a full American breakfast at very reasonable prices, it will never be a problem for you to start the day in the way you like best. At lunch stops, your tour guide will show you where you can find salads, soups, and sandwiches.

Diner time is your chance to try some local food. Sometimes the tour guide will let you have dinner at a restaurant of your own choice. At other times he or she will recommend a restaurant at your hotel. Years of research have taught us which restaurants reliably serve a good choice of delightful dishes at <u>down-to-earth</u> prices.

In Mexico, Alaska, and the Yukon, where your restaurant choice may be limited, we include some meals. The meals provided are clearly stated on the tour pages.

36. According to the passage, most meals are not included in the price of tours mainly because

_____.

    A. meals make up a large part of the tour budget

    B. meal prices vary a lot from place to place

    C. people dislike the menus offered by tour guides

    D. people have different eating habits

37. We can learn from the passage that _____.

A. the hotels where you stay will offer you free breakfast

B. dining information can be obtained from your tour guides

C. you can have a complete choice of local dishes at the hotel

D. a full list of local restaurants can be found on the tour pages

38. Which of the following statements is TRUE?

A. Tour guides are supposed to arrange dinner outside the hotel.

B. Tour guides' recommendations on food are unreliable.

C. Tourists must have lunch in the hotels they stay in.

D. Tourists may taste local dishes during dinner time.

39. The word "down-to-earth" (Line 4, Para.3) most probably means _____.

A. changeable　　　B. expensive　　　　C. reasonable　　　D. fixed

40. Meals are included in the tour price in some places where _____.

A. restaurant choice may be limited

B. there are many nearby restaurants

C. delightful dishes are not served

D. food may be too expensive

TASK 2

Directions: *This task is the same as Task 1. The five questions or unfinished statements are numbered from 41 to 45.*

Some cities have planned their transportation systems for car owners. That is what Los Angeles did. Los Angeles decided to build highways for cars rather than spending money on public transportation.

This decision was suitable for Los Angeles. The city grew outward instead of upward. Los Angeles never built many tall apartment buildings. Instead, people live in houses with gardens.

In Los Angeles, most people drive cars to work. And every car has to have a parking space. So many buildings where people work also have parking lots.

Los Angeles also became a city without a Central Business District (CBD). If a city has a CBD, crowds of people rush into it every day to work. If people drive to work, they need lots of road space.

So Los Angeles developed several business districts and built homes and other buildings in between the districts. This required more roads and parking spaces.

Some people defend this growth pattern. They say Los Angeles is the city of the future.

41. According to the passage, Los Angeles is a city where _____.

A. there is no public transportation system

B. more money is spent on highways for cars

C. more money is spent on public transportation systems

D. public transportation is more developed than in other cities

42. "The city grew outward instead of upward" (Line 1, Para.2) means _____.

    A. the city became more spread out instead of growing taller

    B. there were fewer small houses than tall buildings

    C. rapid development took place in the city center

    D. many tall buildings could be found in the city

43. According to the passage, if a city has several business districts, _____.

    A. people won't have to drive to work every day

    B. there have to be more roads and parking spaces

    C. companies would be located in between the districts

    D. there would be no need to build parking spaces within the districts

44. According to the growth pattern of Los Angeles, homes were mainly built _____.

    A. in the city center   B. along the main roads

    C. around business districts   D. within the business districts

45. The passage is mainly about_____.

    A. the construction of parking spaces in Los Angeles

    B. the new growth pattern of the city of Los Angeles

    C. the public transportation system in Los Angeles

    D. the problem of traffic jams in Los Angeles

TASK 3

Directions: *The following is an instruction of writing a trip report. After reading it, you should complete the information by filling in the blanks numbered from 46 to 50* (**in no more than three words**) *in the table below.*

Trip Reports

    Many companies require their employees to hand in reports of their business trips. A trip report not only provides a written record of a business trip and its activities, but also enables many employees to benefit from the information one employee has gained.

    Generally, a trip report should be in the form of a memorandum（内部通知）, addressed to your immediate boss. The places and dates of the trip are given on the subject line. The body of the report will explain why you made the trip, whom you visited, and what you did. The report should give a brief account of each major event. You needn't give equal space to each event. Instead, you should focus on the more important events. Follow the body of the report with a conclusion.

A Trip Report

Reported by: an employee back from a business trip

Addressed to: his or her immediate   46

Used for:

    1. serving as a written record

    2. giving helpful ___47___ that can be shared by others

Written in the form of: a ___48___

Information to be included in the report:

    1. the places and dates of the trip on ___49___

    2. major events during the trip in the ___50___ of the report

    3. conclusion

TASK 4

Directions: *The following is a list of terms used in railroad services. After reading it, you are required to find the items equivalent to（与……等同）those given in Chinese in the table below. Then you should put the corresponding letters in the brackets on the Answer Sheet, numbered from 51 to 55.*

A—information desk   B—ticket office

C—half fare ticket   D—waiting room

E—excess baggage charge   F—baggage check-in counter

G—security check   H—platform underpass

I—ticket agent   J—departure board

K—railroad track   L—traffic light

M—railroad crossing   N—soft sleeping car

O—hard sleeping car   P—hard seat

Q—baggage-claim area

Examples:（Q）行李认领处　　（E）超重行李费

51.（　　）硬座	（　　）软卧车厢
52.（　　）开车时间显示牌	（　　）信号灯
53.（　　）站台地下通道	（　　）候车室
54.（　　）问询处	（　　）安全检查
55.（　　）半价票	（　　）售票处

TASK 5

Directions: *The following is the Trouble-shooting Guide to a microwave oven. After reading it, you are required to complete the statements that follow the questions, numbered from 56 to 60. You should write your answers (**in no more than three words**) on the corresponding Answer Sheet.*

Problems	Probable causes	Suggested solutions
The display is showing the sign ":".	There has been a power interruption.	Reset（重新设置）the clock.
The fan seems to be running slower than usual.	The oven has been stored in a cold area.	The fan will run slower until the oven warms up to normal room temperature.
The display shows a time counting down but the oven is not cooking.	The oven door is not closed completely.	Close the door completely.
	You have set the controls as a kitchen timer（定时器）.	Touch OFF/CANCEL to cancel the Minute Timer.
The turntable（转盘）will not turn.	The support is not operating correctly.	Check the turntable support is properly in place, and restart the oven.
The microwave oven will not run.	The door is not firmly closed.	Close the door firmly.
	You did not touch the button "START".	Touch the button "START".
	You did not follow the directions exactly.	Follow the directions exactly.

56. What should you do if the display is showing the sign ":"?

Reset _____

57. What is the probable cause if the fan seems to be running slower than usual?

The oven has been put in a _____.

58. What are you advised to do if you have set the controls as a kitchen timer?

Touch OFF/CANCEL to cancel the _____.

59. What is the cause for the turntable to fail to turn?

_____ is not operating correctly.

60. What will happen if you do not touch the button "START"?

The microwave oven _____.

专项训练二

2007 年 12 月真题

Part Ⅲ　Reading Comprehension

Directions: *This part is to test your reading ability. There are five tasks for you to fulfill. You should read the reading materials carefully and do the tasks as you are instructed.*

TASK 1

Directions: *After reading the following passage, you will find five questions or unfinished statements, numbered from 36 to 40. For each question or statement there are four choices marked A, B, C, and D. You should make the correct choice and mark the corresponding letter on the Answer Sheet with a single line through the center.*

The Museum of Contemporary（当代的）Art (MOCA) has started a new series of programs, known as "Art Makes Good Business." It is designed to educate company managers about why art makes good business and how to take full advantage of it.

The event is open to new and current corporate（企业法人的）members of MOCA. An understanding and appreciation of art is becoming a must in today's business world. Art can be a valuable tool for seeking new ways to communicate with customers and raising public awareness of your company's role in the community.

During the coming months the series will look into the relationship between art, business and community. The series will cover how to understand modern art and how art can help improve a company's image. "Art Makes Good Business" speakers will include leaders from the business and art worlds. Bookings are required. Space is limited. For more information call 305-893-6211 or visit www.momanomi.org.

36. The purpose of the museum's new programs is to show _____.

    A. the management of business by artists   B. the role of art in improving business

    C. the education of modern artists   D. the way to design art programs

37. The "Art Makes Good Business" program is intended for _____.

    A. the general public   B. modern art lovers

    C. corporate members of MOCA   D. people involved in art business

38. MOCA members who take part in the programs can learn _____.

    A. to become leaders in business and art worlds

    B. to co-operate with other members of MOCA

    C. the new ways of communication between people

    D. about the relationship between art, business and community

39. Those who want to attend lectures by "Art Makes Good Business" speakers must _____.

    A. make a booking   B. pay additional fees

    C. understand modern art   D. be successful manager

40. This advertisement aims to _____.

    A. improve the relationship between companies

    B. stress the important role of art in education

    C. attract MOCA members to the programs

    D. raise funds for museums of modern art

TASK 2

Directions: *This task is the same as Task 1. The five questions or unfinished statements are numbered from 41 to 45.*

Cars are lots of fun, but they could also be dangerous. We have to be careful when we drive them or ride in them.

It's always a good idea to put on your seat belt when you are in a car. Why? Think about this example: You put an egg on a skateboard（滑板）and give it a push. If the skateboard hits a stone, it will stop, but the egg won't. It will fly through the air, hit the ground and break.

Now, think what would happen if you tied the egg to the skateboard. When the skateboard hits a stone, the egg won't go flying. It will stay safely on the skateboard.

Volvo, a famous Swedish carmaker, was the first to use seat belts in 1949. Air bags are also very important for car safety, because sometimes a seat belt isn't enough. If the car is going really fast and runs into something, seat belts could even hurt the people who wear them.

Most newer cars have air bags in front of and next to the seats. When a car hits something, its airbags will come out quickly—in less than one second—to keep the people inside safe.

41. We have to be careful in driving a car mainly because it could be _____.

    A. little fun   B. a pleasure   C. a lot of trouble   D. a great danger

42. The example of an egg on a skateboard is used to show that _____.

    A. eggs break easily on a moving skateboard

    B. cars should not be stopped suddenly

    C. seat belts are important to safety

    D. driving is a dangerous act

43. Which of the following statements is TRUE?

    A. People with seat belts tied will always be safe in cars.

    B. Volvo was the first carmaker to use seat belts in cars.

    C. Air bags will come out before the cars hit something.

    D. All cars have air bags in front of the seats.

44. According to the passage, air bags are another device that_____.

    A. adds safety to car driving   B. is going to replace seat belts

    C. comes out slowly to function   D. prevents cars from running too fast

45. The best title for this passage is_____.

    A. Buy a Volvo with Airbags   B. Make a Car Safe Inside

    C. Fasten Your Seat Belts   D. Add Air Bags to Cars

TASK 3

Directions: *The following is an advertisement. After reading it, you should complete the information by filling in the blanks numbered from 46 through 50 (**in no more than three words**) in the table below.*

Make our Tourist Information Center your first call when planning your visit to Cheltenham. Our friendly team can provide a wide range of services to make your stay enjoyable and unforgettable. We can book your accommodation（住宿）, from a homely bed and breakfast to a four-star hotel. We can provide tickets for local events and we are booking agents（代理商）for National Express and other local coach companies.

In summer we organize our own various programs of Coach Tours of the Cotswolds, plus regular walking tours around Cheltenham, all guided by qualified guides. We also stock a wide range of maps and guidebooks plus quality gifts and souvenirs（纪念品）. We can help you with advice on what to see, where to go and how to get there.

We look forward to seeing you in Cheltenham.

Tours of Cheltenham

Tour Service Provider: ___46___

Services Offered:

1. booking accommodation.

2. providing tickets for ___47___.

3. booking tickets from National Express and other ___48___.

4. organizing Coach Tours and regular ___49___ in summer.

5. providing various maps, ___50___, gifts and souvenirs.

TASK 4

Directions: *The following is a menu of a mobile phone. After reading it, you are required to find the items equivalent to（与……等同）those given in Chinese in the table below. Then you should put the corresponding letters in the brackets on the Answer Sheet, numbered from 51 to 55.*

A—phone book	B—tools
C—calculator	D—message saving
E—phone setting	F—backlight setting
G—key lock	H—automatic redial
I—sound volume	J—ring type
K—voicemail	L—additional functions
M—own number	N—alarm
O—new message	P—network

Q—delete all

Examples:（C）计算器　　　　　（K）语音信箱

51.（　）自动重拨	（　）本机号码
52.（　）闹钟	（　）音量
53.（　）网络	（　）信息储存
54.（　）工具箱	（　）背景光设置
55.（　）电话簿	（　）话机设置

TASK 5

Directions: *The following is a letter. After reading it, you are required to complete the statements that follow the questions, numbered from 56 to 60. You should write your answers* **(in no more than three words)** *on the corresponding Answer Sheet.*

Dear Guests,

In order to serve you better, we are carrying out a reconstruction program at the hotel, which will improve our fitness（健身）facilities.

We are currently working on our program on the 6th floor. We regret that the tennis court is not in operation.

However, you are still welcome to use the swimming pool. Please change into your swimsuit in your room.

While this program is in progress, drilling（钻孔）work may create some noise during the following time schedule:

9:00 a.m. to 11:00 a.m.

4:00 p.m. to 6:00 p.m.

We apologize for the inconvenience（不便）. Should you require any help during your stay with us, please call our Assistant Manager. He will be at your service any time of the day and night at 6120.

Once again, thank you for your kind understanding and have a pleasant stay!

Yours faithfully,

Arthur White

General Manager

56. What's the purpose of the hotel's reconstruction program?

To improve its _____.

57. Where is the reconstruction work going on at the moment?

On the _____.

58. Where should guests change into their swimsuits before going swimming?

In their _____.

59. Why does the hotel apologize to the guests?

Because of _____ caused by the reconstruction program.

60. Who should the guests turn to if they have any problem?

They should call the _____.

专项训练三

2006 年 12 月考试题

Part Ⅲ Reading Comprehension

Directions: *This part is to test your reading ability. There are five tasks for you to fulfill. You should read the reading materials carefully and do the tasks as you are instructed.*

TASK 1

Directions: *After reading the following passage, you will find five questions or unfinished statements, numbered from 36 to 40. For each question or statement there are four choices marked A, B, C, and D. You should make the correct choice and mark the corresponding letter on the Answer Sheet with a single line through the center.*

A few ways Greyhound can make your next trip even easier.

Tickets by mail.

Avoid lining up altogether, but purchasing your tickets in advance, and having them delivered right to your mailbox. Just call Greyhound at least ten days before your departure. (1-800-231-2222)

Prepaid tickets.

It's easy to purchase a ticket for a friend or family member no matter how many details on how to buy a prepaid ticket.

Ticketing requirement.

Greyhound now requires that all tickets have travel dates fixed at the time of purchase. Children under two years of age travel free with an adult who has a ticket.

If your destination（目的地）is to Canada or Mexico.

Passengers travelling to Canada or Mexico must have the proper travel documents. US, Canadian or Mexican citizens should have birth certificate, passport or naturalization（入籍）paper. If you are not a citizen of the US, Canada or Mexico, a passport is required. In certain cases a visa may be required as well. These documents will be necessary and may be checked at, or before, boarding a bus departing for Canada or Mexico.

36. From the passage, we can learn that "Greyhound" is probably the name of _____.

A. an airline　　　　B. a hotel　　　　C. a website　　　　D. a bus company

37. Why should people call Greyhound for tickets in advance?

A. To avoid waiting in lines at the booking office.

B. To hand in necessary travelling documents.

C. To get tickets from the nearest terminal.

D. To fix the travelling destination in time.

38. What can we learn about the Greyhound tickets?

    A. They are not available for travelling outside the US.

    B. Travellers should buy their tickets in person.

    C. Babies can not travel free with their parents.

    D. They have the exact travel date on them.

39. When people are travelling to Canada or Mexico, a passport is a must for_____.

    A. American citizens   B. Japanese citizens

    C. Mexican citizens   D. Canadian citizens

40. This passage mainly offers information about _____.

    A. how to prepare documents for travelling with Greyhound

    B. how to purchase a Greyhound ticket and travel with it

    C. how to make your trip with Greyhound interesting

    D. how to travel from the US to Canada and Mexico

TASK 2

Directions: *This task is the same as Task 1. The 5 questions or unfinished statements are numbered from 41 to 45.*

    People who work night shifts are constantly fighting against an "internal clock" in their bodies. Quite often the clock tells them to sleep when their job requires them to remain fully awake. It's no wonder that more accidents happen during night shifts than at any other time. Light therapy（光照治疗法）with a bright light box can help night-shift workers adjust their internal clock. However, many doctors recommend careful planning to help improve sleep patterns. For example, night-shift workers often find it difficult to sleep in the morning when they get off work because the body's natural rhythm（节律）fights back, no matter how tired they are. Some experts recommend that night-shift workers schedule two smaller sleep periods—one in the morning after work, and another longer one in the afternoon, closer to when the body would naturally need to sleep. It's also helpful to ask friends and family to cooperate by avoiding visits and phone calls during the time when you are sleeping.

41. Night-shift workers are those who _____.

    A. have to pay on their internal clock   B. need to re-adjust their clock

    C. fall asleep late at night   D. have to work at night

42. In order to remain fully awake at work, people working night shifts should _____.

    A. have longer sleep periods after work   B. make the light darker than usual

    C. try to reset their "internal clock"   D. pay more attention to their work

43. Many doctors think it is helpful for night-shift workers _____.

    A. to sleep with a bright light on

    B. to plan sleep patterns carefully

    C. to avoid being disturbed at work

    D. to sleep for a long time after work

44. Night-shift workers often find it difficult to sleep in the morning because _____.

    A. their internal clock will not allow them to

    B. they are often disturbed by morning visits

    C. they are not trying hard enough to do so

    D. they are too tired to go to sleep well

45. According to the passage, some doctors recommend that night-shift workers should _____.

    A. have frequent visits and phone calls   B. improve their family relationship

    C. have two smaller sleep periods   D. rely mainly on light therapy

TASK 3

Directions: *The following is a letter of complaint. After reading it, you should complete the information by filling in the blanks numbered from 46 to 50 (in no more than three words) in the table below.*

December 10th, 2006

Dear Sirs,

    I know that your company has a reputation（声誉）for quality products and fairness toward its customers. Therefore, I'm writing to ask for a replacement for a lawn mower（割草机）.

    I bought the mower about half a year ago at the Watchung Discount Center, Watchung, Nebraska. I'm enclosing a copy of a receipt for the mower.

    A month after I bought the lawn mower, the engine failed, and it was repaired under warranty（保修期）. So far, I have had the engine repaired four times.

    Now the engine has broken down again.

    I have already spent more than $300 on repairs, and I am beginning to seriously question the quality of your mowers.

    I am requesting that you replace this mower with a new one.

    I hope that you will live up to your reputation of the good customer service that has made your business successful.

Faithfully,

Rod Green

Letter of Complaint

Purpose of the letter: requesting a ___46___ for a lawn mower

Time of purchase: about ___47___ ago

Trouble with the machine: 48
Times of repairs so far: 49
Money spent on repairs: more than   50

TASK 4

Directions: *The following is a list of terms used in modern business management. After reading it, you are required to find the items equivalent to（与……等同）those given in Chinese in the table below. Then you should put the corresponding letters in the brackets on the Answer Sheet, numbered from 51 to 55.*

A—employee turnover
B—life-long employment
C—role conflict
D—profit sharing
E—scientific management
F—comparable worth
G—flexible working hours
H—social support
I—survey feedback
J—core competence
K—public relations
L—group culture
M—wage and salary surveys
N—honesty testing
O—human resource planning

Examples:（I）调查反馈   （A）人员流动

51.（ ）测谎		（ ）工薪调查
52.（ ）社会支持		（ ）终身雇佣制
53.（ ）团队文化		（ ）公共关系
54.（ ）利润分享		（ ）人力资源策划
55.（ ）科学管理		（ ）弹性工作时间

TASK 5

Directions: *The following is a letter applying for a job. After reading it, you are required to complete the statements that follow the questions, numbered from 56 to 60. You should write your answers* **(in no more than three words)** *on the Answer Sheet correspondingly.*

Dear Sirs,

For the past eight years I have been a statistician（统计员）in the Research Unit of Baron & Smallwood Ltd. I am now looking for a change of employment which would broaden my experience. A large and well-known organization such as yours might be able to use my services.

I am 31 years old and in excellent health. I majored in advertising at London University and I am particularly interested in work involving statistics（统计）.

Although I have had no experience in market research, I am familiar with the methods used for recording buying habits and trends. I hope that you will invite me for an interview. I could then give you further information.

I am looking forward to hearing from you soon.

Yours faithfully,

Mike Smith

56. What's Mike Smith's present job?

He's working as a _____.

57. What was Mike Smith's major at London University?

_____.

58. What kind of work does he like to do?

Work involving _____.

59. In what area does he lack experience?

He has no experience in _____.

60. What's the purpose of the writer in sending this letter?

To be invited for _____.

专项训练答案及解析

专项训练一

2007 年 6 月真题

36.【答案】D

【解析】第一段第一句话 "eating habits vary（变化）so much that it does not make sense to include meals in the price of our tours"，可知选 D。

37.【答案】B

【解析】只有 B 正确，由第二段最后一句话 "At lunch stops, your tour guide will show you where you can find salads, soups, and sandwiches" 可知。

38.【答案】D

【解析】只有 D 正确，由第三段第一句话 "Diner time is your chance to try some local food" 可知。

39.【答案】C

【解析】从句子推断出 "down-to-earth" 的意思是 "reasonable"。此句意为：经过多年的调查，我们知道哪些饭店能够以实际合理的价格提供美味的菜肴。

40.【答案】A

【解析】从最后一段第一句话 "In Mexico, Alaska, and the Yukon, where your restaurant choice may be limited, we include some meals" 推出。

41.【答案】B

【解析】第一段最后一句话 "Los Angeles decided to build highways for cars rather than spending money on public transportation"，意思是：洛杉矶决定为汽车修建更多的公路，而不是把钱投资做公共交通运输。

42.【答案】A

【解析】第二段的最后一句话是对 "The city grew outward instead of upward. (这个城市是横向发展而不是纵向发展)" 的解释说明，意思是：洛杉矶决不建很多高层公寓楼，相反，人们主要建的是带花园的房子。选项 A 意思是这个城市会变得更宽阔而不是变高。因此选 A。

43. 【答案】B

【解析】第三段和第四段的意思是说明这个城市需要更多的停车位和道路。因此选 B。

44. 【答案】C

【解析】由第五段和第六段的意思推出。第五段第一句话 "Los Angeles developed several business districts and built homes and other buildings in between the districts" 可以推出。

45. 【答案】B

【解析】这篇文章的主旨是讲洛杉矶的城市发展新模式，所以选 B。

46. 【答案】boss

【解析】由第二段第一句的 "addressed to your immediate boss" 得知。

47. 【答案】information

【解析】第一段最后一句："but also enables many employees to benefit from the information one employee has gained."

48. 【答案】memorandum

【解析】第二段第一句："Generally, a trip report should be in the form of a memorandum..."

49. 【答案】the subject line

【解析】第二段第二句："The places and dates of the trip are given on the subject line."

50. 【答案】body

【解析】第二段倒数第二句："Instead, you should focus on the more important events."

51~55. 【答案】

Examples: (Q) 行李认领处 　　　　(E) 超重行李费

51. (P) 硬座	(N) 软卧车厢
52. (J) 开车时间显示牌	(L) 信号灯
53. (H) 站台地下通道	(D) 候车室
54. (A) 问询处	(G) 安全检查
55. (C) 半价票	(B) 售票处

F—行李登记柜台 　　　　　I—售票代理人

K—铁轨 　　　　　　　　　M—铁轨交叉口

O—硬卧车厢

56. 【答案】the clock

【解析】表格第三列第二行："Reset（重新设置）the clock."

57. 【答案】cold area

【解析】表格第二列第三行："The oven has been stored in a cold area."

58.【答案】Minutes Timer

【解析】表格第三列第五行："Touch OFF/CANCEL to cancel the Minute Timer."

59.【答案】The support

【解析】表格第二列第六行："The support is not operating correctly."

60.【答案】will not run

【解析】表格第一列第六行："The microwave oven will not run."

专项训练二

2007 年 12 月真题

36.【答案】B

【解析】第一段最后一句："It is designed to educate company managers about why art makes good business and how to take full advantage of it."

37.【答案】C

【解析】第二段第一句："The event is open to new and current corporate（企业法人的）members of MOCA."

38.【答案】D

【解析】第三段第一句："During the coming months the series will look into the relationship between art, business and community."

39.【答案】A

【解析】第三段第三句和第四句："'Art Makes Good Business' speakers will include leaders from the business and art worlds. Bookings are required."

40.【答案】C

【解析】综合题。这则广告的目的是为了吸引当代艺术博物馆的会员参与新项目。

41.【答案】D

【解析】第一段第一句："Cars are lots of fun, but they could also be dangerous."

42.【答案】C

【解析】第二段第一句："It's always a good idea to put on your seat belt when you are in a car."

43.【答案】B

【解析】第四段第一句："Volvo, a famous Swedish carmaker, was the first to use seat belts in 1949."

44.【答案】A

【解析】第五段第二句："When a car hits something, its airbags will come out quickly——in less than one second——to keep the people inside safe."

45.【答案】B

【解析】这篇文章讲的是汽车内部的安全设置。

46.【答案】Tourist Information Centre

【解析】第一段第一句："Make our Tourist Information Centre your first call when planning your visit to Cheltenham."

47.【答案】local events

【解析】第一段最后一句："We can provide tickets for local events..."

48.【答案】local coach companies

【解析】第一段最后一句 "...we are booking agents（代理商）for National Express and other local coach companies."

49.【答案】walking tours

【解析】第二段第一句："In summer we organize our own various programs of Coach Tours of the Cotswolds, plus regular walking tours around Cheltenham, ..."

50.【答案】guidebooks

【解析】第二段第二句："We also stock a wide range of maps and guidebooks plus quality gifts and souvenirs（纪念品）."

51~55.【答案】

Examples:（C）计算器   （K）语音信箱

51.（H）自动重拨	（M）本机号码
52.（N）闹钟	（I）音量
53.（P）网络	（D）信息储存
54.（B）工具箱	（F）背景光设置
55.（A）电话簿	（E）话机设置

G—键盘锁   J—铃声类型

L—附加功能   O—新信息

Q—全部删除

56.【答案】fitness facilities

【解析】问题：饭店重建项目的目的是什么？第一段："In order to serve you better, we are carrying out a reconstruction program at the hotel, which will improve our fitness（健身）facilities."

57.【答案】6th floor

【解析】问题：当前重建项目的地点在哪里？第二段第一句："We are currently working on our program on the 6th floor."

58.【答案】room(s)

【解析】问题：游泳前客人在哪里更换泳衣？第三段第二句："Please change into your swimsuit in your room."

59.【答案】the inconvenience

【解析】问题：为什么饭店向客人们致歉？倒数第二段第一句："We apologize for the inconvenience（不便）."

60.【答案】Assistant Manager

【解析】问题：如果客人遇到问题，该向谁求助？倒数第二段第二句："Should you

require any help during your stay with us, please call our Assistant Manager."

专项训练三
2006 年 12 月真题

36.【答案】D
【解析】根据文中最后 "boarding a bus departing for Canada or Mexico" 可知，它指的是公汽公司。

37.【答案】A
【解析】文章第一句话："Avoid lining up altogether, but purchasing your tickets in advance, ..."

38.【答案】D
【解析】第三段："Greyhound now requires that all tickets have travel dates fixed at the time of purchase."

39.【答案】B
【解析】最后一段第二句："If you are not a citizen of the US, Canada or Mexico, a passport is required."

40.【答案】B
【解析】综合题，文中提到了如何购票、购票需求、凭此票旅游注意事项等。

41.【答案】D
【解析】根据短文前两句可知，"night-shift workers" 就是那些值夜班的工人。

42.【答案】C
【解析】短文第四句提到一种光照治疗法，其实就是为了调节他们的内部时钟。"Light therapy（光照治疗法）with a bright light box can help night-shift workers adjust their internal clock."

43.【答案】B
【解析】短文第五句 "However, many doctors recommend careful planning to help improve sleep patterns"，接着说明安排睡眠模式。

44.【答案】A
【解析】为什么值夜班的工人在早上难以入睡？从短文中的举例说明怎样安排睡眠模式可知，原因在于人体内的自然节律，也就是内部时钟。

45.【答案】C
【解析】短文倒数第二句："Some experts recommend that night-shift workers schedule two smaller sleep periods…"

46.【答案】replacement
【解析】短文第一段第二句："Therefore, I'm writing to ask for a replacement for a lawn mower（割草机）."

47.【答案】half a year
【解析】短文第二段第一句："I bought the mower about half a year ago…"

48.【答案】the engine failed

【解析】短文第三段第一句："A month after I bought the lawn mower, the engine failed, ..."

49. 【答案】four

【解析】第三段最后一句："So far, I have had the engine repaired four times."

50. 【答案】$300

【解析】第五段第一句："I have already spent more than $300 on repairs, ..."

51~55. 【答案】

Examples: （I）调查反馈　　　（A）人员流动

51.（N）测谎	（M）工薪调查
52.（H）社会支持	（B）终身雇佣制
53.（L）团队文化	（K）公共关系
54.（D）利润分享	（O）人力资源策划
55.（E）科学管理	（G）弹性工作时间

G—角色冲突　　　　　F—可比价值

J—核心才能

56. 【答案】statistician

【解析】信的第一句："For the past eight years I have been a statistician..."

57. 【答案】Advertising

【解析】第二段第二句："I majored in advertising at London University..."

58. 【答案】statistics

【解析】第二段最后一句："...and I am particularly interested in work involving statistics."

59. 【答案】market research

【解析】第三段第一句："Although I have had no experience in market research, ..."

60. 【答案】an interview

【解析】第三段第二句："I hope that you will invite me for an interview."

第四章　翻译——英译汉

第一节　题型介绍和解题方法指导

题型介绍

　　B 级翻译部分所译材料为四个句子和一个段落，包括一般性内容（约占 60%）和实用性内容（约占 40%）。一般性内容包括：科普、人物、政治、商贸、文化、生活等；实用性内容包括：业务信函、传真、电子邮件、广告、产品与厂家介绍、维护及使用说明等。所涉及的词汇限于《基本要求》词汇表中 B 级（2 500 个）所规定的全部内容。翻译部分得分占总分的 20%。测试时间为 25 分钟。翻译考试题型一般包括选择题和段落翻译两类：第 61~64 题为选择题，题目数量为四题，每题 2 分，共 8 分，每题选项为四种译文，其中一项为标准译文分值，其余三项译文的分值分别为 1.5 分、1 分和 0 分；第 65 题为段落翻译题，一般选择段落篇幅为 70 词左右的文章，题目数量为 1 题，共 12 分。翻译部分主要测试考生以下两个方面的能力：对英语理解的正确性和对汉语表达的通顺性。

解题方法指导

　　英语应用能力 B 级测试的翻译部分的解题一般采用以下步骤：

　　（1）理解阶段：仔细阅读句子，分析句子结构及各部分之间的逻辑关系，判断其是简单句、并列句还是复合句，是否存在某种特殊的句型或特殊的用法，之后再确定其中某些关键词的含义。

　　（2）表达阶段：该阶段建立在译者对原语语言文本的正确理解基础上，译者应清楚源语和目的语之间的差异并掌握一定的翻译理论和技巧。总的来说，翻译的技巧可以分为直译和意译两种。所谓直译是指在忠实传达原文本所表达信息的同时，译文中既保持原文的内容，又保持原文的形式。汉语与英语两种语言存在许多共同之处，许多英语句子的翻译完全可以采取直译的方法。但是，汉语和英语在词汇，句法结构和表达方法上具有很多差异，当由于遵循原文的形式而导致译文中的语意空缺或信息流失时，则应采取意译法，即不拘泥于原文的形式，正确表达原文的内容，又符合目标语言的表达规范。

　　（3）校对润色阶段：检查译文中信息传递是否完整，所涉及的内容有无遗漏；语言是否通顺，是否符合目标语言的表达习惯；有无牵强附会，尽量减少翻译的痕迹；卷面书写是否规范（标点符号是否有误，有无错别字，人名、地点、日期、方位和数字等有无笔误等）。

第二节 历年考点统计、考点解读和解题技巧

单项选择题

考点统计

通过对近几年九套考试命题的分析与研究，多项选择翻译题（第61~64题）所考查的要点大多数是语法结构，比如关系从句、被动语态等。此外还有较多的非谓语动词、各类短语、词类转换等。

时间 考点	2005年 6月	2005年 12月	2006年 6月	2006年 12月	2007年 6月	2007年 12月	2008年 6月	2008年 12月	2009年 6月
从句		3	2	1	1	2	1	1	3
非谓语动词			1		1				
被动		1		1	1	1	1		
否定								1	
虚拟					1				
其他	4		1	1		1	1	2	1

考点解读

在英译汉的翻译过程中，考生对英语原文的正确理解应该是做题的前提和基础。由于这一节的题目（第61~64题）都提供了译文选项供考生挑选，所以考生理解英语的能力的重要性要超过表达能力。根据考点统计结果，结合《高等学校英语应用能力考试大纲（B级）》的基本要求，翻译过程中需重点掌握常用的几项技能：

（1）正确掌握长句子的翻译；

（2）正确掌握从句的翻译；

（3）正确掌握被动句的翻译。

解题技巧

1. 长句的翻译

翻译长句时，首先要弄清楚原文的句法结构，找出整个句子的中心内容及其各层意思，然后分析几层意思之间相互逻辑关系（如因果、条件等），再按照汉语特点和表达方式，正确地译出原文的意思，译文可以不拘泥于原文的形式。长句主要涉及以下几种方法：

（1）顺译法：如果英语原文所述的一连串动作基本上是按动作发生的时间先后安排，或是按逻辑关系安排的，这与汉语表达方式比较一致，因此翻译时一般可按照原文的顺序来翻译。

（2）逆序法：当原句的表达顺序与汉语表达习惯不同甚至完全相反时，可以按照汉语叙事说理的习惯重新组合句子，逆序翻译。

（3）分译法：有时英语原句的表达顺序与汉语不同而且内容层次较多，或者相互间关系并不十分密切时，可考虑不拘泥于原文的语序和表达结构，按照汉语多用短句的习惯，

重新安排叙述层次和结构，有时还可适当增、删个别词语。当然，此种方法须慎用。

2. 从句的翻译

英语注重形合，主从句之间的逻辑关系明确。通过对近几年真题的分析，定语从句、状语从句等出现的频率较多，是考查的重点，因此考生必须正确、重点把握这些从句的译法。

（1）定语从句的翻译

在从句的翻译中，定语从句是最为常见的关系从句之一，是历年B级翻译考试中考查的重中之重。

定语从句可分为限制性定语从句和非限制性定语从句。限制性定语从句对所修饰的先行词起限制作用，在意义上与先行词密不可分，关系代词和先行词之间不用逗号分隔。如被省去，主句的意思就含糊不清，甚至变得毫无意义，因此在翻译时定语词组通常放在先行词之前。而非限制性定语从句同其先行词之间的联系比较松散，它不是先行词必不可分的组成部分，而是对先行词的附加描写或补充说明。非限制性定语从句前常有逗号将它与主句分开。

翻译定语从句具体可以运用下列方法：

1）译成定语词组

限制性定语从句的句法功能是作定语，起修饰、限制先行词的作用，往往译成偏正结构，并需要按照汉语的习惯放到所修饰词的前面，翻译为"……的……"。也就是将定语从句翻译成前置定语，从而将英文中的复合句变成中文的单句。

例如：Our idea is to offer you a place where you can enjoy shopping without interruption by others.

译文：我们的目标是为您提供一个不受他人打扰的购物场所。

解析：本句翻译中把定语从句前置，放到所修饰的先行词前面做定语，更符合汉语的语言习惯。翻译这类从句时经常将关系词省去，在句末加"的"字，放在被修饰项之间。当然，也可视其情况不用"的"字。这种译法在简短的定语从句翻译中尤为常见。

2）译成并列分句

常用的策略是采用分述法将带定语从句的英语复合句译成并列分句，其中分述法是指将主句和从句分开翻译的方法。这往往应用于非限制性定语从句中，因为非限制性定语从句对先行词不起限制作用，只起描述、解释、补充说明作用，翻译时可将其译成一个独立的句子，使译文层次分明、简洁明了。

例如：We are lucky to have the most up-to-date equipment in our laboratory, with which we can complete our research in time.

A. 我们很幸运能够拥有最先进的实验室，可以随时用来进行研究。

B. 很幸运，我们及时地找到了从事研究所需要的最完整的资料和设备。

C. 很幸运，我们实验室拥有最先进的设备，可以用来及时完成研究任务。

D. 非常幸运，我们实验室拥有的先进设备最多，能够完成所有的研究任务。

解析：本题的答案顺序为C—A—D—B。本句中的"with which"引导一个非限制性定语从句，修饰"equipment"。译成了并列分句，简洁明了，重点突出。

3）译为状语从句

有些定语从句在逻辑上与主句有状语关系，表达结果、原因、条件、让步、目的等关系，翻译时可将其译成偏正复合句，这在定语从句尤其是非限制性定语从句的翻译中颇为常见。

（2）状语从句的翻译

状语从句内容丰富，可用来表示原因、条件、目的、让步、时间等功能。英语状语从句的翻译，一般比较容易处理，通常可以直接翻译。但是由于两种语言表达上的不同，在状语从句的安排方面，还是存在着一定的差异。在汉语译文中如何将状语从句置于恰当的位置，使其与主句之间自然地连接，需要考生根据汉语习惯来灵活翻译。

1）时间状语从句

英语中时间状语从句的连接词有：when, since, until, as, as soon as, after 等。翻译的时候，一般翻译在主句的前面。

① 译成相应的时间状语。

② 译成"一（刚、每）……就"的结构。

③ 译成条件句。由于时间状语的引导词除了显示时间关系之外，有时候可以表示条件关系，所以还可以翻译为条件句。

④ 还可译成汉语的并列结构。

2）原因状语从句

英语中原因状语从句的连接词有：because, since, as, now that 等。在翻译的时候，按照中文"先因后果"的习惯，大多数原因状语从句可以放在主句之前翻译。

① 译成表示"原因"的分句，放在主句之前翻译，显示"前因后果"的关系。

② 有时原因状语从句也可以在主句后面，并经常使用汉语的"之所以……是因为"的结构。

3）条件状语从句

英语中连接条件状语从句的连接词常常有：if, unless, providing that, in case, if only 等，常可译为汉语的假设句或补语从句。

① 常翻译在主句之前表示假设。

② 也可以翻译在主句后面，用来补充说明条件。

③ 有时候，还可以根据上下文省略连接词。

4）让步状语从句

表示让步关系的连接词常常有：though, although, even if , whoever, no matter 等。翻译的时候，常可译成汉语的"不管"、"无论"等结构，通常把这些让步状语从句翻译在主句前面。

5）目的状语从句

在英语中，连接目的状语从句的连接词常常有：so that，lest，in case，in order that 等。

① 目的状语从句一般翻译在主句前面，表示"为了"。

② 还可以翻译在主句后面，表示"省（免）得"、"以免"、"以便"、"使得"、"生怕"

等概念。

6）结果状语从句

连接结果状语从句的连词常常有：so that, so...that, such...that 等，通常可以翻译为"结果"，"如此……以至于……"等，可以直接翻译。

3. 被动句的翻译

英汉两中语言中语态的区别较大。被动语态是英语动词的一种变化形式，表示句子的谓语动词和其主语之间存在着逻辑上的动宾关系。被动句的主语实际上是谓语动词动作的承受者。英语被动句把所要说明的人或事物放在主语的位置上，突出了行为的对象或结果。

英语中被动语态较多，而汉语中较少，使用范围较狭窄。因此翻译时，许多被动意义的英语句子一般都习惯于转化成用汉语主动语态表达，或者通过一些表示被动含义的汉语句子如无主句等来表现。

英语被动句的译法比较灵活，翻译时要根据句子的整体结构采用合适的方法来处理。一般来说，英语被动句的翻译可以有以下四种方法：

（1）将被动句译成汉语的主动句

汉语中主动句使用广泛，更强调动作的发出者，有时需要在句前加上施事者。

例如：Most of the questions have been settled satisfactorily.

译文：我们已经圆满解决了大部分的问题。

（2）将被动句译成汉语的判断句

汉语上常用"……是……"这一句式来说明人和事物的客观情况。这种结构在语意上往往具有被动的含义，可以与英语中的被动结构相沟通。一般来说，英语中用来说明客观情况的被动句都可以转译成汉语的这一结构。

例如：This model plane is made by my father.

译文：这架模型飞机是我爸爸做的。

（3）将被动句译成汉语的无主句

汉语的句子可以不带主语，因此，当无须说出行为主体时，可以将英语的被动句翻译成汉语的无主句。一般来说，英语中不带"by"短语并含有情态动词的被动句都可以采用这种译法。翻译时，将原句的主语译成宾语，放在动词后面，也可以加上"把"、"将"、"对"等词将宾语放在动词之前。英语中有些特殊的被动句是由短语动词中的名词作为主语构成的，翻译时可以将原句的主语和谓语合译成汉语无主句。

例如：Wrongs must be righted when they are discovered.

译文：发现了错误一定要改正。

（4）将被动句译成汉语的被动句

当英语被动句在语意上着重谓语动词本身的意义时，可用汉语的被动结构来解释。此时，原文句子的主语一般仍译作主语，在谓语动词前加"被"、"受"、"由"、"为"、"予以"等，或用"为……所"来表示被动意义。有时还可以在原句的主语前加"使"、"把"等来表示被动。

例如：Those who break the rules of the company will be punished seriously.

译文：凡是违反公司规章制度的人都将受到严惩。

（5）常用被动句型的翻译

It is supposed that … 据推测……

It is reported that … 据报道……

It must be admitted that … 必须承认……

It was considered that … 人们认为……

段落翻译题

考点统计

段落翻译测试的文章一般为 70 个词左右，句子不超过 6 句。句子多为简单句、并列句或主从复合句。所涉及的文章题材常为商贸、生活、文化、政治、科普等，内容多为业务往来信函、广告、产品及厂家介绍等。

时间 内容类别	2005年 6月	2005年 12月	2006年 6月	2006年 12月	2007年 6月	2007年 12月	2008年 6月	2008年 12月	2009年 6月
通知							1		
欢迎致辞			1						
商务信函		1		1					
广告、介绍	1				1	1		1	1

考点解读

段落翻译综合考查考生英文的整体阅读能力和汉语的表达能力，是一种主观类考试题型。由于这一试题的英文需要考生自己动手翻译成汉语，因此要求在理解英语的基础上，更强调汉语习惯表达的通顺性。考生在做本节试题时，除了要掌握常用的翻译技巧外（部分可见单项选择翻译的解题技巧），还应从全局入手着重把握以下两个方面：

（1）文章的体裁

（2）英汉的差异

解题技巧

1. 文章的体裁

段落翻译要注意全文在结构上和意义上的整体性，更要注意其所在文章的体裁关系，要尽力在译文中体现原文的风格、格式和语气。例如，广告用语应当尽量简洁、明了、易记忆、口语化，并且要使用大量褒义词，富有一定的煽动性；礼仪致辞有一定的惯用语句，不能太口语化；商务函件的翻译应注意尽量使用正式的书面语言等。如果对原文的体裁分类不清楚，就不能把握译文的质量，不能再现原文的韵味，达到原文的意图。

2. 英汉的差异

英语和汉语属于不同的语系，差别非常明显。英语表达先总后分，先果后因；汉语习惯于先分后总，前因后果。英语多长句、复合句；汉语则常用短句、简单句。英语多被动句；汉语则较少等等。因此，在英译汉的过程中应尽量遵循汉语表达方式，避免出现"中味洋文"。

例如，英语注重省略，避免重复，因此常使用代词替代某些成分。而汉语注重前后相应，有意重复，因此英译汉时要注意英汉之间的相应转换，将英语代词或助动词还原成所代替的成分，重复所替代的内容。

第三节　典型真题分析

单项选择题

1. People now have more leisure time, which is the reason why the demand for services has increased so rapidly.（2006 年 12 月真题）

A. 如今人们有更多的时间去娱乐，从而影响了劳务资源的快速上升。

B. 如今希望有时间娱乐的人越来越多，这是因为服务质量在迅速提高。

C. 如今人们有了更多的闲暇时间，因而对各种服务的需求增长得如此快。

D. 如今人们有了更多的空闲时间，这就是要求迅速提高服务质量的原因。

【解析】本句是主从复合句，包含了一个主句、一个非限定性定语从句和一个同位语从句。主语很简单，重点在后面的非限定性定语从句的翻译，而非限定性定语从句多作为分句翻译，在非限定性定语从句中又套有一个同位语从句"the demand for services has increased so rapidly"指的是对各种服务的需求增长，而非对服务质量的需求。所以最佳答案是 C。

2. All of our four objectives of this trip have been fulfilled, which is more than I had expected.（2005 年 12 月真题）

A. 我们此行四个目标的完成情况比我预期的要好。

B. 我们此行的目标一共有四个，比我预期的还多。

C. 我们此行总共完成了四个目标，比我预期的要多。

D. 我们此行的四个目标均已达到，比我预期的要好。

【解析】选出本题正确答案的关键在于把握由"which"引导的非限定性定语从句修饰"All of … fulfilled"整句话，而不是"objectives"。另外还要注意"All of our four objectives"（我们所有的四个目标）以及"more than"（比……多）两种表达方法的意思。本题最佳答案为 D。

3. For safety, all passengers are required to review this card and follow these instructions when needed.（2006 年 12 月真题）

A. 为了安全，请各位乘客反复阅读本卡片，务必按照各项规定执行。

B. 为了保险起见，请各位乘客务必阅读本卡片，并参照相关内容认真执行。

C. 为了保险起见，要求所有乘客在需要时都能看到这张卡片及以下这些内容。

D. 为了安全，要求所有乘客仔细阅读本卡片各项内容，必要时照其执行。

【解析】本题的句子使用的是被动语态，翻译成无主句的形式。此外，根据上下文可知"for safety"在此强调乘车的安全，"when needed"是分词的独立主格结构，做时间状语，译为"当有必要时"。所以最佳答案是 D。

4. Candidates who are not contacted within four weeks after the interview may consider their application unsuccessful.（2005 年 6 月真题）

   A. 面试后四周内仍未接到通知的求职者可以考虑再申请。

   B. 未在面试后四周内来联系的求职者则可考虑申请是否已失败。

   C. 求职者在面试后四周内不来签订合同则被认为是放弃申请。

   D. 求职者如果在面试后四周内尚未得到通知，则可认为未被录用。

【解析】本题的要点是定语从句的翻译，根据定语从句和主句的关系将该句中的定语从句翻译成条件状语，更为符合汉语的表达习惯。此外，"contact"意为"与……联系，联系……"，"be contacted"应当译成"被联系，得到通知"，"consider"意为"考虑，认为"，在此句译为"认为"最佳，"consider their application unsuccessful"原意为"认为申请不成功"，根据上文的意思应理解为"认为未被录取"。综合考虑，最佳答案为 D。

5. We are confident that we will get rid of those difficulties since government has agreed to give us some help.（2006 年 6 月真题）

   A. 由于政府已经同意给予我们一些帮助，我们有信心克服那些困难。

   B. 自从政府统一给予我们帮助以来，我们才下了脱贫致富的决心。

   C. 政府统一给我们一些帮助，因此我们要下定决心直面困境。

   D. 我们有信心克服困难，争取政府同意给我们一些帮助。

【解析】翻译本句的关键是把握住 since 的用法。"since"在句中引导原因状语，与前面的主句构成了因果关系。同时注意"that"在句中引导宾语从句，说明"confident"的内容。"get rid of"的意思是"排除、去除"。所以选项 A 为最佳答案。

6. Making a speech is an art which is constantly used, and it has to be learned and practiced.（2005 年 6 月真题）

   A. 演讲是一门难得一用的艺术，所以有机会就要学习和锻炼。

   B. 演讲是一门普遍运用的艺术，需要学习和训练才能掌握。

   C. 演讲是一门常用的艺术，而且需要学习和实践。

   D. 演讲这门艺术经常使用才能学会并用于实践。

【解析】本题的翻译要点是定语从句和被动语态。"be constantly used"意为"常用的"，"be learned and practiced"意为"学习和实践"，句子的后半部分"it has to be learned and practiced"中，"it"是代词，代替前面提到的"art"。完整的翻译应该是"这门艺术要通过学习和实践方可掌握"，但因为是一个分句，所以翻译整个句子时，可以省略"这门艺术"。综合考虑，最佳答案为 C。

段落翻译题

1. Card-holders of Holiday Sunshine Hotel automatically become registered members of its Reservation（预订）Network. They are able to enjoy the services offered by its member hotels. We encourage card-holders to use the card as often as possible, and they will be awarded with prizes when their marks（积分）reach a certain amount. Before checking in a

hotel, please always reserve your room first. When you check out, you will only have to pay the member price.（2005年6月真题）

【解析】这段文字是一段广告，介绍了"假日阳光大酒店"的持卡人所能享受的权益。翻译时，考生应首先分析清楚各句的结构，把握好这种广告文字的语气；同时，要注意一些关键词语和短语的翻译："card-holders"意为"持卡人"，"automatically"意为"自动地，机械地"，"registered members"意为"注册会员"，"member hotels"意为"会员酒店"，"award with prizes"意为"获得奖励"，"check in"意为"登记 / 入住"，"check out"意为"结账 / 退房"，等等。

【译文】"假日阳光大酒店"的持卡人自动成为其预订网络的注册会员。他们可以享用各成员酒店提供的服务。我们鼓励持卡人尽量多使用本卡。当持卡人的积分达到一定数量时，他们将获得奖励。在您入住饭店之前，请务必事先预订房间。结账 / 退房 / 离店时，您只需按会员价格付款。

2. We are glad to welcome our Chinese friends to this special Business Training Program. Here, you will have a variety of activities and a chance to exchange ideas with each other. We hope that all of you benefit a lot from this program. During your stay, please do not hesitate to speak to us with questions or concerns. We believe this will be an educational and enjoyable program.（2006 年 6 月真题）

【解析】本题是一段欢迎致辞。在翻译时应注意下列词组的翻译：a variety of 各种各样的、一系列的；exchange 交流、交换；benefit from 受益于……，从……中受益；hesitate 犹豫、不愿；don't hesitate to do... 不要犹豫做某事，直接做……；educational 具有教育意义的。此外，在翻译时考生可根据语境适当地变通词组的翻译或增减词，使表达更通顺，符合中文习惯。

【译文】我们很高兴地欢迎中国朋友参加这个商务培训专修班 / 项目。在这里，你们将会参与一系列的活动，并有机会互相交流 (思想 / 经验)。我希望你们大家都能从中受益。在此期间，如有任何问题或想法，请直接告知我们。我们相信这次培训既有教育意义又轻松愉快。

3. I'm writing to confirm our telephone conversation of Thursday, the 7th, about our visit to your company. Next Monday, December 11th, will be fine for us and we hope that it will suit you, too. My secretary, Miss Mary Brown, and Sales Manager, Mr. Zhang Ming, will be coming in the morning. It's unfortunate that I will not be able to go with them.

Thanks again for giving us this opportunity to visit you.（2006 年 12 月真题）

【解析】这是一封商务函件，因此翻译时注意尽量使用正式的书面语言，如"I'm writing to..."应译为商务信函术语"兹来信确认……"，"your company"为"贵公司"等。翻译要点还有：confirm 确认、证实；our visit to your company 去贵公司参观、拜访；It's unfortunate that... 遗憾的是……；Thanks again for... 为……再次感谢。

【译文】兹来信确认我们在 7 号（星期四）的电话里关于去贵公司参观事宜的商谈内容。12 月 11 日（下周一）的时间很适合我公司，希望也同样合适贵公司。我的秘书玛丽·布朗小姐及销售经理张明先生将于当天上午一同前往贵公司。遗憾的是我不能与他们同行。再次感激给予我们机会拜访贵公司。

4. Production Planner Wanted

Applicants（应聘者）should be college graduates with at least two years' working experience in production control. Good command of mathematics and skills in operating computers are essential. Holders of PRETCO（高等学校英语应用能力考试）certificates are preferred. Please send complete resume in English with one recent photo and expected salary to Post Office Box 67809, Hong Kong.（2004年6月真题）

【解析】这是一则招聘生产计划员的广告，因此翻译时注意尽量使用招聘广告的语言，在文体和语言特点方面与原文保持一致。翻译要点是：标题中"wanted"的意思是"寻找，需要"，在此应译为"招聘"；"production control"表示"生产监控"；"good command"是"熟练掌握"的意思；"holders"意为"拥有者，持有者"；"certificates"意思为"合格证书"；"be preferred"的意思是"更喜欢"，在此可译成"优先考虑"；"expected salary"表示"期望薪金，薪水要求"。

【译文】诚聘生产计划员

应聘者须大学毕业，且在生产监控方面至少有两年的工作经验。精通数学，熟练掌握电脑操作，获得高等学校英语应用能力考试合格证书者优先考虑。有意者请把一份完整的英文简历，一张近照及薪金要求寄到香港67809信箱。

5. *Worktrain* is a website for jobs and learning. It puts the most popular services for job seekers online. This makes it easy for you to get the information you need. At this site, you'll find over 300,000 jobs, plus thousands of training opportunities and information on job markets. And because *Worktrain* uses the power of the Internet, it gives you what you need faster and more easily than ever before.（2007年12月真题）

【解析】该题为网站的介绍。应注意的语言点为："most popular services"在此应译为"最受欢迎的服务"，"information you need"是定语从句，"you need"修饰"information"，"你所需要的信息"，"job seekers"是"求职者"，"training opportunity"意为"培训机遇"，"job market"意为"就业市场"，"faster and more easily"做状语修饰动词"gives"。

【译文】工作培训网是一家以求职与学习为目的的网站。它为求职者提供最受欢迎的在线信息服务，这样你就可以很容易地找到自己需要的信息。在这个网站上，你可以找到超过30万份以上的工作信息，还有数以万计的培训机会与就业市场的有关信息。因为工作培训网借助了强大的网络力量，所以就会比以往任何时候更快更简单地为您提供所需的信息了。

6. We are writing this letter to tell you that up to now no news has come from you about the goods we ordered on May 25th. As you have been informed in our letters, our customers are in urgent need of those machines. They are asking repeatedly for an early delivery（交货）. We hope that you will try your best to arrange all this without further delay.（2005年12月真题）

【解析】简读后确定本文是一封催货信，属于正式的商务信件，考生在翻译时要注意语言简洁、明确，措辞礼貌。翻译本文时需要主要的语言点如下：up to now 到目前为止；urgent 紧急的；inform 通知；arrange 安排；all this 在这里指及时发货。

【译文】我方此次致函的目的是想告诉贵方，到目前为止，我方于5月25日所订货物仍尚未到货。我方已在此前的信函中告知贵方，我方顾客急需那些机器。他们不断要求及早提货。我方希望贵方尽早安排发货，不再延误。

第四节　翻译专项模拟训练及答案解析

专项模拟训练一

61. People's attitudes towards gift giving may vary from country to country.

　　A. 人们的态度是国家之间要送礼物。

　　B. 不同的国家的人对送礼的态度各不相同。

　　C. 国与国之间人们对送礼物的看法不尽相同。

　　D. 各国人们送礼的做法都在变化。

【答案】C—B—D—A

【解析】本题的翻译要点是对"attitude"和"vary"这两短语意思的理解。"attitude"意为"看法"，而不是"态度"、"做法"，"vary"是"各不相同"的意思，并不是"变化"。因此选项 A、B 和 D 均存在不同程度的理解错误。

62. It is better to take your time at this job than to hurry and make mistakes.

　　A. 最好的工作要慢慢找，不要太着急。

　　B. 工作中不要太急，免得出错。

　　C. 干这活最好要慢点，不要匆忙，免得出错。

　　D. 最好要多花点时间在工作上，免得忙中出错。

【答案】C—D—B—A

【解析】本题的翻译要点是"It is better to do sth. than to do sth."和"take your time"。"It is better to do sth. than to do sth."这个句型表示是两件事情的比较，"最好采取……，而不是……"选项 A 理解出错，选项 B 没有把这种比较的意思表达出来，选项 D 没有翻译出"this job"。

63. Not until the problem of talents and funds is solved, is our talking about the project meaningful.

　　A. 不到解决人才和资金问题的时候，无须讨论这项工程的。

　　B. 讨论这项工程有无意义要看人才和资金问题能否得到解决。

　　C. 只有解决了人才和资金问题，讨论这项工程才有意义。

　　D. 解决人才和资金问题与讨论这项工程具有同样重要的意义。

【答案】C—B—A—D

【解析】本题的翻译要点是对"Not until…"这个句型的理解。该句表示强调，意为"直到……才"。选项 D 对句型理解有误。选项 A 和选项 B 没有把强调的语气翻译出来，且选项 A 后半句有漏译现象。

64. It gives us much pleasure to send you the goods asked for in your letter of April 15th.

　　A. 很高兴发去贵方 4 月 15 日来函索购的货物。

B. 我们很高兴寄去你们 4 月 15 日来信询问的商品。

C. 我们十分高兴贵方 4 月 15 日来函询问我们的商品。

D. 我们很高兴贵方来信要求我们 4 月 15 日寄出优质产品。

【答案】A—B—C—D

【解析】本题是一个商务信函中的句子。"asked for" 是定语后置，用来修饰 "the goods"，表示"要求的"，"letter of April 15th" 指 4 月 15 日的信件。选项 D 理解错误，选项 C 并没有把 "send you the goods asked for" 这部分内容翻译出来。选项 B 比较口语，且对 "asked for" 这个短语翻译有误。

65. Buying insurance（保险）is a way in which people can protect themselves against large losses. Protection against fire is one kind of insurance. Large numbers of people pay small sums of money to an insurance company. Although thousands of people have paid for fire insurance, only a few will lose their homes by fire. The insurance company will pay for these homes out of the small sums of money it has collected.

【解析】本题是一段关于保险的说明文题材。翻译难点是 "which" 引导的从句及对一些短语的理解和处理。"protest ... against" 是"保护……免遭"的意思，"small sums of money" 意为"小笔钱"。

【译文】买保险是人们防止重大损失的一种方法。防火也是一种保险。大多数人付一小笔钱给保险公司。尽管数以万计的人都买火险，但是只有极少数人因火灾而失去住所。保险公司从所收集的许多小笔钱中拿出钱付给这些受灾家庭。

专项模拟训练二

61. Not all the milk powder has been sufficiently tested for safety.

A. 所有的奶粉都未进行必要的安全检查。

B. 所有的奶粉都未必进行充分的安全检查。

C. 并非所有的奶粉都进行了必要的检查。

D. 并非所有的奶粉都经过了充分的安全检测。

【答案】D—C—B—A

【解析】本题的翻译要点是 "not all" 和 "sufficiently"。"not all" 是部分否定，不是全部否定。因此选项 A 和 B 是不对的。"sufficiently tested for safety"是指"充分的安全检测"，选项 C 有漏译。

62. During the 1970s, industrial production in these countries increased by 10 percent, compared with 21 percent in Japan.

A. 20 世纪 70 年代，这些国家的工业产品只增加了 10%，与日本相比增加了 21%。

B. 20 世纪 70 年代，这些国家的工业产值只增长了 10%，而日本却增长了 21%。

C. 20 世纪 70 年代，这些国家的工业生产出来的价值只高出了 10%，相比之下日本高出了 21%。

D. 20 世纪 70 年代，这些国家的工业产品只增加到 10%，与日本相比增加到 21%。

【答案】B—C—A—D

【解析】本题的翻译要点是 "increased by 10 percent"。"increased by 10 percent" 意为 "增加了 10%"，如果是 "increased to 10 percent" 则是指 "增加到 10%"。选项 D 理解有误。"compared with 21 percent in Japan" 是指 "相比之下日本增加了 21%"，并不是 "与日本相比……"，选项 A 可排除，选项 C 表述累赘。

63. He owed his failure to bad luck more than capacity.

    A. 他的失败主要是运气不好，但更多有能力因素。

    B. 他把自己的失败归因于运气不好而不是能力有限。

    C. 他失败的原因是不走运大于能力。

    D. 他失败是由于能力不行而不是运气不好。

【答案】B—C—A—D

【解析】本题的翻译要点是对 "owe...to"，"more than" 和 "capacity" 这三个短语意思的理解。"owe...to" 是固定搭配，意为 "把……归因于……"，"more than" 是固定搭配，在本句中意为 "而不是" 的意思，"capacity" 意为 "能力"。因此选项 C、A 和 D 均存在不同程度的理解错误。

64. They failed to recognize that our population is increasing faster than the supply of food and job opportunities.

    A. 他们无法承认人口增长的速度比提供粮食和就业机会还快。

    B. 他们失败的原因是没有认识到人口增长超过了食物和就业的供给。

    C. 他们没有认识到我们人口的增长超过了粮食的供给和就业机会的增加。

    D. 他们失败了，没有认识到人口增长会影响食物的供给，减少就业机会。

【答案】C—A—B—D

【解析】本题的翻译要点是 "fail to recognize that..."，该短语意为 "没认识到……"，并非选项 A、B 和 D 所表述的 "无法承认"、"失败"。

65. It has been half a year since we had the opportunity to serve your car. So, we are inviting you to bring your car into our shop for a free inspection and adjustment at your convenience. We hope that you will accept our offer. Our working hours are between 8:00 a.m. and 4:00 p.m., Monday through Saturday. We are looking forward to serving you again.

【解析】本题是一段售后服务的商业信函，翻译时要注意文体风格。"at your convenience" 是指 "在您方便的时候"，"accept our offer" 意为 "接受我们的建议"，"look forward to" 是指 "期待……"。

【译文】自从上次给您的汽车检修以来，半年过去了。现在我们邀请您在方便的时候将您的车送到我车行，以便对您的车进行免费检查调试。我们希望您接受我们的建议。我们工作时间是周一至周六上午 8:00 至下午 4:00。期待再次为您服务。

专项模拟训练三

61. This is rather for your mother to decide than for you.

    A. 这是你母亲的决定而不是你的决定。

    B. 这取决于你母亲的决定而你不该决定。

C. 这件事情得由你母亲决定而不是你来决定。

D. 这并不是为你而是为你的母亲才这样决定的。

【答案】C—B—A—D

【解析】本题的翻译要点是"rather...than"。"rather...than"连接的是两个并列结构,意为"宁可……而不要……,是……而不是……"。"for sb to decide"表示"由某人来决定","...than for you"后面省略了"to decide"以避免重复。因此选项 B、A 和 D 均存在不同程度的理解错误。

62. It was reported that the construction of the bridge had been held up by flood.

A. 据报道,那座大桥因洪水而停止。

B. 据报道,那座大桥因洪水泛滥而被停止修建。

C. 据报道,那座大桥因洪水泛滥被停止建设。

D. 记者说为了阻拦洪水而修大桥。

【答案】B—C—A—D

【解析】本题的翻译要点是"It was reported that","held up"和"construction"。"It was reported that"是指"据报道",因此选项 D 是错误的。"held up by flood"是指"因洪水泛滥而停止",因此选项 A 是错误的。"construction"意为"修建",不是"建设"。所以选项 C 也可排除。

63. As far as children are concerned, second-hand smoke can only have bad effects on them.

A. 孩子们担心买二手烟会对他们有坏的影响。

B. 就孩子们而言,被动吸烟仅仅对他们有一点影响。

C. 对孩子们而言,被动吸烟危害很大。

D. 对孩子们而言,被动吸烟对他们只有坏的影响。

【答案】D—C—B—A

【解析】本题的翻译要点是"As far as children are concerned"和"second-hand smoke"。"As far as children are concerned"是指"对孩子们而言",所以 A、B 是错误的。"second-hand smoke"是指"被动吸烟",因此选项 A 是错误的。C 虽然大意是对的,但是没有译出"only have bad effects on them"的确切意思。

64. Special attention has been paid to its packing, which we trust will prove satisfactory to your clients in every respect.

A. 我们对包装特别注意,我们相信这既是对客户的尊重,也能使客户满意。

B. 该货物的包装已予以特别注意,相信在各方面都能使您的客户满意。

C. 我们特别注重货物的包装,我们想用它来证明客户对我们是满意的。

D. 我们特别查看了一下包装的情况,结果证明客户对我们非常信任和尊重。

【答案】B—A—C—D

【解析】本题的翻译要点是"Special attention has been paid to its packing"和"in every respect"。"Special attention has been paid to its packing"是指"该货物的包装已予以特别注意",所以 D 是错误的。"in every respect"是指"各方面",选项 A 和 C 都存在误译。

65. I hope you have been able to review the information for new programs (see the last email I

sent you). If you have any questions, please don't hesitate to ask me. Besides, please tell me who will be going to Beijing to meet the new teachers and to guide them on the three-day tour in Beijing. Your early reply will be highly appreciated.

【解析】本题是一个商业信函，翻译时注意文体风格。"don't hesitate to ask me"是指"尽管问，不要迟疑"，"Your early reply will be highly appreciated"意为"盼早日回复"。

【译文】我希望你能看一下关于新项目的情况（请参阅我发给你的上一份电子邮件），如果你有什么问题，请尽管问我。此外，请告诉我，谁将前往北京接待新老师，并陪同他们在北京游玩三天。盼早日回复。

专项模拟训练四

61. She said she would come today, and I expect her at any moment.
    A. 她说她今天要来，我想她随时都会到。
    B. 她说她今天要来，我一直在等她。
    C. 她说她今天要来，我倒希望她什么时候都来。
    D. 既然她说他今天要来，我就等她。

【答案】A—C—B—D

【解析】本题的翻译要点是"I expect her at any moment"。"I expect her at any moment"是指"我随时期待她到来"；所以选项B、C和D都存在问题。选项D前半部分用了"既然"一词，属于增译，原文并没有这层意思。

62. The road department apologized for any inconvenience caused while road improvement was in progress.
    A. 道路部门对道路改造期间所带来的不便表示歉意。
    B. 道路部门为修建道路可能引起的不便进行了了解。
    C. 道路部门辩解说，新近造成的麻烦事因为道路正在改建。
    D. 道路部门对不断改建道路会造成的任何不便表示歉意。

【答案】A—D—B—C

【解析】本题的翻译要点是对"apologize...for"，"inconvenience caused"和"in progress"。"apologize...for"是指"对……表示歉意"，因此选项B、C理解有误。"caused"这个过去分词在本题中修饰"inconvenience"，做定语。"in progress"意为"进行中"，选项D把它译成"不断"是错误的。

63. The following qualifications are required from the candidates for the above position.
    A. 我们要求应聘高职位的求职者需具备以下资历。
    B. 应聘以上职位，需具备下列资格。
    C. 获选人为了高级职位要求自己具备以下资历。
    D. 以下资历是对应聘此职位的候选人的要求。

【答案】B—A—D—C

【解析】本题的翻译要点是"...be required from ...."。"The following qualifications are required from the candidates"是指"应聘者需要以下资格"，"position"参照整个句子的意思，

应是"职位"。

64. As the Christmas season is approaching, it occurs to me that you may need additional assistance in selling gifts from December 18th to 24th.

    A. 随着圣诞节的来临, 我想在 12 月 18 日至 24 日期间给你们多提供一些礼品来卖。

    B. 圣诞节的临近提醒了我, 你们在 12 月 18 日至 24 日期间也许需要卖礼物的店员。

    C. 圣诞节就要到了, 你们可能需要一名助理在 12 月 18 日至 24 日期间卖礼物。

    D. 圣诞节将至, 我想贵店在 12 月 18 日至 24 日期间可能需要出售礼物的临时店员。

    【答案】D—B—C—A

    【解析】本题的翻译要点是对"it occurs to me that..."。"It occurs to me that..."是指"我想到……"。选项 C 没有翻译出这层意思, "need additional assistance"指"需要额外的店员", 选项 A 有误, 选项 C 表述过于口语, 且前半句翻译稍有不当。

65. It is my honor to recommend Mr. Wang for the position of Director of Art Department in your college. Mr. Wang worked in our school for 15 years, and later got his doctor's degree in America. I have known him for many years, and he has impressed me as an academic-minded and hard-working scholar. I believe he will achieve a lot in his new post, and your kind attention to this recommendation would be greatly appreciated.

    【解析】本题是一封推荐信, 翻译时需注意文体风格。"It is my honor to do"意为"很荣幸……", "Director of Art Department"是指"艺术系主任"。

    【译文】我非常高兴地推荐王先生担任贵校艺术系主任。王先生曾在我校工作 15 年, 后来在美国取得博士学位。我认识他已有多年, 我认为他是一位有学问的勤奋的学者。我相信他一定会在新的岗位做出很大的成绩。本推荐信如能得到贵校的重视, 我将不胜感激。

专项模拟训练五

61. An earthquake, which could suddenly happen in places where there are many people, is very harmful.

    A. 地震因为可能会突然发生在人口稠密的地方, 所以是十分有害的。

    B. 地震发生的地方人口稠密, 它是十分有害的。

    C. 那次地震破坏性十分大, 因为它发生在人口稠密的地方。

    D. 地震是十分有害的, 它往往会发生在人口稠密的地方。

    【答案】A—D—B—C

    【解析】本题的翻译要点是对"which"引导的定语从句。本句真正的主干应该是"An earthquake is very harmful", 即"地震是十分有害的"。从句是来修饰"earthquake"。选项 C 明显不对, 选项 B 和原句的主语不一致, 选项 D 没有翻译出"could"所表示的可能性。

62. Hard as he worked, he failed to support the whole family.

    A. 他努力工作, 却未能支持一家人。

    B. 尽管他努力工作, 却养不起一家人。

C. 尽管他努力工作，却没有得到全家的支持。

D. 无论他多么努力工作，也养不起一家人。

【答案】B—D—C—A

【解析】本题的翻译要点是"Hard as he worked"和"support"。"Hard as he worked"，是一个半倒装句，表示让步关系，选项A是一个转折关系。"support the whole family"在这里是"养家糊口"的意思，因此选项A、C均可排除，选项D没有选项B表述确切。

63. Something unexpected has happened which prevents me from keeping my promise.

A. 一些不希望的事情的发生使我不能兑现我的誓言。

B. 一些让我不能遵守诺言的事不希望的发生了。

C. 一些出乎意料的事情的发生使我不能守约。

D. 阻止我免于遵守诺言一些不希望发生的事情还是发生了。

【答案】C—A—D—B

【解析】本题的翻译要点是"Something unexpected"，"prevent sb. from doing..."和"keep my promise"。"Something unexpected"是指"一些未意料到的事情"，并不是选项A、B和D所表述的"不希望"。"prevent sb. from doing..."在这是"避免……发生"，"keep my promise"是指"信守诺言"，因此"prevents me from keeping my promise"是指"使我不能信守诺言"。

64. You may use this machine, on condition that you are able to handle it properly so as not to damage it.

A. 这台机器你可以使用，但如有损坏，你要有条件进行维修。

B. 只要你能正确地使用机器，不损坏它，你就可以使用。

C. 你可以使用这台机器，条件是如有损坏，你能维修。

D. 在有条件的情况下你可以使用机器，千万别损坏它。

【答案】B—C—A—D

【解析】本题的翻译要点是"on condition"，"so as not to"和"handle"。"on condition"引导了一个条件状语从句，选项D将其错译成"在有条件的情况下"。选项C将条件状语从句内容理解错误，把"handle"错译成"维修"，选项A把"so as not to damage it"译为"如有损坏"。

65. Welcome to Beijing, the capital of China. You will discover the main sites of Beijing in a new relaxed manner. The round tour lasts three hours and a quarter. The tour tickets are effective for three days after you buy on the bus. You may break your tour at any stop and continue as you like. The tickets are 50 yuan for adults and 25 yuan for children.

【解析】本题是一段介绍性说明文,翻译时应注意文体风格。"effective"意为"有效的"。

【译文】欢迎来到中国的首都北京。你会发现北京各主要景点都洋溢着一种轻松的新气氛。来回旅程将持续3小时15分钟。车票自上车购买之日起三天内有效。您可在中途任何一站下车或上车。成人票是50元，儿童票是25元。

专项模拟训练六

61. I cannot tell you how sorry I felt when I was informed of your illness.

A. 得知你得了这种疾病，我心里真不知有多难受。

B. 我不会把我听说你生病的消息后的伤心告诉你的。

C. 得知你生了病，我心里真的很难受，但我不会把这一点告诉你的。

D. 得知你生了病，我心里真不知有多难受。

【答案】D—A—C—B

【解析】本题的翻译要点是 "I cannot tell you how sorry" 和 "was informed of"。"I cannot tell you how sorry"，是指 "我无法诉说我有多难受"，选项 B 和 C 理解有问题。"was informed of" 意为 "得知"。选项 A "得了这种病" 不符合原文。

62. Peace and development are the main themes（主题）of the times, an era full of both hope and challenges.

A. 和平与发展是充满了时代希望和挑战的主题。

B. 和平与发展是既充满着希望又充满着挑战的现时代的主题。

C. 和平与发展是时代的主题，这是一个充满了希望和挑战的时代。

D. 和平与发展是这个时代的主题，这个时代既充满着希望，也充满着挑战。

【答案】C—D—A—B

【解析】本题的翻译要点是 "an era full of both hope and challenges"，这个短语补充说明前面的 "times"。翻译的时候最好把这个句子拆开，选项 A、B 和 D 均不符合汉语表达习惯。

63. Would you please tell us the quantity you require so as to enable us to work out the offer?

A. 为了便于报价，能不能请您谈谈你方所需的数量？

B. 你方是否可以告诉我方怎样报价才能得到你方大批订货？

C. 我们只有根据你们所定数量才能报价。

D. 你方是否可以告知所需数量，目的是使我们算出价格？

【答案】A—D—C—B

【解析】本题涉及商务函电的内容，"the quantity you require" 是指 "您所需要的数量"，"you require" 作为后置定语修饰 "the quantity"，"so as to" 做目的状语，表示 "为了……"，"offer" 是商务术语，表示 "报价"。选项 B 理解有误，选项 C 表述不够专业，语气过于口语，选项 D 表述不符合汉语习惯。

64. The hotel also has a special-food restaurant at the east of the courtyard where famous local dishes are prepared by the top chefs.

A. 宾馆还有一个位于庭院东侧、由高级厨师为您准备著名地方菜的餐厅。

B. 宾馆大厅的东侧，有一个由高个子厨师烹制地方名菜的特色餐厅。

C. 宾馆还有特殊风味餐厅，位于庭院东侧，由名厨烹制著名地方菜。

D. 在宾馆东侧的特色风味餐厅内，大厨正为您烹制各种地方菜。

【答案】C—A—D—B

【解析】本题的翻译要点是 "top chefs" 及 "where" 引导的从句。选项 A 没有译出特色风味 (special-food) 餐厅，且表述累赘，不符合汉语表达习惯。"top chefs" 是名厨意思，而不是高个子厨师，所以选项 B 明显错误。选项 D 后半句 "大厨正为您……"，原文中并没有现在进行时这个时态。

65. We have received your offer on June 20th, 2009. We regret that we cannot accept it because of the terms of delivery. We made it clear in our letter that the 500 pairs of shoes should arrive here by July 30th, 2009, and each pair should be packed in a box. If you cannot guarantee these two terms, we have to find other suppliers. We look forward to your immediate reply.

【解析】本题是商务信函，翻译时需注意文体要求。"offer" 意为 "报价"，"terms of delivery" 意为 "交货条款"，"We look forward to your immediate reply" 意为 "望早日回复"。

【译文】贵方报盘已于 2009 年 6 月 20 收到。非常抱歉，由于交货条款问题，我方无法接受此盘。我们在信中已明确表明 500 双鞋子必须在 2009 年 7 月 30 日前抵达，且每双都应有鞋盒包装。如果贵方无法保证这两个条件，我们只能另寻其他供货商。望早日回复。

第五章 写作／汉译英

第一节 题型介绍和解题方法指导

题型介绍

写作／汉译英部分测试考生书写应用性短文、信函，填写英文表格或翻译简短的实用性文字的能力。本部分的得分占总分的 15%。测试时间为 25 分钟。

B 级作文主要包括五个部分。第一部分文案类：备忘录、电子邮件、传真和报告；第二部分招贴类：启事、通知、便条和海报；第三部分宣传类：广告、品牌和商标、简章和商品使用说明书；第四部分书信类：证明、求职、推荐、简历和商务信函；第五部分其他：合同、个人资料和外贸单证。

解题方法指导

（1）在学习过程中，要注重对各类应用性英语短文进行归类，扩大知识面，养成用英语思维的习惯。

（2）熟练掌握各种题材和体裁应用文的写作技巧，正确套用或使用常见应用文格式和语句。在谋篇布局时，一定要考虑各种应用文的写作格式，如书信格式有缩进式和齐头式两种。结构包括以下几部分内容：信头 (letter-head)，日期 (date)，封内名称和地址 (inside name and address)，称呼语 (salutation)，正文 (body of the letter)，结尾敬语 (complimentary close)，写信人签名 (writer's signature) 等。

此外，编号 (references)，烦交行 (attention line)，事由行 (subject line)，附件 (enclosure)，抄送 (carbon copy)，附言 (postscript) 等也是商务书信的组成部分。在写作时一定要切入主题，措辞得当，内容完整。

（3）积累大量有关词汇、短语及句型。积累与写作主题相关的词汇、短语、句型。

（4）熟练掌握语法知识，并在实际运用中加以巩固。写作时应使用通俗易懂、简洁明了的句子，在没有把握的情况下，避免使用复合句式或结构复杂的长句。应该使用自己熟悉的单词、短语和句型，尤其要正确使用时态和语态。写作时无论采用哪一种时态，必须上下兼顾，前后呼应。

（5）制订系统的写作计划，平时反复练习，考前强化训练制订系统的写作计划，把各种题材和体裁的应用文都纳入写作计划，反复练习和模仿。

第二节　历年考点统计、考点解读和应用文写作技巧

考点统计

2002年6月	讲座通知
2002年12月	个人简历
2003年6月	邀请信及回信
2003年12月	填写申请表
2004年6月	索赔函
2005年1月	汉译英填写表格
2005年6月	填写问卷调查
2005年12月	电子邮件
2006年6月	内部通知
2006年12月	留言条
2007年6月	e-mail
2007年12月	英语通告
2008年6月	请假条
2008年12月	感谢信
2009年6月	e-mail

考点解读

从历年的考试试题可看出，B级考试的主要题型为各种实用的书信体裁及表格填写。

应用文写作技巧

（1）掌握格式：熟记各种应用文写作的格式。

（2）积累与写作主题相关的词汇、短语、句型。

（3）熟练掌握语法知识。

（4）熟练掌握各种题材和体裁的应用文写作技巧，正确套用或使用常见应用文格式和语句。

（5）解题步骤：1）审题：确定题型与文体；

　　　　　　　2）列出提纲；

　　　　　　　3）列出关键词；

　　　　　　　4）校对。

第三节　典型真题分析

2007年12月真题

Part V　Writing (25 minutes)

Directions: *This part is to test your ability to do practical writing. You are required to write a*

Notice according to the information given in Chinese. Remember to write it on the Translation/ Composition Sheet.

说明：写一份英语通告，涵盖以下的内容，不要求逐句翻译。

东方电子有限公司为一家中外合资企业，主要生产制造电子产品。该公司将于 2007 年 12 月 26 日（星期三）在我校学生俱乐部举行招聘会。招聘的职位有：办公室文秘、市场营销人员和实验室技术人员。我们希望有兴趣的同学于当天下午 1:30 到 2 号会议室参加招聘会，并携带身份证、个人简历、英语应用考试 B 级合格证书以及计算机等级证书。

Notice

Dong Fang Electronics Ltd. is a joint venture, which_____

_____

_____

_____

_____

_____

Words for reference:

招聘：recruit   身份证：ID card

实验室技术人员：laboratory technician

英语应用考试 B 级合格证书：the certificate of PRETCO (level B)

【真题分析】本题要求写一个通知，要求语言简洁，内容完整。注意写作格式，在上方居中写上 "Notice" 或 "NOTICE" 一词作为标志，正文的右下角写出通知的单位名称或人名，日期放在左下角。出通知的单位以及被通知的对象一般都用第三人称。

【范文】

Notice

Dong Fang Electronics Ltd. is a joint venture, which mainly deals in electronic products. The company will hold a recruit meeting on Wednesday, December 26th, 2007, in the Students Club of our school. The positions are as follows: office secretaries, marketing salesmen and lab technicians. Any student who is interested in these positions is expected to attend the meeting at 1:30 p.m. in No. 2 Conference Room. In addition, please remember to take your ID card, résumé, the certificate of PRETCO (Level B) and the Computer Graded Certificate.

Student Union

December 20th, 2007

【范文点评】本文正文内容完整，表达清楚，格式正确，涵盖了所有信息点。

2007 年 6 月真题

Part V Writing (25 minutes)

Directions: *This part is to test your ability to do practical writing. You are required to write an e-mail according to the information given in Chinese. Remember to write it on the Translation/ Composition sheet.*

假定你是王军，根据以下的内容以第一人称发一封电子邮件。

内容：

1. 发件人：王军

2. 收件人：Anna Brown

3. 发件人电子邮件地址：wangjun11007@hotmail.com

4. 收件人电子邮件地址：anna11008@hotmail.com

5. 事由：王军在网站上卖出了一本书，书名：《电子商务导论》。买家是美国的客户：Anna Brown。

6. 邮件涉及的内容：

（1）感谢对方购买《电子商务导论》。

（2）书已经寄出，预计一周内到达。

（3）希望收到书后在网站上留下反馈意见。

（4）如果满意，希望向其他客户推荐。

（5）最近还会推出一些新书，欢迎选购；再次购买可以享受折扣。

Words for reference

反馈意见：feedback

电子商务导论：*An Introduction to E-commerce*

注意： 内容要写成一个段落，不得逐条罗列。

From: _____

To: _____

Subject: _____

Dear Miss Anna Brown,

_____
_____
_____

Sincerely yours,

【真题分析】这是一封电子邮件，通常包括收件人(To)、发件人(From)、主题(Subject)，然后是正文内容。正文邮件的内容，其书写格式与常规信件相同。

【范文】

From: wangjun11007@hotmail.com

To: anna11008@hotmail.com

Subject: Feedback of the Transaction

Dear Miss Anna Brown,

Thank you for your purchase of *An Introduction to E-commerce* and the book has been sent out and will arrive within one week. We hope you can leave your feedback on line after receiving the book. And we also hope you can recommend the book to other clients if you are satisfied. Besides, we will launch more new books recently on www.ebay.com.cn. You are welcome to place new orders and you can have some discount then.

Sincerely yours,

Wang Jun

【范文点评】本文正文内容完整，表达清楚，格式正确，涵盖了所有信息点，句与句之间，信息点与信息点之间连接顺畅。

2006 年 12 月真题

Part V　Writing (25 minutes)

Directions: *This part is to test your ability to do practical writing. You are required to complete the English Questionnaire（问卷调查）according to the information given in Chinese. Remember to write it on the Translation/Composition sheet.*

根据以下内容填写来访客人的留言表。

内容：

1. 来访客人：李华，男，PPK 公司总经理助理，联系电话：65734363

2. 来访时间：12 月 20 日 上午 10 点

3. 被访客人：Mr. Johnson Smith, 住假日酒店 422 房间

4. 事由：李华来到酒店与 Mr. Johnson Smith 商谈工作，Mr. Johnson Smith 外出

留言：李华约 Mr. Johnson Smith 明天去 PPK 公司洽谈业务。李华明天上午 9:00 驾车来酒店接他。下午安排 Mr. Johnson Smith 参观公司一条新建成的生产线。

Words for reference:

驾车接人：to pick up sb.

生产线：assembly line

总经理助理：assistant to General Manager

Holiday Inn
Visitor's Message
To: Mr./Ms　(1)　Mr. Johnson Smith　　　　　　　　Room No.:　　　　　(2)
While you were out
Mr./Ms.　　　　　　　(3)
Of:　　　　(4)　　　　　　Telephone:　(5) 65734363
☐ Telephone　　　☐ Come to see you
☐ Will call again　　☐ Will come again
☐ Asked you to tell back
Message:
(6)
Clerk:　(7)　Linda　Date:　(8)　　Time:　(9)

注意：请将要求填写在表格中的内容按以下顺序填入答题卡中的 Writing 部分并注明所填内容的顺序号！

(1) Mr. John Smith 　　　 (2)_____

(3) _____

(4)_____ 　　(5) 65734363

(6)_____

_____

_____

_____ 　　(7) Linda

(8)_____ 　　(9)_____

【真题分析】这是一份留言表，考生在做这类作文的时候要紧扣提示中所给条件，将试题中所给的信息全部用上。

【范文】

Holiday Inn

Visitor's Message

TO: Mr./Ms.　(1)　Mr. Johnson Smith　　　Room No.:　(2)　422

While you were out

Mr./Ms.　(3)　Mr. Li Hua, Assistant to General Manager

Of:　(4)　PKK Company　　　Telephone　(5)　65734363

☐ Telephone　　☐ Come to see you

☐ Will call again　☐ Will come again

☐ Asked you to tell back

Message:

(6) Li Hua would like to invite you to discuss business in PKK Company tomorrow, and he will pick you up at the Inn around 9:00 a.m. tomorrow. He would arrange for you to visit his company's newly-built assembly line in the afternoon. Please contact him by phone.

Clerk:　(7)　Linda　Date:　(8)　Dec. 20th　Time:　(9)　10:00 a.m.

【范文点评】该文内容紧扣提示中所给条件，内容表达清晰，语句正确。

2006 年 6 月真题

Part Ⅴ　Writing (25 minutes)

Directions: *This part is to test your ability to do practical writing. You are required to write a*

Memo（内部通知）according to the instructions given in Chinese below. Remember to write it on the Translation/Composition sheet.

说明：假定你是销售部经理 John Green，请以 John Green 的名义按照下面的格式和内容给本公司其他各部门经理写一个内部通知。

主题：讨论 2006 年度第三季度 (the third quarter) 销售计划

通告时间：2006 年 6 月 16 日

内容：本部门已制订 2006 年第三季度的销售计划。将于 2006 年 6 月 19 日下午 1:00 在本公司会议室开会，讨论这一计划。并希望各部门经理前来参加。如不能到会，请提前告知销售部秘书。

Words for reference：

告知：notify

提前：in advance

SALES DEPARTMENT
MEMO

DATE: _____

TO: _____

FROM: _____

SUBJECT: _____

_____

_____

_____

_____

【真题分析】本题要求写一份通知。通知应突出：被通知人、事情、时间、地点、注意事项。因通知所提及的事情一般是计划要做的，时态多用将来时，语态常用被动式。

【范文】

SALES   DEPARTMENT
MEMO

DATE: June 16th, 2006

TO: Managers of every department

FROM: John Green, Sales Manager

SUBJECT: Discussion of the sales plan for the third quarter of 2006

Dear all,

　　Our department has worked out a sales plan for the third quarter of 2006. The meeting for discussion of this plan is going to take place in the conference room of the company at 1:00 p.m.

on June 19th. All managers of different departments are expected to attend the meeting. If you are unable to be present, please notify our secretary in advance.

Looking forward to your presence.

Kind regards,

John Green

Sales Manager

【范文点评】该文基本符合上述要求，内容完整，表达清楚，语言流畅，书写规范，基本没有语言错误。

第四节 写作/汉译英专项模拟训练及答案解析

1. 祝贺信 (Letter of Congratulations) 的写法

Part V Writing (25 minutes)

Directions: *This part is to test your ability to do practical writing. You are required to complete a Letter of Congratulations. Some information is given to you. Remember to write the letter in the corresponding space on the Translation/Composition sheet.*

假如你是李明，你从报纸上看到你的朋友杰克在 IBM 公司获得了一次提升，你对他通过努力取得的成绩表示祝贺，并认为 IBM 挑选到了适当的人担任这一职务。

Words for reference：

提升：promotion   职位：position

【分析】祝贺信一般只有两三段，其结构是首先表达得知消息的高兴心情，同时在表达祝贺外，往往还应对收信人的成功做一些简单评述，最后对收信人的未来表示祝愿和期望。

【祝贺信注意事项】写祝贺信要充满热情、喜悦，说些鼓励、褒扬的话，使对方确实感到温暖和振奋；赞美对方，切实做到实事求是，恰如其分，不要故意拔高，甚至献媚，以致无法起到应有的表示祝贺的目的。祝贺信要做到整洁、大方，用词要恰当、简练，篇幅不宜太长。

【范文】

Dear Jack,

I was delighted to read the news about your promotion at the IBM Company. I know that you earned the promotion through years of hard work, and IBM certainly picked the right person for this position.

It is always a pleasure to see someone's true ability wins recognition. Congratulations and best wishes for your continued success.

Cordially yours,

Li Ming

2. 介绍信 (Letter of Introduction) 的写法

Part V Writing (25 minutes)

Directions: *This part is to test your ability to do practical writing. You are required to complete a Letter of Introduction. Some information is given to you. Remember to write the letter in the corresponding space on the Translation/Composition sheet.*

张明给王强写信介绍他的助手和好友李雷。李雷毕业于北京大学，主修化学。在校学习期间成绩优秀，研究工作也非常出色，被认为是一个有才华、有抱负的年轻人。此次到纽约深造，希望得到帮助和指导。时间：2009 年 10 月 12 日。

Words for reference:

助手：assistant

主修：major in

毕业：graduate

有才华的：intelligent

有抱负的：ambitious

深造：further study

【分析】介绍信要写得简短，应包含被介绍人的姓名、职业以及介绍他们相识的目的、原因。在某种意义上就是恳求友人对第三者给予照顾和帮助，所以还要向收信人表示谢意。

【介绍信注意事项】介绍信写作的格式同一般书信一样。介绍信在选词上要客气，请求他人帮忙不可用命令的口吻。一定要预先在文中向收信人表示感谢，做到礼貌不失礼节。介绍信篇幅无须太长，要简洁；语言要流畅，不要书面语痕迹太重。

【范文】

October 12th, 2009

Dear Wang Qiang,

The bearer of this letter（该持信人），Li Lei, is one of my assistants and good friends.

He graduated from Beijing University, majoring in chemistry. So far as I know, he was the best student in his class and he did exceedingly well in research work.

Since I have known him for three years, I can truthfully say that he is an intelligent and ambitious young man. I am sure he will become an excellent scientist someday if you do give him good service and help him in every aspect while he undertakes further studies in New York.

Your kindness will be warmly appreciated.

Yours faithfully,

Zhang Ming

3. 传真 (Fax Form) 的写法

Part V Writing (25 minutes)

Directions: *This part is to test your ability to do practical writing. You are required to fill in the blanks of a Fax. Some information is given to you. Remember to draw up the fax in the corresponding space on the Translation/Composition sheet.*

假如你是 Peter Reeve，Dragon Trading Ltd. 市场部经理。你现在发一份传真给 Thomas Jones，告诉他你们将定期将年度报告发给他。Thomas Jones 的传真号是 0044-087585，地址是 Great Wall Textiles，UK。日期是 August 5th，2009。

To: _____	From: Peter Reeve
_____	Dragon Trading Ltd.
Fax: _____	Fax: 0065-458764
Date: _____	Pages: 1

MESSAGE:

Dear Mr. Thomas Jones,

_____

_____

Sincerely yours,

Peter Reeve

Marketing Manager

Words for reference:

定期：regularly

年度报告：annual report

【分析】此题考查传真的写法，中文说明已经很清楚，所以只需将相应的中文内容翻译成英文即可。注意用词恰当，语句通顺。传真首页上方一般采用信头，内容包括收发双方的姓名、公司名称、传真号码、日期和页码。并不是所有传真都要使用这种格式，但这种格式给收发双方带来更多的方便。

【传真注意事项】传真正文一般用"be + 动词不定式"这种结构来表示一种按照计划或安排即将发生的动作或行为。考生在做这类作文的时候要紧扣提示中所给条件，将试题中所给的信息全部用上。

【范文】

To: _____Thomas Jones_____	From: Peter Reeve
_____Great Wall Textiles, UK_____	Dragon Trading Ltd.
Fax: _____0044-087585_____	Fax: 0065-458764
Date: _____August 5th, 2009_____	Pages: 1

MESSAGE:

Dear Mr. Thomas Jones,

We are pleased to send you a copy of our annual report regularly.

Sincerely yours,

Peter Reeve

Marketing Manager

B级考试全真试题

第二部分

Practical English Test for Colleges (PRETCO)(LEVEL B)

Part I   Listening Comprehension (15 minutes)

Directions: *This part is to test your listening ability. It consists of 3 sections.*

SECTION A

Directions: *This section is to test your ability to give proper responses. There are 5 recorded questions in it. After each question, there is a pause. The questions will be spoken two times. When you hear a question, you should decide on the correct answer from the 4 choices marked A, B, C and D given in your test paper. Then you should mark the corresponding letter on the Answer Sheet with a single line through the center.*

Example: You will hear: Mr. Smith is not in. Could you please give him a message?

You will read: A. I'm not sure.

B. You're right.

C. Yes, certainly.

D. That's interesting.

From the question we learn that the speaker is asking the listener to leave a message. Therefore, " C. Yes, certainly. " is the correct answer. You should mark C on the Answer Sheet.

[A] [B] [C] [D]

Now the test will begin.

1. A. Never mind.　　　　　　　　　　B. Yes, I am.

   C. No problem.　　　　　　　　　　 D. Here it is.

2. A. I like it very much.　　　　　　　B. That's a good idea.

   C. Thank you.　　　　　　　　　　　D. You're welcome.

3. A. Let's go.　　　　　　　　　　　　B. Don't mention it.

   C. It's delicious.　　　　　　　　　　D. Here you are.

4. A. He's busy.　　　　　　　　　　　 B. He's fine.

C. He's fifty.　　　　　　　　　　　D. He's a doctor.

5.　A. That's difficult.　　　　　　　B. It's sunny today.

C. Yes, please.　　　　　　　　　　D. This way, please.

SECTION B

Directions: *This section is to test your ability to understand short dialogues. There are 5 recorded dialogues in it. After each dialogue, there is a recorded question. Both the dialogues and questions will be spoken two times. When you hear a question, you should decide on the correct answer from the 4 choices marked A, B, C and D given in your test paper. Then you should mark the corresponding letter on the Answer Sheet with a single line through the center.*

6.　A. A telephone.　　　　　　　　B. A watch.

C. A T-shirt.　　　　　　　　　　D. An MP4 player.

7.　A. Travel to Australia.　　　　　B. Start a business.

C. Work part-time.　　　　　　　D. Write a report.

8.　A. Prepare a speech.　　　　　　B. Send an e-mail.

C. Type a letter.　　　　　　　　D. Make a phone call.

9.　A. The first floor.　　　　　　　B. The second floor.

C. The third floor.　　　　　　　D. The fourth floor.

10.　A. In a bank.　　　　　　　　　B. In a bookstore.

C. At the airport.　　　　　　　　D. At a hotel.

SECTION C

Directions: *In this section you will hear a recorded short passage. The passage is printed in the test paper, but with some words or phrases missing. The passage will be read three times. During the second reading, you are required to put the missing words or phrases on the Answer Sheet in order of the numbered blanks according to what you hear. The third reading is for you to check your writing. Now the passage will begin.*

Ladies and Gentlemen,

Welcome to you all. We are pleased to have you here to visit our company.

Today, we will first ___11___ you around our company, and then you will go and see our ___12___ and research center. The research center was ___13___ just a year ago. You may ask any questions you have during the visit. We will ___14___ to make your visit comfortable and worthwhile. Again, I would like to extend a warmest welcome to all of you on behalf of our company, and I hope that you will enjoy your stay here and ___15___.

Part II　Vocabulary & Structure (15 minutes)

Directions: *This part is to test your ability to construct grammatically correct sentences. It* *consists of 2 sections.*

SECTION A

Directions: *In this section, there are 10 incomplete sentences. You are required to complete each one by deciding on the most appropriate word or words from the 4 choices marked A, B, C and D. You should mark the corresponding letter in the Answer Sheet with a single line through the center.*

16. How much does it _____ to take the online training course?

    A. cost   B. give   C. pay   D. spend

17. If you need more information, please contact us _____ telephone or email.

    A. in   B. by   C. on   D. for

18. Mr. Smith used to smoke _____ but he has given it up recently.

    A. immediately   B. roughly   C. heavily   D. completely

19. He was speaking so fast _____ we could hardly follow him.

    A. what   B. as   C. but   D. that

20. Please call me back _____ you see this message.

    A. as well as   B. as early as   C. as far as   D. as soon as

21. We haven't enough rooms for everyone, so some of you will have to _____ a room.

    A. share   B. stay   C. spare   D. live

22. Before _____ for the job, you will be required to take a language test.

    A apply   B. applying   C. applied   D. to apply

23. If you want to join the club, you'll have to _____ this form first.

    A . put up   B. try out   C. fill in   D. step up

24. _____ the rain stops before 12 o'clock, we will have to cancel the game.

    A . As   B. Since   C. While   D. Unless

25. As the price of oil keeps _____ , people have to pay more for driving a car.

    A. to go up   B. going up   C. gone up   D. go up

SECTION B

Directions: *There are 10 incomplete statements here. You should fill in each blank with the proper form of the word given in the brackets. Write the word or words in the corresponding space on the Answer Sheet.*

26. What a (wonder) _____ party it was! I enjoyed every minute of it.

27. The film turned out to be (successful) _____ than we had expected.

28. Readers are not allowed (bring) _____ food and drinks into the library at any time.

29. The manager has promised that she will deal with the matter (immediate) _____ .

30. We are looking forward to (work) _____ with you in the future.

31. Today email has become an important means of (communicate) _____ in daily life.

32. The visitors were (disappoint) _____ to find the museum closed when they rushed there.

33. Because of the (improve) _____ in the road conditions, there have been fewer accidents recently.

34. When you arrive tomorrow, my secretary (meet) _____ you at the airport.

35. John has worked as a sales manager since he (join) _____ this company in 2002.

Part Ⅲ　Reading Comprehension (40 minutes)

Directions: *This part is to test your reading ability. There are 5 tasks for you to fulfill. You should read the reading materials carefully and do the tasks as you are instructed.*

TASK 1

Directions: *After reading the following passage, you will find 5 questions or unfinished statements numbered 36 to 40. For each question or statement there are 4 choices marked A, B, C, and D.You should make the correct choice and mark the corresponding letter on the Answer Sheet with a single line through the center.*

Thank you for your interest in Calibre Cassette (盒式录音带) library. This letter tells you about our service. With it we are sending you an application form, so that you can join if you would like to try it.

Calibre library aims to provide the pleasure of reading to anyone who cannot read ordinary print books because of sight problems. We currently have over 7,000 books available for reading for pleasure, including 1,000 specially for children. All our books are recorded cover-to-cover on ordinary cassettes and can be played on any cassette player. They are sent and returned by post, free of charge.

When we receive your application, we will send you a book and an information tape. They will explain how to use the service. The easy way to use Calibre library is to tell us what sorts of books you like, and we will keep you supplied with books we think you will enjoy. Or you can send us a list of books you would like to read, and we will then send you books from this list whenever possible. In that case you will need to use our website, or buy one or more of our catalogues (目录).

36. According to the first paragraph, the library sends the application form to the readers so that they can _____.

    A. read ordinary books   B. order cassette players

    C. buy Calibre cassettes   D. use the library service

37. Calibre library provides service mainly for people who suffer from _____.

    A. hearing difficulties   B. mental illnesses

    C. sight problems   D. heart troubles

38. The service of sending and returning books by post is _____ .

    A. not available to children   B. paid by the users

    C. free of charge   D. not provided

39. The easy way to use the library service is to _____

    A. inform the library of your name and address

    B. tell the library the sorts of books you like

    C. buy the catalogues of the library

    D. ask the library to buy the books

40. The main purpose of this letter is to _____ .

    A. introduce the library's service to readers

    B. recommend new books to readers

    C. send a few catalogues to readers

    D. express thanks to readers

TASK 2

Directions: *This task is the same as Task 1. The 5 questions or unfinished statements are numbered 41 to 45.*

    People in some countries cannot use their native language for Web addresses. Neither can Chinese speakers, who have to rely on pinyin. But last Friday, ICANN, the Web's governing body, approved the use of up to 16 languages for the new system. More will follow in the coming years.

    The Internet is about to start using the 16 languages of the world. People will soon be able to use addresses in characters (字符) other than those of the Roman alphabet (字母表). The change will also allow the suffix (后缀) to be expressed in 16 other alphabets, including traditional and simplified Chinese characters.

    But there are still some problems to work out. Experts have discussed what to do with characters that have several different meanings. This is particularly true of Chinese.

    Most experts doubt the change will have a major effect on how the Internet is used. "There will be some competition between companies to obtain popular words for addresses."

41. For Web addresses, Chinese speakers now have to use _____ .

    A. pinyin   B. signs   C. numbers   D. characters

42. The approval of the use of 16 languages by ICANN will allow web users to _____ .

    A. change their email address   B. email their messages in characters

    C. have the chance to learn other languages   D. use addresses in their own language

43. The new system will allow the suffix of a Web address to be expressed by _____ .

    A. any native language   B. figures and numbers

    C. Chinese characters   D. symbols and signs

44. Which of the following is one of the problems in using the new system?

    A. Certain characters have several different meanings.

    B. Chinese is a truly difficult language to learn.

    C. People find it difficult to type their address in characters.

    D. Some experts think it is impossible to use Chinese characters.

45. Many experts do not believe that _____.

    A. there are still some problems to work out

    B. there will be competition to get popular addresses

    C. companies are willing to change their web addresses

    D. the change will affect the use of the Internet greatly

TASK 3

Directions: *The following is an advertisement. After reading it, you should complete the information by filling in the blanks marked 46 to 50 (in no more than 3 words) in the table below.*

Hard Work, Good Money

We need:

　Staff (员工) to work in a busy operations center.

　You are to be working in Hangzhou.

We are:

　A rapidly expanding international IT company.

　Based in the UK and USA, with 500 employees worldwide.

We want to:

　Recruit (招聘) staff for our office in Hangzhou.

　Recruit 30 staff members in the first year.

You should be:

　Chinese;

　A college graduate, majoring in Computer Science;

　Flexible, efficient, active;

　Willing to work in Hangzhou;

　Able to work unusual hours, e.g. 7 p.m. to 3 a.m.

You should have:

　Good basic English language skills, holding Level-A Certificate of Practical English Test for Colleges (PRETCO).

　Keyboard skills.

Way to contact us:

　0571-88044066

For more details about the job, please visit our website: www.aaaltd.cn

A Job Advertisement

Recruitment: staff to work in an operations center

Work place: ___46___

Qualifications（资格）:

    Education: college graduate majoring in ___47___

    Foreign language: English, with Level-A Certificate of PRETCO

    Personal qualities: flexible, ___48___, active

Working hours: ___49___, e.g. 7 p.m. to 3 a.m.

Way to get details about the job: visit the website: ___50___

TASK 4

Directions: *The following is a list of terms related to employment. After reading it, you are required to find the items equivalent to（与……等同）those given in Chinese in the table below. Then you should put the corresponding letters in the brackets on the Answer Sheet, numbered 51 through 55.*

A—annual bonus
C—benefit
E—head hunter
G—housing fund
I—job fair
K—labor market
M—minimum wage
O—trial period
Q—welfare

B—basic salary
D—commission
F—health insurance
H—job center
J—job offer
L—labor contract
N—retirement insurance
P—unemployment insurance

Examples: (A) 年终奖　　　　　　　　　(O) 试用期

51.（　）招聘会		（　）最低工资	
52.（　）劳动合同		（　）福利	
53.（　）养老保险		（　）住房基金	
54.（　）猎头		（　）基本工资	
55.（　）劳务市场		（　）失业保险	

TASK 5

Directions: *Here are two letters. After reading them, you are required to complete the answers that follow the questions (No.56 to No.60). You should write your answers (in no more than 3 words) on the Answer Sheet correspondingly.*

Letter 1

December 1, 2009

Dear Mr. John Campbell,

We have received your letter of November 20, 2009 about your latest model of mountain bikes, in which we are very much interested. We believe that they will sell well here in the U.S.A. Please send us further details of your prices and terms of sales. Your favorable quotation (报价) will be appreciated. We look forward to hearing from you soon.

Yours sincerely,

Robert Loftus

Marketing Manager

Letter 2

December 4, 2009

Dear Mr. Robert Loftus,

Thank you for your letter of December 1st inquiring about our latest model of mountain bikes. We are pleased to send you the catalogue (产品目录) and price list you asked for. You will find our quotation reasonable with attractive terms of sales. We are looking forward to receiving your order at the earliest time.

Very truly yours,

John Campbell

Sales Manager

56. What product is inquired about in the first letter?

The latest model of _____.

57. What information of the product does Mr. Robert Loftus ask for?

Further details of the prices and _____.

58. What is enclosed with the second letter?

The catalogue and _____.

59. Who writes the second letter?

John Campbell, _____ manager.

60. What does Mr. John Campbell say about the quotation of the product?

He says it is _____ with attractive terms of sales.

Part Ⅳ   Translation—English into Chinese (25 minutes)

Directions: *This part, numbered 61 to 65, is to test your ability to translate English into Chinese. Each of the four sentences (No.61 to No.64) is followed by four choices of suggested translation marked A, B, C and D. Make the best choice and write the corresponding letter on the Answer Sheet. Write your translation of the paragraph (No.65) in the corresponding space on the Translation/Composition Sheet.*

61. Not until this week were they aware of the problems with the air-conditioning units in the hotel rooms.

 A. 这个星期旅馆里的空调间出问题了，他们没有意识到。

 B. 直到这个星期他们才意识到该修理旅馆房间里的空调了。

 C. 直到这个星期他们才知道旅馆房间里的空调设备有问题。

 D. 他们查不出旅馆房间内空调的故障，这个星期会请人来检查。

62. We sent an e-mail to your Sales Department a week ago asking about the goods we had ordered.

 A. 一周前你方销售部发来电子邮件，询问我方是否需要购买该产品。

 B. 一周前我们给你方销售部发了电子邮件，查询我们所订购的货物。

 C. 一周前我们给你们销售部发了电子邮件，想核查我们要买的货物。

 D. 一周前你方的销售部派人来核实我们的订购货物的有关电子邮件。

63. Candidates applying for this job are expected to be skilled at using a computer and good at spoken English.

 A. 申请该岗位的应聘者应熟练使用计算机并有良好的英语口语能力。

 B. 本项工作的申请人希望能提高使用计算机的能力和善于说英语。

 C. 本工作的受聘人员在应聘前应受过使用计算机的训练并懂得英语。

 D. 申请人在应聘本岗位时有可能被要求使用计算机和说良好的英语。

64. It is widely accepted that the cultural industry has been one of the key industries in developed countries.

 A. 发达国家广泛接受，文化是支撑国家工业发展的关键事业。

 B. 发达国家已普遍接受，文化产业应看成一种关键性的事业。

 C. 大家普遍接受，发达国家应把文化事业看成一种关键产业。

 D. 人们普遍认为，文化产业已成为发达国家的一个支柱产业。

65. Journalist Wanted（招聘记者）

 Student Newspaper is looking for a journalist. Applicants（申请人）should be studying at the university now, and should have at least one year's experience in writing news reports. The successful applicant will be expected to report on the happenings in the city and on campus. If you are interested, please send your application to the *Student Newspaper* office before the end of June. For more information, please visit our website.

Part V Writing (25 minutes)

Directions: *This part is to test your ability to do practical writing. You are required to write a short speech based on the following information given in Chinese. Remember to do your writing on the Translation/ Composition Sheet.*

感谢对方对你的热情款待，你已经访问过天津多次。在过去的访问中看到天津是一个非常美丽的城市。这次访问看到了更加令人欣喜的变化。为此你表示衷心祝贺。为了表示感谢，为大家的健康干杯，为天津将来的成就干杯！

Word for reference:

干杯　cheers

注意：不要逐字翻译。

2010年6月全国高等学校英语应用能力考试（B级）试卷

Practical English Test for Colleges (PRETCO)(LEVEL B)

Part I　Listening Comprehension (15 minutes)

Directions: *This part is to test your listening ability. It consists of 3 sections.*

SECTION A

Directions: *This section is to test your ability to give proper responses. There are 5 recorded questions in it. After each question, there is a pause. The questions will be spoken two times. When you hear a question, you should decide on the correct answer from the 4 choices marked A, B, C and D given in your test paper. Then you should mark the corresponding letter on the Answer Sheet with a single line through the center.*

Example:　You will hear:　Mr. Smith is not in. Could you please give him a message?

　　　　　You will read:　A. I'm not sure.

　　　　　　　　　　　　B. You're right.

　　　　　　　　　　　　C. Yes, certainly.

　　　　　　　　　　　　D. That's interesting.

　　From the question we learn that the speaker is asking the listener to leave a message. Therefore, " C. Yes, certainly. " is the correct answer. You should mark C on the Answer Sheet.

[A] [B] [C] [D]

　　Now the test will begin.

1. A. Just a moment，please.　　　　　B. Fine，thank you.

　C. See you.　　　　　　　　　　　　D. Well done.

2. A. Glad to meet you.　　　　　　　　B. Yes，please.

　C. It may not last long.　　　　　　　D. In twenty minutes.

3. A. Yes，please.　　　　　　　　　　B. On Monday.

　C. I see.　　　　　　　　　　　　　　D. Good-bye.

4. A. No problem.　　　　　　　　　　　B. Many times.

C. I don't know.   D. My pleasure.

5. A. You are welcome.   B. He's nice.

C. It's perfect.   D. It's two o'clock.

SECTION B

Directions: *This section is to test your ability to understand short dialogues. There are 5 recorded dialogues in it. After each dialogue, there is a recorded question. Both the dialogues and questions will be spoken two times. When you hear a question, you should decide on the correct answer from the 4 choices marked A, B, C and D given in your test paper. Then you should mark the corresponding letter on the Answer Sheet with a single line through the center.*

6. A. He's got a headache.   B. He can't sleep at night.

C. He coughs a lot.   D. He doesn't feel like eating.

7. A. Have some food.   B. Clean the table.

C. Make a phone call.   D. Buy a dictionary.

8. A. The sales manager.   B. The information officer.

C. The office secretary.   D. The chief engineer.

9. A. Teacher and student.   B. Manager and secretary.

C. Police officer and driver.   D. Husband and wife.

10. A. Asking the way.   B. Buying a ticket.

C. Checking in at the airport.   D. Booking a room.

SECTION C

Directions: *In this section you will hear a recorded short passage. The passage is printed in the test paper, but with some words or phrases missing. The passage will be read three times. During the second reading, you are required to put the missing words or phrases on the Answer Sheet in order of the numbered blanks according to what you hear. The third reading is for you to check your writing. Now the passage will begin.*

Ladies and gentlemen,

It's a great pleasure to have you visit us today. I'm very happy to have the opportunity to __11__ our company to you.

The company was established in 1950. We mainly manufacture electronic goods and __12__ them all over the world. Our sales were about $100 million last year, and our business is growing steadily.

We have offices in Asia, __13__ and Europe. We have about 1,000 employees, who are actively working to serve the needs of our __14__. In order to further develop our overseas market, we need your help to promote (促销) our products.

I __15__ doing business with all of you. Thank you.

Part II Vocabulary & Structure (15 minutes)

Directions: *This part is to test your ability to construct grammatically correct sentences. It consists of 2 sections.*

SECTION A

Directions: *In this section, there are 10 incomplete sentences. You are required to complete each one by deciding on the most appropriate word or words from the 4 choices marked A , B , C and D. You should mark the corresponding letter in the Answer Sheet with a single line through the center.*

16. I am sorry, but I have a question to _____ you.

    A. treat   B. influence   C. ask   D. change

17. Please give us the reason _____ the goods were delayed.

    A. why   B. which   C. what   D. how

18. Peter will _____ the job as Sales Manager when John retires.

    A. put away   B. take over   C. work out   D. make up

19. There is no doubt _____ he is a good employee.

    A. as   B. who   C. that   D. what

20. I feel it's a great honor for me _____ to the party.

    A. to invite   B. invite   C. having invited   D. to be invited

21. Don't _____ me to help you if you are not working hard.

    A. guess   B. speak   C. plan   D. expect

22. It was two years ago _____ his sister became a doctor.

    A. that   B. where   C. who   D. what

23. The general manager has promised to _____ the matter in person.

    A. get up   B. look into   C. see off   D. put on

24. If you move, you must inform us _____ the change of your address.

    A. with   B. in   C. in   D. of

25. _____ his lecture is short, it gives us a clear picture of the new program.

    A. If   B. Because   C. Although   D. When

SECTION B

Directions: *There are 10 incomplete statements here. You should fill in each blank with the proper form of the word given in the brackets. Write the word or words in the corresponding space on the Answer Sheet.*

26. Thomas was cheerful and (help) _____, and we soon became good friends.

27. The goods that you ordered ten days ago will (deliver) _____ to you tomorrow.

28. Gas prices are (high) _____ here than in other parts of the country.

29. The past decade has seen good economic (develop) _____ in this country.

30. If the engineer (come) _____ here yesterday, the problems would have been solved.

31. While this new law does not (direct) _____ affect the quality of work, it will greatly benefit employees.

32. Now many young people spend several hours a day (talk) _____ on a mobile phone.

33. In China, it is quite (nature) _____ for people to go back home for the Spring Festival.

34. The manager was surprised at the news when he (receive) _____ the phone call yesterday.

35. Advances in medical technology have made it possible for people (live) _____ longer.

Part Ⅲ　Reading Comprehension (40 minutes)

Directions: *This part is to test your reading ability. There are 5 tasks for you to fulfill. You should read the reading materials carefully and do the tasks as you are instructed.*

TASK 1

Directions: *After reading the following passage, you will find 5 questions or unfinished statements numbered 36 to 40. For each question or statement there are 4 choices marked A, B, C, and D. You should make the correct choice and mark the corresponding letter on the Answer Sheet with a single line through the center.*

Online advertising is the means of selling a product on the Internet. With the arrival of the Internet，the business world has become digitalized (数字化) and people prefer buying things online，which is easier and faster. Online advertising is also known as e-advertising. It offers a great variety of services，which cannot be offered by any other way of advertising.

One major benefit of online advertising is the immediate spread of information that is not limited by geography or time. Online advertising can be viewed day and night throughout the world. Besides，it reduces the cost and increases the profit of the company.

Small businesses especially find online advertising cheap and effective. They can focus on their ideal customers and pay very little for the advertisements.

In a word，online advertising is a cheap and effective way of advertising，whose success has so far fully proved its great potential (潜力).

36. According to the first paragraph, buying things online is more _____ .

    A. convenient   B. fashionable

    C. traditional   D. reliable

37. Compared with any other way of advertising, online advertising _____ .

    A. attracts more customers   B. displays more samples

    C. offers more services   D. makes more profits

38. Which of the following statements is TRUE of online advertising?

    A. It has taken the place of traditional advertising.

B. It will make the Internet technology more efficient.

C. It can help sell the latest models of digitalized products.

D. It can spread information without being limited by time.

39. Who can especially benefit from online advertising?

    A. Local companies.   B. Small businesses.

    C. Government departments.   D. International organizations.

40. This passage is mainly about _____ .

    A. the function and the use of the Internet   B. the application of digital technology

    C. the development of small businesses   D. the advantages of online advertising

TASK 2

Directions: *This task is the same as Task 1. The 5 questions or unfinished statements are numbered 41 to 45.*

During our more than 60-year history, with our vast knowledge and experience, *Trafalgar* has created perfectly designed travel experiences and memories.

Exceptional value

Traveling with *Trafalgar* can save you up to 40% when compared with traveling independently. We can find you the right hotels, restaurants, and our charges include entrance fees, tolls（道路通行费）, etc. Because we're the largest touring company with great buying power, we can pass on our savings to you.

Fast-track entrance

Traveling with us means no standing in line（排队）at major sights. *Trafalgar* takes care of all the little details, which means you are always at the front of the line.

Travel with like-minded friends

Because we truly are global, you will travel with English-speaking people from around the world, and that leads to the life-long friendships.

Great savings

We provide many great ways to save money, including Early Payment Discount（折扣）, Frequent Traveler Savings and more.

Fast check-in

Once your booking has been made, you are advised to check in online at our website and meet your fellow travelers before you leave.

41. Because of its great buying power, *Trafalgar* _____ .

    A. can find the cheapest restaurants   B. can pass on its savings to tourists

    C. takes tourists to anywhere in the world   D. allows tourists to travel independently

42. Traveling with *Trafalgar*, tourists do not have to _____ .

    A. bring their passports with them   B. pay for their hotels and meals

    C. stand in line at major sights   D. take their luggage with them

43. Traveling with *Trafalgar*, tourists may _____ .

    A. meet tour guides from different countries

    B. make new friends from around the world

    C. win a special prize offered by the company

    D. have a good chance to learn foreign languages

44. Which of the following is mentioned as a way to earn a discount?

    A. Early payment.   B. Group payment.

    C. Office booking.   D. Online booking.

45. After having made the booking, tourists are advised to check in _____ .

    A. at the hotels   B. at the airport

    C. by telephone   D. on the website

TASK 3

Directions: *The following is a letter. After reading it, you should complete the information by filling in the blanks marked 46 to 50 in no more than 3 words in the table below.*

Dear Sirs,

    I'm writing to tell you that your latest *shipment*（装运）of apples is not up to the standard we expected from you. Many of them are *bruised*（擦伤）, and more than half are covered with little spots. They are classed as Grade A, but I think there must have been some mistake, as they are definitely not Grade A apples.

    We have always been satisfied with the quality of your *produce*（农产品）, which makes this case all the more puzzling. I would be grateful if you could look into the matter. We would be happy to keep the apples and try to sell them at a reduced price, but in that case we would obviously need a *credit*（部分退款）from you. Alternatively, you could collect them and replace them with apples of the right quality. Would you please phone me to let me know how you want to handle it?

Yours faithfully

Finoa Stockton

Purchasing Manager

Letter of Complaint

Produce involved: Grade A (46) _____

Causes of complaint:

    1. many of the apples are bruised

    2. more than half of the apples are covered with (47) _____

Suggested solution:

    1. allow to sell at (48) _____ and give (49) _____ , or

    2. collect them and replace them with apples of (50) _____

TASK 4

Directions: *The following is a list of Shipping Marks. After reading it, you are required to find the items equivalent to*（与……等同）*those given in Chinese in the table below. Then you should put the corresponding letters in the brackets on the Answer Sheet, numbered 51 through 55.*

A— Guard against damp.

C— Keep away from heat.

E— Keep dry.

G— No naked fire.

I— Not to be thrown down.

K— Open in dark room.

M— Poison.

O— This side up.

Q— Use no knives.

B— Handle with care.

D— Keep away from cold.

F— Keep flat.

H— No use of hooks.

J— Open here.

L— Protect against breakage.

N— Take care.

P— To be kept upright.

Examples:（G）严禁明火 　　　　　（H）禁用吊钩

51. (	) 远离热源	(	) 请勿用刀
52. (	) 此面朝上	(	) 此处开启
53. (	) 竖立安放	(	) 暗室开启
54. (	) 小心轻放	(	) 注意平放
55. (	) 不可抛掷	(	) 保持干燥

TASK 5

Directions: *Read the following letter. After reading it, you are required to complete the answers that follow the questions (No. 56 to No. 60). You should write your answers in no more than 3 words on the Answer Sheet correspondingly.*

Dear Mr. Sampson,

I want to thank you very much for interviewing me yesterday for the position of design engineer. I enjoyed meeting with you and learning more about your research and design work.

The interview made me all the more interested in the position and working for XELL Company. I believe my education and work experiences fit nicely with the job requirements, and I am certain I could make a significant *contribution*（贡献）to the company over time.

I would like to re-emphasize my strong desire for the position and working with you and your staff. You provide the kind of opportunity I seek. Please feel free to call me at the following phone number if I can provide you with any additional information: 0811-8222-5555.

Again, thank you for the interview and for your consideration.

Sincerely,

Mary Cruz

56. Why did Mary Cruz write this letter?

    To give thanks to Mr. Sampson for _____ her yesterday.

57. What position did Mary Cruz apply for?

    The position of _____.

58. Which company did the writer wish to work for?

    _____.

59. Why is the writer strongly interested in the position?

    Because the company provides the kind of _____ she seeks.

60. How can the writer be contacted?

    By calling her at_____.

Part IV　Translation—English into Chinese (25 minutes)

Directions: *This part, numbered 61 to 65, is to test your ability to translate English into Chinese. Each of the four sentences (No.61 to No.64) is followed by four choices of suggested translation marked A, B, C and D. Make the best choice and write the corresponding letter on the Answer Sheet. Write your translation of the paragraph (No.65) in the corresponding space on the Translation/Composition Sheet.*

61. If your company insists on your price，we will have to turn to other suppliers for the goods.

    A. 假如贵公司要调整价格，请及早告知我们，以便另做安排。

    B. 假如贵公司提高价格，我们不得不从其他地方另寻货源。

    C. 如果贵公司不给折扣价，我们不得不采用其他方式购货。

    D. 如果贵公司坚持你方报价，我方只能找其他供应商进货。

62. First of all，I appreciate your advice on my decision to go to work in the computer company.

    A. 我首先感谢你们的决定，让我到这家电脑公司来工作。

    B. 我首先感谢你的建议，我已经决定去一家电脑公司工作了。

    C. 首先，很高兴到贵公司来听取你们在计算机方面的意见。

    D. 首先，感谢你对我决定去那家电脑公司工作所给予的建议。

63. Many good movies have been produced recently，but I still prefer to watch old movies because they are more interesting.

    A. 人们对电影是有兴趣的，特别是对老片子，所以我主张放映老片子。

    B. 近来拍了很多好的影片，既古老又饶有趣味，我觉得人人都喜欢看。

    C. 近来制作了很多好影片，但是我还是喜欢老片，因为老片更有趣。

    D. 很多好的影片是最近拍的，但我依然觉得过去拍的影片很有意思。

64. If the new payment methods make it easier for consumers to pay, could they make it easier for criminals too?

    A. 如果这些新的付款方式更便于消费者付款，是否对罪犯也更方便呢？

    B. 如果新的购物方式更容易使消费者满意，难到对罪犯不也是如此吗？

    C. 如果新的购物方式更方便了顾客，不也就更容易使人犯罪吗？

D. 如果新的付款办法便于人们消费，不也就更易于犯罪了吗？

65. Now people have a choice about where they work and what kind of work they'll do. They are faced with the challenge of deciding where to go. They need to know what standard to use in making their decisions. This book provides them with practical advice for making their choices. Meanwhile，they will know what questions to ask，what jobs to look for，and how to make their final decisions.

Part V Writing (25 minutes)

Directions: *This part is to test your ability to do practical writing. You are required to write a notice based on the following information given in Chinese. Remember to do your writing on the Translation/ Composition Sheet.*
The first sentence has been done for you.

说明：以办公室名义写一份有关会议室的使用须知。
内容如下：
1．保持会议室整洁
2．会后请带走您的文件和私人用品，关闭所有电器 (请举例)，关闭会议室所有门窗
3．其他注意事项 (内容自加)
4．表示感谢
5．日期：2010 年 6 月 20 日

Notice

The conference room is available to all, but we need your help to follow the rules listed below:

_____

_____

_____

_____

Practical English Test for Colleges (PRETCO)(LEVEL B)

Part Ⅰ Listening Comprehension (15 minutes)

Directions: *This part is to test your listening ability. It consists of 3 sections.*

SECTION A

Directions: *This section is to test your ability to give proper responses. There are 5 recorded questions in it. After each question, there is a pause. The questions will be spoken two times. When you hear a question, you should decide on the correct answer from the 4 choices marked A, B, C, and D. given in your test paper. Then you should mark the corresponding letter on the Answer Sheet with a single line through the center.*

Example: You will hear: Mr. Smith is not in. Could yon please give him a message?

You will hear: A. I'm not sure.

B. You're right.

C. Yes, certainly.

D. That's interesting.

From the question we learn that the speaker is asking the listener to leave a message. Therefore, "C. Yes, certainly" is the correct answer. Your should mark C on the Answer Sheet.

[A] [B] [C] [D]

Now the test will begin.

1. A. Here you are.   B. That's nice.
   C. Don't worry.   D. It doesn't matter.
2. A. No, you can't.   B. Yes, I am.
   C. Please don't.   D. Fine, thanks.

3. A. No, it isn't.   B. Yes, it is.
   C. Quite well.   D. Thanks a lot.

4. A. Hurry up.   B. Take it easy.
   C. No problem.   D. Mind your steps.

5. A. After you, please.   B. Take care.
   C. This way, please.   D. Sure, I will.

SECTION B

Directions: *This section is to test your ability to understand short dialogues. There are 5 recorded dialogues in it. After each dialogue, there is a recorded question. Both the dialogues and questions will be spoken two times. When you hear a question, you should decide on the correct answer from the 4 choices marked A, B, C, and D. given in your test paper. Then you should mark the corresponding letter on the Answer Sheet with a single line through the center.*

6. A. A writer.   B. A musician.
   C. An engineer.   D. A doctor.

7. A. Very interesting.   B. Rather difficult.
   C. Too simple.   D. Quite good.

8. A. She hasn't got the job.   B. She hasn't passed the exam.
   C. She has got a headache.   D. She has lost her bag.

9. A. On television.   B. In the newspaper.
   C. On the Internet.   D. From a friend.

10. A. Training.   B. Sales.
    C. Service.   D. Quality.

SECTION C

Directions: *In this section you will hear a recorded short passage. The passage is printed in the test paper, but with some words or phrases missing. The passage will be read three times. During the second reading, you are required to put the missing words or phrases on the Answer Sheet in order of the numbered blanks according to what you hear. The third reading is for you to check your writing. Now the passage will begin.*

Good morning, Mr. Blake. Take a seat, please.

Welcome to the ___11___. Before we start, let me give you some idea of what I'd like to talk about with you today ___12___, you'll be given a few minutes to introduce yourself. You can tell us about your education, job ___13___, interests, hobbies, or anything else you'd like to tell us. After that, I'll give you some information about our company and the job you are ___14___. If you have any questions about the job, ___15___ to ask me. I'll be happy to answer them. Now, let's start.

Part II　Vocabulary & Structure (15 minutes)

Directions: *This part is to test your ability to use words and phrases correctly to construct meaningful and grammatically correct sentences. It consists of 2 sections.*

SECTION A

Directions: *There are 10 incomplete statements here. You are required to complete each statement by choosing the appropriate answer from the 4 choices marked A, B, C, and D. You should mark the corresponding letter on the Answer Sheet with a single line through the center.*

16. The report gives a _____ picture of the company's future development.
    A. central
    B. clean
    C. clear
    D. comfortable

17. The company has been producing this model of machine tool _____ 2008.
    A. since
    B. after
    C. for
    D. before

18. Please _____ your report carefully before you hand it in to me.
    A. turn to
    B. bring about
    C. go over
    D. put up

19. The next board meeting will focus _____ the benefits for the employees.
    A. by
    B. for
    C. with
    D. on

20. Breakfast can be _____ to you in your room for an additional charge.
    A. eaten
    B. served
    C. used
    D. made

21. If more money had been invested, we _____ a factory in Asia.
    A. will set up
    B. have set up
    C. would have set up
    D. had set up

22. Even in small companies, computers are a(n) _____ tool.
    A. natural
    B. essential
    C. careful
    D. impossible

23. We were excited to learn that the last month's sales _____ by 30%.
    A. had increased
    B. increase
    C. are increasing
    D. have increased

24. _____ your name and job title, the business card should also include your telephone number and address.
    A. As far as
    B. In addition to
    C. In spite of
    D. As a result of

25. Have you read our letter of December 18, in _____ we complained about the quality of your product?

    A. that   B. where

    C. what   D. which

SECTION B

Direction: *There are also 10 incomplete statements here. You should fill in each blank with the proper form of the word given in brackets. Write the word or words in the corresponding space on the Answer Sheet.*

26. Could you tell me the (different) _____ between American and British English in business writing?

27. John is the (good) _____ engineer we have ever hired in our department.

28. The people there were really friendly and supplied us with a lot of (use) _____ information.

29. You'd better (give) _____ me a call before you come to visit us.

30. Greenpeace is an international (organize) _____ that works to protect the environment.

31. The final decision (make) _____ by the team leader early next week.

32. Have you ever noticed any (improve) _____ in the work environment of our factory?

33. We can arrange for your car to (repair) _____ within a reasonable period of time.

34. It was only yesterday that the chief engineer (email) _____ us the detailed information about the project.

35. We have received your letter of May 10th, (inform) _____ us of the rise of the price.

Part III Reading Comprehension (40 minutes)

Directions: *This part is to test your reading ability. There are 5 tasks for you to fulfill. You should read the reading materials carefully and do the tasks as you are instructed.*

TASK 1

Directions: *After reading the following passage, you will find 5 questions or unfinished statements, numbered 36 to 40. For each question or statement there are 4 choices marked A, B, C and D. You should make the correct choice and mark the corresponding letter on the Answer Sheet with a single line through the center.*

    If you have an *AT&T Business Direct* account, you can have your telephone bill paid automatically each month. You can make payments online with a bank account or use one of the following credit cards (信用卡) : *Visa, Master Card, Discover Network* or *American Express*. When you make an online payment, please follow the instructions given below.

Instructions

1. To make your payment online, click (点击) the "Pay Now" link under the "Account Overview (概

览) " summary.

2. If your business has more than one registered account, first select the account you need from the "Account Number" menu, and then click the "Pay Now" link.

3. If you have never made an online payment before, you will be asked whether you want to make a payment by using a bank account or credit card. Select either "Bank Account" or "Credit Card" from the "Select Payment Method" menu.

The online payment system is available Monday through Saturday, from 7:00 AM to 12:00 AM (Midnight) Eastern Time.

36. An *AT&T Business Direct* account helps you _____.

    A. earn an interest from a bank account

    B. make the first month's payment only

    C. pay your telephone bill automatically

    D. enjoy all the available banking services

37. The payment with an *AT&T Business Direct* account can be made online with _____.

    A. a passport   B. a credit card

    C. a driving license   D. a traveller's check

38. If you have several registered accounts for payment, the first link that you should click is _____.

    A. "Select Payment Method" menu   B. "Account Overview" summary

    C. the "Account Number" menu   D. the "Pay Now" link

39. When making the first-time online payment, you will be asked to _____.

    A. register your online account number B. open several registered accounts

    C. select the payment method first   D. apply for a new credit card

40. The passage is mainly about _____.

    A. how to pay phone bills by *AT&T Business Direct*

    B. how to open an *AT&T Business Direct* account

    C. how to make use of online bank services

    D. how to start a small online business

TASK 2

Directions: *This task is the same as Task 1. The 5 questions or unfinished statements are numbered 41 to 45.*

If you own a car, you are probably considering buying some kind of car insurance (保险). However, when you are actually purchasing car insurance, it can be difficult for you to decide which is your best choice. The ideal buying process is to first research and decide, then purchase.

Research First

Before buying car insurance, you should find out the purpose of your purchase and how the insurance meets your needs.

Decide on Suitable Car Insurance Policies (保单)

A neglected part of car insurance is the part which covers medical bills. Medical payments can add up very quickly in an accident situation, and the insurance should cover the bills incurred (招致) both by you and by the passengers in your car. Make sure you know the full value that your insurance covers.

Purchase the Best Car Insurance for Your Needs

You have a number of choices when it comes to the actual purchase of the car insurance. Each has advantages and disadvantages, and these may be influenced by your individual taste and previous buying experience. Insurance companies may offer you good advice, but prices on the Internet are often better.

41. According to the first paragraph, when buying car insurance, one should first _____.

    A. decide on the number of policies to purchase

    B. do careful research on the different choices

    C. choose the best insurance company

    D. look for the lowest insurance rate

42. The purpose of research is to find out whether the car insurance _____.

    A. includes all the advantages   B. best meets your needs

    C. offers the best rate   D. is easy to purchase

43. When buying car insurance, people often neglect _____.

    A. the damage to the car

    B. the bills paid by the passengers

    C. the part covering the medical bills

    D. the background of the insurance company

44. According to the last paragraph, your choice of car insurance may also be influenced by _____.

    A. your driving habits   B. the kind of car to be insured

    C. the attitude of your family members   D. your own taste and buying experience

45. Which of the following might be the best title of the passage?

    A. Medical Bills Covered in Car Insurance   B. Importance of Buying Car Insurance

    C. Advice on Buying Car Insurance   D. Advantages of Car Insurance

TASK 3

Directions: *The following is a memo. After reading it, you should complete the information by filling in the blanks marked 46 to 50 (**in no more than 3 words**) in the table below.*

MEMO

To: Katherine Anderson, Manager

From: Stephen Black, Sales Department

Date: 19 November, 2010

Subject: Resignation (辞职)

Dear Ms. Katherine Anderson,

I am writing to inform you of my intention to resign (辞职) from G&S Company.

I very much appreciate my four years' working for the company. The training has been excellent and I have gained valuable experience working within an efficient and friendly team environment. In particular, I am very grateful for your personal guidance during these first years of my career.

I feel now that it is time to further develop my knowledge and skills in a different environment.

I would like to leave, if possible, in a month's time on Saturday, 18 December. This will allow me to complete my current job responsibilities. I hope that this suggested arrangement is acceptable to the company.

Once again, thank you for your attention.

Memo
Date: 19 November, 2010
Memo to: Katherine Anderson, ___46___
Memo from: ___47___ , Sales Department
Subject: Resignation
Years of working for G&S Company: ___48___
Reasons for leaving: to further develop ___49___ in another environment
Time of leaving the position: on ___50___

TASK 4

Directions: *The following is a list of different types of advertising. After reading it, you are required to find the items equivalent to (与……等同) those given in Chinese in the table below. Then you should put the corresponding letters in the brackets on the Answer Sheet, numbered 51 through 55.*

A—action advertising

B—airport advertising

C—billboard advertising

D—business advertising

E—direct mail advertising

F—gift advertising

G—lamp post advertising

H—light box advertising

I—local advertising

J—magazine advertising

K—neon light advertising

L—newspaper advertising

M—online advertising

N—outdoor advertising

O—platform side advertising

P—public service advertising

Q—sales promotion advertising

Examples: (P) 公益广告　　　　(K) 霓虹灯广告

51. ( ) 机场广告	( ) 户外广告
52. ( ) 灯箱广告	( ) 杂志广告
53. ( ) 地方性广告	( ) 路灯柱广告
54. ( ) 赠品广告	( ) 直接邮递广告
55. ( ) 行为广告	( ) 报纸广告

TASK 5

Directions: *Read the following two emails. After reading them, you are required to complete the answers that follow the questions (No. 56 to No .60). You should write your answers* **(in no more than 3 words)** *on the Answer Sheet correspondingly.*

Email 1

To: DBL Online

From: Marsha Smith

Subject: Order

Dear Mr. Chapman,

We would like to buy 30 Futura computers, model No. XT 306. Can you ensure delivery (发货) by the 25th of this month?

We would like to confirm that the price is as given in your price list, with a 15% discount (折扣) for new customers. We will make payment upon receiving the goods.

We look forward to receiving your reply.

Sincerely,

Marsha Smith

Email 2

To: WMF

From: Marsha Smith

Subject: Order

Attachment: Purchase order No. J300

Dear Mr. Brown,

Following our telephone conversation this morning, I would like to order 300 washing machines. Could you deliver the items according to the purchase order?

Please send the items by express freight (快运).

I would like to confirm that the prices remain unchanged, and include a 10% discount.

As before, we will pay by check within 15 days after receiving the goods.

Best wishes,

Marsha Smith

56. What does Marsha want to buy in the first email?

_____.

57. What is the delivery date of the goods required in the first email?

By _____ of this month.

58. According to the first email, what discount does Marsha get as a new customer?

_____.

59. How did Marsha Smith contact Mr. Brown before she order the washing machine?

She contacted him through _____ in the morning.

60. According to the second email, how should the goods be shipped as Marsha requested?

By_____.

Part IV Translation—English into Chinese (25 minutes)

Directions: *This part, numbered 61 to 65, is to test your ability to translate English into Chinese. Each of the four sentences (No. 61 to No. 64) is followed by four choices of suggested translation marked A, B, C, and D. Make the best choice and write the corresponding letter on the Answer Sheet. Write your translation of the paragraph (No. 65) in the corresponding space on the Translation / Composition Sheet.*

61. As a matter of fact, your product will sell well if the advertisement is convincing.

A. 事实上，如果广告令人信服的话，你们的产品会很畅销。

B. 事实上，由于人们相信广告，你们的产品会卖出好价钱。

C. 实际上，尽管广告做得较差，你们出售的产品还是好的。

D. 实际上，要是广告能说服人，你们产品就能卖出好价格。

62. On account of rapid increase of trade with China, we have recently established a new branch there.

A. 由于最近在中国设立了新公司，我们增开了在中国的贸易账户。

B. 由于对华贸易的高速增长，我们最近在中国设立了新的分公司。

C. 为适应对华贸易的快速增长，我们新公司最近在中国隆重开业。

D. 为了在中国建立一家新公司，我们需要重新开设一个贸易账户。

63. It seems that women are now more attracted to the convenience of online shopping than they used to be.

A. 现在看来，利用网络购物的女性与过去相比，人数越来越多。

B. 看起来网上购物更加容易了，现在比过去更能吸引现代女性。

C. 现代的妇女与传统的妇女比较起来，似乎更加喜欢网络购物。

D. 看起来，如今的妇女比起过去更加为网络购物的便捷所吸引。

64. There was a heated discussion about customer service at the meeting until the manager came

up with a great idea.

A. 经理提出的关于客户服务的好主意，在会议上引起了大家的热烈讨论。

B. 经理到会之前，会议还在对那个客户提出的合理建议进行热烈的争论。

C. 会议就客服问题进行了热烈讨论，直到经理提出一个绝妙主意才停止。

D. 会议一直在热烈讨论客服问题，直到结束时经理才想出了一个好主意。

65.

Ladies and gentlemen, I am happy to introduce to you Mr. Wang Qiang, our new sales manager.

He is an expert in sales and marketing. For the last three years, Mr. Wang has worked for JHS Company.

Today he will explain to you what our company expects you to do. He will be meeting each of you to discuss your monthly sales plans in the following days and he is ready to answer any questions you might have.

Part V Writing (25 minutes)

Directions: *This part is to test your ability to do practical writing. You are required to write a letter of application according to the following instructions given in Chinese. Remember to do your writing on the Translation/Composition Sheet.*

说明：假定你叫王林，根据下列内容写一封求职信。

写信日期：2010 年 12 月 19 日

内容：

1. 从 2010 年 12 月 10 日的《中国日报》上获悉 ABC 公司招聘办公室秘书职位的信息；

2. 毕业于东方学院（注：专业自拟），获得多种技能证书；

3. 曾在 DDF 公司兼职，熟悉办公室工作，熟练使用电脑；

4. 随信附上简历；

5. 希望能获得面试机会。

注意信函格式。

Words for reference

《中国日报》：*China Daily*

工商管理：Business Administration

证书：certificate

附上：enclose

B 级考试模拟试题

第三部分

Model Test 1

Part I Listening Comprehension (15 minutes)

Directions: *This part is to test your listening ability. It consists of three sections.*

SECTION A

Directions: *This section is to test your ability to give proper responses. There are five recorded questions in it. After each question, there is a pause. The question will be spoken twice. When you hear a question, you should decide on the correct answer from the four choices marked A, B, C and D given in your test paper. Then you should mark the corresponding letter on the Answer Sheet with a single line through the center.*

Example: You will hear: Mr. Smith is not in. Could you please give him a message?

You will read: A. I'm not sure.

B. You're right.

C. Yes, certainly.

D. That's interesting.

From the question we learn that the speaker is asking the listener to leave a message. Therefore, "C. Yes, certainly." is the correct answer. You should mark C on the Answer Sheet.

[A] [B] [C] [D]

Now the test will begin.

1. A. I'm fine.   B. It's Tuesday.

   C. I feel thirsty.   D. I've been here.

2. A. You are welcome.   B. I'm very busy.

   C. Of course.   D. That's right.

3. A. I heard it yesterday.   B. Sorry to hear that.

   C. Yes. What a pity!   D. Yes, he had.

4. A. A nice day.   B. A new type of computer.

   C. By taxi.   D. It's very kind of you.

5. A. The matter is very important.   B. I'm very busy.

   C. The food is terrible.   D. I fell down the steps just now.

SECTION B

Directions: *This section is to test your ability to understand short dialogues. There are five recorded dialogues in it. After each dialogue, there is a recorded question. Both the dialogues and questions will be spoken twice. When you hear a question, you should decide on the correct answer from the four choices marked A, B, C and D given in your test paper. Then you should mark the corresponding letter on the Answer Sheet with a single line through the center.*

6. A. It's too late now.   B. They don't want to take train.

  C. There are no trains now.   D. They won't miss the train.

7. A. They're eating fruit.   B. They're preparing for a pie.

  C. They're having breakfast.   D. They're drinking beer.

8. A. Noisy.   B. Worst.   C. Convenient.   D. Comfortable.

9. A. In the street.   B. At the police station.   C. On the phone.   D. In a restaurant.

10. A. 6 yuan.   B. 12 yuan.   C. 7 yuan.   D. 2 yuan.

SECTION C

Directions: *In this section you will hear a recorded short passage. The passage is printed in the test paper with some words or phrases missing. The passage will be read three times. During the second reading, you are required to put the missing words or phrases on the Answer Sheet in order of the numbered blanks according to what you hear. The third reading is for you to check your writing. Now the passage will begin.*

  John was playing with a ball in the street. He ___11___ it too hard and it broke the window of Ms. Green's house. The ball ___12___ inside. Ms. Green came to the window with the ball and shouted at John. So John ___13___, but he still wanted his ball back. A few ___14___ later, John returned and knocked at the door. When Ms. Green answered it, he said, "My father's going to come and ___15___ your window very soon."

Part II Vocabulary & Structure (15 minutes)

Directions: *This part is to test your ability to construct meaningful and grammatically correct sentences. It consists of two sections.*

SECTION A

Directions: *In this section, there are ten incomplete sentences. You are required to complete each one by deciding on the most appropriate word or words from the four choices marked A, B, C and D. You should mark the corresponding letter on the Answer Sheet with a single line through the center.*

16. The policeman said that the young man was _____ for the accident.

    A. responsibility   B. recent   C. result   D. responsible

17. Much of what he says _____ not true.

    A. does   B. do   C. is   D. are

18. I _____ an old friend on the way home yesterday.

    A. meet   B. met   C. have met   D. had met

19. Many people felt great sorrow when they heard that the brilliant young actor _____ a heart attack at the age of 25.

    A. died from   B. died of   C. died for   D. died to

20. The classroom needs _____.

    A. clean   B. to clean   C. to be cleaned   D. being cleaned

21. I like him because he makes me _____.

    A. to laugh   B. laughed   C. laugh   D. laughing

22. We have _____ rainfall this year than last year.

    A. less   B. little   C. fewer   D. few

23. We have found _____ difficult to memorize so many words.

    A. it   B. this   C. which   D. that

24. The movie is _____ more interesting than the one I recommend to you.

    A. rather   B. very   C. much   D. so

25. None of us expected the president to _____ at the party. We thought he was still in hospital.

    A. turn in   B. turn down   C. turn out   D. turn up

SECTION B

Directions: *There are ten incomplete statements here. You should fill in each blank with the proper form of the word given in the brackets. Write the word or words in the corresponding space on the Answer Sheet.*

26. With the _____ (develop) of tourism, more and more people are traveling all over the world.

27. If your credit is good, you will be allowed _____ (use) the credit card.

28. If you drive too fast in this speed-limit area, you will _____ (fine) ￥200.

29. Thank you for your letter of April 15, _____ (tell) us what really happened in the US on April 10.

30. Although you may not _____ (success) in the beginning, you should still go on trying.

31. Last year, customers _____ (buy) a total of 90-million books from the book center.

32. On hearing the good news that we got the first place in the competition, we all got _____ (excite).

33. The _____ (late) model of the racing car will be on display at the exhibition this week.

34. The professor recommended that Richard _____ (read) more philosophy books.

35. Nurses should treat the sick and wounded with great _____ (kind).

Part III Reading Comprehension (40 minutes)

Directions: *This part is to test your reading ability. There are five tasks for you to fulfill. You should read the reading materials carefully and do the tasks as you are instructed.*

TASK 1

Directions: *After reading the following passage, you will find five questions or unfinished statements numbered from 36 to 40. For each question or statement there are four choices marked A, B, C and D. You should make the correct choice and mark the corresponding letter on the Answer Sheet with a single line through the center.*

How often one hears children wishing they had grown up, and old people wishing they were young again. Each age has its pleasures and its pains, and the happiest person is the one who enjoys what each age gives him without wasting his time in useless regrets.

Youth is a time when there are few tasks to make life difficult. If a child has good parents, he is fed, looked after and loved whatever he may do. It is impossible that he will ever again in his life be given so much without having to do anything in return. In addition, life is always presenting new things to the child—things that have lost their interest for older people because they are too well-known. But a child has his pains: he is not so free to do what he wishes to do; he is continually being told not to do things, or being punished for what he has done wrong.

When the young man starts to earn his own living, he can no longer expect others to pay for his food, his clothes, and his room, but has to work if he wants to live comfortably. If he spends most of his time playing about in the way that he used to as a child, he will go hungry. And if he breaks the laws of society as he used to break the laws of his parents, he may go to prison. If, however, he works hard, keeps out of trouble and has good health, he can have the great happiness of building up for himself his own position in society.

36. People can experience happiness if they _____.

    A. are no longer young

    B. value the present

    C. become old and have much experience

    D. always think of the past and regret it

37. When people were young, they used to _____.

    A. face a lot of difficulties

    B. have few things to think about and take on

    C. be in charge of many businesses

D. look after their younger sisters and brothers

38. The pains of children lie in the fact that _____.

A. no one helps them make right decisions

B. they are often beaten by their parents

C. they can not be accepted and praised by others

D. they are not allowed to do what they like to do

39. Children are usually happy because _____.

A. old people lose interest in them

B. they are free to do wrong

C. they are familiar with everything going on around them

D. things are new to them

40. Which of the following is NOT needed for a young man to be happy?

A. Hard work.　　　　　　　　　　　B. Being free from troubles.

C. Wealth.　　　　　　　　　　　　D. Health.

TASK 2

Directions: *This task is the same as Task 1. The five questions or unfinished statements are numbered from 41 to 45.*

When young people get their first real jobs, they face a lot of new, confusing situations. They may find that everything is different from the way things were at school. It is also possible that they will feel uncomfortable and insecure in both professional and social situations. Eventually, they realize that university classes can't be the only preparation for all of the different situations that <u>arise</u> in the working world.

Perhaps the best way to learn how to behave in the working world is to identify a worker you admire and observe his behavior. By doing so, you will be able to see what it is that you admire in this person. For example, you will observe how he acts in a crisis. Perhaps even more important, you will be able to see what his <u>approach</u> to day-to-day situations is.

While you are observing your colleague, you should be asking yourself whether his behavior is like yours and how you can learn from his responses to a variety of situations. By watching and learning from a model, you will probably begin to identify and adopt good working habits.

41. The young people who just graduated from school may not behave well in the working world because _____.

A. they were not well educated at school

B. what they learn in university classes is not adequate for their new life

C. the society is too complicated to adapt to

D. they failed to work hard at school

42. In the last sentence of Para.1, the word "arise" means _____.

A. come into being　　　B. bring about　　　C. go up　　　D. cause to happen

43. The best way to learn how to behave in the working world is _____.

A. to find a worker and follow him closely

B. to find a person you respect and see how he acts in different situations

C. to find a person you admire and make friends with him

D. to make the acquaintance of a model you admire

44. In the last sentence of Para. 2, the word "approach" means _____.

A. means of entering

B. way of coming near

C. speaking to someone for the first time

D. method of doing something

45. The passage could be best entitled _____.

A. Learn, Learn and Learn Again

B. One Is Never Too Old to Learn

C. Learn from a Model

D. Learn Forever

TASK 3

Directions: *The following is an advertisement for Disney vacation. After reading it, you should complete the information by filling in the blanks marked from 46 to 50 (in no more than three words) in the table below.*

Disney Vacation

Experience two great theme parks in one great resort—Disney's California Adventure Park and right next door Disneyland Park. Just footsteps away, extraordinary entertainment, shopping and dining await in the Downtown Disney District. And when you and your family stay at one of the hotels of the Disneyland Resort, you're right in the middle of all the magic! And now, one child receives a free Disneyland Resort Park Hopper Ticket with each adult ticket purchased in a Disney vacation package. You can go back and forth between Parks as often as you like.

Discover the friendly faces and magical places of the Disneyland Resort and see why this spectacular destination has more vacation magic than you could ever imagine!

Disney Vacation
There are two great theme parks in the great resort: Disney's California Adventure Park and __46__.
In the Downtown Disney District you can have extraordinary entertainment, __47__ and __48__.
And now, one child receives a __49__ Disneyland Resort Park Hopper Ticket with each __50__ ticket purchased in a vacation package.

TASK 4

Directions: *After reading the list, you are required to find the items equivalent to（与……等同）*

those given in Chinese in the table below. Then you should put the corresponding letters in the brackets on the Answer Sheet, numbered from 51 to 55.

[A] — exchange rate   [B] — foreign exchange certificate

[C] — selling rate   [D] — change

[E] — credit card   [F] — currency

[G] — service charge   [H] — traveler's cheque

[I] — mail transfer   [J] — Bank of China

[K] — coin   [L] — remittance

[M] — cash   [N] — ATM

[O] — memo

51. (   ) 手续费   (   ) 中国银行

52. (   ) 硬币   (   ) 外汇券

53. (   ) 信用卡   (   ) 旅游支票

54. (   ) 卖价   (   ) 电汇

55. (   ) 自动取款机   (   ) 货币

TASK 5

Directions: *The following is a letter. After reading it, you are required to complete the answers that follow the questions, numbered from 56 to 60. You should write your answers **(in no more than three words)** on the Answer Sheet correspondingly.*

Dear Mary,

It was certainly grand of you and Tom to come and see me off! I know it wasn't easy for you to get to the airport at such an early hour, so I appreciate it all the time.

Flying over water can get dreadfully boring after the first few hours, and your book of detective stories comes in very handy. It was sweet and thoughtful of you to think of it.

The flight was uneventful and we arrived in Beijing on scheduled time. Lucy and Lily met me at the airport, and we went straight to their charming little house. I know I am going to love here; I'm living together with my sisters!

I'll write to you again, Mary. In the meantime, my thanks to you and Tom for your many kindnesses to me—and my love to you both, always!

Yours,

Kate

56. What kind of letter is it?

It's a letter of _____.

57. How did Kate go to Beijing?

By _____.

58. When did Mary and Tom get to the airport?

_____ in the morning.

59. What present did Mary give Kate?

_____ of detective stories.

60. Who went to the airport to meet Kate in Beijing?

_____.

Part Ⅳ Translation—English to Chinese (25 minutes)

Directions: *This part, numbered from 61 to 65, is to test your ability to translate English into Chinese. Each of the four sentences (No. 61 to No. 64) is followed by four choices of suggested translation marked A, B, C, and D. Make the best choice and write the corresponding letter on the Answer Sheet. Write your translation of the paragraph (No. 65) in the corresponding space on the Translation/Composition Sheet.*

61. The production of our factory increased by 18 percent over that of the previous year.

　　A. 我们工厂的产量比前年增加了 18%。

　　B. 我们工厂的产量比前年增到 18%。

　　C. 我们工厂的产量比上一年增加了 18%。

　　D. 我们工厂的产量比上一年增到 18%。

62. Had she found the right buyer, she would have sold the house.

　　A. 只有找到了正式的买方，她才能售出房子。

　　B. 要是找到了合适的买方，她就会把房屋售出了。

　　C. 如果找到了合适的买方，她就已经把房屋售出了。

　　D. 她已经找到了正式的买方，并会把房屋售出。

63. These two dresses have little in common in style except for the colors and patterns of the cloth.

　　A. 除了布的颜色和图案相同外，这两条裙子的式样没什么相同之处。

　　B. 这两条裙子款式很少相同，除了布的颜色和图案。

　　C. 这两条裙子除了布的颜色和图案相同外，没什么相同的。

　　D. 除了布的颜色和图案不同之外，这两条裙子式样也很不同。

64. It is obvious that Mary can hardly understand the instructions of the washing machine she is reading.

　　A. 玛丽显然看不懂她正在阅读的洗衣机说明书。

　　B. 玛丽费了很大劲才看懂本来很明显的洗衣机指令。

　　C. 显然，玛丽努力去理解她正在阅读的洗衣机指令。

　　D. 显然，玛丽再费劲也看不懂她正在阅读的洗衣机说明书。

65. Ladies and Gentlemen,

Merry Christmas!

This is the first Christmas day since our company's opening here. Looking back over the previous year, I am grateful to you all for your great efforts which have made it possible for the company to make unexpected high achievements. On behalf of the board of directors, I would like to thank you again. Looking ahead, I believe we will have an even brighter future.

Part Ⅴ Writing (25 minutes)

Directions: *This part is to test your ability to do practical writing. You are required to write an e-mail based on the following information given in Chinese. Remember to do the writing on the Translation/Composition Sheet.*

写信人：Li Qiang   电子邮件地址：liqiang@126.com
收信单位：Reservation Office   电子邮件地址：groupsales@aston.com
入住时间：2003 年 12 月 25 日至 27 日   写信时间：2003 年 12 月 20 日
预订房间：一个带浴室的单人房间，三个带浴室的双人房间。将于 12 月 26 日下午租用会议室一间，进行业务洽谈。请尽早回复，告知是否有空房、房价及是否需要预付押金等。

Here is the e-mail form:

To:

E-mail address:

From:

Subject:

Date:

Dear Sir or Madam,

Words for reference:

空房：vacancy

预付押金：pay a deposit

Model Test 2

Directions: *This part is to test your listening ability. It consists of three sections.*

SECTION A

Directions: *This section is to test your ability to give proper responses. There are five recorded questions in it. After each question, there is a pause. The question will be spoken twice. When you hear a question, you should decide on the correct answer from the four choices marked A, B, C and D given in your test paper. Then you should mark the corresponding letter on the Answer Sheet with a single line through the center.*

Example: You will hear: Mr. Smith is not in. Could you please give him a message?

You will read: A. I'm not sure.

B. You're right.

C. Yes, certainly.

D. That's interesting.

From the question we learn that the speaker is asking the listener to leave a message. Therefore, "C. Yes, certainly." is the correct answer. You should mark C on the Answer Sheet.

[A][B][C][D]

Now the test will begin.

1. A. Sorry, I have no idea.　　　　　　　　B. It's opposite to the park on a busy road.

　C. In a bookstore.　　　　　　　　　　　D. It was excellent.

2. A. Yes, he was.　　　　　　　　　　　　B. No, he wasn't.

　C. Yes, he called.　　　　　　　　　　　D. Yes, he did.

3. A. It's my birthday present.　　　　　　　B. Four times a year.

　C. I think it's worth reading.　　　　　　　D. Two dollars.

4. A. At the corner of the street.　　　　　　B. Of course. Go ahead.

　C. We finished the fifth dialogue of text A.　D. You left early yesterday.

5. A. It's fashionable.　　　　　　　　　　　B. It's too expensive.

　C. It's on sale.　　　　　　　　　　　　　D. It's 50 dollars.

SECTION B

Directions: *This section is to test your ability to understand short dialogues. There are five recorded dialogues in it. After each dialogue, there is a recorded question. Both the dialogues and questions will be spoken twice. When you hear a question, you should decide on the correct answer from the four choices marked A, B, C and D given in your test paper. Then you should mark the corresponding letter on the Answer Sheet with a single line through the center.*

6. A. Classmates.   B. Headmaster and teacher.

   C. Father and daughter.   D. Teacher and student.

7. A. She wants to go with the man.   B. She has time every night.

   C. She is not willing to go.   D. She has no time.

8. A. 8:30.   B. 9:00.   C. 9:30.   D. 10:00.

9. A. Australia.   B. China.   C. Japan.   D. Mexico.

10. A. On Thursday.   B. On Monday.   C. On Saturday.   D. On Wednesday.

SECTION C

Directions: *In this section you will hear a recorded short passage. The passage is printed in the test paper with some words or phrases missing. The passage will be read three times. During the second reading, you are required to put the missing words or phrases on the Answer Sheet in order of the numbered blanks according to what you hear. The third reading is for you to check your writing. Now the passage will begin.*

When you were six years old, you had 20 teeth. These are called milk-teeth. After you are six, your milk-teeth begin to ___11___. They're making way for a new ___12___. As new teeth come in, they cut off the ___13___ supply to the milk-teeth. After a while, the milk-teeth fall out. By the time you are 25, you should have a whole new set of teeth. And you'll have 12 ___14___ teeth. In all, you'll have ___15___ teeth in each jaw.

Part II Vocabulary & Structure (15 minutes)

Directions: *This part is to test your ability to construct meaningful and grammatically correct sentences. It consists of two sections.*

SECTION A

Directions: *In this section, there are ten incomplete sentences. You are required to complete each one by deciding on the most appropriate word or words from the four choices marked A, B, C and D. You should mark the corresponding letter on the Answer Sheet with a single line through the center.*

16. It is _____ of you to go into the dark room by yourself at midnight.

    A. efficient   B. proud   C. bold   D. greedy

17. I think nobody wants to have their new car _____.

    A. repair   B. repairing   C. to repair   D. repaired

18. Pupils failing to _____ their homework are asked to stay after the class.

    A. hand in   B. hand out   C. hand down   D. hand over

19. —How about visiting the Summer Palace this weekend?

    —That _____ good, but I have a lot of work to do.

    A. sounds   B. smells   C. appears   D. looks

20. They decided to teach the naughty boy a good _____.

    A. thing   B. task   C. lesson   D. class

21. The weather _____ fine for many days this month.

    A. is   B. has been   C. had been   D. was

22. It's necessary that the problem _____ in some way or other.

    A. is settled   B. was settled   C. be settled   D. has been settled

23. All the students in our class passed the English final text _____ him.

    A. besides   B. except for   C. except   D. without

24. My teacher speaks to me _____ she were my mother.

    A. even though   B. if   C. even if   D. as if

25. It was America _____ launched the war against Vietnam.

    A. that   B. when   C. whom   D. which

SECTION B

Directions: *There are ten incomplete statements here. You should fill in each blank with the proper form of the word given in the brackets. Write the word or words in the corresponding space on the Answer Sheet.*

26. Next week we _____ (sign) the sales contract with the new supplier.

27. It is true that traditional meals are _____ (healthy) than fast foods.

28. I asked her not _____ (tell) others anything about our research until the end of the week.

29. Many Chinese people are spending plenty of time in _____ (learn) English.

30. _____ (Frank) speaking, Mr. Black is a person that can be trusted.

31. By this time next year the Smiths _____ (live) in this city for ten years.

32. I would rather you _____ (speak) English with me now in such a embarrassed situation.

33. My mother is a music fan and she enjoys _____ (sing) very much.

34. Eric has made the _____ (decide) to go to the US for further study.

35. This medicine is highly _____ (effect) in treating liver cancer if it is applied early.

Part III Reading Comprehension (40 minutes)

Directions: *This part is to test your reading ability. There are five tasks for you to fulfill. You should read the reading materials carefully and do the tasks as you are instructed.*

TASK 1

Directions: *After reading the following passage, you will find five questions or unfinished statements numbered from 36 to 40. For each question or statement there are four choices marked A, B, C and D. You should make the correct choice and mark the corresponding letter on the Answer Sheet with a single line through the center.*

Do you remember a time when people were a little nicer and gentler with each other? I certainly do and I feel that much of the world has somehow gotten away from that. Too often I see people rushing into elevators without giving those inside a chance to get off first, or never saying "thank you", when others hold the door open for hem. We get lazy, and in our laziness we think that something like simple "thank you" does not really matter. But it can matter very much. The fact is that no matter how nicely we dress or how beautifully we decorate our homes, we can not be truly elegant unless we have good manners, because elegance and good manners always go hand in hand. If fact, I think of good manners as a sort of hidden beauty secret. Haven't you noticed that happens, but it does. Take the long-lost art saying "thank you", like wearing a little make-up or making sure you hair is neat. Getting into the habit of saying "thank you" can make you feel better about yourself. Good manners add to your image while an angry face makes the best-dressed person look ugly.

36. What does the writer say about the people of the past?

    A. They were nicer and gentler.

    B. They paid more attention to their appearance.

    C. They were willing to spend more money on clothes.

    D. They were more aware of changes in fashion.

37. What does the writer think of the people today?

    A. They are less rude.   B. They are less polite.

    C. They are less pretty.   D. They are less happy.

38. According to the speaker, how can we improve our image?

    A. By decorating our homes.   B. By being kind and generous.

    C. By wearing fashionable clothes.   D. By putting on a little make-up.

39. According to the author, saying "thank you" _____.

    A. does good to yourself   B. deserves respect

    C. is a piece of cake   D. will make you pretty

40. What is the passage mainly about?

    A. The art of saying "thank you".   B. The secret of staying pretty.

    C. The importance of good manners. D. The difference between elegance and good manners.

TASK 2

Directions: *This task is the same as Task 1. The five questions or unfinished statements are numbered from 41 to 45.*

There are many ways to learn about people of other lands. One way is to study the clothing other people wear.

For thousands of years, people in different parts of the world have worn very different types of clothing. There are four big reasons for this.

One reason might be religion. In many Moslem countries, women must wear veils to hide their faces. The veil must be worn in public. Veils are part of the Moslem religion.

The second reason is that different materials are used in different countries. For instance, in France the materials used in clothing may be cotton（棉）, silk, wool, or many other man-made materials. Most people in China wear cotton.

The ways clothes are made are also very different. This is another reason why people dress differently. Western countries rely on machines to make most of their clothing. Someone living in India can use only hand power to make the clothing he needs.

World-wide differences in customs also lead to differences in clothing. A Mexican farmer wears a straw hat with a brim up. In China, a farmer wears a straw hat with a brim down. Both hats are used to protect the farmers from the sun. Some of these customs have come down through thousands of years.

41. If you want to learn about the difference about people in the world, you _____.

    A. may be surprised by the ways people wear hats

    B. may study the different types of clothing people wear

    C. should know the four big reasons given in the passage

    D. should know the ways to study other lands

42. In many Moslem countries, women have to _____ in public.

    A. wear more clothes than men　　　　B. protect their faces from being hurt

    C. wear religious clothing　　　　　　D. cover their faces with veils

43. Which of the following is the reason for the differences in clothing?

    A. Most people like silk clothes.

    B. Man-made materials are invented to make clothes.

    C. Cotton is the common material for clothing.

    D. Materials used for clothes differ from country to country.

44. The third reason for the difference in clothing is _____.

    A. different ways of making clothes　　B. different materials

    C. different types of dressing　　　　　D. different religions

45. The two examples of wearing hats are given in the last paragraph to show _____.

    A. the long history of some customs　　B. the effect of customs on dressing style

    C. the correct way of wearing straw hat　D. the function of wearing straw hat

TASK 3

Directions: *The following is an advertisement. After reading it, you should complete the information by filling in the blanks numbered from 46 to 50 (**in no more than three words**) in the table below.*

Welcome to Hong Kong Disneyland!

The long-anticipated Hong Kong Disneyland, the 11th Disney-themed Park in the world and the first in China, successfully opened to the public on September 12, 2005 after six years of planning and construction. Disneyland is the world's most famous themed amusement park and one of the most visited sites in the world. The park will feature four differently themed lands similar to those of other Disney parks: Main Street, USA; Adventure land; Fantasyland and Tomorrow land. It will also feature a daily parade and night fireworks. Hong Kong Disneyland will offer two types of tickets.

HK $295 per adult during the weekdays and HK $350 on weekends and holidays; children's tickets (aged between 3 and 11) will be priced at HK $210 during weekdays and HK $250 on weekends and peak holidays; online booking or direct purchase at gate is available.

46. When did Hong Kong Disneyland open to the public?

Hong Kong Disneyland opened to the public on _____.

47. How many Disney-themed parks are there in the world up until now?

Up until now, there are _____ in the world.

48. What are the two types of tickets?

Tickets during weekdays and on _____.

49. What are two ways of buying tickets?

Direct purchase at gate or _____.

50. How much should two adults and a child pay for thickets on Sunday?

They should pay _____ for tickets.

TASK 4

Directions: *The following is a list of some film-related terms. After reading it, you are required to find the items equivalent to（与……等同）those given in Chinese in the table below. Then you should put the corresponding letters in the brackets on the Answer Sheet, numbered from 51 to 55.*

A—film industry

C—first-run cinema

E—film library

G—release

I—shooting schedule

K—production

B—movie theatre

D—film society

F—premiere

H—distributor

J—banned film

L—continuous performance cinema

M—exterior 　　　　　　N—adaptation

O—script 　　　　　　　P—director

Q—cinematograph

Examples:　（ G ）release 准予上映　（ Q ）cinematograph 电影放映机

51.（　　）首轮影院	（　　）循环场电影院
52.（　　）电影资料馆	（　　）电影工业
53.（　　）首映式	（　　）摄制计划
54.（　　）制片	（　　）发行人
55.（　　）电影协会	（　　）导演

TASK 5

Directions: *There are two business letters below. After reading them, you are required to complete the answers that follow the questions, numbered from 56 to 60. You should write your answers **(in no more than three words)** on the Answer Sheet correspondingly.*

Letter One

Jan. 25，2009

Dear Mr. Guan Li,

　　From your advertisements we know that you are making transformers（变压器）in a variety of types. We are interested in your products. Would you please send us the details of the products? If possible，please send us some pictures of the products.

　　Looking forward to your early reply.

Yours sincerely,

Louis Smith

Letter Two

Feb. 14, 2009

Dear Mr. Louis Smith,

　　It's our pleasure to submit the attached quotation（报价）for your review and consideration. Here enclosed are some pictures of our latest types of transformers. This quotation package consists of the following:

　　Section 1：Price list for transformers

　　Section 2：Types of transformers

　　Section 3：Technical specification

　　In the price list you can see we are giving you the lowest prices and offer our best goods. We also think it better to offer you a 5% discount on purchases of more than ten units.

　　Please advise if you have additional questions.

Yours sincerely,

Guan Li

56. What products are the two letters dealing with?

    _____.

57. What does Mr. Louis Smith ask for in his letter?

    _____ and pictures of the goods.

58. Apart from a price list of the goods, what else does Mr. Guan Li offer in his quotation package?

    Types of the goods and _____.

59. How many transformers must Mr. Louis Smith buy to get a discount of 5%?

    _____ of them.

60. What are also included in Guan Li's letter apart from the quotation package?

    Some _____.

Part Ⅳ Translation—English to Chinese (25 minutes)

Directions: *This part, numbered from 61 to 65, is to test your ability to translate English into Chinese. Each of the four sentences (No. 61 to No. 64) is followed by four choices of suggested translation marked A, B, C, and D. Make the best choice and write the corresponding letter on the Answer Sheet. Write your translation of the paragraph (No. 65) in the corresponding space on the Translation/Composition Sheet.*

61. It is necessary that the amount of fat in your food be limited.

    A. 食物中有限的脂肪是很必要的。

    B. 有限的脂肪是食物中的必要因素。

    C. 食物中的脂肪含量应该是有限的，这是很必要的。

    D. 对身体很有必要的脂肪，往往在食物中是有限的。

62. Linda was wearing her usual sunglasses and a toothy smile.

    A. 琳达戴着平常的太阳镜，上面印有露齿的笑容。

    B. 琳达戴上平时的太阳镜的时候，露齿而笑。

    C. 琳达戴着平时老戴的太阳镜，露齿地笑着。

    D. 琳达带着笑容和太阳镜。

63. We would like to have samples of various sizes of your product together with the lowest prices.

    A. 我们宁愿有各种规格的产品样品，加上最低价格。

    B. 和最低价一起，我们想要你们不同型号的产品。

    C. 我方希望得到贵公司各种规格的产品样品及其最低售价。

    D. 我方希望获得你们各种形状的样本，加之最低价格。

64. Bicycles are cheaper to purchase and operate than cars, which have to be fueled and housed.

A. 购置和使用自行车比既要加油又要为其配备车库的汽车便宜得多。

B. 购买和使用自行车比汽车便宜，因为汽车需要油，还要车库。

C. 廉价的自行车比既要加油又要车库的汽车更需要购置和操作。

D. 自行车要比汽车购置和使用起来更廉价，这是一种不得不加油和供给车库的车。

65. Peking Opera has often been introduced abroad as a representative type of China's traditional operas. It was formed in Beijing about 200 years ago mainly on the basis of Hui (of Anhui Province) and Han (of Hubei Province) operas, but also absorbing some points from other local operas. The latter half of the 19th century and the early 20th century were an important period in the development of Peking Opera.

Part Ⅴ Writing (25 minutes)

Directions: *This part is to test your ability to do practical writing. You are required to write an e-mail based on the following information given in Chinese. Remember to do the writing on the Translation/Composition Sheet.*

通知

兹定于 10 月 24 日（星期五）上午 9 点在教学楼 401 室，由 Henry Smith 博士给经济管理系 2009 级 37 班上英语公开课。全体英语老师务必出席。欢迎其他系教师参加。

系主任办公室
2009 年 10 月 20 日

Words for reference:
教学楼：Teaching Building
英语公开课：an open English class
经济管理系：Economic Management Department

Model Test 3

Directions: *This part is to test your listening ability. It consists of three sections.*

SECTION A

Directions: *This section is to test your ability to give proper responses. There are five recorded questions in it. After each question, there is a pause. The question will be spoken twice. When you hear a question, you should decide on the correct answer from the four choices marked A, B, C and D given in your test paper. Then you should mark the corresponding letter on the Answer Sheet with a single line through the center.*

Example: You will hear: Mr. Smith is not in. Could you please give him a message?

You will read: A. I'm not sure.

B. You're right.

C. Yes, certainly.

D. That's interesting.

From the question we learn that the speaker is asking the listener to leave a message. Therefore, "C. Yes, certainly." is the correct answer. You should mark C on the Answer Sheet.

[A] [B] [C] [D]

Now the test will begin.

1. A. It's hard to say.
   C. The same to you.
   B. It's very difficult.
   D. I think it's a good idea.

2. A. It's three kilograms.
   C. You should do it another way.
   B. It takes two weeks.
   D. You should have it weighed first.

3. A. It's Linda's.
   C. Linda borrowed it from the library.
   B. It's for Linda.
   D. I lent it to Linda.

4. A. It's out of the question.
   C. With pleasure.
   B. Yes, I would.
   D. It's nothing.

5. A. I don't think so.
   C. That's too bad.
   B. Oh, I'm sorry.
   D. I'm afraid not.

SECTION B

Directions: *This section is to test your ability to understand short dialogues. There are five recorded dialogues in it. After each dialogue, there is a recorded question. Both the dialogues and questions will be spoken twice. When you hear a question, you should decide on the correct answer from the four choices marked A, B, C and D given in your test paper. Then you should mark the corresponding letter on the Answer Sheet with a single line through the center.*

6. A. A nurse.　　　　　　　　　　　B. A teacher.

 C. A doctor.　　　　　　　　　　　D. Not mentioned.

7. A. A shop assistant.　　B. A secretary.　　C. A waitress.　　D. A policewoman.

8. A. He broke the window to enter his house.

 B. He opened a window to enter his house.

 C. He broke the window but entered the wrong house.

 D. He entered the house from the back door.

9. A. He will not go swimming.　　　　B. He didn't go swimming.

 C. He is tired of swimming.　　　　　D. He likes swimming very much.

10. A. A bus station.　　B. A train station.　　C. A hospital.　　D. An airport.

SECTION C

Directions: *In this section you will hear a recorded short passage. The passage is printed in the test paper with some words or phrases missing. The passage will be read three times. During the second reading, you are required to put the missing words or phrases on the Answer Sheet in order of the numbered blanks according to what you hear. The third reading is for you to check your writing. Now the passage will begin.*

Now back to the news. An early morning fire ___11___ the historic Geller House today. It destroyed the third floor of the building, but firefighters ___12___ the first and second floors. There were only a few elderly people living in the building at the time, and they were carried out to ___13___.

Several fire departments were called to the ___14___. When we asked the Fire Chief how the fire started, he answered that most likely a burning cigarette caused it. The Fire Chief promised to ___15___ examine the cause.

Part Ⅱ Vocabulary & Structure (15 minutes)

Directions: *This part is to test your ability to construct meaningful and grammatically correct sentences. It consists of two sections.*

SECTION A

Directions: *In this section, there are ten incomplete sentences. You are required to complete each*

one by deciding on the most appropriate word or words from the four choices marked A, B, C and D. You should mark the corresponding letter on the Answer Sheet with a single line through the center.

16. She found _____ rather difficult to cooperate with Jane.

    A. it is   B. that   C. he is   D. it

17. When _____ his homework, he heard someone singing.

    A. he does   B. he doing   C. doing   D. did

18. The meeting will begin at 9:00 according to the _____.

    A. calendar   B. schedule   C. column   D. diagram

19. The flower needs _____.

    A. to water   B. watered   C. watering   D. being watered

20. Little _____ that the girl has fallen in love with him.

    A. he knows   B. he doesn't know

    C. does he know   D. doesn't he know

21. Encourage children to _____ some of their pocket money to buy Spring Festival presents.

    A. set out   B. take off   C. put aside   D. give in

22. I don't know if he is _____ to come to my birthday party.

    A. possibly   B. likely   C. probably   D. maybe

23. People won't go out after dark because they are afraid of _____.

    A. attacking   B. being attacked   C. having been attacked D. attacked

24. Since the introduction of the new technique, the production cost _____ greatly.

    A. reduces   B. is reduced   C. is reducing   D. has been reduced

25. This is the small village _____ our president was born.

    A. which   B. where   C. that   D. as

SECTION B

Directions: *There are ten incomplete statements here. You should fill in each blank with the proper form of the word given in the brackets. Write the word or words in the corresponding space on the Answer Sheet.*

26. A lot of people do believe that smoking will _____ (definite) bring great harm to our health.

27. Last week Jim received a written _____ (invite) to a dinner from Mr. Green.

28. Of all the books in this library, this one is the _____ (good).

29. They discussed with me for hours, _____ (try) to persuade me to give up my plan.

30. If you are a manager, you should handle the customers' complaints in a _____ (friend)

way.

31. Eric will go back home as soon as he _____ (finish) his tasks.

32. It seems that the production of this company have _____ (great) increased this month.

33. Now the number of people who are working at home on the Internet _____ (be) still very small.

34. My friend Linda was _____ (luck) enough to get the chance to work in the world-famous company.

35. I wish I _____ (be) as tall as you.

Part Ⅲ Reading Comprehension (40 minutes)

Directions: *This part is to test your reading ability. There are five tasks for you to fulfill. You should read the reading materials carefully and do the tasks as you are instructed.*

TASK 1

Directions: *After reading the following passage, you will find five questions or unfinished statements numbered from 36 to 40. For each question or statement there are four choices marked A, B, C and D. You should make the correct choice and mark the corresponding letter on the Answer Sheet with a single line through the center.*

As people continue to grow and age, our body systems continue to change. At a certain point in your life your body systems will begin to weaken. Your strength may become weaker. It may become more difficult for you to see and hear. The slow change of aging causes our bodies to lose some of their ability to bounce back from disease and injury. In order to live longer, we have always tried to slow or stop this change that leads us toward the end of our lives.

Many factors decide your health. A good diet plays an important role. The amount and type of exercise you get is another factor. Your living condition is yet another. But scientists studying aging problem want to know: Why do people grow old? They hope that by studying the aging medical science they may be able to make the length of life longer.

There is nothing to be afraid of as old age comes. Many consider the later part of life to be the best time for living. Physical activity may become less, but often you get better understanding of yourself and the world.

What we consider old age now may only be middle age some day soon. Who knows, with so many advances in medical science happening so quickly, life <u>span</u> may one day be measured in centuries, rather than in years.

36. When people become aging, they will lose some of their ability to bounce back from disease and injury, "bounce back" here means _____.

   A. to improve in health after one's disease and injury

B. to recover from disease and injury

C. to jump after recovering

D. to run fast

37. In order to live longer, _____.

    A. we have to try to be on a diet   B. we should keep in high spirits

    C. we should try to do more exercise   D. we should postpone the process of aging

38. Why are some scientists interested in studying aging problem?

    A. They want to increase the general ability of our bodies.

    B. They may be able to find a better way of our life.

    C. If they can pin down the biochemical process that makes us age, there will be hope for extending the length of life.

    D. They want to find out if there is a link between how efficiently a cell could repair itself and how long a creature lives.

39. Many consider the later part of life to be the best time of living, because _____.

    A. they have a very good understanding of themselves and the outside world

    B. they consider their life has been a successful one

    C. they have come through the battle of life safely

    D. they have nothing to do all day long only to watch their grandchildren growing up around them

40. According to the passage, "span" means _____.

    A. longevity   B. a length of time

    C. a long period of time   D. a long distance from one place to another

TASK 2

Directions: *This task is the same as Task 1. The five questions or unfinished statements are numbered from 41 to 45.*

Two sisters, Mildred Hill, a teacher at the Louisville, Kentucky Experimental Kindergarten, and Dr Patty Hill, the principal of the same school, together wrote a song for the children, entitled "Good Morning to All". When Mildred combined her musical talents, as the resident expert on spiritual songs, and as the organist for her church, with her sister's expertise in the area of kindergarten education, "Good Morning to All" was sure to be a success.

The sisters published the song in a collection entitled "Song Stories of the Kindergarten" in 1893. 31 years later, after Dr Patty Hill became the head of the Department of Kindergarten Education at Columbia University's Teacher College, a gentleman by the name of Robert H. Coleman published the song, without the sisters' permission. To add insult to injury, he added a second verse, the familiar "Happy Birthday to You".

Mr. Coleman's addition of the second verse popularized the song and, eventually, the sisters' original first verse disappeared. "Happy Birthday to You", the one and only birthday song, had altogether replaced the sisters' original title, "Good Morning to All".

After Mildred died in 1916, Patty, together with a third sister named Jessica, sprang into action and took Mr. Coleman to court. In court, they proved that they, indeed, owned the melody. Because the family legally owns the song, it is entitled to royalties from it, whenever it is sung for commercial purposes.

41. The song "Happy Birthday to You" was originally written for _____.

    A. the kids in kindergarten   B. the children in elementary school

    C. the teenagers in middle school   D. the adults

42. The phrase "to add insult to injury" in line 4, paragraph 2 probably means _____.

    A. to one's disappointment   B. to be even worse

    C. to be troublesome   D. to one's surprise

43. Finally, what happened to the song "Good Morning to All" after the addition of the second verse?

    A. It was even more popular than before.

    B. It was no longer sung by the children in kindergarten.

    C. The composers, Mildred and Patty, gave up their rights to own the song.

    D. It was gradually replaced by the addition, having a new name "Happy Birthday to You".

44. What was the purpose of the legal action taken by Patty and Jessica?

    A. Commercial uses of the song should be forbidden.

    B. No one could use the song except the Hills.

    C. They wanted to put Mr. Coleman into jail.

    D. They asked for the recognition of being the real owners of the song and its royalties.

45. This passage is mainly about _____.

    A. why "Good Morning to All" was replaced by "Happy Birthday to You"

    B. how the song "Happy Birthday to You" was composed

    C. the history of the song "Happy Birthday to You"

    D. why the song "Happy Birthday to You" is popular

TASK 3

Directions: *The following is a short passage. After reading it, you should complete the information by filling in the blanks marked from 46 to 50 (in no more than 3 words) in the table below.*

I run manufacturing company with about 350 employees, and I often do the interviewing and hiring myself. As I see it, there are four keys to getting hired:

Firstly, prepare to win. Getting hired is no longer a once-in-a-lifetime experience. Employment experts believe that today's graduates may have a lot of pressure. But if you're prepared, the pressure is on the other folks, the one who haven't done their homework. Secondly, never stop learning. Work on your weaknesses and develop your strengths. To be able to compete, you've got to keep learning all your life. And then, believe in yourself, even when no one else does. Don't ever let anyone tell you that you can't accomplish your goals. Who says you're not tougher, harder working and more able than your competitors? At last, find a way to make a difference.

From my standpoint, that's what it's all about.

Key to getting hired:

The writer is a manager who often does the ___46___ himself.

Four keys to getting hired:

1) Prepare to win. Getting hired isn't a ___47___ experience.

2) Never ___48___.

3) ___49___, even when no one else does.

4) Find a way to ___50___.

TASK 4

Directions: *The following is a list of some terms used in business English. After reading it, you are required to find the items equivalent to（与……等同）those given in Chinese in the table below. Then you should put the corresponding letters in the brackets on the Answer Sheet, numbered from 51 to 55.*

A—dealer   B—promising

C—moderately   D—insurance

E—freight   F—enclose

G—illustrated   H—by separate post

I —irrevocable L/C   J —place

K—prompt shipment   L—invite

M—standing credit   N—reference

O—firm

Examples:（O）商行   （I）不可撤销信用证

51. （ ）定额贷款	（ ）商人
52. （ ）保险	（ ）适度地
53. （ ）订货	（ ）即装
54. （ ）邀请	（ ）封入
55. （ ）有希望的	（ ）另邮

TASK 5

Direction: *The following is an announcement. After reading it, you are required to complete the statements that follow the questions, numbered from 56 to 60. You should write your answers (in no more than three words) on the Answer Sheet correspondingly.*

Announcement

The swimming pool of Shanghai University will be open to the public on July 10th this year.

Time: 8:00 a.m.— 8:00 p.m.

Fee: RMB 2 yuan/hr for an adult

RMB 1 yuan/hr for a child

Please bring your own swimming suits.

Shanghai University

---

56. When will the swimming pool begin to be open to the public?

57. What time will the swimming pool close?

58. How much will a grown-up pay if he stays in the swimming pool for 2 hours?

59. How much will two children pay if they stay in the swimming pool for 3 hours?

60. What do you need to bring when you go to the swimming pool?

Part IV Translation—English to Chinese (25 minutes)

Directions: *This part, numbered from 61 to 65, is to test your ability to translate English into Chinese. Each of the four sentences (No. 61 to No. 64) is followed by four choices of suggested translation marked A, B, C, and D. Make the best choice and write the corresponding letter on the Answer Sheet. Write your translation of the paragraph (No. 65) in the corresponding space on the Translation/Composition Sheet.*

61. The boss broke his rule against singing last night.

    A. 昨晚老板打破惯例，唱了点。   B. 老板昨晚破例唱了歌。

    C. 老板昨晚破例没唱歌。   D. 昨晚老板破了唱歌的禁令。

62. Metal, iron in particular, is known to be an important material in building.

    A. 大家知道，金属，特别是铁，已知在建筑上是一种重要材料。

    B. 大家知道，金属，特别是铁，是建筑方面的重要材料。

    C. 金属，铁很特殊，是重要建筑方面的材料。

    D. 金属，尤其是铁，它是建筑中的重要材料，这是众所周知的。

63. Having taken her breakfast, the writer sat in the study among her morning letters.

    A. 作家吃完早饭就坐着研究早上来的信件。

    B. 吃了早饭之后，作家就坐在书房里，周围都是早上来的信件。

    C. 在书房里吃过早饭之后，作家就坐在早上来的信件之中。

    D. 吃过早饭后，作家就坐在书房里处理早上来的信件。

64. Two copies of our estimate you required in your letter of June 13 will be sent to you in a few days.

    A. 我们会在几天后的 6 月 13 日寄上贵公司信中要求的两份报价单。

    B. 两份估单会按 6 月 13 日的要求给你寄过去。

    C. 我们会在近日内寄上贵公司 6 月 13 日来信中要求的两份估单。

    D. 估计这几天会寄出 6 月 13 日要求的两份信。

65. It's always a pleasure to hear from an old friend again. We are still making our famous "Boss" pressure cookers, and we are pleased to tell you that we have been able to improve their quality without any increase in price. Here are the latest price list and catalogues（产品目录）. Please telephone us when you receive this letter. We look forward to your order at an early date.

Part Ⅴ Writing (25 minutes)

Directions: *This part is to test your ability to do practical writing. You are required to complete the following English resume. Some related information is given to you. Remember to write the message in the corresponding space on the Answer Sheet.*

简历

全名：赵勇全

性别：男

出生日期：1968 年 1 月 1 日

出生地：中国上海北京路 24 号

国籍：中国

婚姻状况：单身

健康状况：良好

电话：021–5980643

当前通讯地址：中国上海杭州路 20 号

学　历：

1976—1982　北京路小学

1982—1988　16 中

1988—1992　就读于上海复旦大学英文系，1992 年获英语学士学位

1992—1995　　就读于北京清华大学英文系，1995年获英语硕士学位

工作经历：

1995年7月—1998年5月　上海《解放日报》当实习记者

1998年6月至今　北京《中国日报》（英文版）记者

证明人：上海华南路12号复旦大学人事部经理李华

Words for reference：

性别：gender　　国籍：nationality　　婚姻状况：marital status

健康状况：health　　英语学士学位：B.A. degree in English

人事部经理：personnel manager

Resume

Full name: _____

Gender: ___

Date of birth: ____

Place of birth: _____

Nationality: <u>Chinese</u>

Marital status: _____

Health: <u>Excellent</u>

Tel No.: <u>021-5980643</u>

Present/Permanent address: <u>20 Hangzhou Road, Shanghai</u>

Educational records:

1976—1982　<u>Beijing Road Elementary School</u>

1982—1988　<u>No. 16 Middle School</u>

1988—1992 _____

1992—1995 _____

Working experience：

July, 1995 — May, 1998 _____

June, 1998 — present _____

Reference: _____

Model Test 4

Part I Listening Comprehension (15 minutes)

Directions: *This part is to test your listening ability. It consists of three sections.*

SECTION A

Directions: *This section is to test your ability to give proper responses. There are five recorded questions in it. After each question, there is a pause. The question will be spoken twice. When you hear a question, you should decide on the correct answer from the four choices marked A, B, C and D given in your test paper. Then you should mark the corresponding letter on the Answer Sheet with a single line through the center.*

Example: You will hear: Mr. Smith is not in. Could you please give him a message?

You will read: A. I'm not sure.

B. You're right.

C. Yes, certainly.

D. That's interesting.

From the question we learn that the speaker is asking the listener to leave a message. Therefore, "C. Yes, certainly." is the correct answer. You should mark C on the Answer Sheet.

[A][B][C][D]

Now the test will begin.

1. A. I want a seat near the window. B. Yes, you can.
   C. That's right. D. No, you can't.
2. A. About 80 miles. B. About 80 pages.
   C. About one and a half hours. D. Almost a year.
3. A. Yes, I have phoned them. B. Yes, they all do.
   C. Yes, they have phoned me. D. Yes, I do.
4. A. I will be expecting you, then. B. You may do as you like.
   C. I'm glad to see you. D. Me too.
5. A. I like swimming. B. It's like a ship.
   C. It's too cold. D. It's going to be wet and windy.

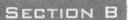

SECTION B

Directions: *This section is to test your ability to understand short dialogues. There are five recorded dialogues in it. After each dialogue, there is a recorded question. Both the dialogues and questions will be spoken twice. When you hear a question, you should decide on the correct answer from the four choices marked A, B, C and D given in your test paper. Then you should mark the corresponding letter on the Answer Sheet with a single line through the center.*

6. A. 9:23.　　　　B. 9:37.　　　　C. 9:07.　　　　D. 9:20.

7. A. A librarian.　　B. A cashier.　　C. A telephone operator.　　D. A typist.

8. A. He is a shoe repairer.　　　　B. He is a guide.

　　C. He is a broadcaster.　　　　D. He is a repairman.

9. A. His mother liked it but his father didn't.　　B. They both liked it.

　　C. His father liked it but his mother didn't.　　D. Neither liked it.

10. A. 13 hours.　　B. 8 hours.　　C. 9 hours.　　D. 14 hours.

SECTION C

Directions: *In this section you will hear a recorded short passage. The passage is printed in the test paper with some words or phrases missing. The passage will be read three times. During the second reading, you are required to put the missing words or phrases on the Answer Sheet in order of the numbered blanks according to what you hear. The third reading is for you to check your writing. Now the passage will begin.*

Now that I have been in college for a few weeks, I'm ___11___ that it is not as bad as I thought it would be. Firstly, I have ___12___ new friends from all parts of the country. We all have classes together and go to the same parties. ___13___, I have been able to become more independent. Lastly, I have learned to be more ___14___ for my actions. I know that homework always comes first and that my ___15___ must wait until all my work is done.

Part II Vocabulary & Structure (15 minutes)

Directions: *This part is to test your ability to construct meaningful and grammatically correct sentences. It consists of two sections.*

SECTION A

Directions: *In this section, there are ten incomplete sentences. You are required to complete each one by deciding on the most appropriate word or words from the four choices marked A, B, C and D. You should mark the corresponding letter on the Answer Sheet with a single line through the center.*

16. My children are looking forward to _____ a trip to Beijing next week.

    A. make   B. be making   C. making   D. have made

17. All _____ to Hong Kong were delayed because of bad weather.

    A. fly   B. flights   C. flyings   D. flies

18. It is high time you _____ your membership dues.

    A. paid   B. pay   C. will pay   D. to pay

19. I missed the morning train because I slept _____.

    A. over   B. of   C. in   D. through

20. All the ideas _____ into realities in the near future.

    A. will be turned   B. will turn   C. would be turning   D. is turning

21. _____ aloud is a very useful way to learn English.

    A. Read   B. Reads   C. Reading   D. Being read

22. The government has _____ a committee to investigate this matter in local elections.

    A. set out   B. set to   C. set up   D. set about

23. _____ what to do, the man telephoned the police.

    A. Not known   B. Not knowing   C. Don't know   D. Knowing not

24. The fact _____ exercise is good for health is known to all.

    A. which   B. what   C. that   D. it

25. When you _____ back to Beijing next month, let me know the exact date.

    A. will come   B. had come   C. be coming   D. come

SECTION B

Directions: *There are ten incomplete statements here. You should fill in each blank with the proper form of the word given in the brackets. Write the word or words in the corresponding space on the Answer Sheet.*

26. If my English teacher hadn't helped me, I _____ (fail) in the final examination last term.

27. This philosophy book is worth _____ (read) for many times.

28. We have to find new ways to _____ (strength) the relationship with the US.

29. If I _____ (be) you, I wouldn't buy that expensive diamond ring.

30. Although the small town has been changing slowly, it looks quite _____ (difference) from what it was.

31. This wonderful book _____ (write) by a young writer in Germany last year.

32. Due to the fact that light travels _____ (fast) than sound, lightning is seen before thunder is heard.

33. The fast _____ (develop) of the local economy has caused serious pollution in this county.

34. Jim, as well as his two elder brothers, _____ (teach) in Harvard University now.

35. As soon as I _____ (get) there, I'll telephone you.

Part III Reading Comprehension (40 minutes)

Directions: *This part is to test your reading ability. There are five tasks for you to fulfill. You should read the reading materials carefully and do the tasks as you are instructed.*

TASK 1

Directions: *After reading the following passage, you will find five questions or unfinished statements numbered from 36 to 40. For each question or statement there are four choices marked A, B, C and D. You should make the correct choice and mark the corresponding letter on the Answer Sheet with a single line through the center.*

In China, when you meet a friend in the street, you would say, "Where are you going?" or "Have you eaten yet?" But in England people don't do that. In fact, if you ask an English person these questions, he might think that is his business, not yours. And the common saying "Mind your own business." will come naturally to his mind.

Now what do people say in England when they meet? They generally talk about the weather. They might say, "Lovely weather, isn't it?" or "It is a bit colder than yesterday, isn't it?" On another day they might look up at the sky and say, "Look like rain, doesn't it?" or "Terrible weather!" or all sorts of things like that.

You may wonder why everybody talks about the weather in England. The reason is very simple: Britain is a very small island country, and in a country like that the weather changes very often and very quickly. Even on a sunny day many people go out and carry an umbrella or raincoat with them. "Just to be on the safe side," they say.

36. In China, when people meet their friends in the street, they usually ask "Where are you going?" because _____.

　　A. it is necessary for them to know where their friends go

　　B. that is a way to show their politeness

　　C. they are interested in other people's business

　　D. they care for their friends

37. If a Chinese ask an Englishman this question "Have you eaten?", the Englishman might _____.

　　A. think that Chinese wants to invite him to dinner

　　B. not answer the question

　　C. be very happy

　　D. think it has nothing to do with other people

38. When people in England meet with each other, they usually talk about _____.

    A. clothes   B. umbrellas   C. the weather   D. the sky

39. In Britain everybody talks about the weather because _____.

    A. the weather is changeable in that country

    B. they are only interested in weather

    C. they can't talk about other things in public

    D. the weather report is often wrong

40. The weather changes very often in Britain because _____.

    A. the country has many big forests   B. the country is a very large dryland

    C. the country is a small island   D. the country's sky is not clean

TASK 2

Directions: *This task is the same as Task 1. The five questions or unfinished statements are numbered from 41 to 45.*

    Man has a big brain. He can think, learn and speak. Scientists used to think that man is different from animals because he thinks and learns. They know now that animals—dogs, rats and birds—can learn. So scientists are beginning to understand that men are different from animals because they can speak. Animals cannot speak. They make noises when they are afraid, or hungry, or unhappy. Apes（类人猿）are our nearest cousins. They can understand some things more quickly than human beings, and one or two have learned a few words. But they are still different from us. They can never think about the past or the future. Language is a wonderful thing. Man has been able to develop civilization because he has language. Every child can speak his own language very well when he is four or five—but no animal learns to speak. How do children learn? Scientists do not really know. What happens when we speak? Scientists do not really know. They only know that man can speak because he has a big brain.

41. The passage is mainly about _____.

    A. why animals can learn   B. why man is different from animals

    C. why animals cannot speak   D. why man has a big brain

42. Scientists think that the difference between animals and man is _____.

    A. animals cannot learn   B. animals cannot speak

    C. animals cannot think like us   D. animals do not have their own language

43. Now, scientists still don't really know _____.

    A. whether animals can think about the past and the future

    B. how children learn and what happens when we speak

    C. why animals can understand some things more quickly than human beings

    D. at what age, a child can speak his language very well

44. According to the passage, language has played a very important part in _____.

A. teaching apes a few words
B. expressing ourselves well

C. understanding the animals
D. developing our civilization

45. The passage tells us that man can speak because _____.

A. he is different from animals
B. he can read and write

C. he can learn and think
D. he has a big brain

TASK 3

Directions: *The following is a passage about how to make hamburgers. After reading it, you should complete the information by filling in the blanks marked from 46 to 50 (**in no more than three words**) in the table below.*

How to Make Hamburgers

Making hamburgers is really very simple. All you need is a pound of minced（剁或绞碎的）beef which you mix with the other things—salt and pepper, a teaspoon of mustard（芥末）, and an egg as well. You break the egg in a bowl, and mix all the things together with a fork. When it is smooth and well-mixed, make round hamburgers from the mixture, and roll them in some flour. Then you need a frying pan（煎锅）and some oil. Fry the hamburgers on both sides for about 15 minutes until they are brown. When they are ready, get some soft bread rolls and cut them in half. Put the hamburgers inside them and eat them as soon as possible.

How to Make Hamburgers
Ingredients（成分）:
a pound of beef, salt, pepper, a teaspoon of mustard, an egg, flour, oil
Method:
(1) Break the ___46___ in a bowl, and mix all the things together.
(2) When it is ___47___, roll them in some flour.
(3) ___48___ the hamburgers on both sides for about 15 minutes until they are brown.
(4) Get some ___49___ and cut them in half.
(5) Put the hamburgers ___50___ the bread rolls.

TASK 4

Directions: *The following is part of personal information. After reading it, you are required to find the items equivalent to（与……等同）those given in Chinese in the table below. Then you should put the corresponding letters in the brackets on the Answer Sheet, numbered from 51 to 55.*

A——blood type

B——postal code

C——sex

D——height

E——date of birth
F——native place
G——date of availability
H——association
I—— health condition
J—— place of birth
K——marital status
L——work experience
M——married
N——current address
O——family status
P——ethnic group

Examples: （ I ）健康状况 　（ F ）籍贯

51. （　　）性别		（　　）家庭情况	
52. （　　）婚姻状况		（　　）出生日期	
53. （　　）民族		（　　）目前住址	
54. （　　）工作经历		（　　）血型	
55. （　　）已婚		（　　）身高	

TASK 5

Directions: *The following is a letter of self-recommendation. After reading it, you should give brief answers that followed the questions numbered from 56 to 60. You should write your answers (in no more than three words) on the Answer Sheet correspondingly.*

May 7, 2009

Dear Dean Green,

I have learnt from your school newspaper that you are seeking a Chinese teacher for a short-term Chinese course run by your department. I am wondering whether you consider my application for the position as I wish to gain some academic background from your college.

I am a male visiting scholar of 45 from China. I graduated from Jilin University, China, specializing in physics. But I sometimes attended lectures in the Chinese Department, and I am fond of the Chinese classics. Every week, I can afford to teach Chinese conversation for ten periods as I am on vacation now.

You may obtain further information about my fitness for the position by telephoning the dean of the department where I am working.

Hoping that you'll offer me the opportunity of an interview and I shall do my best to make the appointment a success.

Yours sincerely,
Deng Ming

56. What is the position the writer wants to apply for?

    It is a _____ for a short-term Chinese course run by a school department.

57. What is the writer?

    He is a _____ of 45 from China.

58. Where did he graduate?

    He graduated from _____.

59. How long can he teach Chinese conversation every week?

    _____ periods.

60. What's the writer's name?

    _____.

Part IV Translation—English to Chinese (25 minutes)

Directions: *This part, numbered from 61 to 65, is to test your ability to translate English into Chinese. Each of the four sentences (No. 61 to No. 64) is followed by four choices of suggested translation marked A, B, C, and D. Make the best choice and write the corresponding letter on the Answer Sheet. Write your translation of the paragraph (No. 65) in the corresponding space on the Translation/Composition Sheet.*

61. What they have in common is that they have a high object in life.

    A. 他们的共同点是他们在生活中都有很高贵的物品。

    B. 他们的共同之处是他们的生活目标很高。

    C. 他们的共同之处在于他们有一个很高的生活期望值。

    D. 他们共同拥有的是生活中置于很高地位的东西。

62. It is well-known that electricity can be transmitted from where it is produced to where it is needed.

    A. 大家知道，电可以从发电的地方输送到需要的地方。

    B. 众所周知，把电从发电的地方输送到需要的地方是可以的。

    C. 可以把电从发电的地方输送到需要的地方，这是已经知道的。

    D. 这是很了解的，电从生产电的地方到需要它的地方是可以的。

63. Jiuzhaigou is noted for its varieties of exotic plants and flowers, rare birds and animals.

    A. 九寨沟上有一告示，爱护奇花异草、珍奇鸟兽。

    B. 九寨沟以奇花异草、珍奇鸟兽而著名。

    C. 进入九寨沟要注意，不要破坏奇花异草、珍奇鸟兽。

    D. 九寨沟以奇花异草而闻名，但少有珍奇鸟兽。

64. Mr. Wang was too experienced a businessman to accept the first offer.

    A. 为了接受第一次报盘，王先生有了一次非常丰富的商人经历。

    B. 王先生是位经验非常丰富的商人，他不可能接受第一个报价。

    C. 王先生是一位有经验的商人以至于不能接受第一次报价。

    D. 王先生是一位接受第一次报价的非常有经验的商人。

65. One good thing about our chopsticks is that we can reach for what we'd like to eat at tables; it wouldn't be so convenient with knife and fork. I understand friends from western countries do not approve of reaching over the table for things when you have dinner parties in your own country. But in China we don't mind. Make yourselves at home, please. Help yourselves!

Part Ⅴ Writing (25 minutes)

Directions: *This part is to test your ability to do practical writing. You are required to complete an application form. Some related information is given to you. Remember to write the message in the corresponding space on the Translation/Composition Sheet.*

李佳，出生于 1978 年 1 月 7 日，女，未婚，中国籍，住在中国上海华山路 1922 号（出生地同上）。现任助理经理，去新加坡旅游，计划停留 4 天，申请日期是 2003 年 9 月 17 日。

Singapore Visa Application Form

Full Name: _____ Chinese Character: _____

Date and Place of Birth: _____

Gender: _____

Marital Status: _____

Nationality: _____ Nationality at Birth: _____

Permanent Address: _____

Occupation: _____

Reason for Visit: _____

Proposed Duration of Stay: _____

Signature: _____ Date: _____

Model Test 5

Directions: *This part is to test your listening ability. It consists of three sections.*

SECTION A

Directions: *This section is to test your ability to give proper responses. There are five recorded questions in it. After each question, there is a pause. The question will be spoken twice. When you hear a question, you should decide on the correct answer from the four choices marked A, B, C and D given in your test paper. Then you should mark the corresponding letter on the Answer Sheet with a single line through the center.*

Example: You will hear: Mr. Smith is not in. Could you please give him a message?

You will read: A. I'm not sure.

B. You're right.

C. Yes, certainly.

D. That's interesting.

From the question we learn that the speaker is asking the listener to leave a message. Therefore, "C. Yes, certainly." is the correct answer. You should mark C on the Answer Sheet.

[A] [B] [C] [D]

Now the test will begin.

1. A. I shouldn't be late just now.   B. I was not late.

   C.I was late for the concert.   D. I was on time.

2. A. I'm sorry.   B. It's nothing.

   C. Sure. What is it?   D. Oh, which one?

3. A. Everything seems to be going fine.   B. I agree with you.

   C. No, I don't think so.   D. Nothing.

4. A. Yes, I look tired.   B. Yeah, I'm sure.

   C. I've got a headache.   D. Don't mention it.

5. A. That's right.   B. I enjoyed it.

   C. No, I didn't.   D. Yes, I think so.

SECTION B

Directions: *This section is to test your ability to understand short dialogues. There are five recorded dialogues in it. After each dialogue, there is a recorded question. Both the dialogues and questions will be spoken twice. When you hear a question, you should decide on the correct answer from the four choices marked A, B, C and D given in your test paper. Then you should mark the corresponding letter on the Answer Sheet with a single line through the center.*

6. A. In a hotel.   B. In the ticket-ordering hall.

   C. In a restaurant.   D. On a plane.

7. A. 8:13.   B. 8:30.   C. 8:00.   D. 9:00.

8. A. Teacher and student.   B. Manager and client.

   C. Manager and staff.   D. Patient and doctor.

9. A. The woman would like to leave the window open.

   B. The woman will not open the window.

   C. The window is closed.

   D. They will close the window.

10. A. By train.   B. Neither train nor bus.

    C. Get on this bus.   D. Wait for the next bus.

SECTION C

Directions: *In this section you will hear a recorded short passage. The passage is printed in the test paper with some words or phrases missing. The passage will be read three times. During the second reading, you are required to put the missing words or phrases on the Answer Sheet in order of the numbered blanks according to what you hear. The third reading is for you to check your writing. Now the passage will begin.*

  The first time that China fully ___11___ an Olympic Games was at the Los Angeles Games in 1984. The Chinese team was made up of 250 athletes, ___12___ whom had been to an Olympic Games before. The team made an ___13___ step for China, not only into the Olympics, but also into international sports. The first ___14___ medal of the L.A. Olympics was won by a Chinese athlete ___15___ Xu Haifeng in the men's free pistol event.

Part II Vocabulary & Structure (15 minutes)

Directions: *This part is to test your ability to construct meaningful and grammatically correct sentences. It consists of two sections.*

SECTION A

Directions: *In this section, there are ten incomplete sentences. You are required to complete each*

one by deciding on the most appropriate word or words from the four choices marked A, B, C and D. You should mark the corresponding letter on the Answer Sheet with a single line through the center.

16. Knock _____ the door before you enter the room.

    A. over   B. for   C. at   D. in

17. The bicycle _____ by Mr. Zhang's brother now.

    A. has been repaired　B. is being repaired   C. is repaired   D. has repaired

18. When my son was a child, he _____ ice cream, but he doesn't like it now.

    A. used to like   B. was liking   C. use to like   D. used to liking

19. Only after half a year _____ to find the result of my experiment in his lab.

    A. I begun   B. I had begun   C. have I begun   D. did I begin

20. People are coming to understand that easy access to _____ is often the key to success in this highly developed society.

    A. information   B. an information   C. the information   D. informations

21. I prefer to live in the countryside rather than _____ in a city.

    A. to live   B. live   C. living   D. lived

22. John had an argument with Tom, _____ was known to all.

    A. what   B. this   C. that   D. which

23. _____ frightened me was a loud crash from the next room.

    A. How   B. What   C. That   D. Why

24. It's better to avoid _____ downtown during the rush hour.

    A. to drive   B. having driven   C. driving   D. to be driving

25. It is no use _____ over the split milk.

    A. to cry   B. crying   C. cry   D. cried

SECTION B

Directions: *There are ten incomplete statements here. You should fill in each blank with the proper form of the word given in the brackets. Write the word or words in the corresponding space on the Answer Sheet.*

26. To learn things well and to develop our various _____ (able), we need a lot of practice.

27. By the time John retires, he _____ (work) for 30 years.

28. I remember _____ (pay) for the job, but I have forgotten the exact amount.

29. There are many _____ (different) between the two languages.

30. Since the beginning of this term, Jack has shown some _____ (improve) in both his reading and writing.

31. By the time he was 12, Edison _____ (begin) to make a living by himself.

32. We had difficulty in _____ (find) a parking place.

33. Rich people are not _____ (necessary) happy.

34. This factory is short of _____ (experience) workers.

35. I am looking forward to _____ (meet) her.

Part III Reading Comprehension (40 minutes)

Directions: *This part is to test your reading ability. There are five tasks for you to fulfill. You should read the reading materials carefully and do the tasks as you are instructed.*

TASK 1

Directions: *After reading the following passage, you will find five questions or unfinished statements numbered from 36 to 40. For each question or statement there are four choices marked A, B, C, and D. You should make the correct choice and mark the corresponding letter on the Answer Sheet with a single line through the center.*

Every day we read a lot of books, from our textbooks to some magazines or romantic stories. Have you ever thought about the speed or the rate of reading?

Some people read very rapidly; others read very slowly. A rapid reader may say, "I read a long story in one evening." However someone who reads slowly perhaps say, "I read slowly, but carefully. And I am familiar with every detail（细节）." So who do you think is the better reader? The slow reader or the rapid reader?

In my opinion, the key question is not the speed. That is to say, we cannot draw a conclusion that the rapid reader is the good reader, or the slow reader is good. It depends on what we are reading and what's our purpose of reading. If you are a rapid reader, you may be a good reader when you read a story book for fun, and it will not take you too much time. But when you have to read a textbook or a research report, you'd better slow your speed and read it word by word to avoid making any possible mistake. On the other hand, if you are a slow reader, you may be a good reader when you read some directions for making something. But you will waste a lot of time to read a simple story.

So before reading, you'd better think about what you are reading and what you are reading for.

36. According to the author, who is the good reader?

    A. The slow reader.   B. The rapid reader.   C. It is not mentioned.   D. It all depends.

37. From the passage, we know that when we read a story book, we'd better _____.

    A. read it rapidly   B. read it slowly

    C. remember every detail   D. read it in one evening

38. What should be read slowly?

    A. A romantic story.   B. A magazine.   C. A joke.   D. A research report.

39. What should be read rapidly?

    A. A textbook.   B. A research report.

    C. A love story.   D. Some directions for making something.

40. For a reader, what is the most important?

    A. A good book.   B. Avoiding any mistake.

    C. The purpose of reading.   D. Reading many books.

TASK 2

Directions: *This task is the same as Task 1. The five questions or unfinished statements are numbered from 41 to 45.*

    The food we eat seems to have profound effects on our health. Although science has made enormous steps in making food more fit to eat, it has, at the same time, made many foods unfit to eat. Some research has shown that perhaps 80% of cancer is related to the diet as well. Different cultures are more prone to contract certain illnesses because of the food that is characteristic in these cultures. That food related to illness is not a new discovery. In 1945, government researchers realized that nitrates（硝酸盐）and nitrites（亚硝酸盐）, commonly used to preserve colour in meat, and other food additives, caused cancer. Yet, these carcinogenic（致癌的）additives remain in our food, and it becomes more difficult all the time to know which things on the packaging labels of processed food are helpful or harmful.

    The additives which we eat are not all so direct. Farmers often give penicillin（青霉素）to beef and poultry, and because of <u>this</u>, penicillin has been found in the milk of treated cows. Sometimes similar drugs are administered to animals not for medicinal purposes, but for financial reasons. The farmers are simply trying to fatten the animals in order to obtain a higher price on the market. Although the Food and Drug Administration (FDA) has tried repeatedly to control these procedures, the practices continue.

41. What is the main topic of the passage?

    A. Food and our health.   B. Food and additives.

    C. Food and cancer.   D. Food and culture.

42. All of the following statements are true EXCEPT _____.

    A. 80% of cancer is caused by problems related to food

    B. researchers have known about the potential danger of food additives for many years

    C. we eat some of the food additives directly and some indirectly

    D. drugs are always given to animals for medicinal purposes

43. Why do farmers give drugs to their animals?

    A. To speed up the growth of animals.   B. To make the animals fatter.

    C. To make the animals' meat fit to eat.   D. To make the animals' meat rich in nutrients.

44. It can be inferred from the passage that _____.

A. scientists have made all the food fit to eat

B. only in recent years have people found that food is related to one's illnesses

C. all kinds of cancer are related to the diet

D. some additives are harmful to our health

45. The word "this" in the second sentence of paragraph 2 most probably refers to _____.

A. farmers

B. penicillin

C. beef and poultry

D. the fact that farmers often give penicillin to beef

TASK 3

Directions: *The following is a passage about the Nobel Prize. After reading it, you should complete the information by filling in the blanks marked from 46 to 50 (in no more than three words) in the table below.*

The Nobel Prize

The Nobel Prize was founded by Swedish inventor Alfred Nobel. Nobel died in 1896 and left his fortune of about US $9.2 million to a fund to honour people who have helped other human beings. Jelinek won this year's Nobel Prize for Literature, and she was the nineth woman winner since the prize was first awarded in 1901.

The Nobel Prize
Alfred Nobel was the founder of ___46___.
The fortune Nobel left to a fund was about ___47___.
___48___ won this year's Nobel Prize for ___49___.
The year Nobel Prize was first awarded: ___50___.

TASK 4

Directions: *The following is part of information on traffic. After reading it, you are required to find the items equivalent to (与……等同) those given in Chinese in the table below. Then you should put the corresponding letters in the brackets on the Answer Sheet, numbered from 51 to 55.*

A——traffic regulation

B——safety island

C——fly-over/overpass

D——parking lot

E——license plate/number plate

F——emergency lane

G——one-way street

H——filling station/petrol station

I——no through way/dead end

J——drunk driving

K——break down

L——rush/ peak hour

M——taxi rank/taxi pick-up point/taxi stand

N——accident

O——traffic jam

P——pedestrian crossing/ zebra crossing

Examples: （ N ）事故　　　（ O ）交通堵塞

51. （　　）此路不通	（　　）高峰期
52. （　　）加油站	（　　）车牌
53. （　　）酒后驾驶	（　　）抛锚
54. （　　）单行道	（　　）应急车道
55. （　　）停车场	（　　）安全岛

TASK 5

Directions: *The following is a reply to a request. After reading it, you should give brief answers that followed the questions numbered from 56 to 60. You should write your answers (in no more than three words) on the Answer Sheet correspondingly.*

A Reply to a Request

Dear Mark,

It was good to hear from you once again. Preparations are underway to welcome you and Anna when you arrive in California on March 5. Our staff has been hard at work to create an imaginative campaign to launch Adonis, and we are eager to share our ideas with you.

As you requested, we have been able to reserve a double suite in the same hotel you and Anna stayed in last year. The reservations will be confirmed directly by the hotel. You will be hearing from them several days before you leave Florida.

I have notified all the department heads of your visit, and we have scheduled meetings with major retailers here on the West Coast. The response so far has been enthusiastic, and our new Adonis campaign should be just as successful as the Magic Mask campaign was last year.

If there is anything else I can do for you, please let me know. I will meet you and Anna at the airport on Friday evening, March 5, at 10:00. Have a good flight!

Regards,

Fred Hutton

56. Which state will Mark and Anna leave?

_____ .

57. When will Mark and Anna arrive in California?

_____ .

58. What is their new product?

_____ .

59. How about the response so far?

_____ .

60. Who will meet Mark and Anna at the airport?

_____ .

Part Ⅳ Translation—English to Chinese (25 minutes)

Directions: *This part, numbered from 61 to 65, is to test your ability to translate English into Chinese. Each of the four sentences (No. 61 to No. 64) is followed by four choices of suggested translation marked A, B, C, and D. Make the best choice and write the corresponding letter on the Answer Sheet. Write your translation of the paragraph (No. 65) in the corresponding space on the Translation/Composition Sheet.*

61. I went to a supermarket soon after arriving in Japan and was shocked at the price of vegetables.

　　A. 我到达日本后不久，去了一家超市，其蔬菜的价格使我感到震惊。

　　B. 逛了超市后不久我即来到日本，我被蔬菜的价格震惊了。

　　C. 当到达日本后，我立即去了一家超市，我被蔬菜的价格震惊了。

　　D. 我去了超市不久，我到达日本，对当地的蔬菜价格感到震惊。

62. She has put on a lot of weight since she got out of the hospital.

　　A. 自从出院以来她挑起了工作的重担。　　B. 自从出院以来她长胖了很多。

　　C. 因为她出院了，所以挑起工作的重担。　　D. 因为她出院了，所以长胖了许多。

63. This contract will enter into force after the seller confirms that the export license of men's ties is valid.

　　A. 在卖方证实男士领带出口许可证有效之后，本合同才能生效。

　　B. 在卖方确认男士领带出口许可证有效之后，本合同生效。

　　C. 本合同在卖方确认男士领带出口许可证有效之后发生效力。

　　D. 本合同只有在卖方确认男士领带出口许可证有效后才有约束力。

64. Much as we may pride ourselves on our taste, we are no longer free to choose the things we want because of advertising everywhere.

　　A. 尽管我们可以自夸自己的品位，但广告无处不在，我们已经无法独立自主地作出自己的选择了。

　　B. 正如我们可以自夸自己的品位一样，我们想不再自由地选择是因为无处不在的广告。

　　C. 当我们可以自夸自己的品位的时候，无处不在的广告已使我们不再自由地选择了。

　　D. 我们可以自夸自己的品味，但到处都是广告，我们不再自由地作出自己的选择了。

65. This e-dictionary is made in Hong Kong. It has a large vocabulary of 1 million English words and phrases. The dictionary is controlled by advanced computer technology which is also the latest technical result of the company's 20-year research. The body is made of light metal. Therefore, it is small in size and convenient to carry. Besides, it is easy to operate. The price is reasonable. It is a wise choice for English learners.

Part V Writing (25 minutes)

Directions: *This part is to test your ability to do practical writing. You are required to write a telephone message according to the following information given in Chinese. Remember to write it on the Translation/Composition Sheet.*

以秘书 Mary 的名义，给 Mr. Brown 写一份电话留言，包括以下内容：

来电人：ABC 公司的 Mr. Green

来电时间：2009 年 12 月 18 日上午 9:00

事由：Mr. Green 将于明天上午 9:00 到 Mr. Brown 的办公室商谈广告设计合作事宜。如果时间不合适请 Mr. Brown 回电话协商。

Model Test 6

Directions: *This part is to test your listening ability. It consists of three sections.*

SECTION A

Directions: *This section is to test your ability to give proper responses. There are five recorded questions in it. After each question, there is a pause. The question will be spoken twice. When you hear a question, you should decide on the correct answer from the four choices marked A, B, C and D given in your test paper. Then you should mark the corresponding letter on the Answer Sheet with a single line through the center.*

Example: You will hear: Mr. Smith is not in. Could you please give him a message?

You will read: A. I'm not sure.

B. You're right.

C. Yes, certainly.

D. That's interesting.

From the question we learn that the speaker is asking the listener to leave a message. Therefore, "C. Yes, certainly." is the correct answer. You should mark C on the Answer Sheet.

[A][B][C][D]

Now the test will begin.

1. A. It is 16:40.
   C. Yes, the meeting is late.
   B. Yes, I think so.
   D. About three minutes.

2. A. It is a very large hospital.
   C. It is far away from here.
   B. It is not far from here.
   D. It is about two kilometres.

3. A. Not at all.
   C. I missed the bus.
   B. Because he was sick.
   D. The class was late.

4. A. You are welcome.
   C. Sorry, I will have a meeting.
   B. That is all.
   D. Yes, of course.

5. A. He is handsome.
   C. He is healthy.
   B. His favourite sport is tennis.
   D. He is a doctor.

SECTION B

Directions: *This section is to test your ability to understand short dialogues. There are five recorded dialogues in it. After each dialogue, there is a recorded question. Both the dialogues and questions will be spoken twice. When you hear a question, you should decide on the correct answer from the four choices marked A, B, C and D given in your test paper. Then you should mark the corresponding letter on the Answer Sheet with a single line through the center.*

6. A. Vegetables.　　　B. Clothes.　　　　C. Books.　　　　D. Fruit.

7. A. Teacher and student.　　　　　　B. Policeman and thief.

 C. Manager and staff.　　　　　　　D. Patient and doctor.

8. A. 25 dollars.　　　B. 30 dollars.　　　C. 70 dollars.　　　D. 10 dollars.

9. A. In a company.　　　　　　　　　B. In a hospital.

 C. On a bus.　　　　　　　　　　　D. In a department store.

10. A. The woman can buy the ticket.

　B. The woman will go there by taxi.

　C. The woman will go there by bus.

　D. The ticket the woman wants to buy is not available.

SECTION C

Directions: *In this section you will hear a recorded short passage. The passage is printed in the test paper with some words or phrases missing. The passage will be read three times. During the second reading, you are required to put the missing words or phrases on the Answer Sheet in order of the numbered blanks according to what you hear. The third reading is for you to check your writing. Now the passage will begin.*

　　With the end of the term coming, many college students are ___11___ preparing papers. However, let's ___12___ at how they "write" their papers. Some college students ___13___ by themselves, but many just download articles from the Internet, do some editing, and then put them ___14___ and "finish" their papers. This phenomenon prevails. The Internet brings us boundless ___15___ but sometimes it kills creativity.

Part II Vocabulary & Structure (15 minutes)

Directions: *This part is to test your ability to construct meaningful and grammatically correct sentences. It consists of two sections.*

SECTION A

Directions: *In this section, there are ten incomplete sentences. You are required to complete each*

one by deciding on the most appropriate word or words from the four choices marked A, B, C and D. You should mark the corresponding letter on the Answer Sheet with a single line through the center.

16. It was in that lab _____ they did the chemical experiment.

    A. which   B. where   C. that   D. what

17. When you come tomorrow afternoon, I _____ the painting.

    A. will finish   B. shall be finished   C. will have finished   D. have finished

18. Nobody but Tom and Mary _____ the secret.

    A. know   B. knows   C. have known   D. is known

19. The medicine has many functions, _____ are unknown to us.

    A. some of that   B. some of them   C. some of which   D. some of what

20. Though the horses got off with a good start, it was not long _____ most of them were out of the race.

    A. before   B. after   C. when   D. until

21. The doctor recommended that he _____ a rest for a few days.

    A. has   B. will have   C. have   D. had

22. He gave up his job _____ for his family and for himself.

    A. both   B. all   C. much   D. little

23. Have you heard the news _____ she failed in the English exam again?

    A. which   B. if   C. that   D. whether

24. China is larger than _____ in Asia.

    A. other countries   B. all the countries

    C. any country   D. any other country

25. When _____ about his qualifications for the position, Tom kept silent.

    A. being asked   B. asked   C. asking   D. to be asked

SECTION B

Directions: *There are ten incomplete statements here. You should fill in each blank with the proper form of the word given in the brackets. Write the word or words in the corresponding space on the Answer Sheet.*

26. To see a place with one's own eyes is better than any _____ (describe).

27. Vegetation and wildlife _____ (kill) recently in this region owing to the pollution.

28. He looks quite _____ (health) but, in fact, he suffers from many diseases.

29. With the question _____ (settle), they went home.

30. We are going to Florida as soon as we _____ (finish) taking our final exams.

31. Your luggage is overweight. So an _____ (add) charge should be paid.

32. This shop can meet all your _____ (require).

33. Most students _____ (obtain) 160 credits by the time they graduate.

34. _____ (comparison) with what it was, it has improved greatly.

35. After studying the system carefully, they reached a _____ (conclude).

Part Ⅲ Reading Comprehension (40 minutes)

Directions: *This part is to test your reading ability. There are five tasks for you to fulfill. You should read the reading materials carefully and do the tasks as you are instructed.*

TASK 1

Directions: *After reading the following passage, you will find five questions or unfinished statements numbered from 36 to 40. For each question or statement there are four choices marked A, B, C and D. You should make the correct choice and mark the corresponding letter on the Answer Sheet with a single line through the center.*

Solar energy for your home is coming. It can help you as a single home owner. It can help the whole country as well. Whether or not solar energy can save your money depends on many things. Where you live is one factor. The type of home you have is another. Things like insulation present energy costs and the type of system you buy are added factors.

Using solar energy can help save our precious fuel. As you know, our supplies of oil and gas are very limited. There is just not enough on hand to meet all our future energy needs. And when Mother Nature says that's all. The only way we can delay hearing those words is by starting to save energy now and by using other sources, like the sun.

We won't have to worry about the sun running out of energy for another several billion years or so. Besides beginning an endless source of energy, the use of the sun has other advantages as well. The sun doesn't offer as many problems as other energy sources. For example, fossil fuel plants add to already high pollution levels. With solar energy, we will still need sources of energy, but we won't need as much. That means we can cut down on our pollution problems.

With all these good points, why don't we use more solar power? There are many reasons for this. The biggest reason is money. Until now, it was just not practical for a home owner to put in a solar unit. There were cheaper sources of energy. All is changing now. Experts say that gas, oil and electricity prices will continue to rise. The demand for electricity is increasing rapidly. But new power plants will use more gas, oil and coal. Already in some places the supply of electricity is being rationed. Solar energy is now in its infancy. It can soon grow to become a major part of our nation's energy supply.

36. Which statement best expresses the main idea of the passage?

    A. Something about Solar Energy and pollution.

    B. Solar Energy.

    C. Energy and Pollution.

    D. Energy and Money.

37. Solar energy can help us save _____.

    A. the earth and natural resources

    B. Mother Nature

    C. the sun

    D. our precious fuel

38. The sun is an endless source of energy; it will not run out of it for _____.

    A. several million years

    B. several hundred years

    C. several billion years

    D. several thousand years

39. Which of the following statements is correct?

    A. Energy from coal would not pollute our living environment.

    B. Energy from natural gas would not pollute our living environment.

    C. Energy from the sun would not pollute our living environment.

    D. Energy from oil would not pollute our living environment.

40. Solar energy is now in its infancy, _____.

    A. but it will be considered as an important part of our nation 's energy supply

    B. yet we will build more power plants

    C. and the supply of electricity will be rationed

    D. but we don't need to practice energy rationing now

TASK 2

Directions: *This task is the same as Task 1. The five questions or unfinished statements are numbered from 41 to 45.*

Television, or TV, the modern wonder of electronics, brings the world into your own home in sight and sound. The name television comes from the Greek word "tele", meaning "far", and the Latin word "videre", meaning "to see". Thus, television means "to see far". Sometimes television is referred to as video, from a Latin word meaning "I see". In Great Britain, the popular word for television is "telly".

Television works in much the same way as radio. In radio, sound is changed into electromagnetic waves which are sent through the air. In TV, both sound and sight are changed into electromagnetic waves. Experiments leading to modern television took place more than a hundred years ago. By the 1920s, inventors and researchers had turned the early theories into working models. Yet it took another 30 years for TV to become an industry.

As an industry, TV provides jobs for hundreds of thousands who make TV sets and broadcasting equipment. It also provides work for actors, technicians, and others who put on programs.

Many large schools and universities have "closed-circuit" television equipment that will telecast lectures and demonstrations to hundreds of students in different classrooms. And the lectures can be video-taped to be kept for later use. Some hospitals use TV to allow medical students to get close-up view of operations.

In 1946, after World War II, TV began to burst upon the American scene with a speed unforeseen even by the most optimistic leaders of the industry. The novelty of seeing TV pictures at home caught the public's fancy and began a revolution in the world of entertainment. By 1950, television had grown into a major part of show business. Many film and stage stars began to perform on TV as television audiences increased. Stations that once telecast for only a few hours a day sometimes telecast around the clock in the 1960s.

41. "… others who put on programs" means that _____.

　　A. people get on their clothes with programs printed on

　　B. people prepare and present the programs on TV

　　C. people like the programs

　　D. people acted in the TV programs

42. "… to allow medical students to get close-up view of operations" suggests _____.

　　A. the students can have view of operations with enlarged details

　　B. the students can operate through TV

　　C. the students were allowed to learn operations

　　D. TV is being used by students

43. "… TV began to burst upon the American …" indicates that _____.

　　A. in 1946 TV sets exploded in American families

　　B. TV may injure people

　　C. TV suddenly became available to many American families

　　D. TV was very popular in 1946

44. "TV pictures at home caught the public's fancy …" tells us _____.

　　A. TV pictures are better than movies

　　B. TV pictures can be seen at home

　　C. TV pictures can hurt people's eyes

　　D. TV pictures had aroused people's interests

45. "… sometimes telecast around the clock in the 1960s" means _____.

　　A. TV telecast used to have a round clock

　　B. people watch TV with around clock nearby

　　C. TV telecast 24 hours a day in the 1960s

　　D. TV was on show every day

TASK 3

Directions: *The following is a job-wanted advertisement. After reading it, you should complete the information by filling in the blanks marked from 46 to 50* **(in no more than three words)** *in the table below.*

He, B.A., majored in Japanese, 2-year experience as a tourist guide in a travel agency; communicative, caring, active; for a position of teaching at any high school or college; salary required at least RMB 2,000 per month. Tel: 010-12345678 E-mail: hjf2009@hotmail.com

His degree: ___46___

He is an experienced ___47___.

His personality: ___48___

He wants to find a job as a ___49___ at any high school or college.

His ideal payment for each month is no less than ___50___.

TASK 4

Directions: *The following is some signs for obligation. After reading them, you are required to find the items equivalent to（与……等同）those given in Chinese in the table below. Then you should put the corresponding letters in the brackets on the Answer Sheet, numbered from 51 to 55.*

A —— No Scribbling

B —— No Littering

C —— No Angling

D —— No Admittance

E —— No Bills

F —— No Spitting

G —— No U Turn

H —— Keep Off the Lawn

I —— Pet Is Not Allowed

J —— Improper for Kids

K —— Cameras Forbidden

L —— Staff Only

M —— Consecutive Curves Ahead

N —— School About, No Horn

O —— Do Not Proceed Beyond Rail

P —— Please Keep Hands Off

Examples: （ I ）请勿带宠物入内　　（ P ）请勿动手

51. （　　）禁止调头	（　　）游客止步
52. （　　）不准垂钓	（　　）请勿越过栏杆
53. （　　）请勿在此招贴	（　　）少儿不宜
54. （　　）请勿在此涂写	（　　）学校附近，禁止鸣笛
55. （　　）请勿乱扔果皮纸屑	（　　）闲人免进

TASK 5

Directions: *There is a passage. After reading it, you should give brief answers to the five questions (No. 56 through No. 60) that follow. The answers should correspondingly be written on the Answer Sheet.*

To the curious and the courageous, the sea still presents the challenge of the unknown, for ignorance is still the distinguishing characteristic of man's relation to the sea. But now, more than ever, necessity urges us onward in our exploration of the sea. We now have submarines capable of staying under water for many months holding missiles capable of destruction many times greater than those used in World War II. For strategic reasons, therefore, we need urgently to learn more about the ocean bottom. Quite apart from the threat of war, another necessity presses us to learn to master the sea. That necessity is basic to life itself: food. The lives of 2/3 of the world's people are wholly dictated by that basic necessity; they are oppressed by hunger and by the weakness and disease which hunger generates. Out of the sea we can extract food to relieve the hunger of these millions of people and give dignity to their lives. We must turn to the sea, because the bounty of the land has limits.

56. What is the passage mainly about?

_____

57. Which word can be used to describe man in his knowledge about the sea?

_____

58. Why do modern submarines present a greater threat?

_____

59. What is the other reason for which we should learn to master the sea?

_____

60. The passage indicates that the land _____.

Part IV Translation—English to Chinese (25 minutes)

Directions: *This part, numbered from 61 to 65, is to test your ability to translate English into Chinese. Each of the four sentences (No. 61 to No. 64) is followed by four choices of suggested translation marked A, B, C and D. Make the best choice and write the corresponding letter on the Answer Sheet. Write your translation of the paragraph (No. 65) in the corresponding space on the*

Translation/Composition Sheet.

61. There was so little water left that only small children and patients were given some.

   A. 只有小孩和病人分到一些，其余的人就没有水喝了。

   B. 仅剩下很少的水了，小孩和病人分到了水。

   C. 余下的水很少，所以只有小孩和病人才能分到一些。

   D. 所有剩下的水都分给小孩和病人了。

62. The last being gone, we could do nothing except spend the night in the mountain village.

   A. 最后一班公交车已经开走了，我们没办法只能留在山村过夜了。

   B. 眼看最后一班公交车已经开走，我们就在山村过夜了。

   C. 眼看最后一班公交车已经开走，我们没什么事好做，就在山村住了一晚。

   D. 没能赶上最后一班公交车，我们别无他法，只能在山村过夜了。

63. There are a number of issues with imports and exports that must be taken into consideration when conducting foreign trade.

   A. 做对外贸易时必须考虑若干有关进出口的问题。

   B. 有相当数量的问题要和进出口一起考虑，才能做对外贸易。

   C. 考虑进出口贸易时存在大量的有关问题。

   D. 做对外贸易的人需要考虑大量进出口问题。

64. Try hard as he will, he never seems able to do the work satisfactorily.

   A. 他是愿意努力工作，但他却从来都不满意工作。

   B. 尽管他是愿意努力工作，但是他好像从来都不能使他的工作令人满意。

   C. 他愿意努力工作，也好像从来都不能使他的工作令人满意。

   D. 像他希望的那样尽心尽力，不过他好像从未对他的工作满意过。

65. A company in the US believes it has found a method to make houses with paper. About ten years ago the company supplied a number of the newest paper houses as urgent housing for thousands of farm workers in California. Today, the paper houses are still holding up well. The builders now guess that the houses will have a useful life of at least 15 or 20 years.

Part Ⅴ Writing (25 minutes)

Directions: *This part is to test your ability to do practical writing. You are required to complete a letter of complaints. Some information is given to you. Remember to write the letter in the corresponding space on the Translation/Composition Sheet.*

收信人：光华商店经理

内容：上星期你在该商店买了一台洗衣机，刚用了一星期机器就运转不畅，噪音较大，因此要求退款。

Words for reference：

洗衣机：washing-machine   退款：refund

Model Test 7

Directions: *This part is to test your listening ability. It consists of three sections.*

SECTION A

Directions: *This section is to test your ability to give proper responses. There are five recorded questions in it. After each question, there is a pause. The question will be spoken twice. When you hear a question, you should decide on the correct answer from the four choices marked A, B, C and D given in your test paper. Then you should mark the corresponding letter on the Answer Sheet with a single line through the center.*

Example: You will hear: Mr. Smith is not in. Could you please give him a message?

You will read: A. I'm not sure.

B. You're right.

C. Yes, certainly.

D. That's interesting.

From the question we learn that the speaker is asking the listener to leave a message. Therefore, "C. Yes, certainly." is the correct answer. You should mark C on the Answer Sheet.

[A] [B] [C] [D]

Now the test will begin.

1. A. It's over there.   B. It's 10:00 now.   C. It's too late.   D. It's 14:00.

2. A. It doesn't matter.   B. I caught a cold.   C. It matters a lot.   D. I don't like it.

3. A. Yes, I do.   B. Never mind.   C. Of course not.   D. Why not?

4. A. She was going to come, but then changed her mind.

B. No, she hasn't.

C. Yes, she is.

D. I will tell her.

5. A. Sorry, I don't want to.   B. Yes, I agree with you.

C. It is far from here.   D. I don't know where it is.

SECTION B

Directions: *This section is to test your ability to understand short dialogues. There are five recorded dialogues in it. After each dialogue, there is a recorded question. Both the dialogues and questions will be spoken twice. When you hear a question, you should decide on the correct answer from the four choices marked A, B, C and D given in your test paper. Then you should mark the corresponding letter on the Answer Sheet with a single line through the center.*

6. A. June 22.　　　　B. June 20.　　　　C. June 18.　　　　D. June 30.

7. A. He does nothing in his spare time.　　　B. He sits down quietly in his spare time.

　 C. He enjoys reading in his spare time.　　　D. He does his homework.

8. A. Windy.　　　　B. Not bad.　　　　C. Too cold.　　　　D. Snowing.

9. A. Weather.　　　　B. Smoking rooms.　　　　C. Winter sports.　　　　D. Smoky rooms.

10. A. At a bank.　　　　B. On a plane.　　　　C. At an office.　　　　D. At a post office.

SECTION C

Directions: *In this section you will hear a recorded short passage. The passage is printed in the test paper with some words or phrases missing. The passage will be read three times. During the second reading, you are required to put the missing words or phrases on the Answer Sheet in order of the numbered blanks according to what you hear. The third reading is for you to check your writing. Now the passage will begin.*

What is the use of ___11___? It's like asking what is the use of going to university—if you're asking in that tone of voice, you probably shouldn't do it. But, ___12___ my diary once or twice proved useful, when I was involved in a libel（毁谤罪）suit where I had to give ___13___ about a night eight years before. Normally, I can't remember what I did eight years before, but I was able to fish out（摸索出，掏出）the diary for a ___14___ account. But it would be mad to keep a diary just for occasional ___15___.

Part II Vocabulary & Structure (15 minutes)

Directions: *This part is to test your ability to construct meaningful and grammatically correct sentences. It consists of two sections.*

SECTION A

Directions: *In this section, there are ten incomplete sentences. You are required to complete each one by deciding on the most appropriate word or words from the four choices marked A, B, C and D. You should mark the corresponding letter on the Answer Sheet with a single line through the center.*

16. The play was wonderful and I wish I _____ to it with you.

    A. had gone   B. would go   C. went   D. have gone

17. Professor White had us _____ compositions every Friday.

    A. writing   B. write   C. written   D. to write

18. Like the old, _____ respected in some countries.

    A. the female is   B. a female is   C. a female are   D. the female are

19. _____ his cold, he came first in the athletics meet.

    A. Regardless of   B. Despite   C. In spite   D. Besides

20. If I _____ out of ink, I would have finished writing the paper.

    A. shouldn't run   B. haven't run   C. hadn't run   D. didn't run

21. _____ he is a hard-working person, he has not been successful in business.

    A. Since   B. Although   C. Unless   D. However

22. These students won't go unless their instructor _____ soon.

    A. comes   B. has come   C. came   D. will come

23. They spent the whole day _____ strawberries in the wood.

    A. pick   B. to pick   C. picking   D. picked

24. There was so much noise that the speaker couldn't make himself _____.

    A. hearing   B. to hear   C. being heard   D. heard

25. Twenty dollars _____ obviously too much to pay for such a small item.

    A. were   B. are   C. is   D. have been

SECTION B

Directions: *There are ten incomplete statements here. You should fill in each blank with the proper form of the word given in the brackets. Write the word or words in the corresponding space on the Answer Sheet.*

26. Making sure the _____ (safe) of the plane is the pilot's responsibility.

27. He warned them _____ (not leave) until the class was over.

28. It is necessary that an efficient worker _____ (accomplish) his work on time.

29. The car was repaired but not quite to the owner's _____ (satisfy).

30. All my bags _____ (examination) when I entered the country.

31. He can lift heavy weights because of his _____ (strong).

32. Although I don't go in for sports, I enjoy _____ (watch) football matches.

33. The woman is _____ (fortune) in having an ideal husband.

34. When I arrived at the theatre, all the tickets _____ (sell) out.

35. We are studying the _____ (possible) of building a new shipping center outside the town.

Part Ⅲ Reading Comprehension (40 minutes)

Directions: *This part is to test your reading ability. There are five tasks for you to fulfill. You should read the reading materials carefully and do the tasks as you are instructed.*

TASK 1

Directions: *After reading the following passage, you will find five questions or unfinished statements numbered from 36 to 40. For each question or statement there are four choices marked A, B, C and D. You should make the correct choice and mark the corresponding letter on the Answer Sheet with a single line through the center.*

The White House is the home of the President of the United States and his family. It wasn't called the White House until Teddy Roosevelt named it in 1901.

James Hoban designed the White House in 1792. He was awarded the job because he had won a contest sponsored by the government. His design had been selected as the best.

President John Adams was the first to live in the White House. When he and his wife, Abigail moved in, it was a huge mansion in the middle of a swamp. Many of the rooms were unfinished. Abigail used the famous East Room as a drying room for laundry. More rooms were decorated every year. Rare shrubs and trees were planted on the grounds.

Yet, all this work was for nothing. In the war of 1812, the British burned the mansion to the ground. The White House was rebuilt in 1817. The beauty of its decorations and furnishings has been growing ever since.

36. Which of the following would be the best title for the passage?

   A. President John Adams and the White House   B. White House Today

   C. A House Full of History   D. White House Before 1812

37. The White House was sponsored by the government. This means that the government
_____.

   A. received the prize   B. held the contest

   C. did the designing   D. was against having a contest

38. James Hoban won the job of building the White House because _____.

   A. his plan of the house seemed better than the others'

   B. he was the best-known architect of his time

   C. he organized the contest

   D. he applied for the job to the government

39. Which of the following statements is TRUE according to the passage?

   A. The present building of the White House has been standing for almost two centuries.

   B. It was James Hoban who first got the idea of building the White House.

   C. The number of the rooms in the White House has been growing ever since it was built.

D. The White House got its name at the turn of the century.

40. We can infer from the passage that the White House was first built _____.

    A. on a low and damp site

    B. among trees and flowers

    C. on a small island

    D. on a small hill

TASK 2

Directions: *This task is the same as Task 1. The five questions or unfinished statements are numbered from 41 to 45.*

After a busy day of work and play, the body needs to rest. Sleep is necessary for good health. During this time, the body recovers from the activities of the previous day. The rest that you get while sleeping enables your body to prepare itself for the next day.

There are four levels of sleep, each being a little deeper than the one before. As you sleep, your muscles relax little by little. Your heart beats more slowly, and your brain slows down. After you reach the fourth level, your body shifts back and forth from one level of sleep to another.

Although your mind slows down, from time to time you will dream. (Scientists who study sleep state that when dreaming occurs, your eyeballs begin to move more quickly although your eyelids are closed). This stage of sleep is called REM, which stands for rapid eye movement.

If you have trouble falling asleep, some people recommend breathing very slowly and very deeply. Other people believe that drinking warm milk will help make you <u>drowsy</u>. There is also an old suggestion that counting sheep will put you to sleep!

41. A good title for this passage is _____.

    A. Sleep   B. Good Health   C. Dreams   D. Work and Rest

42. The word "drowsy" in the last paragraph means _____.

    A. sick   B. stand up   C. asleep   D. a little sleepy

43. This passage suggests that not getting enough sleep might make you _____.

    A. dream more often   B. have poor health   C. nervous   D. breathe quickly

44. During REM, _____.

    A. your eyes move quickly

    B. you dream

    C. you are restless

    D. both A and B

45. The average number of hours of sleep that an adult needs is _____.

    A. approximately six hours

    B. around ten hours

    C. about eight hours

    D. not stated here

TASK 3

Directions: *The following is an advertisement. After reading it, you should complete the information by filling in the blanks marked from 46 to 50 (**in no more than three words**) in the* *table below.*

Foreign English Teachers

We need **8** foreign English teachers.

♦ If you are a native English-speaker.

♦ If your weekends or your holidays are available (During Jan. 20—Feb. 16, 2010).

♦ If you have related teaching experience for **KIDS** (8~14 years old).

♦ If you are interested in teaching.

Please contact us—the most prominent training school of **Shanghai New Oriental**!

The better job the more bonuses!

TEL: 13761279417 Susan

(Weekdays only, please! Thank you.)

FAX: 65446793

ADDRESS: No.321, Wudong Road

(the crossing roads of Jipu Road and Wudong Road)

Contact before: Jan. 15, 2010

Foreign English Teachers

Requirements for the job applicants（应聘者）:

1) We need 8 __46__ English-speakers.

2) The job involves working on __47__ or __48__ during Jan. 20~Feb. 16, 2010.

3) We want to employ the __49__ foreign English teachers for kids of 8~14 years old.

4) If you have any questions or want to get further information about the job, you can contact us before __50__.

TASK 4

Directions: *The following is part of Information for the World Expo. After reading it, you are required to find the items equivalent to（与……等同）those given in Chinese in the table below. Then you should put the corresponding letters in the brackets on the Answer Sheet, numbered from 51 to 55.*

A —— Expo Emblem

B —— Expo Logo

C —— Expo Mascot

D —— Expo Souvenir

E —— Expo Park

F —— the Expo Site

G —— Theme Pavilion

H —— International Pavilion

I —— Enterprise Pavilion

J —— the Expo Village

K —— the Expo Center

L —— Expo Dining Center

M —— Symposium

N —— Expo First-aid Center

O —— Volunteers

P —— International Convention Center

Examples: （ C ）世博会吉祥物　　（ M ）专题讨论会

51. （　　）志愿者	（　　）世博园
52. （　　）世博急救中心	（　　）企业馆
53. （　　）世博会徽标	（　　）世博餐饮中心
54. （　　）国际会议中心	（　　）世博会纪念品
55. （　　）世博园区	（　　）主题馆

TASK 5

Directions: *There is an article about myths in job-hunting. After reading it, you should give brief answers that followed the questions numbered from 56 to 60. You should write your answers (in no more than three words) on the Answer Sheet correspondingly.*

Job-hunting Myths（误区）

"Don't defeat yourself by accepting common myths", says the head of an international company.

Myth 1: If there's nothing available in your field, change careers.

Fact 1: That's one of the worst things you can do. You compete against others with experience, and you will not approach your old salary level on a new job.

Myth 2: Lower your salary demands. You'll be more attractive to employers in an uncertain economy.

Fact 2: People who ask for less are viewed as "low property". If you are considered as anything less than first-class, you are not likely to be hired.

Myth 3: Workers over 50, it will be very hard to find another job.

Fact 3: Workers over 50 win new jobs almost as quickly as youngsters do. Today's employers place a premium（额外价值）on experience.

Myth 4: Bring up salary as quickly as possible in the first interview.

Fact 4: That's a fast way to be removed（取消）from consideration. It tells employers you are more concerned with yourself than with the company.

Myth 5: You can only get interview between 9:00 a.m. and 5:00 p.m. on weekdays.

Fact 5: Employers are often available before and after regular hours when the office is quieter. If you get an interview then, you've got the employer's concentrated attention.

56. What is the disadvantage of changing your career?

You will not reach the _____.

57. What is likely to happen if you are not considered as first-class?

It's less possible for you to _____.

58. Why do old people still have an equal chance to get a new job?

Because _____ is appreciated.

59. What will happen if you ask for a high salary in the first interview?

You will probably lose the chance _____ the job.

60. What is a better time for an interview?

Not during _____.

Part IV Translation—English to Chinese (25 minutes)

Directions: *This part, numbered from 61 to 65, is to test your ability to translate English into Chinese. Each of the four sentences (No. 61 to No. 64) is followed by four choices of suggested translation marked A, B, C and D. Make the best choice and write the corresponding letter on the Answer Sheet. Write your translation of the paragraph (No. 65) in the corresponding space on the Translation/Composition Sheet.*

61. He wants all countries in the Group of Twenty to coordinate their separate efforts to strengthen their economies.

A. 他呼吁所有二十国集团国家把他们分散的努力协调起来壮大他们的经济。

B. 他要二十国集团国家共同努力把他们分散的资源协调起来加强经济实力。

C. 他呼吁二十国集团中所有成员国家集中力量，共同致力于加强集团国的经济建设。

D. 他让二十国组织所有国家统一目标，独立行事，加强经济合作。

62. POD has been a number one provider of exhibition display stands and our range of exhibition equipment is second to none.

A. POD 名列展台提供商第一，我们的展览设施无与伦比。

B. POD 是一家展台提供商，我们的展览设施仅次于第一。

C. POD 一直是最好的展台提供商，我们生产最优质的展览设备。

D. POD 是第一家展台提供商，我们的展览设施生产线无与伦比。

63. No matter how complicated the problems may seem to be, he always finds ways to solve them.

A. 无论怎么复杂，这些问题似乎可能让他试着寻找办法解决。

B. 无论事情怎么复杂，这些问题似乎可能是有的，他总是在找办法解决。

C. 无论事情怎么复杂，他总是能找出办法解决。

D. 无论问题看起来怎么复杂，他总能找到解决办法。

64. Leaders of the world's wealthiest nations have promised 20 billion dollars to improve food security in poor countries.

A. 世界最富裕国家的领导人已经承诺要拿出 200 亿美元改善穷国的食品安全。

B. 世界最富裕国家的领导人已经承诺要用 200 亿美元改善穷国的食品安全。

C. 世界富国领导说了算。他们承诺在贫穷的国家投 200 亿美元搞食品安全。

D. 在世界上，最富裕的国家就是领导。他们已经承诺要拿出 200 亿美元改善穷国的食品安全。

65. Advertising is part of our daily life. To realize the fact, you have only to leaf through a magazine or newspaper or count the radio or television commercials that you hear in one evening. Most people see and hear several hundred advertising messages every day. And people respond to the many devices that advertisers use to gain their attention.

Part V Writing (25 minutes)

Directions: *This part is to test your ability to do practical writing. You are required to complete a Notes Left. Some information is given to you. Remember to write the Notes Left in the corresponding space on the Translation/Composition Sheet.*

杨：

　　明天的会议因举办讲座延期召开，特告，并转告有关人员。

大海
星期五下午

Model Test 8

Directions: *This part is to test your listening ability. It consists of three sections.*

SECTION A

Directions: *This section is to test your ability to give proper responses. There are five recorded questions in it. After each question, there is a pause. The question will be spoken twice. When you hear a question, you should decide on the correct answer from the four choices marked A, B, C and D given in your test paper. Then you should mark the corresponding letter on the Answer Sheet with a single line through the center.*

Example: You will hear: Mr. Smith is not in. Could you please give him a message?

You will read: A. I'm not sure.

B. You're right.

C. Yes, certainly.

D. That's interesting.

From the question we learn that the speaker is asking the listener to leave a message. Therefore, "C. Yes, certainly." is the correct answer. You should mark C on the Answer Sheet.

[A] [B] [C] [D]

Now the test will begin.

1. A. 9:10.   B. No, it isn't.

   C. In the office.   D. What's wrong with you?

2. A. That's all right.   B. Yes, look at him.

   C. Yes, it is.   D. It's beautiful.

3. A. It's not your business.   B. Great.

   C. He is hungry.   D. Sorry, I don't know.

4. A. The computer doesn't work.   B. The computer is very helpful.

   C. He felt tied.   D. It is over there.

5. A. No, it's not good.   B. So do I.

   C. Yes, it is.   D. I don't know.

SECTION B

Directions: *This section is to test your ability to understand short dialogues. There are five recorded dialogues in it. After each dialogue, there is a recorded question. Both the dialogues and questions will be spoken twice. When you hear a question, you should decide on the correct answer from the four choices marked A, B, C and D given in your test paper. Then you should mark the corresponding letter on the Answer Sheet with a single line through the center.*

6. A. 8:15.　　　　B. 8:45.　　　　C. 9:45.　　　　D. 9:15.

7. A. Teacher.　　　B. Nurse.　　　　C. Saleswoman.　　　D. Doctor.

8. A. To the man's office.　　　　　B. To the manager's house.
   C. Home.　　　　　　　　　　　D. To the manager's office.

9. A. He is going to visit Hong Kong.　　B. Hang Kong isn't worth a visit.
   C. Hang Kong is worth visiting.　　　D. Another place is worth visiting.

10. A. The woman runs slowly.　　　　B. The woman couldn't.
    C. The woman runs too fast.　　　　D. The woman runs very well.

SECTION C

Directions: *In this section you will hear a recorded short passage. The passage is printed in the test paper with some words or phrases missing. The passage will be read three times. During the second reading, you are required to put the missing words or phrases on the Answer Sheet in order of the numbered blanks according to what you hear. The third reading is for you to check your writing. Now the passage will begin.*

Jill bumped into a young zoologist（动物学家）called Adam Briton who absolutely loved crocodiles. One of the things that ___11___ him about crocodiles was that as part of their ___12___ behaviors, they fight with other crocodiles and regularly ___13___ limbs（肢体）. What amazed him was that crocodiles ___14___ in dirty, bacteria-filled water, and yet they never seem to get infections—their limbs heal ___15___.

Part II Vocabulary & Structure (15 minutes)

Directions: *This part is to test your ability to construct meaningful and grammatically correct sentences. It consists of two sections.*

SECTION A

Directions: *In this section, there are ten incomplete sentences. You are required to complete each one by deciding on the most appropriate word or words from the four choices marked A, B, C and D. You should mark the corresponding letter on the Answer Sheet with a single line through the* *center.*

16. Documents _____ with chemicals will not become yellow with age.

    A. treating   B. be treated   C. treats   D. treated

17. His grandfather is looking forward to _____ to his native place some day.

    A. return   B. being returned   C. returning   D. be returning

18. The doctor told the new nurse _____ to do.

    A. what   B. how   C. that   D. as

19. _____ from the top of the mountain, the city is very beautiful.

    A. To see   B. Seen   C. Saw   D. Seeing

20. _____ he was seriously ill, I wouldn't have told him the truth.

    A. If I knew   B. Did I know   C. If I know   D. Had I known

21. He must be in the building because he was seen _____ the building just now.

    A. entering   B. enter   C. to enter   D. having entered

22. In 2006, she was elected _____ chairman of the Student Union.

    A. an   B. a   C. \\   D. the

23. I saw Mr. Zhang a moment ago. He _____ to Germany.

    A. can't go   B. couldn't have gone

    C. mustn't go   D. mustn't have gone

24. He looks similar to his father. What's more, his words are _____ his father.

    A. as few as   B. as little as   C. as less as   D. as fewer as

25. Is this the city _____ you visited last year?

    A. when   B. where   C. which   D. what

SECTION B

Directions: *There are ten incomplete statements here. You should fill in each blank with the proper form of the word given in the brackets. Write the word or words in the corresponding space on the Answer Sheet.*

26. John not only learnt Chinese but also _____ (know) the difference between his culture and ours.

27. The secretary worked late into the night, _____ (prepare) a long speech for the president.

28. I was frightened because I had never seen him in such _____ (angry) before.

29. She put on the dress once again and wondered if she could have the sleeves _____ (short).

30. Robert said that he wouldn't mind _____ (do) the job for me.

31. It is required that every employee _____ (come) in his uniform before 8:30 a.m.

32. The flat _____ (consist) of three rooms, with a kitchen and bathroom.

33. The next morning he packed up his _____ (person) belongings and checked out of the hotel.

34. Ask for help if you have difficulty _____ (understand) the passage.

35. There is a great _____ (differ) between a second-rate company and an international company.

Part III Reading Comprehension (40 minutes)

Directions: *This part is to test your reading ability. There are five tasks for you to fulfill. You should read the reading materials carefully and do the tasks as you are instructed.*

TASK 1

Directions: *After reading the following passage, you will find five questions or unfinished statements numbered from 36 to 40. For each question or statement there are four choices marked A, B, C and D. You should make the correct choice and mark the corresponding letter on the Answer Sheet with a single line through the center.*

I was telling my boy Tony the story of the hare（野兔）and tortoise（乌龟）. In the end I said,

"Son, remember: slow and steady, but wins the race. Don't you think there's something to learn from the tortoise?"

He opened his eyes wide. "Do you mean next time when I'm entering for the 60-meter race, I should wish that Billy and Tom and Sandy would all fall asleep half-way?"

I was shocked. "But the tortoise didn't wish the hare would fall asleep!"

"He must have wished that," Tony said. "Otherwise how could he be so stupid as to race with the hare? He knew very well the hare ran a hundred times faster than he himself did."

"He didn't have such a wish," I insisted. "He won the race by perseverance（坚韧不拔）, by pushing on steadily."

Tony thought for a while. "That's lie," He said. "He won because he was lucky. If the hare hadn't happened to fall asleep, the tortoise would never have won the race. He could be as steady as you like, or a hundred times steadier, but he'd never have won the race. That's for sure."

I gave up. Today's children are not like what we used to be. They are just hopeless.

36. The writer argued with his son because _____.

A. he liked tortoises while his son liked hares

B. they disagreed about whether the tortoise was stupid

C. he liked the story of the hare and the tortoise while his son didn't

D. he tried to teach his son the moral lesson of the story but the son rejected it

37. Tony believed that the tortoise _____.
    A. won the race by his own effort   B. took a risk by agreeing to race
    C. was not given a fair chance in the race   D. won the race by chance
38. Billy and Tom and Sandy must be _____.
    A. boys who were unknown to Tony' father   B. boys Tony had run races with before
    C. boys Tony had never raced with before   D. boys Tony did not expect to race with again
39. When the author says "I gave up" at the end, he means _____.
    A. he gave up his belief in the moral idea of the hare-and-tortoise story
    B. he gave up arguing with Tony
    C. he gave up Tony as a hopeless child
    D. he gave up trying to keep up with the new generation
40. According to the passage, who do you think learnt a lesson?
    A. The tortoise.   B. The hare.   C. Tony.   D. Tony's father.

TASK 2

Directions: *This task is the same as Task 1. The five questions or unfinished statements are numbered from 41 to 45.*

Why don't birds get lost on their long flights from one place to another? Scientists have puzzled over this question for many years. Now they're beginning to fill in the blanks.

Not long ago, experiments showed that birds rely on the sun to guide them during daylight hours. But what about birds that fly at night? Tests with artificial stars have proved that certain night — flying birds are able to follow the stars in their long-distance flights.

A dove had spent its lifetime in a cage and had never flown under a natural sky. Yet it showed an inborn ability to use the stars for guidance. The bird's cage was placed under an artificial star-filled sky. The bird tried to fly in the same direction as that taken by <u>his outdoor cousins</u>. Any change in the position of the artificial stars caused a change in the direction of his flight.

But the stars are apparently their principal means of navigation. When the stars are hidden by clouds, they apparently find their way by such landmarks as mountain ranges, coast lines, and river courses. But when it's too dark to see these, the doves circle helplessly, unable to find their way.

41. The reasons why birds don't get lost on long flights _____.
    A. have been known to scientists for years   B. have only recently been discovered
    C. are known by everyone   D. will probably remain a mystery
42. During daylight hours, birds _____.
    A. fly aimlessly   B. rely on landmarks
    C. use the sun for guidance   D. are more likely to get lost
43. By "his outdoor cousins" the author means _____.
    A. other experimenters   B. the other doves of the same brood

C. doves under the natural sky   D. other birds in general

44. The experiment with the dove indicated that _____.

A. birds have to be taught to navigate

B. a bird that has been caged will not fly long distances

C. some birds cannot fly at night

D. some birds seem to follow the stars when they fly at night

45. In total darkness, doves _____.

A. use landmarks   B. don't know which way to fly

C. fly back home   D. wait for the stars to appear

TASK 3

Directions: *The following is a letter. After reading it, you should complete the information by filling in the blanks marked from 46 to 50 (in the table below).*

Dear Kathy,

Now I'm sending you a copy of the final program schedule of the conference, together with a map of the location of St. Martin's College.

Please note also that there has been an exchange between meetings. Those meetings for Friday morning will be replaced by those for Saturday afternoon. I hope this will not cause you any problem.

If you are going to present a page, please let me have an abstract（摘要）of it as soon as possible. The deadline for the abstract is Monday, 23, March.

The entire conference fee (3 days) is $120. You may send the fee to the conference organizer according to the above address or just pay on arrival.

Looking forward to meeting you soon.

Yours sincerely,

Dr Smith

Professor of Collins University & Organizer of the Conference

Information about a conference at Collins University

Place of the Conference: ___46___

Change in the schedule: Meeting for Friday morning will be held on ___47___

The time for receiving an abstract: no later than ___48___

Conference fee: ___49___

Receiver of the conference fee: ___50___

TASK 4

Directions: *After reading the following list, you are required to find the items equivalent to*

（与……等同）those given in Chinese in the table below. Then you should put the corresponding letters in the brackets on the Answer Sheet, numbered from 51 to 55.

[A] — ambulance   [B] — credit card

[C] — website   [D] — catalogue

[E] — on vacation   [F] — metro

[G] — download   [H] — be clearly marked and priced

[I] — network games   [J] — traffic jams

[K] — magazine cover   [L] — house to let

[M] — IT   [N] — campus life

[O] — sale discount

51.（　　）明码标价   （　　）信息技术

52.（　　）网络游戏   （　　）杂志封面

53.（　　）度假   （　　）销售折扣

54.（　　）校园生活   （　　）救护车

55.（　　）商品目录   （　　）房屋出租

TASK 5

Directions: *The following is a letter. After reading it, you should give brief answers that followed the questions numbered from 56 to 60. You should write your answers (in no more than three words) on the Answer Sheet correspondingly.*

Dear Miss White,

Following my telephone conversation with you yesterday, we have decided that we would prefer to go to Cambridge for our holiday rather than Birmingham. Of the hotels you suggested, we think that Red Inn would suit us best.

We should like to stay there for two nights from the 23rd, July. Our party will consist of two families, that is, two couples and three boys. Therefore, we shall require two double rooms and a three-bedded room for the kids.

I enclose the completed booking form and check to cover the deposit（押金）of £25 per person required at the time of booking. I should be glad to receive confirmation of booking at your earliest convenience.

Yours sincerely,

Frank Simpson

56. What is the purpose of the letter?

To book _____ for holiday.

57. Where has the writer finally decided to go for holiday?

To _____.

58. Which hotel do the party prefer to live in during their holiday?

59. How many rooms do they want to book in all?

_____.

60. How much is the deposit for them to book all the rooms?

_____.

Part Ⅳ Translation—English to Chinese (25 minutes)

Directions: *This part, numbered from 61 to 65, is to test your ability to translate English into Chinese. Each of the four sentences (No. 61 to No. 64) is followed by four choices of suggested translation marked A, B, C and D. Make the best choice and write the corresponding letter on the Answer Sheet. Write your translation of the paragraph (No. 65) in the corresponding space on the Translation/Composition Sheet.*

61. Not only I but also Jane and Mary are tired of having one meeting after another.

    A. 我、珍妮和玛丽都很疲倦，无法在一次会议后再参加一次会议。

    B. 一个会议接着一个会议，不仅我厌烦，珍妮和玛丽也都厌烦。

    C. 除我以外，珍妮和玛丽先后参加了两次会议，觉得很劳累。

    D. 不仅我，还有珍妮和玛丽有开不完的会，搞得筋疲力尽。

62. Seen from the TV tower at night, the city looks even more magnificent with all its lights on.

    A. 夜晚，电视塔上的灯都装上了，城市看上去显得更美丽。

    B. 夜晚在市里看电视塔，因为所有的灯都亮了，所以显得更华丽。

    C. 夜晚，从电视塔上望出去，所有的灯都亮了，城市显得更辉煌。

    D. 夜晚，在电视塔上看这座城市，要是所有的灯都亮的话，城市看起来就更加壮观。

63. His ignorance of the company's financial situation results in his failure to take effective measures.

    A. 他对公司的财务状况毫不理会，自以为措施有效，以致失当。

    B. 他对公司的财务状况一无所知，结果未能采取有效措施。

    C. 他采取的措施无效，使得公司的经营状况更加恶化。

    D. 他不了解公司的金融状况，结果采取的措施失败了。

64. As far as an Advertising and Sales Manager is concerned, excellent oral English is also a necessary requirement.

    A. 广告部和销售部经理都要求员工必须有良好的英语口语能力。

    B. 对广告和销售经理而言，娴熟的英语口语能力也是必要的条件。

    C. 广告部经理和销售部经理认为，熟练的英语口语能力也会是必需的。

    D. 广告部经理和销售部经理所关心的是员工也必须要有很高的英语水平。

65. Flexible working hours were invented in Germany in the late 1960s, but reached Britain only in 1972. The system allows workers to start and finish work whenever they want, with only two requirements. Firstly, all workers must be present for certain "key" times in a day, and

secondly, all workers must work an agreed total number of hours per week.

Part V Writing (25 minutes)

Directions: *This part is to test your ability to do practical writing. You are required to complete a Letter of Thanks. Some information is given to you. Remember to write the letter in the corresponding space on the Translation/Composition Sheet.*

广州大学教师向明去美国纽约大学考察回国后，向该大学物理系 Prof. Howell 致谢，感谢他在向明逗留纽约的那一周所给予的热情和帮助。

Words for reference:

美国纽约大学：State University of New York

物理系：Physics Department

殷勤招待：hospitality